K.N. Shields grew up in Portland, Maine. He graduated
from Dartmouth College and the University of Maine
School of Law. He continues to reside along the coast of
Maine with his wife and two children.

THE
SALEM
WITCH
SOCIETY

K.N. SHIELDS

sphere

SPHERE

First published in the United States in 2012 by Crown Publishers,
a division of Random House, Inc., New York
First published as a paperback original in Great Britain in 2013 by Sphere

A CIP catalogue record for this book
is available from the British Library.

ISBN 978-0-7515-4910-2

Typeset in Granjon by M Rules
Printed and bound in Great Britain by
Clays Ltd, St Ives plc

Papers used by Sphere are from well-managed forests
and other responsible sources.

MIX
Paper from
responsible sources
FSC® C104740

Sphere
An imprint of
Little, Brown Book Group
100 Victoria Embankment
London EC4Y 0DY

An Hachette UK Company
www.hachette.co.uk

www.littlebrown.co.uk

This book is dedicated to
Cathy, Penelope, and Aidan

PART I

June 14, 1892

Apart from the fact that the reconstitution of the crime for oneself is the only effective method, it is the only interesting one, the only one that stimulates the inquirer and keeps him awake at his work.

Dr Hans Gross, Criminal Investigation

1

At the sound of footsteps in the alley, Maggie Keene dimmed the gas lamp and sidled up to the room's only window. She eased the curtains aside, her fingers barely touching the paper-thin material for fear it might tear and crumble. The gap between two neighboring tenement houses allowed a slice of moonlight to pierce the narrow passageway below. A man in a brown derby hurried past, stepping over the remains of a smashed crate. The splintered boards lay scattered on the ground like animal bones bleached a ghastly white by long exposure.

Maggie cupped a hand against the glass and peered in the other direction. There was still no sign of John. Her eyes drifted past the lights of the Grand Trunk Railway Station, down toward the waterfront of Portland, Maine. The harbor was a dark canvas, interrupted only by a scattering of ships' lamps bobbing on the tide. She smiled at a faint memory: fireflies hovering over a field on a summer night. She clung to the image for a few seconds until the distant lights began to blur. The laudanum mixture made her feel remote and empty. It threatened to lull her to sleep until a familiar pain twisted in her gut. A vague, unformed prayer sped through her mind, begging God to let her be all right.

She reached for the small brown medicine bottle on the nightstand. Against the light of the gas jet, Maggie saw that it was almost empty, even though John had given it to her only yesterday. It helped the cramps, but she worried that she'd be doubled over again when she woke, the same as most mornings that week.

She sat on the edge of the bed and gazed around the room, searching for a distraction from the pain. The place bordered on spare, but it was clean, with a sitting area, a fireplace, and even a private water closet. The only thing she missed was a clock.

John had promised to be back no later than midnight. Maggie knew he'd return, since he paid for the room. He'd even left behind his precious notebook, the one he was always patting his coat for, making sure it was safe in his pocket. The desire to peek inside it washed over her, but she let that thought tumble back into the deep. Even if she could undo the book's locked clasp, she had never been to school and struggled with even simple passages from a child's primer. Another cramp snaked its way through her gut. She drained the last of the little brown bottle, then poured a glass of water to rinse the taste from her mouth.

Maggie wished John would hurry up and get back. Then he could finally show her what he'd been hiding. He would reveal to her the truth of all things; that was how he'd phrased it. Then they would toast his shattering success. Just John puffing himself up, of course, but the thought still made her smile. It would be nice to celebrate something more than turning out a drunk stiff's pockets and finding loose change. She reached for the black hat she'd bought that day and looked at her reflection in the window. It was impossible to tell from the faint image staring back, but she knew she was paler than usual.

The sound of a step on the outside stairs stirred her back to the moment. There was the quick ascent of boots, and she met him at the door as the knob twisted.

'I was starting to wonder,' she said. 'Everything all right?'

'Everything is' – he struggled for several seconds to produce the right word – 'perfect.'

He had these moments of silent effort, and Maggie had already learned to act as if she didn't notice the awkward pauses. John brought her forward onto the landing. He slipped into the room and extinguished the light. Maggie heard him fumbling in the dark before he reappeared and led her down the stairs

'So where are we going anyways?'

'Patience, my dear. You'll see . . . soon enough.'

'Always such a mystery with you.'

He smiled. 'Behold, I show you a mystery; we shall not all sleep . . . but we shall all be changed. In a moment, in the twinkling of an eye . . . at the last trump: for the trumpet shall sound, and the dead . . . shall be raised incorruptible, and we shall be changed.'

'What are you on about? Better not start preaching at me.'

He gave a chuckle. 'Just a bit to start you on the way.'

Maggie's mind was drifting into the haze of the laudanum; she didn't take any notice of how thin and raspy his laugh sounded. It held no warmth or humor and was instantly swallowed up by the night air. She stumbled on the uneven ground and then felt John's grip on her arm as he guided her into the darkness.

Deputy Marshal Archie Lean stood in the Portland Company's cavernous machine shop. He wasn't quite as trim as when he'd first joined the police a decade ago, but he still retained the sturdy build developed in his youthful days as a boxer and rugby football player. He doffed his hat and tugged on a handful of sandy hair, as if he could somehow forcibly extract an explanation from his spinning mind. Lean pulled out his notebook and glanced at his earlier jottings under the heading of 6-14-92. Halfway down the page, he caught sight of two lines of poetry that he didn't recall writing: 'She seemed a thing that could not feel / The touch of earthly years.' He crossed out the lines. Lean needed to focus his thoughts, so he lit a cigarette, his fourth in the hour since he'd first seen the body. Maybe he could make it the rest of the day without another. His wife hated the smell on him, but he knew that Emma wouldn't mind once she heard what he'd seen tonight.

Dr Steig had stepped out a few minutes earlier, and Lean was now alone with the woman's body for the first time. The wooden floor planks had been pried up and removed, exposing a roughly circular patch of dark earth about eight feet in diameter upon which the body now lay. A pitchfork stood before him, plunged into the dirt. Two of the prongs ran straight through the young woman's neck, pinning her to the ground. She was on her back, arms out to the sides, her legs spread apart. A burned-out lump of candle tallow sat just below her right foot. She still wore her long black skirt, dark hose just visible at the ankles, and black leather shoes. Her white blouse, black coat, and several other garments had been removed and stacked neatly several yards away. Although she was naked from the waist up, that had not been immediately apparent at a distance. Two long cuts crisscrossed her chest. Blood, drying darkly, covered nearly all her torso, though her arms were a ghostly white. Her right arm was severed at the wrist, a pool of blood where the missing hand should be.

The deputy was no stranger to bodies that had met a violent end. They were mostly men, older ones who had lived out a decent portion of their allotted years. At least it seemed that way, since they typically led hard, unforgiving lives that aged them prematurely and sped them on to their ends. Doubtless, Maggie Keene was on a similar road that would have robbed her of any final traces of hope and innocence in a short time, but earlier that night she had been young and alive.

Lean noted a fifteen-ton Cleveland crane overhead. The machine was suspended above, resting on rails on either side of the room so it could move heavy steel pieces and equipment the length of the building. The crane's great hook held a chain from which a massive circular gear dangled at eye level. The large iron cog would soon help drive some powerful engine across great distances, but now it hung motionless and silent.

Facing him, scrawled along the side of the gear, was a series of chalk letters: KIA K'TABALDAMWOGAN PAIOMWIJI. It was too long to be any sort of worker's note for some special component for the rail car they were building. He supposed it was either foreign or perhaps some sort of code. The letters were printed in his notebook already. He took a deep drag and let the cigarette smoke linger in his lungs a few seconds more as he prepared for another inspection of the body, hoping to notice something new and telling. Soon Mayor Ingraham would arrive, and Lean would be called upon to explain what steps had been taken, what he made of the scene, and the plan for apprehending the murderer. He could answer the first question.

As one of Portland's three deputy marshals, Lean was in a small minority of citizens with a telephone in his home. After receiving the call, he had hurried down to meet the first patrolman who'd answered the watchman's frantic whistle. Other officers had since swept through the building, but Lean had kept them away from the body. He'd ordered the first patrolman to stand guard over the watchman inside the latter's shack, quarantining the only two known witnesses to the horrific details of the body. The dozen or so other buildings that made up the

Portland Company's rail car manufacturing grounds had been searched as well. He'd used the telephone in the company office to speak with the marshal and then sent word to the station to call in every available patrolman. Almost every one of Portland's three dozen police officers was now out on foot, searching for signs of the killer.

He looked down at the body once more. The passage of time since Lean had first viewed the corpse did nothing to alleviate the unexpected despair he'd felt when he first stood over the young woman's body and her face had still been warm to the touch. Even that last hint of life had since been stolen away. Now the woman's soul was one more hour removed from this world. The wide, unknowing look on her face remained, and the senseless horror of it all weighed on Lean. He fought down the urge to yank away the pitchfork still planted in her neck.

2

Dr Virgil Steig was a slight man of about sixty with a neatly trimmed mustache and beard gone mostly white. From where he stood by the entrance to the machine shop, the doctor could hear the gentle sloshing of the harbor against the wharf pilings just a good stone's throw away. The various buildings of the locomotive foundry and machine works were crammed into ten waterfront acres near Portland's East End. At the sound of approaching horseshoes and the clatter of carriage wheels over the cobblestones, the doctor returned his attention to the land. He let his gaze drift past the carriage to the open space before him, then up to the dome of the Grand Trunk Railway. Dr Steig stepped away from the machine shop door, ready to greet the mayor's landau as it arrived at the entrance to the Portland Company. A uniformed patrolman moved across the compound and opened the carriage door. The ample frame of Mayor Darius Ingraham disgorged itself from the cab.

'Dr Steig. I should have known,' the mayor said between heavy breaths. 'The officer didn't mention it was you.'

'Would you have come if he had?'

'This is no hour for jokes. Why the hell am I here?'

'I thought you'd want to see this, in a manner of speaking. It's going to cause quite a stir: a young woman.' Dr Steig led the mayor toward the front door.

'Prostitute?'

'Yes.'

'That's something. I mean, it could be worse.'

'Don't get your hopes up,' said Dr Steig.

'Who's the investigator?'

'Lean.'

The mayor drew in his breath.

'You appointed him,' said the doctor.

'There were other considerations.'

'Aren't there always?'

The mayor seemed to weigh the need to defend himself but settled for, 'Where is he?'

'Inside with the body.'

'I don't know; he seems bright enough,' the mayor said.

'Plenty bright. Not the most seasoned.'

'He's been around a few years.'

'I have scars older than him.' The doctor turned and reached for the doorknob. 'I just think this case might warrant someone with a bit more expertise.'

'It's just a dead whore, Virgil.'

'And *Macbeth* is just a play about a Scotsman. All the same, better prepare yourself for what you're about to see.' Dr Steig led the way inside. Deputy Marshal Archie Lean was standing twenty paces ahead.

'Holy Mother of God!' The mayor drew a handkerchief and clapped it to his mouth.

'Not by a long shot,' Lean said.

The mayor moved forward with halting steps. 'Who is she?'

'Maggie Keene,' Lean said. 'One of Jimmy Farrell's newer girls. Usually works North Street.'

Mayor Ingraham tapped his cane on the ground. 'Oh, just wait until news of this gets out. Blanchard and his temperance fanatics will drag me over the coals. A dead whore, some bloody killer roaming about— '

'And a watchman too drunk to notice anything.' Lean saw the mayor grimace. The Maine Temperance Union had been firing broadsides against the mayor since the day he took office. Newspapers with Republican leanings routinely ran stories accusing him of failing to enforce the Maine Liquor Law that – on paper, anyway – had banned the sale, and nonmedicinal use, of alcohol since 1855. There were even allegations of payoffs by the larger Irish gangs that controlled much of the flow of booze into Portland.

'Why isn't Marshal Swett here anyway?' asked the mayor.

'Prefers not to conduct business before breakfast,' Lean said.

'Takes a better photograph after a full night's sleep,' Dr Steig added.

Mayor Ingraham stared at them in disbelief, his jowls starting to quiver.

'I did speak with him on the telephone,' Lean said with the unenthused voice of a man obeying dubious orders. 'He wants the men to scour the docks and alleys, dredge up whatever drunks and vagrants they can. Find one with no memory of the last few hours, some blood on him, and that's our man.' He took a deep drag on his cigarette. 'Apart from those few still on watch outside, I've got everyone out looking.'

'Good,' Mayor Ingraham said. 'So we throw out the net and examine the haul.'

'You think they'll find him?' Dr Steig said.

'I don't know what to think about . . . whatever you call this.'

'Someone killed a whore.' The calm was returning to the mayor's face. 'Someone in the grip of extreme passion. Wouldn't you agree?'

Lean shrugged. 'It's more than just a guy getting rough; a beating 'cause the girl wouldn't give his coins back after he can't finish up his business. Or worse yet, the horse bolts the gate before the starter's pistol.'

'All such pleasant imagery aside, I agree,' said Dr Steig. 'This doesn't appear to be a blind rage or a drunken fit. The presentation of the body is all wrong.'

Mayor Ingraham frowned at the opinion. 'What, then? What sort of man would do such a thing?'

Lean could almost picture the images that must have been running through the mayor's mind. The editorial cartoons would show a caricatured, blurry-eyed Irish watchman and paint the mayor hoisting the whiskey jug for the ape-faced brute to drink from. Now the mayor's eyes lit up at the prospect of pinning this

11

all on something other than demon rum and his failure to curb the flow of alcohol.

'We'll roust Farrell's joint,' Lean said. 'See if the other girls will talk. She's dressed rather fancy for the work; maybe her friends will know who she was getting so dudded up for.'

'You don't sound hopeful,' Dr Steig said.

Lean crushed his cigarette beneath his heel. 'Never seen anything quite so . . .' He failed to finish the thought before being interrupted by the sound of a carriage approaching.

'Now what?' the mayor said. 'The photographer?'

'Can't be,' Lean said. 'I only sent for him twenty minutes ago.'

Dr Steig cleared his throat. 'I know who it is. A thought occurred to me after I saw the body, and I telephoned for someone. Now, it's a rather unusual step I'm suggesting.'

'Why not?' said the mayor, his voice leaden with disappointment. 'Desperate times and all that rot.'

'There's a man recently returned to Portland. The grandson of my old commander, Major Grey. The young man was a student in some of my anatomy classes. Would've made a great surgeon, actually—'

'Cyrus Grey? Wait a minute – that scrawny red-Indian boy of his?' A look of puzzled doubt landed on the mayor's face.

'Only on his father's side. Anyway, knowing the family and all, I followed his career, the odd bit of news and whatnot. He joined the Pinkertons, gained a bit of notoriety there.'

Lean snorted. Ever since Allan Pinkerton had famously uncovered a plot against President Lincoln during the war, the private detective and security force of the Pinkertons – with their pompous symbol of the all-seeing eye – had been held to be a notch above all other police forces. But since that success thirty

12

years earlier, Lean considered that the Pinkertons' true talent, exposed in their operations infiltrating unions as strikebreakers, was for cracking skulls rather than using their own.

'Deputy, do you recall, about a year ago, news of Jacob Rutland, the Boston shipping magnate whose young daughter went missing?' Dr Steig asked.

'Heard something. Pinkertons got her back, didn't they?'

'Their men were brought in but made no further headway than the city police. Another week went by, and still no trace of the girl. Nothing at all. In desperation they called in this fellow.'

'Desperation?' Mayor Ingraham's eyebrow arched.

'His methods are a bit unorthodox.'

This did nothing to smooth the mayor's forehead. 'Smoke signals and spirit visions?'

'Quite the contrary,' Dr Steig said. 'He's known to employ a rather modern, scientific approach. Where the other detectives couldn't find a hair of the girl after two weeks, this fellow brought her home alive within forty-eight hours.'

'I don't recall hearing anything about that,' Mayor Ingraham said.

'He was also involved in the Athenaeum burglaries,' Dr Steig said, 'and the Bunker Hill murders.'

'That was him?' Mayor Ingraham exchanged a long look with Lean.

'Can't say I care much for involving some Pinkerton with half-cooked ideas about police work.' Lean imagined much time being wasted by some fool using uncertain techniques such as taking fingerprint samples and rambling on about the Frenchman Bertillon's system of identifying criminals by their precise body measurements. 'But I suppose there's no harm in talking to him,'

13

Lean said. 'We're already rounding up derelicts, and I can take some men over to Farrell's after sunup.'

'Agreed, then,' the mayor said. 'Though not a word of this to anyone. I don't want it known about town that we're consulting, in desperation, with this Indian fellow. Has a name, does he? Chief Something-or-Other?'

'Just Grey. Perceval Grey.'

The three of them stood, waiting for the machine-shop door to open and this Perceval Grey to reveal himself.

'Where is he already?' Mayor Ingraham said.

'Perhaps that wasn't him after all,' Dr Steig said.

'Could be a reporter. Better have a look. Cover the body, just in case.' The mayor reached out and took Lean by the arm. 'I don't want any newspapermen stealing a look at that ... that travesty.'

3

The doctor's newly arrived hansom sat twenty yards away, the driver still atop the cab. There was no sign of anyone else until the driver nodded his head to the side. Lean saw the dark outline of a tallish man standing near the watchman's shack, staring down the alley that ran between the long machine and erecting shops of the Portland Company. Dr Steig wandered forward to his carriage, the mayor and Lean following behind.

'What's he doing?' asked the doctor.

The driver shrugged. 'Whatever it is, he's been at it since we got here.'

'Grey?' the doctor called out. The man answered by holding up a hand, one finger extended skyward. Then he turned and stared at the small outbuilding that served as the watchman's shack.

Lean was only thirty years old and fit enough, but this night was unusually cold and wet for mid-June. A driving storm of the type usually reserved for September or October in New England had ripped through during the prior afternoon, and the dampness was making his knees stiffen. He stomped his feet on the stones underfoot, forcing the blood to move along. After several more moments, Perceval Grey finished whatever he was doing and approached the others.

'Dr Steig, I was pleasantly surprised to receive your message.' Grey took the doctor's hand in both of his own. Lean noticed a caution in the movement, then recalled the doctor's mention that Grey had been a student. Of course he would know of the doctor's weakness in his right arm, the Civil War wound that had ended his career as a surgeon and still caused tremors in that hand.

Grey stepped back and regarded the other two guests. 'Mayor Ingraham and Detective Sergeant . . . '

'Deputy Marshal Lean.' Lean glanced down at his front, looking to see if his badge or pistol was somehow visible. Neither was.

'Deputy Marshal?' Grey cocked an eyebrow. 'Rather an odd title for an investigating officer. Barring a stagecoach robbery, that is.'

Lean studied Perceval Grey as the man talked. Grey's eyes were dark and focused, giving no hint of the late hour. He was only slightly taller than his guests, though his height was accentuated by his thin, angular frame. His complexion was tan, but

15

not as dark as Lean expected. His face held sharp features topped by short black hair parted on the right and slicked back under a fine beaver-felt derby. Lean wasn't exactly sure of what he expected to see of this half-blood Pinkerton, but it wasn't the man before them, dressed in a black dinner coat, charcoal waistcoat, and black tie, the four-in-hand still tightly knotted. The suit was so well tailored that the man could be taking in a concert at Kotzschmar Hall with the mayor rather than responding to a murder investigation in the dead hours of the morning.

'Thank you for coming so quickly. You see, something's happened and ... well ...' Dr Steig cleared his throat. 'Grey, the thing is, we were hoping you might be able to assist us in a matter.'

'Actually, I'm not planning on taking on any full inquiries at this time; I'm here in Maine on a sabbatical from practical work. But for you, Doctor, I am willing to provide a quick overview of the prostitute's murder.' Grey's face was perfectly reserved as he made the announcement. 'Peculiar for the killer to enter through the front door, in plain view of the night watchman's shack – and possible other witnesses passing at a distance,' Grey said.

'Well, the watchman admits he was asleep inside the shack. And, in any event, our man entered a side door.' Lean nodded in that direction. 'Busted a pane of glass to reach the lock.'

'Interesting.' Grey headed for the door to the machine shop.

'Wait. My note made no mention of a murder, let alone a prostitute. Rasmus?' The doctor looked to his driver, who held up his hands in a display of innocence.

Lean's entire body tensed.

'What's this?' The mayor stepped back from the others. 'I demand an explanation!'

'It's hardly reasonable to expect a complete explanation of the case until I've examined the murder site. Through here, is it?'

'I mean the murder, a prostitute – how did you know?'

Grey ignored the mayor and disappeared inside the doorway.

There was a brief silence as each of the men contemplated Perceval Grey's remarks. A crooked smile settled itself within the confines of Dr Steig's neatly trimmed beard. 'You see, gentlemen – Grey can be of considerable assistance in pursuing this matter, if we can just overcome his reluctance.'

'I don't trust him,' said the mayor. 'Don't see how he could possibly know those details unless he's had some involvement in the crime. What do you say, Lean?'

'Perhaps we should head inside and see what this Grey makes of the scene.'

Lean led the way inside, where they found Grey standing just a short distance into the shop, not yet in sight of the body.

He turned to them. 'Who has set foot at the scene?'

Dr Steig answered, since he was standing closest. 'Present company, the first officer, and the watchman. Additional officers have examined the rest of the compound.'

'That's right,' said Lean. 'You see, what I find most peculiar about the body is that the killer must have intended—'

Grey held up a hand. 'I must insist on silence as to all opinions, particularly those addressing the killer's methods or motives, until I've finished examining the evidence.'

'Oh, come now, time is against us in this,' said the mayor. 'The quicker you understand the nature of this, the better.'

Grey tilted his head with the air of a music teacher suffering the haphazard notes of an untrained child. 'If you learn nothing else tonight, remember this: one of the greatest threats to a successful inquiry is letting yourself be led afield by a preconceived theory. The absurdly concocted theories of others can irreparably taint one's objectivity. Even casual statements will conjure up familiar notions and memories of similar crimes, causing unwarranted importance to attach to irrelevant facts. The mind becomes set on finding what it now expects to see and fails to perceive that which is actually present.'

Lean could see the mayor bristling at the very idea of being lectured to. 'Is that what they teach you in the Pinkertons?'

'No. One of the things I tried, unsuccessfully, to teach them in my brief tenure there.'

'All the same, Grey, believe me when I say you've never seen a case similar to this one, I mean to have a—'

Grey halted Lean again with a raised hand.

'Suit yourself,' Lean said. 'Right this way.' The tarp, which Lean had set atop the upright hay fork earlier, remained in place. It reminded him of a soldier's field tent from a long-abandoned battlefield, the canvas hanging limp and uneven from a single pole. Lean had only ever seen pictures of such sights, the Civil War having ended twenty-seven years earlier, before his first memories. It also reminded him of other images from that time, photographs of Portland.

Grey stopped beside him and announced the very same thought. 'Like one of the old tents they set out after the Great Fire.'

Even though Lean had been a toddler at the time, he had seen so many photographs and engraved images and heard so many tales that the event was seared into his mind almost as clearly as if it had happened only a month ago. A boy's mishap with matches near stored fireworks on the Fourth of July, 1866, had quickly turned into a disaster. The resulting flames had ignited Brown's sugar factory, and the fire then cut a swath through two hundred acres of Portland Neck, destroying two thousand buildings in the heart of the city. Ten thousand people were left homeless, with many forced to live temporarily in a makeshift village of canvas tents along the emptied grounds at the base of Munjoy Hill. The city rose up from the ashes within three years, refashioning itself more grandly in brick-fronted Victorian splendor.

'Let's hope this scene isn't quite so disastrous as that great inferno,' Grey said. 'Maybe we can salvage some few clues after all the inexcusable trampling of the evidence.'

'I didn't want anyone nosing around, stealing a glimpse of the scene,' Mayor Ingraham said.

Seeing Grey's dubious stare, Lean added, 'I was careful not to disturb the body.'

He helped Grey remove and dispose of the canvas. Grey stared at the body for a full minute, almost perfectly still. Finally he pulled a pencil and a thin notepad from his side pack and began to sketch and scribble as his head turned in all directions, his eyes shooting back and forth.

'You're planning to photograph the body?'

Lean nodded. 'Our man should be here shortly.'

Several minutes later Grey's notepad disappeared into his bag. He took up a lamp, and he began to circle the body, pausing briefly where Maggie Keene's clothes had been neatly stacked. He proceeded to kneel down on the wooden flooring near the bloody stump of the right wrist. With his pencil he reached forward and poked at a small lump sitting on the blood-soaked ground. He traced a very small circle in the air around the end of the right arm. 'One candle burned down by the right foot, another here.

She was on the ground when her hand was removed. The blade cut into the earth.' He stood again and pondered the area around the severed wrist. 'Significant bleeding here, Dr Steig, yet less of a stream than I would have expected from a sudden amputation.'

'Likely dead before the hand was severed,' answered Dr Steig. 'No pressure. The blood simply pooled.'

'The cuts on the chest were also inflicted posthumously?' asked Grey.

The doctor shrugged. 'I'll know more when we get the body to the hospital.'

Perceval Grey continued to circle the corpse. 'Lean, this pitchfork – you'll need to confirm whether this is factory property. Did the workers leave it close by, or did our man bring it himself just for this purpose?' Grey moved a few more steps before pausing again at the young woman's head, where he held his lamp close to examine her features. After studying the ground, Grey knelt and stretched forward until his own face was within inches of hers. He turned to Dr Steig.

The doctor nodded. 'Yes, the tongue's been cut out.'

Lean stared in near shock as he watched Grey move close enough so that his lips were almost touching the dead woman's. Grey gave several hearty sniffs before pulling away.

'Takes the tongue to stop her talking. But then why her right hand, too? Does he mean to keep her from . . . ' Lean was mostly thinking aloud but noticed Grey and Dr Steig waiting on him to finish the thought. 'Maybe to keep her from writing as well. To keep her from revealing something. But why bother to cut the hand off after she's already dead? Makes no bloody sense.'

'Interesting observation,' mumbled Grey. He regained his footing and moved along, careful not to tread on the damp earth surrounding the body. Upon reaching her left foot, he stooped and peered at the ground. His stare moved in a line away from the body's left side, and he inched along in that direction.

'Two bloody marks, faint partial curves of the heel.' Grey pulled out his tape measure and noted the length of a dim reddish outline just visible on the floor. 'Matches the footprints he left in the earth by her body.'

Lean moved closer and saw the traces of blood. He set his own foot down parallel to the faint bloody outline of the killer's heel. 'Small feet.'

Grey was now measuring the distance between the prints.

'Based on his stride, our man is rather short – five foot two, more or less. And these are not hesitant steps. He was going somewhere.' Grey moved in the direction of the bloody footprints. Several yards ahead he stopped and held his lamp low as he gazed about.

'Ha! Here we are.' He pointed to a sheet of metal leaning against a workbench.

Lean and Dr Steig moved closer to see what looked like traces of blood, smeared in a thin horizontal line, then back again at a downward angle.

'Almost looks like a seven,' noted Dr Steig.

Grey shook his head. 'No, he's made the angle too severe.'

'Angle?' Lean blew his nose and shoved the balled-up hand-kerchief back into his coat pocket. 'He's just wiping the blood off his fingers.'

'If you bother to look closely, you'll see a larger spot here. His thumb was planted, then drawn across. Then a second smudge, smaller. A new finger planted where the first line ended. Separate actions. Deliberately placed. He's not wiping; more like he's drawing.'

Lean turned his frown from the bloody lines to Grey. 'What on earth is he drawing?'

'And why?' added the doctor.

'An interesting question, Doctor, and one, I believe, that you may be the most suited to answer as we pursue this inquiry. But in answer to the deputy, I believe that our man is fashioning some sort of diagram. What it represents I cannot yet say.' Grey lifted up the sheet of metal to get a better look.

'That's not the only puzzle he's left for us.' Lean took several steps back toward the body and waved at the gear hanging from the overhead crane. 'You've ignored these chalk letters. Could be some sort of cipher. Or else Greek or some such.'

'Or nonsense,' Dr Steig said. 'It's no foreign language I've ever seen.'

'I haven't ignored it at all. And no, it's not foreign. Quite the contrary – an indigenous tongue.'

Lean felt his face wrinkle. 'A what, now?'

'A native tongue. The language of the Abenaki tribes of Maine and New Hampshire.'

Dr Steig grinned. 'Well then, a wonderful coincidence that I called you here.'

'Coincidence?' Grey appeared almost offended by the word. 'No. More likely your mind held some faint memory of having seen the language. An inkling that made you think to summon me in the first place.'

Lean edged forward. 'So what does it say?'

'*Kia K'tabaldamwogan paiomwiji.*' Grey studied the language for another moment. 'I haven't spoken it in many years. I'd say: "You ... your reign, or maybe kingdom, has arrived."'

Within seconds it hit Lean. '"Thy kingdom come"?'

Grey nodded at Lean. '"Thy kingdom come."'

'The killer is an Indian,' Ingraham declared.

Grey held up a finger. 'The killer can write in the Abenaki language. Nothing more is yet proved.'

Lean gave a small snort. 'The evidence is quite damning, Grey. You must be sorry to see that he's one of your people.'

Grey regarded him for a long moment, and Lean felt that, in some sense, his own measure was being taken. Perhaps he'd insulted the man somehow. 'It's no reflection on you, of course. Don't let that concern you.'

Grey turned back to the chalk writing once more and said in a detached voice, 'At the moment my only concern is with the one glaring question that is truly confounding me.'

'Just the one question, eh?' Lean couldn't resist smirking at the effortless way Grey tossed out his conceits.

'Yes. Given the horrific and sensational display our man has set out for us here ... how is it that we have never heard any news of his first victim?'

4

'First victim?' Mayor Ingraham called out from where he'd been standing aside, watching the proceedings with evident distaste.

'What the devil are you on about?' asked Lean.

'Tell me, Deputy, do you introduce the missus as your second wife?'

'What? No, I've only been married once.'

'Precisely. You simply don't designate something as number

two if there's never been a number one.' Grey began to pace on a short course between the body and the metal sheet with the bloody lines. 'He burned two candles. Left the stubs at the right foot and right hand. Two points of five on the body; hands, feet, and head splayed out in a pentagram. The angle formed by those two extremities matches those bloody streaks he drew.'

'Like a star,' Lean said, picturing his young son's drawings, crisscrossing pencil lines forming a warped, five-pointed figure in a paper sky.

'Add to that he's gone to the trouble of quoting the Lord's Prayer. But only the second line. That makes three separate markings he's left behind. All indicating a connection with the number two.'

'What does it mean?' asked Dr Steig.

Grey shook his head. 'A compelling puzzle. And once we have gleaned all we can from this location, I believe we will be forced to turn our attention to finding the first victim. Our man is going through quite a bit of trouble to paint us a picture. And right now we are missing half the canvas. We need to understand more of what he has done.'

'Well,' said the doctor, his eyes alight, 'I should hope to learn something more once I get a proper look at the body.'

Lean paused from his frantic note taking. 'I know you've got your own examination room, Doctor, but we'll have to do this one by the book. Maine General Hospital.'

The doctor nodded agreement as the sound of approaching carriage wheels grew louder.

'Must be the photographer. You can take the body as soon as he's done,' said Lean.

'Then we can join you at the hospital after we collect one more piece of evidence and interview the watchman,' said Grey.

'I thought you were otherwise occupied. Could only offer a quick review,' Lean said. 'Why the sudden change? That Abenaki writing give you a personal interest?'

'My willingness to take on this inquiry is born not of any personal interest but rather of pure and utter fear.' Grey stepped close and stared into Lean's eyes. 'Fear that the police department will conduct the investigation with the same lack of perception and imagination that they typically display. Fear that, given the complexity of this matter, the murderer will go free as a result.'

The two detectives remained fixed against each other until Dr Steig interrupted. 'Lean, shouldn't you see about the photographer?'

'Yes,' Grey agreed, 'you may want to go and safeguard his expensive equipment. There are criminals about, you know!'

'Your man's quite a charming fellow,' Lean said as he walked to the exit with Dr Steig and the mayor.

The doctor smiled. 'He can actually be rather engaging, once you get to know him.'

'Let's hope it doesn't come to that.'

Outside, Dr Steig's driver was busy helping the photographer unload his cumbersome gear. Mayor Ingraham motioned to his own driver, parked across the courtyard.

'Gentlemen, I shall gladly leave the postmortem and the rest to you. The vision of the body is already enough to trouble my sleep for some time to come. Good night, Doctor.' The mayor then turned his attention to Lean. 'Deputy, I shall eagerly await word of your investigation's progress.'

Lean couldn't mistake the mayor's meaning. This was his

investigation alone; neither Dr Steig nor Perceval Grey would be held to answer for the failure to apprehend the murderer. Forty-five minutes later, Lean watched the doctor's carriage rumble away into the darkness. The photographer had finished his work, and Dr Steig was heading to the west end of town to conduct the autopsy. Lean glanced to his left, not yet seeing the first hint of morning at the far edge of the ocean. A few faint sounds drifted up from the easternmost wharves as the Portland waterfront stirred to life.

Inside, Perceval Grey waited, pitchfork in hand, by the exposed circle of earth that had held the corpse minutes earlier. It had taken both men to wrest the grisly tool from the ground and free the body.

'Say, standing there near a puddle of blood with a dark look in your eyes and a hay fork in hand – you remind me of someone,' Lean said.

Grey handed the pitchfork over to Lean. 'Such a wit for a police officer. Further proof that you have missed your true calling.'

'Oh, and what might my true calling be?'

'Anything other than a police officer.'

Lean offered a weary smile. 'Tonight I might just agree with you.' He brandished the pitchfork. 'What do you have in mind?'

'Here.' Grey gestured to the exposed earth where the woman's head had been. 'Away from where the blood has softened the soil.'

Lean cocked an eyebrow.

'I've marked on the prongs just how far into the earth our man was able to penetrate.'

Lean noticed the white chalk line about five inches high on the iron prong. 'Got it in pretty good, didn't he?'

'Especially when you consider that the dirt is hard packed and he had to get it through her neck. If my suspicions are true, we're dealing with a man possessed of remarkable strength.'

'And yet a little fellow by his stride and shoe size.' Lean had hardly slept in almost twenty-four hours, but the thought that this experiment might help draw the picture of the man they were looking for, as well as the prospect of being shown up by some murderous little runt, suddenly invigorated the deputy. He doffed his woolen coat and tossed it aside, spit into his palms, and practiced his grip on the long wooden handle.

'Come now, Lean.'

'A moment. Need to stiffen the sinews, summon up the blood, and all that.' He swung his arms side to side, readying for a full-bodied effort. Lean jerked the pitchfork up with both arms so that the prongs loomed for a second before his eyes, then he drove it straight down with every bit of strength he could muster. A groan escaped him as the iron tips bit into the hard dirt.

Grey knelt down to mark the same prong. 'A valiant effort. But you're an inch and a half shy of our man's mark.'

'Damn. I gave it my all.' Lean examined the disparity in the chalk marks and let out a low whistle. 'What sort of fiend are we dealing with?'

'Don't be too critical. Your effort was fueled by curiosity and a touch of pride. Our man's was motivated by something deeper and wholly more violent.' Grey set the pitchfork aside, then motioned for Lean to lead the way. 'Now the side entrance.'

'Broken glass underfoot,' Lean noted as they exited the machine shop by its side door. The top half held tall three-over-three glass panes. The right one in the bottom row had been shattered.

Grey examined the panes from both sides before following Lean into the alleyway between the long machine shop and the shorter erecting shop that ran parallel. It was dark there; the electric light post set a few feet away was out. Grey held his lamp high, examining the scene around the side door.

'This is where they entered.' Lean began to step forward.

'A moment, please.' Grey edged sideways along the machine shop's outer wall, then moved in a half circle around the door, eyes fixed on the ground. When he completed his path, he turned his attention toward the unlit streetlight.

'Watchman said it went out tonight. A bird struck it,' Lean said.

Grey made a curt noise in response. Lean thought it was a laugh, though there had been an element of anger in the sound. He watched Grey move several yards past the lamppost and kneel. His lantern revealed a dead pigeon.

'Interesting.' Grey squatted, set the lamp down, and examined the dead bird from several angles. 'Meant to look like it had flown into and busted the light.'

'You suspect foul play?' Lean allowed himself a smile. 'Perhaps the bird was a witness.'

'An accomplice, actually. An unwilling one, but an accomplice nevertheless. See here, the neck was twisted. And it was originally placed closer to the streetlamp and side door.' Grey motioned to the ground nearby, where Lean could see several scuff marks in the dirt. 'The watchman walks with a limp?'

'Yes. You think he's involved?'

Grey answered only with a noncommittal tilt of his head before he stood, lamp in hand, and started walking down the alley toward the front of the Portland Company and the watchman's shack. He paused briefly at a corner of the erecting shop where another, perpendicular alley ran away from the machine shop. Grey continued on, often bending down with the lamp inches from the ground, peering at some seemingly invisible object for long moments. Then he would spring up and stride forward or backtrack several steps and repeat the process. After several minutes he returned to the corner of the erecting shop's building.

'Here. The killer stood here. The watchman's door is visible. Come, Lean, notice on the ground one set of firmer footprints, with scuffling all about. He waited for a long while, grew restless, and shifted his feet around. He was here long enough to smoke four cigarettes at intervals.' Grey bent down and picked up a hand-rolled cigarette butt.

'There's only three butts,' Lean noted.

'Four matches.'

Grey unwrapped the last bit of the cigarette and held the exposed tobacco to his nose. Lean thought he saw a flash of surprise on Grey's face. He dropped the material and bent to collect the two remaining butts. He examined each, turning them all around to inspect them from multiple angles.

'What do you see?' Lean asked.

'It's nothing important. He was still smoking the last when something occurred, caused him to move.' Grey dropped one of the cigarettes to the ground as the other disappeared into a jacket pocket. Before Lean could ask another question, Grey turned and moved down the narrow perpendicular alley with his lamp held low to the ground. 'He dashed away.'

Lean picked up the discarded cigarette butt and sniffed it. It had an unusual, acrid scent that was mildly offensive. He slipped it into his shirt pocket, then followed after, pausing wherever Grey had. He too could make out the occasional imprint of a foot. At the end of the short alley, the ground turned to cobblestone.

'Well, that's the end of that,' Lean said.

Grey shook his head and handed his lamp to Lean. 'Keep the light abreast of me but stay four feet from the side of the building.'

Lean followed the instructions as Grey got close to the ground and proceeded, sometimes on hands and knees, his head bobbing and swaying this way and that as he moved along. Lean watched, totally perplexed, but dutifully holding the lamp closer when asked. Grey would pause to examine loose rocks or pluck strands of weeds from the earth, which he would then peer at and sniff. There was something almost wild about Grey's behavior, and Lean became conscious of the fact that anyone observing them would have thought them both mad.

'What exactly are you doing?'

Grey answered without diverting his gaze from the ground. 'Our man wishes to conceal himself in the night. It's human instinct to move along walls. Moving quickly, he's bound to leave traces. Like so.'

Lean swung the lamp close and peered at Grey, who reached into the crevice between two cobblestones, his index finger now marked with a dark smudge. Grey gave it a smell.

'Tobacco ash. The same mix.' He stood and brushed off his knees. 'He came along here, as far as the corner, anyway.'

They continued until they reached the corner, where they had a fine view of the Portland Company's front courtyard, including the watchman's shack. In the lit windows, they could plainly make out the watchman and the patrolman who had first

30

responded to the scene. Grey walked ahead, stopped, stepped aside, and retrieved a half-smoked cigarette from the ground. He smelled it to confirm the contents, examined the external appearance, then slipped it into his pocket.

'He's trying not to be seen, yet he heads straight for the watchman?' Lean stared ahead at the outbuilding. 'He's mad.'

'I suspect not. But the answer is waiting in there,' Grey said as he strode toward the small shack.

'Tell me, Tibbets, how long has that limp of yours been keeping you from making your regular rounds?' Grey asked.

'What? Not at all. I make my rounds like I'm supposed to. Every hour.' The stocky, balding watchman shifted about in his seat as his eyes darted back and forth between Grey and Lean, looking futilely for some safe harbor. Lean thought the man appeared drunk; his words were slow and careless.

'Come now, your limp is pronounced. The night's damp. Sitting here in your shack only stiffens the joints further. No one is blaming you for this.'

'I'm paid to go every hour—'

'Your boss doesn't need to hear any of this,' said Lean, 'so just answer the question.'

The watchman rubbed his fingertips together, contemplating his options while staring into the dark gaze of Perceval Grey. 'All right then, as you say. It ain't so bad usually. Just this past week's been worse than ever. I've been promising my wife I'll go down to the druggist shop for them drops her sister's always carping on about helping the rheumatism in her hands—'

Grey held up his own hand to stop the unnecessary tale. 'Just a week, then? Before then you were making your rounds timely?'

'Yeah.' The man's shoulders slumped, and he sighed, a combination of relief and defeat. 'Been doing one roundabout soon as I get here and another before sunup. If I'd known that something like this would happen, I'd have said something, let someone else take my rounds. But I can't lose the work, you know?'

'You needn't trouble yourself,' Grey said. 'Walking your rounds would not have saved that girl. Now, let's have a look at your bottle.' The watchman's eyes went wide and his lips parted, but the protest of temperance died in his throat. With something of an effort, he leaned down to an overturned wooden crate and retrieved a bottle from inside. Grey examined the bottle, removed the loose cap, sniffed the contents, and handed it over to Lean. 'The closure is of interest.'

Lean glanced at the bottle's top. It was not the more common lightning-type closure that had a metal wire toggle atop the stopper. This one was a loop seal: a disk with a metal loop on top and a rubber convex bottom forced into the mouth of the bottle. It was favored by bootleg bottlers since it was cheaper, but it was only a one-timer, not reusable like the lightning type. Once it was yanked out by means of a small hook, the rubber stopper expanded, rendering it impossible to completely reseal. Lean also sniffed the bottle; it smelled of cheap beer, though a bit off. Unlike the stopper, the bottle would have been used many times over and might not have been cleaned after its last use.

'It's just beer, no booze. And you see I only drank half it anyways,' said the watchman.

'Fortunate for you. You've been drugged. If you'd emptied the bottle, you'd still be unconscious. You bring the same kind every night?' Grey said.

'Most every.'

'You open it before your first inspection of the property?'

'Nah, I wait till after the first walk round. Done about ten o'clock.' The watchman wiped his lips with the back side of his hand. 'Work up a thirst and all.'

'What time did you hear the bird crash into the lamp by the machine shop's side door?'

'Right about ten twenty.' He stopped short and stared suspiciously at Grey.

'You looked at your pocketwatch?'

'No, but the Montrealer gets in at ten past ten. And it was just a bit after that I heard a bunch of fellas wandering this way from off the train. Carrying on loud enough to get me up to take a look. Could practically smell the Canadian Rye on 'em all the way up here. They made it a few hundred yards from the station 'fore they seen they were heading toward the ocean instead of the city.'

'So you noticed the light was out, went to investigate, realized that the bird had busted the lamp, and returned here. Then what?'

'Same as I've already said ten times. I was feeling sleepy. Must have dozed off. Next thing, I hear a sound – a scream, maybe. Took my lamp and stick. Saw a candle flame in through the window of the machine shop. Went inside, and that's when I saw this man running for the side door. Didn't get a good look at him. I would've gone after him, but then I seen her lying there. And that's all.'

Grey motioned to Lean, passing off the watchman.

'All right, you're free to go now. We'll be in touch if we need anything else,' Lean said.

'There is one more thing you can do to help,' added Grey.

'Anything. Anything at all.'

'Don't talk about this to anyone. Only a few souls know any details of tonight. Start talking and you're liable to draw attention to yourself. Reporters first, but then, perhaps, from the fiend who did this.' Grey arched his eyebrows in warning.

The watchman nodded mutely before gathering up his things and bumbling out the door.

'You believe him?' Lean asked.

'He never had a hand on the girl, in any event.' Grey waved his hand at the small room. 'No hint of her perfume when we entered. Nor do I think he was complicit in the break-in.'

'A bit of fragrance wouldn't do him any harm.' Lean flipped through a small stack of loose papers on the desk. 'If he'd been in on it, he could have broken that window to hide using his keys.'

'If the killer had the watchman's assistance, he wouldn't have needed that elaborate distraction with the dead bird.'

'You're certain our killer planted the dead bird?' Lean asked.

'Birds don't fly into streetlights at night, Deputy. Our killer was prepared. He needed to ensure that the watchman was not awake during the crime. But the killer couldn't dope the watchman's beer until after the bottle was opened. That would happen only after completing his first circuit. And he wouldn't leave his shack to make another inspection until almost sunrise.'

'So the bird and the broken lamp were bait,' Lean said. 'The killer needed to draw him out for a few minutes after he completed his first walk.'

'Precisely. Busting the lamp darkened the pathway and got the watchman's attention. He came to investigate. And while he did, the killer sprinted around the back of the building, slipped unseen into the shack, and drugged the bottle.'

'Rather elaborate scheme,' Lean said.

'And, therefore, it provides several important clues. Not the least of which is that our killer was very familiar with the immediate area and with the watchman's routine. He must have been lingering nearby for several nights at least.'

'Or else he invented the distraction on the spot. And he's the sort who always carries a dead pigeon for just such an occasion,' Lean said with a smirk.

'A troubling development in either case.'

Lean glanced at his pocketwatch. 'We should be on our way. Dr Steig's probably started his examination without us.'

5

The cab carrying Lean and Grey hurtled along Congress Street, with only splashes of light from the streetlamps to reveal the scene. This was Portland's principal avenue, the only one that ran the entire three-mile length of the Neck, as the peninsula was called. It was a city of slopes, curves, and dips carved by glaciers and now crisscrossed by a network of angled streets and blocks, unfettered by any sense of regularity and uniformity. Portland's maze of cobbled roads was the result of two and a half centuries of fishermen and merchants driven by immediate necessity and that economy of steps that occurs naturally in a place where winters often lasted five months out of the year. Lean enjoyed the view at this hour: the public façade that met the commercial and social needs of the world stripped bare to reveal the city in dark repose. It was a scene reserved for those restless souls who were still awake, whether by choice, duty, or desperation.

Lean returned his attention to his notes from the crime scene. Fatigue was setting in, and he worried that his attention was fading; perhaps he'd failed to record some crucial fact. He glanced at Grey, whose closed eyes and serene countenance betrayed no hint of the same concerns that plagued Lean.

'Tell me something, Grey. It seems impossible that you could have known it was a prostitute that had been murdered. The mayor's worried. Thinks we have stumbled upon the very man we seek.'

Grey chuckled. '"Stumbled" would be an apt description.'

Lean sat, awaiting an explanation.

'Oh, it's all quite simple. Your presence could only mean that a crime had been committed. I know that Dr Steig occasionally performs postmortems for the city. His presence indicated that violence had been done. Knowing the doctor's commitment to his patients, it's a simple deduction that if this victim were still alive, Dr Steig would have been away attending her.'

'You said "her." How did you know the prostitute bit?' asked Lean.

'Ah, I gleaned that from the mayor's attendance.'

Lean opened his mouth to comment, but Grey cut him off. 'I only mean that the mayor certainly wouldn't be about at three in the morning for a simple murder. The victim was someone of social significance, or else the murder was so sensational it warranted his immediate involvement. I observed his comportment. He was not outraged or distressed as he would be if some woman of substance had been murdered. Rather, his movements displayed a gross aversion to this entire matter.'

Grey motioned as if wafting a smell toward his nose. 'Also, I detected inexpensive perfume when shaking the doctor's hand.

He had touched the victim, a woman. So what type of woman, not earning the sympathy of our municipal leaders and wearing cheap perfume, is out at night, in danger of meeting her end in a manner so startling as to rouse the mayor?'

'All plain enough when you explain it that way.'

Grey turned his face toward the small window, glancing at the buildings as they passed. 'Everything that can be observed offers the opportunity to draw conclusions as to what must have occurred previously.'

As they turned off onto Bramhall Street and topped a short rise, Maine General came into full view. The four-story brick hospital, fronted by a spirelike tower, was still faint in the dawn light. The cab moved down Brackett Street to the hospital compound's side entrance.

'One more thing, though. Inside the machine shop, you made a comment about my wife. I don't wear a wedding band.'

'A man can be viewed the same as a crime scene. His appearance, his habits, his expressions, the questions he asks. They all reveal clues to his nature and his history. It's just a matter of training oneself to note these traits, then cataloging them in the memory, contrasting them against those of different social classes, professions, and generations.'

'And so you figured I'm married. What else have you deduced about me?'

'It's not really my place to say.'

'We've already stood together over a woman's naked corpse, discussing her lunatic killer. I think we can speak openly.'

The cab drew to a halt, and the men hopped down.

'Very well, then. I should congratulate you on the impending birth of your child.'

Lean stopped dead in his tracks. 'How . . . ? Remove your hat a moment.'

Grey did so, with a bemused caution.

'No horns on you. So how the devil did you know that? Dr Steig said something.'

Grey smirked. 'There's no magic trick. As I said, my conclusions about you follow the same path as the adduction of proof in a criminal inquiry. Drawing from the truth of one fact the existence of those other facts that most probably preceded it.'

Lean stared at him, silently demanding a more concrete explanation.

'In this instance your hat and your shoes.'

'What of them?' Lean inspected what looked to be a perfectly innocent bowler.

'The hat is on the far side of its better days but has been well tended. The ribbon about the base of the crown has been replaced recently, and the felt has been brushed within the past day.'

'So?'

'Having observed you over the past several hours, I note that you are not overly attentive to the finer points of your own grooming.' Grey gestured toward Lean's coat pocket, from which dangled his crumpled handkerchief. 'The care of your hat indicates a woman who takes pride in your appearance. A mistress is more concerned with her own. It's a wife who takes such pains with a man's hat. And yet your shoes haven't been polished in days – weeks, even. You have an attentive wife but one who can reach the hat rack with much greater ease than she can bend to retrieve your shoes. A disorder of the spine is unlikely in a young woman. An altogether happier condition explains the known facts.'

'Fair enough. Still,' said Lean with a trace of a smile, 'how long ago did you get into town?'

'Two months.'

'You're safe by three months. But if you're still around in October and the babe comes out with jet-black hair . . .'

Grey chuckled and approached the pair of double doors at the rear of the hospital. Lean was close behind but paused to turn his attention to the horizon. The hospital sat atop the northern ridge of Bramhall Hill at the terminus of Portland's scenic Western Promenade. This location at the base of Portland's Neck gave a full view of the peninsular city's only abutting neighbor, the town of Deering. Farther off in the distance, Lean could see the White Mountains of New Hampshire, the peaks now tinged a pleasant rose by dawn's outstretched fingertips.

Lean turned his back on the panorama and walked up the two short steps to the doors. Fully aware of the scents that awaited him, he drew a last deep breath of the fresh air. He pulled the door open and glanced up, thinking a relief frieze of screaming, tormented souls above the lintel would have been more appropriate than the bare wall of bricks he saw there.

Formaldehyde mingled in the air with carbolic acid. Behind it all, Lean could still smell the ingrained stench of dead bodies. Maggie Keene was laid out on an examination table. The corpse had been stripped, and the young woman's clothes were arranged on a sideboard. A sheet covered her from the pelvic bone to the ankles. Her abdomen was nearly as white as the hospital linen.

'As far as I can see, there was no struggle.' Dr Steig held a scalpel and used it to point to the features of the body as he spoke.

'No blood under the fingernails. No bruising or scraping at the back of the skull, her back, or elbows to indicate she was forcibly thrown down. Consistent with blood patterns at the scene. She was already lying down when the pitchfork struck her. The neck wound was fatal and, I suspect, the first inflicted.'

'Could she have been strangled before?' Lean asked.

Dr Steig shook his head. 'There's a lack of hemorrhaging of the facial tissue. Also, the prongs missed the trachea, so I was able to observe that the tissue surrounding the larynx is undamaged. Nor was the hyoid bone fractured.' The doctor's scalpel gleamed in the light of the gas lamps as it hovered over the two dark holes punched into Maggie Keene's throat. 'The right external jugular vein was nicked and opened to half an inch; the left common carotid artery was punctured and hemorrhaged. Death would have been instant.'

'She was unconscious, or near to it, at the time of death,' Grey said. 'I detected an odor near her mouth.'

'Could be chloral hydrate,' Dr Steig said, then indicated the area of the missing hand. 'It took the murderer three cuts to sever the right wrist. She was palm down, and I'd say the first blow was the highest there on the radius. The chip into the bone is shallow, a tentative blow. The second came in lower, and then the third blow succeeded.'

'A hatchet?' asked Lean.

'Given his strength, our man wouldn't need three blows with a hatchet,' Grey said.

Dr Steig nodded. 'Furthermore, from the marks on the bone and the other cuts on the flesh, I'd wager the weapon to be more of a cutting blade, and curved. Still, he's using it to hack more than cut. No surgical skills employed here.'

Lean smiled a bit. 'Well, there's one bright spot anyway. We can eliminate Jack the Ripper as a suspect.'

Grey answered absentmindedly as he bent in to examine the body. 'Though it's generally thought the Ripper had some medical training, at least one of the postmortem physicians, a Dr Bond, opined that the killer didn't have even the technical skill of a butcher or a horse slaughterer.'

'I was only joking, of course,' Lean said.

Grey turned his attention back to the body. 'What about the two cuts to the torso?'

'Probably the same instrument was used,' Dr Steig said.

There were two long cuts upon the young woman's chest. The first ran from below the neck down to her abdomen, ending above and to the left of her navel. The second wound began above her right breast and sloped down to the left. The result was an imperfect, slanted cross sliced into her torso.

'From the angle I'd say he was close to her and on her right, slashing away from himself,' Grey said. 'And again, with her already dead, there would be minimal splatter.'

'Yes, particularly from these cuts. Strictly superficial wounds,' Dr Steig said.

Lean pondered that last bit of information. 'Then why cut her at all? She's already dead. And they'd be deep wounds if they were struck in anger.'

'Clearly our killer was not swept up by emotions. Like everything else at the scene, these wounds were calculated,' Grey said.

Lean asked, 'Was she assaulted, Doctor?'

'No apparent wounds to the generative organs. No signs that a sexual act was even attempted. No rips or tears on any of the garments. Nothing out of the ordinary there.'

'I'd say that fact itself is out of the ordinary, given her line of work,' Lean said.

'But the penetration of the flesh with the pitchfork, the cutting between the exposed breasts,' Grey said. 'Possible indications of a violent, sexual motive.'

'Doubt it,' Lean said. 'She remained dressed below the waist. Skirt, petticoat, chemise, the whole lot still on.'

'Perhaps he meant to attempt the act, but the watchman, still reeling from the effects of his drugging, stumbled in and ended the proceedings too early.'

'Pssh,' Lean snorted. 'She was dead already—' Understanding flashed into his mind, and he groaned. 'Must you make this any more revolting than it already is?'

'I cannot make this anything,' Grey said. 'The facts exist as they are. We can only reveal the truth, and that is exactly what we must do, no matter how disturbing it may be. I'm merely pointing out that we have not yet established a motive. And while the lack of an assault, as well as some of the other details, speak against the attack's being sexually motivated, it would be premature to eliminate some depraved carnal design.'

Lean's dumbfounded look revealed his struggle to take in the full measure of what the man was saying.

'I assume you are not familiar with Krafft-Ebing's research,' Grey said.

'A friend of yours?'

Grey smirked. 'That such conduct may be inexplicable to you, or to society in general, does not make it impossible. We mustn't lose sight of the fact that in all probability we are dealing with a highly disturbed individual.'

'I'm being reminded of that fact more and more.'

'You may not be far off the mark, Grey,' Dr Steig said. 'Look at her right rib cage.'

The dark layer of dried blood that covered much of the torso was smeared away in a roughly circular patch two inches in diameter around a large, molelike protrusion.

'A witch's tit,' declared Lean after examining the odd bump of skin.

Dr Steig pointed with his scalpel. 'Teeth marks in the smeared area. Like he was—'

'Suckling at it.' Grey reached for a magnifying glass from the tray of surgical instruments and examined the bloodied skin surrounding the dark protuberance. 'We should prepare a cast for teeth marks. No facial hairs deposited here by the killer.'

'I did remove two separate hairs from above. They were plastered into the blood on the rib cage. Too long and fine for a beard. Both appear black.'

'The watchman scared him off, so he had no time to clean himself up,' said Lean. 'Rushing away, he'd be quite a savage sight – lower face covered in blood.'

'Some blood on his hands also,' said Dr Steig. 'He took hold of her shoes and left a bloody thumb mark there.'

Grey moved to the sideboard to inspect the right shoe. He lifted his leather satchel over his head and set it down close by. Lean came over to observe as Grey took some filament paper and a small vial of liquid from his kit. He placed drops on the paper before placing it onto the bloody thumbprint to collect an impression. With a pair of tweezers, Grey set it between two glass slides, which he then clamped together.

'Fingerprinting, right?' Lean said.

'Yes. Galton has worked out a system of classification. Unlike the remainder of the man's dangerously misguided notions, this appears to possess scientific merit.' Grey deposited the slides into a hard case that he returned to a compartment within his kit. 'When we locate a suspect, perhaps we'll be able to obtain another sample for comparison.'

Dr Steig began his cuts to the torso in order to examine the internal organs and the contents of her stomach. Grey moved closer to the examination, while Lean elected to remain by the side table and made a point of closely examining the neatly folded pile of Maggie Keene's clothing. He caught a scent and raised her shirt to his face and inhaled. An underlying current of stale sweat lingered in the fabric, but it was overpowered by Maggie's cheap perfume. Morbid though it seemed, Lean found it a welcome relief from the surrounding odors and took another breath. Next were her white gloves, both of them. The killer had removed them before proceeding with his grisly work.

Lean held the right glove, itself like a hollow, phantom version of the dismembered and missing right hand. There was something on the glove, near the tip of the pointer finger. Lean examined it beneath the light of the gas jet. The fingertip was red, but there was something peculiar about the stain. The coloring did not look consistent with a stain from dipping the surface into blood. It looked incomplete, as if it had been absorbed and soaked through more thickly in spots. Lean turned the glove inside out and had his answer.

He interrupted the narrative of the doctor's examination to show them his discovery. The stain had originated from within the glove. Grey took the glove and then held it up against where blood had dried on Maggie Keene's body. The contrast was clear.

The glove's stain had dried deep red, while the blood on the body had already turned an iron-rich reddish brown.

'Is it blood at all?' asked Lean.

'A spectrometer test of some scrapings would tell us,' said Dr Steig.

'It looks more like ink,' Grey said. 'Red ink.'

Lean glanced down into the opened chest cavity of Maggie Keene. His stomach nearly revolted. He was in desperate need of sleep, food, coffee, and fresh air, and so he announced he would need to get back to the Portland Company.

'I still have the internal organs to go, but my report should be ready tomorrow,' Dr Steig said.

'I recommend just the clear medical facts,' Grey said. 'Let's leave our more speculative comments out of the official record for now. Do you agree, Lean?'

'Of course,' Lean said with a nod. He stood there in the fetid air of the underground morgue alongside a dead prostitute, the body mutilated by a meticulously scheming, pitchfork-wielding lunatic who liked to quote the Bible one minute and suckle at witches' tits the next. He glanced up at the windows where, a world away, daylight existed.

6

Lean tromped up the stairs to his family's second-floor apartment on Hanover Street. He had stopped along the way at a police call box and learned that several drunks and vagrants had been rounded up but there were no good suspects among them.

After reaching the landing, Lean let his head rest against the doorframe for a moment. Inside was the unmistakable sound of Owen's feet thudding across the apartment's wooden floors, and he heard his wife call out for the boy to stop running. Lean turned the knob and lurched into the entryway. The smell of frying rashers washed over him, and he also detected the scent of coffee hovering in the air. His stomach growled in anticipation. He deposited his coat and hat on the rack and took several steps into the main room.

He needed sleep, but first he'd sit down for a minute with a book. Something to set his mind straight again. He paused at the bookcase, perusing the titles. He considered the Whitman he'd purchased just after the poet's death three months earlier. But at this moment he wasn't up for the challenge. He needed something with recognizable patterns, something that adhered to the rules of classic poetic measures. He opted for a more sympathetic volume of Longfellow. Book in hand, Lean slumped into his favorite chair. He bent forward to untie his shoelaces, but before he could reach that far, he was met by the full-bore charge of his five-year-old boy.

'Daddy's home!'

'Hello, boy.'

Owen catapulted into his father's midsection, knocking him back into the chair. Within seconds the boy had scrambled down to the floor and was off again, pounding away across the room.

Lean could feel his eyelids sagging. He fought against it and was rewarded with the sight of Emma walking toward him, still in her morning robe, her long, dark curls not yet put up for the day. She was smiling, but even in Lean's exhausted state he could recognize the thinly veiled mixture of relief and frustration in her deep brown eyes.

'Daddy's home,' she repeated at a mere fraction of the volume of her son's prior announcement.

Lean smiled, and his hand moved to her belly, where his wide-spread fingers pressed gently against her dress, feeling the taut, bulging skin beneath the fabric.

'How's the wee one this morning?'

'Good,' Emma said. 'Quiet, though. She was wondering where her father was.'

'She?'

'Just a thought.'

'It's a good thought.'

Lean heard a scraping on the floor as his wife used her foot to slide a stool in front of him. With a herculean effort, Lean raised his feet enough to slip them onto the stool. He peeked out from under a drooping eyelid and contemplated his scuffed shoes.

'Have we any polish?'

'They are a bit rough, aren't they? I'm sorry. I'll get to them before tomorrow.'

'Oh, don't worry over it.'

'Asks for polish, the first time in his life he's ever mentioned shoe polish, then he says not to mind it. You're a right piece of mischief, Archie Lean. And you've been smoking again. I smell that stink on you.'

At the mention of the offending odor, Lean's hand drifted up to his shirt pocket. He felt the little nub of the killer's cigarette butt. 'You'd forgive me if you only knew.' His voice was faltering, giving in to sleep.

'I forgive you anyway.' Emma ran her fingertips across his

forehead, brushing his thick, straw-colored hair to one side. 'I'll get you some eggs, and there's rashers still warm.'

As Emma went into the kitchen, Lean withdrew the killer's cigarette and held it to his face once more. He wrinkled his nose. It was a strange herbal mixture that he didn't recognize. Was that it – was that the look he'd seen flashing across Grey's face when he sniffed the tobacco? The surprise of recognition?

'What the devil's he hiding?' Lean let the cigarette drop back into his pocket. He reached over to the side table and laid a hand on his volume of Longfellow, but he couldn't muster the energy to pick it up.

'I thought you'd be back sooner,' Emma said from the kitchen.

'I will be,' he said.

'Be what?' Emma wandered over to the doorway.

'Back soon. Promise.'

'Fair enough, love.' She chuckled, then called for Owen in a low voice.

As he drifted off, Archie Lean felt a rough tugging at his foot and then heard a loud thud. He peeked with one eye to see his son sprawled out on the floor, an unpolished brown oxford-tie shoe clutched triumphantly in the boy's stubby fingers.

It was midafternoon when Lean hopped down from the carriage. A crowd had assembled outside the police station, on the Myrtle Street side of the City Hall building. As he weaved and pushed his way through to the steps, he saw two reporters smoking by the doors.

'Hey, Archie,' called out Dizzy Bragdon, a short, wiry man

with glasses that didn't hide a lazy eye, 'how about some details on the murder? Is it true he slashed her throat?'

'No, it was—' Lean had to stop himself short, wary of revealing any details that might panic or inflame the public. 'I got nothing for you right now.'

'So it was an Indian, right? He tomahawk her?' said the second reporter.

'Where'd you hear that?'

'We all saw the writing down there with Marshal Swett this morning. Fellow from the *Advertiser* recognized it as Indian.'

'Is it true she was scalped?' Dizzy asked.

'What? No – that's ridiculous. Don't print that.'

'Hey, come on, Arch, give us something. One of Farrell's girls, right? Killer take care of business before he done her?'

Lean walked on. Inside was a bit quieter, though there was still a buzz of conversation. He noticed an unusual number of uniformed patrolmen and double the regular number of complainants and unsavory types being questioned or escorted in or out of the building. Lean stopped at the front desk. 'Anything promising?'

'They're coming out of the woodwork. Swearing up and down about every crazy rumor out there,' said Officer Bushey, a stocky veteran whose mustache covered most of his lower face. 'Mayor's been asking for you.'

Lean made his way upstairs to Ingraham's office. Behind his polished mahogany desk, the mayor glanced up from his morning paper.

'You're a right mess.' He motioned toward Lean's face and tossed him a handkerchief.

Lean had been rattled awake forty-five minutes earlier and was still wearing the same, now crumpled, four-button brown-check cutaway suit from last night. As he'd fumbled about for his shoes and hat, his wife had managed to stuff a handkerchief with a hard-boiled egg and a handful of warmed-over rashers into his coat pocket. Lean had devoured the offering in just a few bites on the ride to Myrtle Street.

'This whole mess is about to spill over. Tell me you've got something.' The mayor's eyebrows shot up, and his bulbous head wobbled in anticipation. Lean sat down and rattled off every bit of evidence that he and Grey had uncovered.

'That bit about a first murder seems something of a leap.'

Lean nodded. 'Grey's a sharp man. Very sharp. But I'm not convinced about that either.'

'Sounds a bit of a distraction to me. An attempt to divert our attention. I knew involving that bloody half-breed was a mistake. The killer's an Indian, and that doesn't suit him very well, now, does it?'

'I think he may know something more than he's letting on,' Lean said.

'He's protecting his own. To be expected, of course.'

'They're going to need more protection than that. Once the afternoon extras hit the stands and word gets out that an Indian killed a white woman, even if she was a whore, the streets won't be safe for any of them.'

The mayor grimaced. 'The last thing we need is angry mobs roaming the streets. We need to find this lunatic quickly. He's Indian – what else do we know?'

'He's dark-haired. Short – five foot two, give or take, yet unusually strong. He's familiar with the area near the Portland Company. Probably had a room nearby for the past week at least, based on his knowledge of the night watchman's schedule.'

Mayor Ingraham pulled open a desk drawer and withdrew a tumbler and a bottle of whiskey. Lean watched him pour a hefty dram and drain it.

'Some short, dark mystery man with a room on Munjoy Hill.' The mayor poured himself another drink, but his agitation prevented his hand from closing the gap with his spittle-flecked lips. 'Not exactly promising. You need to find an Indian with blood on his clothes. And fast.'

'We don't think the killer would have had much on him, actually. Given she was lying down and the angle of the cuts. Though he likely had some blood on his face from where he was ...' Lean trailed off when he caught sight of the mayor's horrified face staring back at him. It took Lean a moment to realize that his own mouth was gaping open in duplication of the killer's activities.

'Enough with all these gruesome details and Grey's theories,' said the mayor. 'Horseshit. This dead whore and an Indian killer is all one great steaming pile. It'll stink worse if it gets out we asked an Indian for help. Grey knows more than he's saying? So find out what it is. Then he's through with this business. Understood?'

Lean nodded and headed for the door.

7

Grey sat in a stuffed chair in his dark study. He had never bothered to open the shades after returning from the postmortem that morning. Feeble sunlight crept in around the edges of the tall windows. He held the killer's fourth cigarette, only half smoked, in a pair of pincers close to his face. Grey turned the hand-rolled bit of evidence, examining it from every angle. Two sets of sharp indentations were set at the base of the cigarette – teeth marks. The killer had clenched the cigarette with his teeth, perhaps while he hurried around the building toward the timekeeper's shack. An inch farther up were two almost imperceptible impressions, one on each side of the stick, where the man had squeezed it between his knuckles.

Grey went to the corner worktable where his microscope and racks of test tubes sat. He put the cigarette underneath an electric lamp. Next he placed a small pan over a standing gas jet on the table. He struck a match and lit the gas, turning the flame down to almost nothing. He held the first of the killer's cigarette butts collected earlier that morning and set it in the pan. He pulled up a tall chair and sat before the burner. After fifteen seconds the paper began to brown and thin wisps of smoke curled upward. Grey closed his eyes and leaned forward, his hands gripping the edge of the table. The bitter odor was familiar, though he hadn't smelled it in decades. He inhaled deeply and released a short bark of a cough. His eyes flickered, then closed again. He continued to draw slow, full breaths as the memories came.

He feels the cold, but only in that distant way that doesn't matter to a child at play. He's kneeling in the snow, before a blanketed slope, with several other Indian boys. Each one holds a flat wooden board to be aimed down the thin, cleared tracks on the hillside in the game of snakes.

The air is crisp, and his father's voice carries clear across the snow, calling him home. His father is still alive, and coming closer in his old wool coat and hat. He makes a run for it, and the pleasant thrill of escape consumes him until a careless step sends him tail over head into the snow. His father's arms raise him up, and they trudge along through a world of gray skies and white earth punctuated with dark tree trunks.

'I have to be a hawk with you.' His father is speaking English, though he knows that was not the truth, not when they were alone. 'You're a clever boy. But you must always look ahead, always think what is next. The ground can shift under your very feet. You must always know where your next step will be. Your next three steps.' He cocks his head to see his father's face. There's a smile in the man's eyes, no anger, and so he buries his face in the solid shoulder for warmth and draws in that unpleasant smell: wet wool with old tobacco lingering underneath.

Back inside the winter cabin, he is wrapped in an old woolen blanket. The fire roars, lighting the dark walls of wood planks, where dried mud and hay fill the gaps. A film of gray-blue smoke hovers close to the low ceiling. The skin of his legs tingles, itching from his body's sudden shift back toward a living warmth.

His mother, fair-skinned and beautiful, reads from an English book, her words musical, rising and falling with the story. There are knights and ladies and great beasts. He gazes up past her pale eyes, aglow in the firelight, to the drifts that rise from his father's pipe. The smoke curls into hints of shapes, and he imagines the breath of a fiery dragon. He puffs out his chest, drawing in the smoky breath and making it part of him, tasting the bitter, almost medicinal smell of his father's tobacco. He smiles.

Grey stared at the plate in front of him. The cigarette was only cold ashes, and all visible signs of the smoke had dissipated. The scent lingered in his memory as he looked toward the windows. The light around the curtain was different now. He stood up, steadied himself against the edge of the worktable for a moment, then strode across the room. Grey snatched his hat from the rack and slipped on his lightweight frock coat before heading out the door. He made no effort to soften his descent as he thudded down the stairs, welcoming the feel of the unyielding wooden treads and the almost palpable sound of his own footsteps in the narrow stairway.

Lean entered Delavino's smoke shop near the corner of Middle and Exchange. A large sign in the window advertised the fashionable new brand of Turkish Treasures cigarettes. He moved past displays of colorfully illustrated cigar boxes, chewing tobacco, patent medicines, and spruce gum. Posters lined the walls, calling out for him to enjoy the delights of Duke's Preferred Stock and White Rolls. There was even a small display of Cameos, though Lean couldn't recall ever having seen a woman inside this shop in all his years of coming to Delavino's.

At the counter, Lean was greeted by the sweaty pate and smiling eyes of the proprietor.

'Deputy, good to see you. How many today?' He turned away and reached toward the stacks of cigarette boxes on the shelves behind the counter. The man's thick fingers tripped along the rows of Allen & Ginter products until they reached the Richmond Straight Cuts.

'Just one pack ought to do it, Tino.' Lean's eyes roamed over the shop as he dug in his pocket for change. Under a banner declaring her famous phrase 'Ta-ra-ra-Boom-de-ay' was Lottie Collins, the toast of the English music halls, her right leg kicking high to reveal her stocking and garter, tempting all who passed to try Phillips Guinea Gold cigarettes.

'There is something else you can help me with.' Lean drew the killer's cigarette butt from his pocket. 'What can you tell me about this? It's not regular tobacco – got a funny scent to it.'

'Well, it's hand-rolled, eh. So it could be all sorts.' He took a whiff, then another. 'Oh, this is Indian tobacco. It's native, a wild-growing herb.'

'You sell it?'

Tino gave a dismissive shake of his head. 'Of course, for you I can get some if you like. Not the kind of thing people here are willing to pay for. But then' – Tino rolled the butt between his fingers – 'it's perfectly fine rolling paper. Not cheap. For whatever that's worth to you.'

'Thanks. Very helpful.' Lean took the butt back and pocketed it.

'If you're interested in the Indians, there's a new series of Duke cards, famous Indian chiefs. Your boy might like them.'

'Maybe next time.' Lean moved to the door.

'Yes, always next time.' The proprietor took up his newspaper and rattled it loudly after Lean. 'If I'm still in business, I can sell you just the one pack again.'

The landlady, Mrs Philbrick, blocked the doorway at the two-story brick house on High Street, chin out and arms folded across her chest. 'Mr Grey hasn't been accepting visitors. Has strict instructions that he's not to be disturbed.'

Lean showed his badge, but the revelation that he was a police deputy did little more than earn a raised eyebrow. 'In any event he's not in at the moment. You missed him by five minutes.'

'Do you know where he's gone?'

'Mentioned something about the B&M.'

Within minutes Lean reached his destination on Commercial

Street, where he paid the cab fare and headed toward the Boston & Maine depot. Ahead, by the station doors, a fair-skinned twelve-year-old boy dressed in a fringed buckskin shirt and a feathered headdress too large for him was handing out flyers to passengers entering the station.

'Mohegan Indian Medicine Show. Camp Ellis every night this week.' The boy waved a flyer toward Lean's face. 'Need a night of amusement? Free shows, trick-shooting displays, authentic dances, medicine demonstrations. Everything's first class, all the way. Hear Chief White Eagle lecture on the historic customs of his tribe.'

This was where Grey was heading. Inside the station Lean bought a ticket for the Old Orchard Beach train. Out on the platform, the conductor announced last call. Once he saw that it was only a two-car train, Lean made no move to board. Grey would certainly spot him in such close quarters. He turned back and studied the timetables. Another train left for Old Orchard in forty-five minutes. He'd wait and follow on behind so he could observe Grey's activities in secrecy.

8

The late-afternoon sun filtered into the top floor of the three-story brick building on Temple Street that housed the Maine Temperance Union's headquarters. Simon Gould, in his late forties but still powerfully built and with a soldier's bearing, lifted a coffeepot from its silver platter. He caught sight of his own marred face, the burned tissue reflecting clearly in the vessel's gleaming surface.

'A prostitute was killed last night,' Gould said.

'One less whore corrupting our streets,' said Colonel Ambrose Blanchard as he held out his fine white porcelain cup. 'So foul a life leads to so foul an end. No doubt that the demon alcohol lured her so far from redemption.'

As Gould filled the colonel's cup, the curvature of the coffee-pot twisted his stern visage, growing the dead, milky orb of his right eye to grotesque proportions. Gould finished pouring and placed the pot down, freeing himself from the uncomfortable sight of his old wound.

'They found her down at the Portland Company.' Gould retook his seat. 'With a pitchfork through her neck.'

The colonel was silent for a moment. He frowned, and his gray, thistly eyebrows threatened to form a tangled knot above his austere face. 'Was there ... anything else?'

'She was laid out like a pentagram. Her right hand was missing.'

The elder man set his cup down on its saucer with a sharp clank. He cursed as the steaming coffee splashed over the side, scalding his hand. 'You think it's him?'

'He talked of some such things,' Gould said, 'once or twice, when he was in one of his agitated states.'

'You told me he was gone. That he would not be a concern ...'

'Perhaps he's come home.' Gould saw the colonel glare at him in response and added, 'To Portland, that is.'

'Why?' Blanchard finally asked. 'The hand taken, it's like ...'

'That book of his,' said Gould.

'Maybe, but we need to know whether he had anything to do with that whore's death.' The colonel walked to a bookcase filled with a mix of leather- and cloth-bound volumes. Several picture frames stood on the shelves as well, most showing the colonel with small groups of people, often shaking hands with various municipal or state leaders. 'Find out whether he's been here. And find that book before anyone else does.'

'The police have no idea. They're looking for an Indian.'

'Good, but we must take an active hand in this. None of us are safe now. No one can know who he is.' The colonel set the picture facedown on the shelf. 'Or who he ever was.'

Helen Prescott and her eight-year-old daughter, Delia, arrived at Dr Steig's at six thirty. The servant took their coats. Helen wore a stylish walking costume of English serge with double box plaiting and apron drapery in the front. The dark blue material complemented her fair skin and blue eyes. She wore her rich brown hair up in a popular style, knotted and braided but long enough, in her case, to cover the back of her neck. Helen gave a soft rap at the study door, then entered.

Dr Steig looked up from his desk, where he was pecking away, mostly left-handed, on his Daugherty Visible typewriter. Delia skipped across the room, doing a twirl to show off her fancy cashmere jersey dress, before giving Dr Steig a hug.

'Thank you, sweet child. What a surprise.'

'You did invite us for dinner,' Helen reminded him.

'Oh, heavens, forgive me. Just gotten distracted with something. Why don't we dine out?'

'Can we?' Delia asked.

'If you need to get that done first, I could do the typing for you,' Helen said.

'What? No, this is nothing. I can finish it later.'

'It's not a problem, Uncle Virgil. I could have it done for you in no time.' She approached to get a look at the document.

58

Dr Steig released the paper from the typewriter. 'Not at all, dear. It's nothing. A sensitive matter. I need to attend to it personally.' He set the paper atop several pages of notes, then deposited the bunch in the top right drawer of his desk.

Once Helen was close enough, she noticed the circles beneath her uncle's eyes. 'Are you feeling all right? You look as though you haven't slept.'

'I'll be fine. Get a good night's rest tonight. It's just this pressing matter.'

Helen took a half step back, her nose wrinkling as she puzzled it out. 'It's that awful business in the papers, isn't it? At the Portland Company.'

'Not appropriate to discuss in front of Delia.'

'Yes, Delia,' Helen said. She showed him a sarcastic smile. 'Or any other fragile ears.'

'I'm certainly not going to discuss it while we dine.' He rose and moved toward the coatrack by the door.

'Then you can tell me all about it later.'

'Police business, dear. Highly confidential.'

'That's never stopped you before,' Helen said with a glance back at Dr Steig's desk. 'So it must be terribly gruesome.'

9

An hour after leaving Union Station, Lean reached the town of Old Orchard Beach and made his transfer. While he rode the narrow-gauge dummy train that shuttled him several miles from that summer resort town to the beachfront depot at Camp Ellis, he read two newspapers he'd bought. The *Eastern Argus* declared, WOMAN MURDERED AT PORTLAND CO. and HORRIBLY MUTI-LATED BODY — POLICE SEEK INDIAN SUSPECT. Not to be outdone, the *Daily Advertiser* screamed, BLOODY MURDER THE WORK OF INDIANS, and RIPPER-STYLE KILLING BY BLOOD-THIRSTY RED SAVAGE.

After reading the stories twice through, Lean turned his attention to the passing scenery as the open-air train rattled along the dunes. It moved through the evangelical summer community of Ocean Park, then past the salt marshes, where Goose Fair Creek emptied into Saco Bay. Lean stared out to his left at the Atlantic. The sun, less than half an hour from setting, lit the beach and the ocean water from behind him. He had managed to telephone his house from the station to explain he wouldn't be home until late, and now he thought of returning here next weekend to give Emma a well-deserved day of leisure.

Two miles on, past an empty landscape of dunes and long stretches of scrub pines, the dummy train deposited Lean and a load of fellow travelers at Camp Ellis. The spot was a sandy point capped with a long rock jetty extending straight out into the ocean from the north bank of the slow-moving Saco River. He could hear the festive noises coming up from the show grounds closer to the beach. As the couples and families moved past him, Lean glanced over to where three long wagons were parked under a shady stand of trees. Close to two dozen men loitered about there in small clumps. There was not a single woman or child among them, and Lean noticed several bottles and flasks making the rounds. Apparently he wasn't the only man who'd been reading the shocking Indian allegations that had flooded every newspaper in the state that afternoon.

He hurried after the crowd of spectators, wanting to blend in on arrival and avoid being spotted by Grey. The show consisted of several large tents, stages, fenced pens for horsemanship displays, and booths spread out over a few acres of grounds bounded in by the Saco River and the Atlantic Ocean. For the next half hour, Lean searched through the stalls and among the crowds for Grey. As daylight faded, oil lamps hanging from posts all around the grounds were lit. In one great fenced-in area, a small crowd of performers reenacted a battle scene where white settlers, to the rousing cheers of the crowd, fought off a circling party of warriors on horseback. Lean moved on and passed a painted tepee where a kindly faced middle-aged Indian woman by the name of Sister Neptune told fortunes. She also sold various powders and potions designed to ward off the very evils she foretold.

Elsewhere a small stage was set aside to entertain young children, whose number had dwindled as the sun went down and some families set off for the return trip on the dummy train. A puppet show told some story involving a giant eagle and Glooskap, the man created from nothing, an Algonquin Indian trickster hero. A riding display included the famous Sable Island Ponies, said to be untamable. Nearby, an attractive Indian woman with long braids and a fringed buckskin suit, decorated with purple and white wampum beads, made trick rifle shots, including an over-the-shoulder target practice performed with a hand held mirror.

On closer inspection Lean noticed that a superb juggler in full warrior regalia, handling four razor-sharp tomahawks, turned out to be a white man. The fact did little to dampen his appreciation of the man's skill. He moved on, passing booths where vendors hawked Indian oils, ointments, and syrups. The big seller was the

Sagamo Indian Elixir. As Lean approached a raised platform near the entrance to the grounds, he recognized the old Indian he'd seen on the flyer earlier. The man, announced as Chief White Eagle, praised the elixir as a great pain reliever that remedied everything from cold stomach to jaundice, dropsy, and stranguary.

As Lean approached, he caught sight of Grey staring straight back at him. Grey, dressed in a charcoal frock coat with dark striped pants and holding a fancy steel-gripped walking stick, wandered over as the Indian began his pitch.

'Finally, Lean. Why on earth didn't you just take the earlier train?'

'Enjoying yourself, then?'

'Not at all. A horribly disappointing display. Half the performers are not even Indians. And I can promise you that if any Mohegan Indians were still alive and here today, they wouldn't be dressed in these costumes, which have no business anywhere east of the Mississippi.' Grey waved in the direction of a passing performer wearing a full headdress with strands of feathers at the back running all the way to his knees. 'It's a complete fraud and mockery of actual Algonquian Indian culture.'

'It's just a show, Grey.'

'So was throwing Christians to the lions.' Grey gestured toward the nearby medicine display. 'It's not wholly a loss. Old Chief White Eagle is, despite his name, an authentic and very knowledgeable individual.'

'Knowledgeable about what? Why are you here, Grey?'

'The same reason as you, I suspect.'

'I'm investigating you.'

'I stand corrected.' He gave Lean a bemused look. 'I'm attempting to solve Maggie Keene's murder.'

'I need to know what you're hiding from me. Why come all the way here? You could have visited any tobacconist in Portland to learn about the cigarettes you pocketed. It's Indian tobacco. Grows wild.'

'The scientific name is lobelia. I brought a sample. Unfortunately, the chief could tell me nothing specific about the blend our killer used.'

'What, then? Do you suspect that someone from the show is the killer?'

Grey shook his head. 'It was a slim possibility. But all the performers and workers arrived here from New Hampshire only two days ago. Our killer spent a week studying the Portland Company and the watchman. Everyone here was in Portsmouth each night last week, Concord the week before that.'

Lean regarded him for a long moment. 'You've never thought the killer's an Indian at all, have you? Convince me of the same. Otherwise ... well, the mayor wants you off this investigation.'

'I see. I have Indian blood, and you're convinced the killer is an Indian. I can't be trusted.'

Lean shrugged. 'Who else would leave an Indian message? Why can't you admit the obvious?'

'The evidence hasn't yet proved the race of the killer,' Grey said.

'It's good enough for me.'

'It appears you're not alone.'

There was an angry shout behind Lean, followed by a murmur of panicked excitement that boiled up into a frenzy in mere seconds. When he turned, Lean recognized the group of two dozen men he'd seen near the train depot approaching in a mob, several carrying clubs. One of the men swung his stick as he passed a booth, toppling the wooden support and sending the overhead sign crashing down. A middle-aged man stepped forward from the crowd of peaceful patrons. 'Enough of that now! This is a family event. There are women and children about!'

His objection earned the man a violent shove, and he went sprawling down into the dirt. Other visitors began scurrying out of the way, and parents herded their children off in the direction of the train.

Lean glanced about, getting his bearings and assessing his options. 'They've swallowed their fill of liquid courage. There'll be no reasoning with that lot.'

'So how do you intend to handle them?'

'Same as a wild dog. Smack 'em hard in the snout – set 'em running before they know what to make of you.' Lean drew his pistol.

10

'What's all this, then?' The show boss, a portly white man in a top hat, chomping away at a cigar, appeared next to Chief White Eagle. A look of alarm passed over his face as he took stock of the mob.

Lean identified himself, pistol in hand.

'That won't be necessary, Deputy. I know how to handle these people.'

Grey approached. 'Which of your products has the highest portion of alcohol?'

'What, now? As the sign says, my good man, all of our

products are strictly wholesome vegetable products. Not a drop of alcohol in the lot.'

'Your show and your people are about to be in serious trouble. I need something flammable.'

The boss smiled and shook his head. 'Pardon me, gentlemen. Your concern is appreciated, but I have customers to attend to.' The boss grabbed an empty crate and overturned it to use as a speaking platform.

Grey turned away to inspect the various bottles. Chief White Eagle reached into a box and drew out two bottles of the Sagamo Elixir. 'This'll burn plenty.'

Grey thanked the old man, then held out a hand toward Lean. 'Lend me your matches. Hold them off for a couple of minutes – I'll send up an alarm.'

Lean handed over his matches, and Grey hurried from the scene. The mob had paused its forward motion to watch the show boss. From an inside pocket, the man drew a short white baton, which he waved about as he prepared to address the crowd.

Voices called out from the mob: 'Go back where you came from!' 'Take your bloody savages with you!' 'They ain't welcome here!'

'Gentlemen! Gentlemen!' the boss cried. 'How good of you to come. You're just in time. Tonight is the—'

A beer bottle flew from the crowd, striking the show boss in the chest. The man went down in a heap. Lean fired one shot into the air, which brought a sudden silence to the rumble of the mob.

'Deputy Marshal Lean of the Portland police. I order you to disperse immediately!'

'One of these Indians killed that girl, and he's going to swing for it!' yelled one man.

'Turn him over and no one else will get hurt!' shouted another.

'No one's turning anyone over. Now, I'm warning you — this is a criminal assembly. Anyone failing to disperse will be arrested.'

A man who seemed to be a leader of the mob stepped up to Lean and announced, 'This ain't Portland. You're out of your territory.'

Lean extended his arm, pressing the pistol against the man's forehead. He waited a moment, the entire mob and dozens of onlookers all staring at him. Then he released the hammer on his pistol and drew it back slowly from the man's forehead.

A nervous smile appeared on the man's face. 'Now, step aside and let us do what's right.'

A sudden rage welled in Lean's gut and rushed up past his chest. His hand flashed forward and rammed the butt of the pistol into the man's forehead, splitting open a thin, bloody seam. The man buckled and went down. Two other fellows came forth with violence still on their faces, but they only moved to help their comrade off the ground. Lean sensed the steam going out of the mob. Once again he ordered them to disperse and then made the mistake of holstering his pistol.

With a rumbling growl, a young man from the mob came hurtling forward, arms wheeling. A well-timed left to the man's face dropped him at Lean's feet. Two more men rushed him, and Lean tried to square his feet, but the young man on the ground had clasped on to his leg. Lean threw an off-balance punch as the first reached him, then went down as the second assailant tackled him.

Grey had dashed away, circling around the developing mob scene. He rushed along the sand dunes, his steel-handled walking stick in one hand while his other rested on the bottles in his coat pocket. Grey moved toward the three long wagons where the mob had congregated earlier. He set his walking stick against the shortest wagon in order to free the draft horses and tether them to a nearby tree. In the back were several empty wood casks that the men had used as seats. Grey smashed one of these into kindling on the ground, then doused it with Sagamo Elixir. He broke off a match, struck it, and dropped it onto the wood. Once it lit, he snatched up a thin burning board and turned toward the wagon. He splashed the wooden frame with just enough to cause alarm to the owners, without actually damaging the structure. The point was to startle the mob, not actually cut off their escape. He lit the wagon, and a thin streak of blue-tinged flames spread along the edge.

'What the hell you think you're doing?'

A hand gripped Grey by the shoulder and spun him around. A thickset ogre of a man, well over six feet, with raging, whiskey-soaked eyes, took a wild swing. Grey ducked out of the way as he dropped the fiery brand and the bottle. He seized his walking stick and delivered an over-the-head strike. The man blocked it with a treelike forearm, snapping the stick in half.

The man shook off the blow and threw a roundhouse that connected with Grey's ribs, wobbling him. Before Grey could react, the man grabbed him and slammed him to the ground next to the burning wagon. Grey caught sight of the Sagamo Elixir. He crawled under the wagon, snatching the bottle as he went. The man grasped Grey's left ankle and pulled. Grey tipped the bottle and filled his mouth with what tasted like turpentine spiked with sugar. As the man dragged him from under the wagon, Grey reached for the burning board he had used to light the wagon.

The man hauled Grey to his feet, then drew back a massive fist to finish him off. Grey, still holding the noxious liquid in his mouth, stuck the burning brand directly between their faces and sprayed the Sagamo Elixir. The man fell to the ground, screaming as he slapped at burning bits of hair. Grey seized another small cask from the wagon and smashed it down on the man's crown.

He hauled the unconscious body a safe distance from the wagons, then tossed the cask onto the fire and watched the smoke drift skyward. He cupped his hands to his mouth and shouted, 'Fire! Fire! The wagons are on fire!' He repeated this twice more, collected his broken walking stick, and disappeared into the trees.

11

An hour after the confrontation with the mob, Lean sat in a mid-size tent with his ankle wrapped in a cool compress. Grey's fire had startled the mob into thinking their means of escape had been sabotaged. The spirit of the attack had been broken, and the men had fled into the night. The whole affair ended quickly, keeping major injuries to a minimum on both sides. Lean suffered a twisted ankle in the melee and also came away with bruised knuckles. Now he and Grey were inside a makeshift museum of Indian artifacts that served as a bunkhouse for the performers after the shows. Chief White Eagle was present, as well as several Abenaki men of various ages who were around a table, smoking and playing cards. The kind-faced fortune-teller, Sister Neptune, was tending to Lean after taking care of some other cuts and bruises. Also present was the attractive Indian sharpshooter, who, Lean observed, was taking a keen interest in Grey's minor scrapes.

The fortune-teller handed Lean a clay mug. 'Drink this. It will help keep the swelling down.'

'Thank you, Sister Nep—'

'Agnes. Just call me Agnes. Least I can do for your help out there. That could have been a load of trouble.'

Lean took a sip and nearly spit it out. 'My God! Tastes like cat piss.'

'Well, when you move about the way we have to, you learn to make do with what's at hand.' Agnes smiled at Lean's incredulous look. 'Don't worry, it's a simple herb-and-bark tea.'

Lean forced down a second sip, then handed the mug back. He stood up and limped over to Grey. 'We should be going.'

Grey glanced at his pocketwatch. 'I doubt the train will be coming back after all this. And the road to Old Orchard won't be safe for us to walk tonight. Besides, you're in no condition to be moving about on that ankle.'

'I told my wife I'd be home,' Lean said.

'Listen to your friend,' said Agnes. 'After all, a husband who's late is better than one with a cracked skull.'

'We'll bunk here on spare cots. Your wife will understand,' Grey said.

One of the card players passed a bottle to Lean. 'If you're staying, you might as well have something real to take care of the pain.'

Lean took a swig and felt the harsh warmth rush down into

his chest. He handed the bottle to Grey, who passed it along without drinking.

Chief White Eagle spoke in a quiet voice. 'I don't know any called Grey. What was your father's name?'

'He went by Poulin. Joseph Poulin.'

The chief nodded in recognition. Lean was not surprised by the name, being familiar with the practice of Indians in Maine to assume names showing a French-Canadian influence.

'I knew him,' said one of the other men at the card table. He paused and peered at Grey. 'I remember you now too. Wouldn't have known you if you hadn't said the name, but now I see it plain enough. Scrawny kid, you were.' The man stubbed out his cigarette. 'I was there the day they found your father. When they pulled him out of the water below the falls. He was a good man, though I suppose you know that well enough.'

'Thank you. I don't actually recall. Awfully long time ago.'

Lean stared at Grey, astonished to hear that his father had drowned when Grey was just a boy. Even more surprising was that Grey hadn't so much as blinked at the mention of such a tragic event from his childhood.

'Let us not dwell on the troubles of yesterday.' The chief moved toward the smoking circle around the card table. He motioned Grey and Lean to join them.

'Yeah. Not when there's today's troubles to worry about,' said the man who had spoken of Grey's father.

Lean shook his head. 'I expected a few minor incidents after news spread of the killing in Portland. But nothing so big, not such a mob over a prostitute's death.'

'She was still white, and we're still not,' said one of the Abenaki men.

70

'Men's passions are like a massive boulder perched on a mountainside,' said Chief White Eagle. 'In a civilized society, they seem held in place, solid among the rocks. But things have a natural inclination to return to the lowest point. A man's basest instincts are no exception. Often only the smallest push can set them in motion. And old hatreds are as steep as any slope I have ever seen.'

'Welcome to the reservation, Deputy,' said the other man as he raised his glass and let out a sorry laugh. 'Sorry to tell you, but it sits square at the bottom of a great, wide mountain.'

More drinks were poured, and a long-stemmed pipe was passed around. It took Lean a moment to get a proper handle on the bowl. He wasn't used to pipes in general and had never smoked one of this length and shape. Lean's new friends all had a good chuckle over his struggle. When it came to Grey, he examined the pipe in his own grip, took a small puff, then passed it on.

Some of the other men spoke in low tones in Abenaki. Grey was trying to follow their conversation, but with limited success. Chief White Eagle noticed this.

'They wonder at how far you have gone from the old ways. They think perhaps you look down on us, think we put on these costumes and play at make-believe for the amusement of the white men.'

Grey shrugged. 'Everyone has to earn a living. I don't begrudge any of you that. Though I do question the honesty of the images that you portray here.'

Chief White Eagle thought about that for a moment before answering Grey. 'We all take on identities that are not true to ourselves. Sometimes we choose to become what the world expects to see of us, who the world thinks we should be. Perhaps you think it reflects poorly on you. You wonder, if this is how the white man sees all of us, then how does he see you?'

Grey gave the chief a bit of a smile, raised the cup that had been poured for him earlier, and took a small drink. The others around the circle were more enthusiastic with the bottles, and before long the stories turned to past episodes of troubles encountered as they moved among white people. Most of these ended without harm, though the mention of the infamous beating to death of an elderly Penobscot man named Denny caused a stir.

'And what about Old Stitch?' said an Indian man.

'That wasn't murder,' said another. 'The old witch just drank herself to death.'

Lean looked up. The name of Old Stitch stirred a faint memory in him.

'No, but it was murder years ago when they burned her house out,' said the first man.

'She wasn't even an Indian,' argued the second.

Agnes held up a palm to quiet the two men. 'It just shows that the white man's hatred isn't reserved for us. Anyone who lives apart from their ways, in harmony with nature, seeking to learn from the earth rather than be her master, is to be feared.'

As the Indian men went on with their stories, Lean turned to Agnes. 'Old Stitch. That name's familiar. Tell me about her.'

'I knew her a long time ago. She was a fortune-teller like me. Only she worked as a spirit medium.'

'And she died recently?'

'She made potions, and she drank a lot. Probably grabbed the wrong bottle.'

'Why was she called Old Stitch?' asked Lean.

'Her real name was Lucy. Old Stitch because she made her name crafting poppets.'

'Puppets? What, like Punch and Judy stuff?'

'Poppets,' Agnes said. 'Cloth dolls, the kind you might stick a pin in.'

'She have a last name?' Lean asked.

'I can't tell you what it was.'

'And what about that business years ago? There was a fire, and someone was killed.'

'That's the story. They tried to kill her one time. In the early days, when her and the boys were working out of Back Cove.'

'The boys?'

'Yes, her two kids – different fathers, of course. And hardly an ounce of kid in them. They earned what little keep they got.'

'How so?'

Agnes's eyes drifted up. 'Her customers would ride out over Tukey's Bridge to see her down there by the cove. When they left, one boy would be in the woods nearby and tail them back. He'd signal the other at the far end of the bridge. That one would follow the carriage to their houses to spy on them, eavesdropping, reading mail, then sealing the letters back up. When a customer came for a second visit, Old Stitch could tell them so many details about their lives that they'd believe anything she said.'

'Seems a harmless bit of graft.'

'Harmless for the clients,' Agnes said. 'Not them boys. Blamed them for her lot in life and made sure they knew it. If she got paid, they would eat. Maybe. Them two were thinner than shadows. Lived on whatever they could steal, catch, or dig out of the cove mud. If they couldn't get what she needed on a customer, they'd feel it on their backs. She kept them in absolute fear. Had poppets of each of them that she'd threaten to burn. It went on like that for years. Until they burned her out.'

'Who did?' Lean asked.

'Some church folk got wind of her ways. Came down with torches crying witchcraft and bloody murder. After that, she came along and traveled about with us for a while. A few years later and she was back at the cove, talking to spirits and selling medicines to all sorts of ladies.'

'So someone died in the fire.'

'One of her boys. The little one, I think.' A hint of sadness lingered in Agnes's voice.

12

Grey stood on a large, flat rock two hundred yards out on the jetty. He ignored the local fishermen farther along the rocks, working the outgoing tide for the striped bass that fed at the mouth of the Saco River. He stared across the water, dull beneath a slew of morning clouds. Free from the distracting smells and sights of the Indian encampment, he refocused on the scene at the Portland Company: Maggie Keene laid out like a pentagram on the dark, exposed earth. Why would the killer go through the tremendous effort to pry up the floorboards? It would have been quite a task even for several men with the right tools. He gave his mind a shove in the direction of the murder inquiry and then let it go. To his annoyance his thoughts kept circling back to the night before and the mob of club-wielding locals. His mind raced on to another image of armed men, decades earlier.

The men spoke politely to his mother, but he could not ignore the menace of the shotgun held casually on the shoulder of one man. Another man collected their family possessions into a sack. The cabin door hung loose in the frame. They were hustled along, out into a four-wheeled carriage. There was the crack of a whip, and the carriage bolted forward. He glanced back at the cabin, all dark and empty like a discarded shell. He clung to his mother as they sped along the bumpy road. He started to ask for his father before he saw his mother's glistening eyes and remembered everything.

'Where are we going?'

'To your grandfather's.'

'*N'mahom?*'

'No, your white grandfather. In Portland.' She laid a warm palm on his cheek and smiled through her tears.

Lean glanced at his pocketwatch: half past seven. He favored his swollen ankle as he navigated the uneven granite blocks that made up the jetty. His head ached, and he felt unsteady from drinking too much the night before. He continued his slow progress until Grey was only twenty yards ahead, facing out to sea with his hands behind his back.

'Any sign of that bear?'

It took Grey a moment to react and turn toward Lean. 'What bear?'

'The one that slipped into the tent last night and shit in my mouth.' Lean managed a feeble smile before he turned his head and spit into the ocean, trying to clear out the taste of cheap whiskey and Indian tobacco. Lean watched the waves slosh against the side of the jetty. '"Break, break, break, / On thy cold gray stones, O Sea! / And I would that my tongue could utter / The thoughts that arise in me.'"

Grey looked aside at Lean.

'You never did tell me why you came here. What you were looking for?' Lean waited for a response, then added, 'A killer's on the loose. If you know something that will help bring him in, you have to tell me. Whether he's one of your people or not.'

'My people? I was seven years old the last time I lived with Indians. After that, I spent years sequestered with the finest tutors in Portland and Boston, until I was socially skilled enough to no longer be an embarrassment to my grandfather. Then I was sent packing to the finest schools and colleges in New England. Once old enough to direct my own education, I spent six years in Europe studying under the greatest criminalists in London and Paris. Even Professor Gross in Vienna. A tenuous statement at best, to call the Indians my people. You needn't worry about any old sympathies of mine.' Grey turned and began to walk along the top of the jetty, back toward shore. 'None of us is the child he was at age seven.'

Lean let the words hang in the air as he followed behind. There was a gravity in Grey's voice that convinced him the man was sincere. 'Fair enough, Grey. Then tell me why the killer's not an Indian. The message above the body was in Indian, for heaven's sake.'

'Taking the simplest view of facts is certainly a wise course.' Grey stopped and pulled a notebook from his side bag. 'Provided you have all the facts.' He wrote the message from the Portland Company and held it out for Lean to see.

'The chalk message was *Kia K'tabaldamwogan paiomwiji*. But

76

I noticed that something about the writing wasn't quite right. Old Chief White Eagle, or whatever his true name is, confirmed it. "Thy kingdom come." *Kia* means "thy" or "your," but adding it to this sentence is unnecessary. The "K" at the start of *K'tabaldamwogan* already functions as the possessive pronoun. As written, the killer's message really is more like "Thy kingdom of yours come." It's grammatically incorrect. An amateur's mistake. The author has studied the language, perhaps, but is not a native speaker.'

'Maybe he's an Indian who simply can't write well,' Lean said.

'I don't think so.' Grey motioned to the middle word. 'He also used an "o" toward the end of *K'tabaldamwogan*. An Abenaki would have used this symbol.' Grey traced a figure eight on the page. 'It represents a nasal vowel not found in English. Though it's approximated in English with an "o", a native writer would have used the figure eight.'

'Hardly conclusive. Rather trivial details to conclude that the killer is not an Indian.'

'Trivial details are often the most telling.' Grey returned his notebook to his bag and starting toward the shore again. The pair reached the beginning of the jetty and paused on the sand. 'And so,' Grey continued, 'I have not yet formally eliminated the possibility that an Abenaki is indeed the killer. But there's a false element here. I can't yet put my finger on it, but something doesn't fit with an Indian as the killer.'

'That may be enough for you, but I have to do my duty and follow the evidence as I see it. If you're going to pursue your theories ... well, I won't try to stop you. So long as you do it quietly.'

Grey nodded and tipped his hat.

13

A full day later, Archie Lean sat outside Mayor Ingraham's City Hall office. He mentally sorted through the dozens of reports and letters, many anonymous, that had landed on his desk from people with suspicions as to Maggie Keene's killer. Eventually the secretary's voice summoned him.

Lean closed the office door behind him, and Mayor Ingraham stared up from his large desk. 'Where have you been all morning?'

'Following up on tips. Plus a stop back at the consulate.' Among the other trouble caused by news of the murderer's race, a man attached to the Spanish consulate had been mistaken for an Indian and assaulted.

'Well, forget about that for now.' The mayor handed over a letter. 'This came to my house this morning.'

Lean opened it and saw a message written in blocky letters, which he read aloud. '"I am writing so you will know your errors. Of course I'm not an Indian! The Master is above all others. I stand with the Master, above them. The black man serves the Master. In the third month, the month of the Master's power, you will see the truth and know I hold the Master's power. You will know this in time."'

Lean looked up from the page. 'The strangest of the lot, but I've seen a dozen—'

'This came with it.' Ingraham's face was pale as he set a small folded section of leather on his desk. With a pen he lifted the flap open to reveal a dark object.

It looked like a bit of meat. Lean moved closer for a look.

'Dr Steig's come by already. It's the tip of a human tongue, and it would match the section cut out of Maggie Keene's mouth. The man's a savage.'

'Yet he's angry at being made out as an Indian.'

'Mad that he's been revealed,' the mayor said.

'If that's true, then why would he leave Indian writing at the scene?' Lean read through the killer's note once more. 'He mentions something happening in the third month. So is this the second month? Maybe Grey was right about an earlier murder.'

'And more to come, from the sounds of it.' The mayor gestured toward the leather patch that held Maggie Keene's tongue. 'This was delivered to my front step. Do you understand? This madman came to my house, Lean. Find him.'

Lean folded the leather back over the tongue and picked it up, along with the letter. He started to speak, but the mayor cut him short. 'There's nothing more to discuss, Deputy.'

Lean took the ten-minute walk to Grey's apartment on High Street. As he approached the building, he noticed a grubby-faced boy of about ten perched on the granite steps, a shoeshine box next to him.

When Lean started up the steps, the boy piped up. 'You're the cop come to see Mr Grey, then?'

'Yes. How'd you know?'

'Mr Grey said you'd look like a cop, with scuffed-up shoes.'

Lean chuckled. 'Did Mr Grey have anything useful to say?'

'He said I should charge you ten cents for a shine and this message.' The boy took a small folded note from his pocket and waved it.

Lean reached into his pocket to find a dime, then took the

note. It was a rectangle of heavy-grade paper folded over with an ornate capital 'G' pressed into the red wax seal. Lean broke it open with his thumbnail. 'Dr Steig's – 9 tonight. We begin in earnest.'

Lean looked up; the boy was already halfway down the block, shine box under his arm.

'Hey, kid! What about my shoes?'

14

Tom Doran stood silent in the dim light of Maine General's morgue. His selection of suits was somewhat limited, since tailoring to his size was expensive. Still, he wanted to dress for the somber occasion and had selected a decent imported worsted in a dark brown corkscrew pattern. It was not the first time he had ever been there. Working as muscle for Jimmy Farrell ensured that he made the trip down to claim a body every so often, whenever trouble broke out with McGrath's outfit or some newcomers looking to make a name. Other times it would be a scrape between a few of Farrell's young toughs, each with more thirst than brains. Sooner or later one would pull a blade. But this was the first time in almost twenty years he had come to collect the body of a woman.

'Right this way.' The morgue attendant led Doran past the covered bodies on the first two tables. He set his papers on the edge of the last table and lifted the sheet, folding it down to reveal nothing lower than the young woman's chin. Tom Doran stared at the underfed face. His eyes moved over the sheet. It was hard to believe that such a small frame had actually held an entire soul just two days before.

Doran drew a gold picture locket from his coat. It looked absurdly small as he rolled it about in his massive, callused hand. Eventually he noticed that the attendant was staring, waiting for eye contact to be made. Doran nodded. 'That's her.' He tried not to think too much about where he was, tried to let his mind go blank.

The attendant replaced the sheet and gathered up his papers. He stared down at his clipboard while he talked. 'Full name?'

'Margaret Keene.'

'You're family?'

'Ahh ... employer.'

'She have any family?'

'No.'

'Address?'

Doran paused. Maggie moved around a lot, finding rooms or a spare bed wherever she could. Same as most of the girls. Of course, the answer didn't really matter anymore, so Doran just picked a recent lodging. 'Merrill Street.'

'Occupation?' The attendant peeked over his glasses as he asked the last question.

'Domestic,' said Doran. He kept his voice flat, not caring whether the little man believed him.

'If you can just mark here on the bottom line.'

'I can sign my name,' answered Doran, who focused and proceeded to do so. 'I can take her now? If I bring my wagon around to the back door?'

'Oh, legally I can't release the body to anyone other than a licensed undertaker. City ordinance. And of course there's the standard two-dollar fee associated with the handling and the paperwork and whatnot, additional charges depending on where the body is delivered. Or we could make the arrangements and take care of things.'

'Arrangements?'

'Pauper's grave. It's what's usually done for . . . domestics.'

Doran stared at the man, who looked away and cleared his throat.

'That is, it's done sometimes when there's no family.'

Doran produced two dollar bills and slapped them down into the attendant's hand. 'I'll be back with the undertaker directly.'

As soon as Doran was out of sight, the attendant rang a thin bell cord. Within a minute a boy appeared at the doorway. The attendant handed him a quickly scrawled note.

'Take this to Dr Steig at the Soldiers' Home.'

15

Helen Prescott's eyes darted over the audience in the reading room on the first floor of the Portland Public Library. The twenty-eight-year-old assistant researcher at the Maine Historical Society was in charge of organizing the summer lecture series and had worn one of her handsomer suits for this evening's event. The Assabet cloth was trimmed with Hercules braid and had a pointed waist, diagonally buttoned and trimmed to match the skirt, also braided in six wide rows along with knife plaiting at the bottom.

The chairs were almost filled, and she glanced at the clock. It was just after eight. Her daughter, Delia, was staying with a neighbor for the evening, and Helen had promised to be home no later than nine thirty. Her boss, the speaker for tonight's topic, nodded to signal his readiness, and Helen moved to the lectern at the front of the room.

'Ladies and gentlemen, friends of the Portland Public Library and the Maine Historical Society, and those who simply have a morbid curiosity.' Helen threw a smile at the audience of several dozen and was greeted with polite laughter. 'I'd like to welcome you to the second of our Wednesday-evening lectures remembering the bicentennial of the 1692 Salem witchcraft trials. So now, without further ado, I present the society's chief historian, Mr F. W. Meserve.'

Helen sat where she could observe her boss, the audience, and also see into the lobby. The library was closed, but the front door was unlocked for any late arrivals to the lecture. She watched Meserve arrange himself at the podium. He was a paunchy fellow in a well-worn tweed coat. Thick glasses sat atop his upturned nose. A mustache with arrow-sharp tips stretched out across his pale, flabby face. Helen always had difficulty shaking the image of a highly literate mole that had burrowed up into a closet of ill-fitting clothes, then wandered blindly into the library.

'As we discussed last time, the witchcraft delusion of 1692 has rendered the name of Salem infamous throughout the world. Those who know nothing else of the history and character of New England surely know, and are pleased to remind us, that our Puritan ancestors hanged witches. We are familiar with the setting in Massachusetts, two hundred years ago: how political and religious persecutions, along with early hardships here, left the Puritan settlers with a gloomy, superstitious view of the world. To them, anything strange or outside the normal course of events was attributed to supernatural powers. They believed that the devil, having failed to prevent the progress of Christianity in Europe, had withdrawn into the American wilderness, to rule over his pagan Indian allies.'

Helen heard the library front door open and close, followed by what she thought were hesitant footsteps. She craned her neck and waited for the person to come into view. It was a man in a dark wool coat with a flat cap pulled forward and wearing dark, tinted glasses. He paused for a second, looked in the doorway, and then moved off to a nearby bookshelf that held volumes related to the lecture series. Helen returned her attention to the lecture.

'I had planned to continue on with the course of chronological events,' Meserve said. 'However, given the excitement caused within the city by the recent tragedy at the Portland Company, I thought I might seize this opportunity to speak on a related topic: the role of the Maine Indians in the Salem witch trials.'

The crowd members were a sufficiently staid lot that this announcement generated a murmur of anticipation. Helen was pleasantly surprised as well, not at the substance of the change in topic but by the fact that Meserve was claiming to have seized the opportunity. Not that her boss was a timid man, but he was so methodical and ponderous in his work that in her few years' acquaintance she couldn't recall him ever seizing an opportunity, a moment, or anything else to speak of.

'Though it is hard to imagine in our modern times, the wilderness of that age was a hostile place, home to a strange race of savages that were widely believed, even by the scholars of the day, to be worshippers of the devil. Within decades,' Meserve went on, 'provocations on both sides led to a series of devastating wars. By the time of the witchcraft trials, there was hardly a town, or even a family, in all New England untouched by the violence. We Portlanders understand that history, our frontier town having been raided by Indians in 1676 and then wiped from the map in 1690. In fact, several of the most prominent figures in the Salem tragedy had close connections to Maine or were even refugees from here after those brutal Indian attacks. This fear of the Indians created such anxiety and paranoia in the minds of the populace that the stage was well set for the tragedy of Salem Village.'

Helen was having a hard time focusing on the lecture. She knew that Meserve was doing his usual good job of quickly summarizing in minutes what seemed to occupy hundreds of pages in Charles Upham's bloated and rambling two-volume opus, *Salem Witchcraft*. Instead she found her gaze returning to the lobby, where the latecomer seemed transfixed by the bookcase dedicated to treatises on Salem and the general history of witchcraft. There was something disturbing in his demeanor.

'It was during an early examination of Martha Corey that one of the afflicted girls added a new element of terror to the proceedings. She cried out that she could see a "black man" whispering to the accused. This dark figure was understood by all to be the devil, or his servant. The term "black" was commonly meant to refer to the dark complexion of the natives. This marked the first open connection between the two deadly threats facing the English: the spiritual war waged on them by the devil and the devastating attacks recently launched by the Indians along the northeastern frontier.

'The scope of the witchcraft investigations shifted dramatically again on April nineteenth, when teenager Abigail Hobbs, who already had a reputation for odd behavior, confessed to being a witch. She stated she had first seen the devil and had signed his book four years earlier while living here to the eastward at Casco Bay. Satan had taken the shape of a black man in a hat. This confession of the devil's initial appearance at what is now Portland, a place of great conflict in both the Indian wars, proved to the people of Salem that there was a common source for the assaults launched by both the witches and the Abenakis.

'The next day Ann Putnam Jr. reported seeing an apparition of a minister who tormented her and tore her to pieces. She said his name was George Burroughs and that he had killed his first two wives as well as Reverend Lawson's wife and child. Further, he had bewitched a great number of soldiers to their deaths on Sir Edmund Andros's eastern Maine expedition years earlier.

'It is very likely that information on Burroughs had been provided by another of the afflicted teenage girls, Mercy Lewis. One of the more active accusers, she was a small child in Portland when our town was overrun by Indians in 1676. Several of her uncles, cousins, and grandparents were killed. Her own parents escaped with her to an island in Casco Bay with a party led by Burroughs, before moving to safety in Massachusetts. The Lewis family returned seven years later, and she actually lived in Burroughs's house in Maine at some point. She would have been very well acquainted with the rumors and gossip that surrounded the man.'

The sound of a book slapping against the floor of the lobby finally gave Helen enough reason to excuse herself from the lecture. Once in the lobby, she saw that the man had not yet retrieved the fallen book. She took a deep breath, trying to restrain her ire. After all, perhaps the man wore those tinted glasses due to some malady of the eyes that prevented him from picking it up. The more likely explanation was that he was drunk, or otherwise just too much of a discourteous lout to bother.

As she approached, she felt a twinge of remorse upon noting the wide scar that was visible around his eye despite the dark glasses. 'Is there something I can help you with?'

The man looked at her and offered a thin, humorless smile. He was middle-aged, with short blond hair and a hard face. She couldn't see his eyes, but the rest of his expression betrayed no real trace of interest in her. 'No.'

It was a plain dismissal, and Helen was speechless for a moment. Her irritation at the man's callousness returned even more forcefully for having been held in check.

'The library does actually close at eight o'clock on Mondays. Of course, you're more than welcome to stay for the lecture.'

'Thank you, no.' He took a thin brown volume from the shelf. 'Tell me, is this your full collection on the subject of occult matters?'

'No. Were you looking for something in particular?'

'Yes. An older book. Quite a bit older than these, I think.'

'What's the title?' Helen asked.

'I'm afraid I can't recall.'

'The author?'

The man shook his head.

'Well, I really don't think I can help you tonight.'

'But you do have additional books? Older ones?'

Helen nodded. 'In our special-collections room upstairs.'

The man looked toward the staircase, his body leaning enough to make Helen think he might actually walk off in that direction.

'The head librarian will be available around ten in the morning to help you.' Helen motioned toward the front door. 'Now, I really should be getting back to our speaker.'

'This book here' – the man motioned toward a shelf – 'there's a slip noting it's on loan from a private library. But the owner's name is missing.'

'Some patrons with extensive collections have loaned volumes to support our lectures on the Salem witch trials.'

'Personal collections? I'd like to see the names of those people.'

'Oh, I'm afraid I can't do that. Several have contributed on the condition of anonymity.' Helen felt the weight of the man's gaze on her, although more than once his head turned slightly as he glanced away from her. Helen listened, hoping someone was approaching, but in her gut she knew that the opposite was true. The man was looking to make certain there was no one else.

'I assure you, if I could locate what I'm looking for in a private library, the owner would be very interested in speaking with me. Of course, someone who could provide assistance in contacting those parties would be compensated as well.'

Helen shifted on her feet and then cleared her throat, wanting to be sure she could address the man in a firm tone. 'I'm really very sorry, Mr ... I didn't catch your name.'

'It's not important.'

The man's tepid smile sent a chill through Helen. She felt he was looking at her with no more regard than he had shown for the book he'd discarded on the floor earlier.

'As I said, the library is closed. So I must insist.' Helen again gestured toward the exit.

The man ignored the motion. 'I'm very sorry to have kept you.'

Helen's chest was tight with a swelling fear that she couldn't trace to the man's words or even his tone of voice. His apology was a blatant lie, and, more important, she knew he meant that to be obvious. Helen nodded and returned to her seat in the reading room.

Meserve rambled on, oblivious to Helen's confrontation. 'The connection between the witches and the threat of Indian attacks was made even clearer by the testimony offered by the likes of Mary Toothaker. She confessed to the charges, blaming her great fear of the Indians. She reported that the devil had appeared to her as a tawny man and promised to save her from the Indians and that she should have further happy days with her son, who had been wounded in the war. She admitted that her fear led her to sign the devil's book, stating he had given her a piece of birch bark on which she made a mark.

'Other testimony from afflicted women also underscored the satanic connection to the northern Indians. A maidservant, Mercy Short, who had previously been taken captive by the Abenakis in 1690 and held for half a year, was at the Boston jail one day and had an argument with the imprisoned witch Sarah Good. Afterward Mercy Short began to have the same fits as the afflicted Salem girls. In later months Mercy would describe the devil as a short and black man, not like a Negro but rather of a tawny Indian complexion. The book he wanted her to sign held covenants and signatures of those who served the devil, all written in red. During her fits she was described by Cotton Mather as being in captivity to the witches' specters. Mercy reported visions of Frenchmen and Indian chiefs among the specters who tormented her. They would torture her with burnings, as if she were being roasted at the stake.

'This sort of imagery – visions of witches roasting victims on spits – was common among the descriptions provided by the afflicted girls. This was a torture sometimes inflicted by the Indians and reported home by colonists who had been redeemed from captivity. The Salem accusers would also report witches threatening to "knock them on the head" if they would not sign the devil's book. That was recognized as a common phrase used by Indians. Another threat by the witches is that they would tear the afflicted girls to pieces if they did not sign. Apart from the common fate of having one's scalp ripped from his head, other stories of Indian tortures, such as victims' fingers being severed one by one and chunks of flesh carved from their bodies, into which wounds the Abenakis would stick burning pine-tar brands, were often repeated among the colonists.'

Helen glanced at the lobby once more. Her brow creased as she tried to remember if, after returning to her seat, she had heard the soft bang of the front door closing.

16

Lean arrived at Dr Steig's shortly before nine and was shown to the consulting room.

'Deputy Lean, good of you to come.' Dr Steig rose from behind his desk. 'Truth be told, I wasn't sure you'd make it.'

'That is,' Grey said from where he stood looking out the window, 'according to today's editions, the police have assured us they're already pursuing leads to locate the crazed Indian who killed Maggie Keene.'

'Well, those reports may have been a bit off track. New information having come to light and all. Though I still suspect he's a lunatic.' Lean withdrew a small box from his coat pocket and set it on Dr Steig's desk. 'Maggie Keene's tongue. Sorry, Doctor, I didn't know what else to do with it.'

'I assume your presence here means that His Honor had a strong reaction to the message.' Grey glanced at Lean.

'Earlier he'd ordered me to end your involvement in this case.'

'Well, fortunately for me, and for those members of the public who are opposed to being murdered and dismembered, I don't answer to your superiors.'

Lean held up a conciliatory hand. 'But after the tongue arrived at his doorstep, he was more open to considering some of your views on the case. For the record, he insists your involvement in this investigation remain unreported. As dangerous and mad as our killer is, the mayor still has his own reputation to consider.'

'Dangerous and mad.' Dr Steig blew a thin plume of cigarette smoke toward the ceiling, then tipped his ashes into the tray. 'According to the *Daily Advertiser*, the killer's not only insane but a syphilitic degenerate. They're guessing the condition was contracted from a prostitute, explaining his selection of victim and the savagery of his vengeful attack.' Dr Steig's face was turning a shade of red as he spoke, his tone growing more severe. 'It's the same old pigheaded biases. Branding all those who suffer psychological infirmities as a threat to society. They're all criminals whose own sins have brought on their condition. A syphilitic degenerate – why, there have been more city councilors than murderers in this city over the past fifty years who fit that description.' Dr Steig was about to continue, but the cigarette in his left hand burned down during his rant and singed his fingers. 'Damn!'

Lean was not wholly surprised by the reaction. He'd been in the doctor's study before and read the framed letter on the wall appointing Dr Steig to run the Portland Soldiers' Home. It was from the Civil War hero and former governor of Maine, Joshua Chamberlain. The two had been colleagues at Bowdoin College after the war. Chamberlain had served as president while Dr Steig, his wounded arm limiting his surgical skills, had become a professor of anatomy and later neurology. The letter hanging in the study reflected the shared attitude of those two old soldiers: that those who'd suffered psychologically in the battles that had saved the Union deserved medical treatment as much as those who'd lost limbs. Confining these men to barren asylum cells was condemnation, not care. Unfortunately, that attitude was never widely shared by the taxpaying public. Lean sympathized with the doctor's position, but then again, he had seen the kinds of damage that could be done by those whom he considered to be mad.

'Be that as it may, Doctor, our killer's message certainly points toward insanity.' He withdrew the note received with the tongue and read it aloud. '"I am writing so you will know your errors. Of course I'm not an Indian! The Master is above all others. I stand with the Master, above them. The black man serves the Master. In the third month, the month of the Master's power, you will see the truth and know I hold the Master's power. You will know this in time."'

Dr Steig waved his hand about, thinking as he spoke. 'There's arrogance there. As if he's lowering himself to even bother pointing out our ignorance. The note's preoccupied with setting out a hierarchy of sorts. He indicates subservience to a master but then claims superiority over the Indians because the master rules over them and he, the killer, stands with the master. All rather confused.'

Grey nodded. 'I agree. But what is clear, and most important in the note, is that he intends to keep killing. The next murder will likely be even more sensational – a display of his power.'

'So what do we do?' Dr Steig's tone hinted at a growing frustration.

'Unless we learn more about this man, I think it will be fruitless to try to decipher his message,' Grey said. 'If we're to stop him, we're going to have to reconstruct this puzzle from the ground up. Now that the mayor is supporting our effort, at least privately, we'll have the use of police resources in conducting a canvass of the boarding rooms in the vicinity of the Portland Company.'

Lean shrugged. 'That was done already. No one in the area saw anything the night of the murder.'

'Not surprising. Our man would have taken every precaution not to be seen that night. But we have the advantage of knowing he was in the vicinity not solely on that night but for as long as a week prior. So the questions that need to be asked, of every landlady or family renting a room, of every grubby child in the streets playing at bases or jack stones, are these: Has a short, dark-haired man been renting a room thereabouts in the past week or two? And if so, was he the type who kept strange hours? And did he pay in advance through at least Sunday, then disappear with no forwarding address?'

'There must be dozens of rooms to let in that area,' Dr Steig said.

'A right piece of work,' Lean agreed.

'We mustn't be daunted by the specter of difficult times ahead,' Grey said. 'I expect this inquiry may prove severely taxing before its conclusion. It's not to be undertaken with anything less than the utmost commitment.'

Lean held his tongue for a moment even as he bristled at the implication. 'I'm sworn to protect this city, Grey. My commitment to catching this murderer is not in question.'

Grey nodded. 'Accepted. And though my reasons are not so succinctly stated as your own, I can assure you likewise.'

'Then we're agreed, gentlemen,' Dr Steig said. 'Now, where do we begin?'

'Where every criminal inquiry must begin,' Grey said, 'with the facts. We're mostly in the dark, but we do have some prospects. We already know some of his physical characteristics. I believe we have four additional fields of inquiry. First, the victim. Why was she selected, and has she left us any clues behind? Second, the location. Certainly a conscious choice, given the amount of preparation involved. But why was it selected? Third is the mechanism of death. We do not know the significance of the weapons used. And lastly, what can we learn of that prior killing which our man appears to acknowledge?'

Dr Steig was scribbling in a notebook, his right forearm planted against the edge of his desk to steady his writing hand. 'So first,' he said, 'why Maggie Keene?'

'She's a prostitute,' Lean said. 'Perhaps the papers are right on this one. The man may simply have a grudge against whores.'

'The savagery of the killings certainly speaks to more than a mere grudge. There's fervor of the type associated with a . . . ' Dr Steig pondered the correct classification.

'A religious fanatic,' Lean suggested. 'It fits with the chalk message. And the cuts in her chest, forming a cross. He was punishing her for her sins.'

Grey gave a hesitant shake of his head. 'But why Maggie Keene in particular? Our man planned everything else in detail. It stands to reason that the choice of victim was also premeditated. And, if so, she may have been acquainted with him prior to her death.'

'Maybe he felt wronged by her in the past,' Lean said.

Grey shrugged. 'Or maybe he fancies girls with freckles.'

'Or witch's tits. He was certainly intrigued with it,' the doctor added.

'An interesting detail. What do you make of that?' Grey asked.

Dr Steig puffed on his cigarette and pondered the question for a moment. 'Obviously I have never treated anyone who's committed such an act as this. But I have seen men, deeply troubled, who have had irrational, violent urges. Despite this man's evident capacity for organizing his thoughts and actions, I presume he is a highly tormented fellow. He may have certain desires he knows are wrong, yet he cannot ignore them. These could cause a great conflict within him. Eventually his anger becomes too much to bear, and he lashes out, punishing the very person, or type of person, that is the object of his immoral fascinations.' The doctor shrugged. 'It's just a thought. I cannot pretend to understand truly the workings of this man's mind.'

After a long pause, Grey nodded as if he'd made some type of decision. 'It's a plausible theory, but for now it's only that. What else about Maggie Keene? What clues as to her killer's identity has she left behind for us? If she'd seen him before, she may have mentioned him to her associates before her death.'

'We questioned Farrell's other girls. They weren't talking,' Lean said.

Grey said, 'This Tom Doran who collected the body. You said you knew him, Doctor.'

'Yes. In fact, he was one of my first patients here.'

'He works as muscle for Farrell's operations?' Grey asked.

Lean nodded. 'If any of the other girls are talking about Maggie's death, he should know what they're saying.'

'How soon can we arrange to question him?' Grey asked.

'I would expect to see him at the funeral tomorrow,' Dr Steig said.

'Farrell's not the type to show his face and admit any kind of involvement in this sort of thing. So we should be able to see Doran alone,' Lean said.

'I think I can get him to talk openly,' Dr Steig added.

'Excellent. Now to our second point. What evidence did our man leave as a result of his prolonged presence in the area?' Grey asked.

'Canvassing the boarding rooms again' – Lean tried to conceal his lack of enthusiasm for the task – 'for any eyewitnesses who put him in the area that week. There are some patrolmen I can rely upon to be discreet as to our actual suspicions. The last thing we need is another round of violence, this time against short, dark-haired men.'

Grey nodded. 'Our third point. Whether the exact location of the crime reveals any connection to the killer.'

'Perhaps a former employee. Maybe injured or fired?' Dr Steig said.

'A simple enough question for the owners and foremen,' Lean replied.

'That reminds me – what of the pitchfork left near the body?' Grey asked.

'The workers knew nothing about it. Didn't belong there.'

'Interesting.' Grey took several steps away from the window and then returned. He traced a star on the glass with his index finger. 'We cannot assume a former worker. We should also ask if they have received any threats from outside the company.'

'A competitor?'

'Possibly. Or our man could even be some type of Luddite. The Portland Company is at the forefront of building steam locomotives. Not everyone is thrilled about such developments. The railroads signify change; that frightens some people.'

'I could see arson or some such,' Lean said, 'but cutting up a prostitute?'

'I only mention the possibility in light of our man's choice of weapon.'

'The pitchfork.' The oddity of that detail had struck Lean before, but it was easy to lose sight of it amid all the bizarre details of the crime scene. He realized that he hadn't fully considered the symbolism of that weapon. 'Stuck right in the ground like that. Peeling back the boards, to expose the soil underneath. It does have a primitive, rustic quality.'

'And finally,' Grey said, 'the first murder.'

Lean held up a finger. 'Assuming there was such a murder. You said yourself it was queer that we've heard nothing of it. Perhaps there was no other murder. If our man's a lunatic, he could have left those two candles and two bloody lines for no reason at all.'

'Unlikely. Everything at our scene was calculated. There was a first murder; and now he's practically boasting of a third to come.' Grey thought for a moment. 'If we remain ignorant, it is because the victim has not yet been found or the body was not thought suspicious. A third possibility is that we are simply too far removed to have word of the event.'

'He certainly meant for Maggie Keene's body to be found right off. And if his note means he committed the first murder last month, I'd guess enough time has passed for the first one to be discovered,' Lean said.

Dr Steig nodded his agreement. 'And if the first victim was left in any condition like Maggie, the discovery would have raised an outcry.'

'It stands to reason,' Grey said. 'So let us assume that a body, probably dismembered, has been discovered, more or less one month ago. But it was far enough away that we've heard not a whisper of it.'

'Could be anywhere,' Lean said.

'So we actively pursue the first three areas of inquiry while we cast our net for the last. If the earlier murder was anything like Maggie Keene's, it was investigated by a detective or sheriff some-where. I have contacts in most of the larger cities between here and Manhattan. North of Portland is a different story.'

'I know every county sheriff and town police chief within a hundred miles,' Lean said.

Grey began to pace, his first outward display of excitement since the discussion started. 'Then we telephone or telegraph them. Nothing specific, since we can't be sure if the details will be the same for the first victim. But we ask about murders: peculiar circumstances, mutilations, possible dismemberments. We start close by. I'll contact Portsmouth, Concord, Worcester, and Boston.'

'I'll check Bangor, Lewiston, Augusta, and Bath,' Lean said. 'And if we come up empty-handed?'

'There is the possibility that we won't solve this matter until we learn more about our killer's methods.'

Lean stared at him, grasping the dire meaning of Grey's plan. 'You mean wait until there's another murder.'

17

Helen returned the last of the lecture chairs to its rightful place. She glanced up at the clock on the far wall. Mr Meserve had gotten long-winded, as she feared he might. When she let the lecture guests out, it was raining. Finding a cab would be difficult, meaning she wasn't going to keep her promise of getting home before Delia was asleep. She paused a moment by the front desk. The rain beating on the windows made it hard to be sure whether she had heard a faint noise overhead.

Then she heard the sound again and recognized it. One of the small second-floor windows had a loose clasp that often came unhitched and would rattle in the wind. She hoped not too much rain had come in. Helen switched on the electric lights by the stairs and walked up to the landing. Moving down the dim hallway, she caught sight of a light under the door to the special-collections room. The librarian was notorious for forgetting to extinguish the lights when she left for the evening. Helen moved forward, turned the handle, and stepped into the room.

She flinched as if she'd been slapped. A dark figure stood near the far end of the room. He was visible in profile, facing a bookshelf that also held a half-shuttered lamp. Helen tried to force her throat shut and strangle the scream, but it was too late. Her cry splintered the silence, and the figure darted around the corner. A second later he stepped forward again.

Helen bolted back the way she'd come, down the stairs, one hand clutching up her skirt. The panicked rush kept her from hearing any sounds of pursuit, but she knew he was coming. Her feet thudded down onto the first-floor landing, and she began to turn for the exit but then forced herself to veer off down the hall. She would never outrace him to the front door. The head librarian's office had a lock. Helen's hand shot out and grabbed the knob. It slipped under her sweaty palm but turned. She pushed the door open. Her eyes dashed back to her left. The man reached the landing and came toward her.

Helen threw herself into the room and slammed the solid oak door behind her. The key was in the lock, and she turned it, letting herself breathe only after she heard the click, then clutched the key to her chest. The knob rattled. The door shook in its frame as the man abused the handle. Helen looked around and seized a heavy candlestick from a side table. The door went silent. She held her breath and was rewarded with the faint sound of footsteps moving away. The wood of the door felt cool as she pressed her ear against it. The front door of the library banged shut. Helen hurried to the window overlooking the front exit on Congress Street. A dark shadow splashed away across the wide avenue.

She unlocked the office door and, with the candlestick still lodged in her grip, ran across the lobby to bolt the front door. She dashed to the telephone at the front desk and picked up the receiver. What would she say? She hadn't actually seen the man's face upstairs. She couldn't swear he was the same man she had confronted earlier in the lobby. She'd be there for hours while the police asked questions she couldn't answer. Her thoughts flashed to Delia – she had to get home. Helen hung up the phone. Uncle Virgil would know what to do. She would ask him in the morning.

Helen let her neighbor out and locked the door behind her. She went back through the kitchen to make sure the rear door was also locked, then hurried upstairs. She peeked into Delia's room. The curtain was open, and a sliver of rain-soaked moonlight fell through the window to reveal the girl's sleeping face. Helen went to her own room and worked her way through the process of removing her several layers. She pulled on a muslin robe with a bosom of fine tucks and box pleats, trimmed with embroidery, then returned to her daughter.

When she lifted the covers to climb into bed, Helen saw that Delia was clutching a picture frame. She eased the girl's grip and slid the picture away. It showed a handsome man with a bushy mustache standing behind a chair. A seated Helen Prescott, younger and smiling, looked out at the world. 'Bastard,' she said, then grimaced at the sound of her voice in the still room.

'Mother?' Delia's head turned, but her eyes remained shut.

'Shhh. Go back to sleep.' Helen set the picture down and slid under the covers. She wrapped her arm around Delia and held her close. She felt the girl's gentle breathing, close enough that Helen could let her own heart slow, falling into rhythm with that of the dreaming child.

18

Tom Doran stared straight ahead, his eyes focusing on the ragged rectangle carved into the earth. Nearby, someone in the cluster of Farrell's girls was crying. Next to the mound of dark earth, the priest was reading a psalm. Doran recognized it, but the words simply swirled around him, then moved on unhindered.

"'Why standest thou afar off, O Lord? Why hidest thou thyself in times of trouble? The wicked in his pride doth persecute the poor.'"

The box that held Maggie was nothing fancy. It hadn't cost much, and Doran felt a twinge of guilt over that, but then again, it was no worse than the coffin for his own wife two decades earlier. Besides which, Maggie was in a better place, and she wouldn't begrudge him that pine box. The other girls might complain, but Doran knew the loud grief coming from that group would dwindle and die over the next couple of weeks. After that, Maggie Keene might get remembered in a drunken toast on some night when the girls got together for a cup of cheer after a good bit of business. And that would be the whole of it.

The priest's voice rattled on. "'His mouth is full of cursing and deceit and fraud: under his tongue is mischief and vanity. He sitteth in the lurking places of the villages: in the secret places does he murder the innocent; his eyes are privily set against the poor. He lieth in wait secretly as a lion in his den.'"

Doran's gaze wavered and fell upon the box itself. She was in there, lifeless and still. Whatever made her who she was had gone out of the face he'd seen in the morgue. Doran closed his eyes and tried to picture her as she'd looked while alive. The image soon blurred and twisted until he was instead seeing his own Mary, staring back at him with soft eyes.

'"Thou hast seen it; for thou beholdest mischief and spite, to requite it with thy hand: the poor committeth himself unto thee; thou art the helper of the fatherless. Break thou the arm of the wicked and the evil man: seek out his wickedness till thou find none."'

Tom Doran clenched his fists hard enough that his ragged fingernails dug into his palms. When that didn't work, he raised his left hand to his mouth and bit into a knuckle. Soon the pain and the faint taste of blood were enough to banish the thoughts.

'You don't think she's in any further danger?' Dr Steig asked.

'Well, I told them they should have more than a lone woman locking up the place at night,' Lean said, recalling that morning's meeting with the doctor's rattled niece and the head librarian. 'But from this same fellow? I don't think so. He wasn't a regular visitor, unfamiliar with the library. Strikes me as an isolated occurrence. Troubling, but not likely to be repeated.'

'Thank you again, Lean. After all this, the idea of a madman on the loose, then my own niece being threatened. You don't suppose there's any chance?'

'The thought struck me, but her man was of average height and blond.'

'In the lobby, yes, but she never saw the face of the one who chased her,' said the doctor.

'Probably the same man.' Lean shifted his feet on the grass, not yet wanting to interrupt the scene below even though the ceremony was clearly finished. 'Ready?'

'Let's give him a minute,' Dr Steig said.

Lean glanced over his shoulder at the doctor's hansom cab, which had brought them across the river to the Catholic cemetery in Cape Elizabeth. Through the window he could make out Grey, sitting in the shade with his telescope in hand, perusing the scenery with his back to the cemetery.

'Doran's this way,' noted Lean.

'You think Doran's our man, then?'

'Of course not.'

'Good,' Grey said, 'then it's agreed we shouldn't both be wasting our time staring at him.'

'Oh, and you think the killer is lurking about behind some tree, come to see his girl off.' Lean rolled his eyes.

The doctor gave a shrug. 'He obviously attached a great degree of significance to her death and to her body after death. Not implausible to think he still feels some perverse sense of union with her.'

'Fine.' Lean turned back to Grey. 'Any luck, then?'

Grey held his telescope aimed along the tree-lined sidewalk, looking toward where Vaughan's Bridge led back across the Fore River to the West End of Portland. 'Not unless our man is successfully disguised as an old woman walking a constipated mutt.'

'Here he comes,' said Dr Steig.

Lean turned to see a massive, rusty-haired man trudging toward them. Grey secured his telescope inside the carriage, then climbed down to join the others.

'There's something I can help you with, Doc?' Doran asked, tipping his hat.

'Perhaps, Tom. We need some information about Margaret Keene.'

Doran's eyes narrowed, and he glanced at Lean, then Grey.

'It's all right, Tom. You can talk freely in front of my colleagues,' Dr Steig said.

'I'm not in the habit of talking to the police.'

'Just a few questions,' Lean said.

Doran glanced back and forth among their faces. 'Right. What do you need to know?'

'You picked her up from the morgue. So she was one of Farrell's girls?' Lean said.

Doran nodded.

'Farrell paid the morgue fees?'

'I did.'

'Why?' Lean asked. 'Were you friendly with her?'

Anger flashed in Doran's eyes but subsided after Dr Steig cleared his throat.

'Not like that. Just because she deserved better. She was a good kid. Could get a little mean when she'd had a few drinks. But mostly she was a nice girl. Just wanted to have things a little better. Always talked about getting off of Munjoy Hill. Said she'd wind up with a big place looking over the river.'

'She was half right,' Grey said.

'So you have any thoughts on who might have done this?' Lean asked.

Doran shook his head. 'If it ain't some madman like the papers say, then I don't know.'

'Gotten herself up a bit fancy. New hat, gloves. She have something special working?'

'Nothing much. Just some guy passing through. Big talker, I heard, promising her a better life and all. Nothing new. She was a dreamer, though. Mighta fallen for that whole bit.'

'Hear anything about him being rough with her?' Lean asked.

'If I'd heard any such, the man would've been in the ground himself, afore he could do this to Maggie.' Doran nodded back toward where the gravediggers were shoveling in the dirt.

'Those other girls that were here. They know any more about this new guy?'

'Don't think those girls really know much,' Doran said.

'"Those" girls?' Grey said. 'There's someone else who might?'

'She had a friend. Called her cousin, but I think she was just a gal from the next town over back home. Families knew each other kind of thing.'

'Where can we find this . . . ?' Lean left the question of a name hanging.

'Boxcar Annie. Something of a loose bird. She used to be around a lot up on the hill. I went looking for her myself yesterday, but she's cleared out. Heard she's taken up with some of McGrath's crew. Down off Pleasant Street.'

'Tom,' Dr Steig said, 'do you know anyone, maybe a customer coming around a lot, who carries a kind of blade with a good curve to it?'

'Curve? What, like the tip of a bowie knife?'

'No. A good section of the blade would have something of a curve to it.' Dr Steig cupped his hand like the thin edge of a waning moon. 'So you could cut with it, but really more useful for slashing down or hacking away at something.'

A look of recognition flickered in Doran's eyes along with the slightest hint of a smile. 'Like an old billhook, you mean.'

'A what?' Grey's voice held an unexpected sharpness.

'A billhook.'

'You know anyone who carries something like that?' asked Lean.

'Not in the city.'

'Where, then?' asked Grey.

'Just about any farm in the state. For cutting hedges or stripping down saplings and such.'

Grey looked on as if expecting some further explanation.

'Tom here was a farmer years ago,' explained the doctor.

'It was a fair piece back. Didn't agree with me.'

'Hear the livestock didn't much care for it either,' added Lean.

A tired sigh escaped Doran's throat. He offered nothing more and glanced at his shoes.

'All that's a lifetime ago, eh, Tom?' said Steig.

Doran just nodded toward the doctor.

'Gentlemen?' Dr Steig raised his eyebrows. Grey was deep in thought, so Lean answered for the two of them, nodding his assent. The doctor reached out and shook Doran's hand. 'Thank you, Tom. Very helpful.'

A minute later, as the carriage hurried down Spring Street, past the broad, tree-lined yards of the West End and into the more densely packed city blocks, Lean called up to the driver to head for City Hall.

'I think perhaps we pay this Boxcar Annie a visit tomorrow.' He waited for a response, but there was only the rattling of the cab. 'Well, Grey, do you agree about seeing her?'

'Hmm? Yes, of course. This prostitute friend. I'll leave that to you, Deputy.' Grey turned to the doctor. 'What was that piece about livestock?'

'Livestock? Oh, Doran. He used to be a tenant farmer, but he was a slave to the bottle,' answered Dr Steig. 'Not an uncommon affliction among his countrymen, especially for one who's had the troubles he's had.'

'So one morning after a real hard night at it,' added Lean with a hint of a smirk, 'some poor old heifer comes wandering in too close to Doran's window, bursting to be milked and mooing like mad over him leaving it for so long. Well, Big Tom stirs out of his drunk in such a foul mood that he storms right out into the yard, hauls off bare-handed, and slugs that old milk bag right across the skull. Dropped her down dead on the spot.' Lean chuckled at the thought of it, then noticed that neither of his companions was smiling.

'Not quite so amusing when you know the whole of it,' grumbled Dr Steig.

Lean shrugged his shoulders at Grey, who had gone strangely quiet, peering off into some distant, solitary space. 'Something about Doran bothering you?'

'No,' answered Grey as the cab came to a stop. He leaped to the cobblestones. There was a sudden vigor in his voice as his long strides carried him down the sidewalk. 'Something about a bill-hook!'

19

Helen Prescott pushed the rattling book cart from the circulation desk toward the stacks on the first floor of the Portland Public Library. Although she was officially employed as an assistant researcher in the historical society on the third floor, when her duties were light she would come downstairs to lend a hand. The library was not crowded, typical for lunchtime on Friday, but she still imagined a dozen pairs of eyes tracing her noisy path across the room. There had been little sleep when she got home on Wednesday night. The sound of heavy steps halting for a moment somewhere on the street outside at two in the morning had been enough to stir her from a fitful dream and cause her to peek from the bedroom window for any signs of the intruder lurking outside her home. She had gone to work the next morning just long enough to report the incident and await the arrival of Deputy Lean, the police detective her uncle had contacted. Although she had seen not a trace of the intruder since two nights earlier, she could still not shake the feeling that he was nearby, watching her.

Helen was finishing her reshelving when she heard the clang of the front door, followed by purposeful footsteps moving toward the front desk. She stooped down to peer through the narrow gap above a row of books. A tallish man in a charcoal suit appeared at the circulation desk. She studied him and decided he didn't match the outline of the man she'd seen two nights before. Helen felt a wave of relief as the man removed his dark felt hat to reveal his jet-black hair. He was studying the displayed program for the library's lecture series with a focus on Charles W. Upham's 1867 work *Salem Witchcraft: With an Account of Salem Village & a History of Opinions on Witchcraft and Kindred Subjects.* Helen strode back to the desk, studying the man as she approached. He was tall and thin, with a very tan complexion. She thought he had a deeply honest face, but not in a simple, straightforward way. Even as he stood there, just waiting, he seemed to be intently focused on some faraway thought. All in all, she thought him rather handsome, and she even managed a tentative smile as she asked the man if there was anything she could help him find.

'Yes, I'm in need of some information regarding, coincidentally enough,' he said with a motion toward the displayed program, 'witches. Particularly the superstitions and folklore surrounding witchcraft.'

Although the man's expression was pleasant, his dark eyes bored into her. Helen felt he was reading her as plainly as the program. Her smile faded, and she threw a glance down at the desk, her frantic eyes finding the letter opener she'd placed within easy reach when she came in that morning. 'Any particular time period? We have some rare, older texts published in the sixteenth century that might interest you.' Her hand slid unseen across the desktop, toward the letter opener.

'No, actually I'm looking for something more recent. From just the past ten years or so.'

Helen gave him directions to the second floor and the small section there on folklore and mythology, as well as a nearby section featuring writings on spiritualism, a subject that had grown steadily over the past two decades.

'If you can't find what you're looking for there, you can see Mr Meserve on the third floor. In conjunction with our lecture series commemorating the bicentennial of the Salem Witch Trials, we have amassed a rather impressive selection of related works, many on loan from some of the city's finest private collections.'

The man showed no interest in that bit of information. He gave her an awkward smile and thanked her. Helen watched him move to the stairs and then out of sight. The similarity in this new request, coming so hard on the heels of the intruder's request two nights before, left goose bumps on her arms. She glanced about and grabbed a small stack of items that needed to be reshelved. Once she reached the second floor, Helen maneuvered into an aisle opposite the main room, where she saw the man's back. A stack of four or five texts was set on the table in front of him. She listened as he flipped the pages at quick, regular intervals. The pattern continued for a few minutes before the man started on a new book. The interruption broke the spell, and Helen forced herself to head back down to the circulation desk.

A half hour later, she invented another task and returned to the second floor in search of a volume on Greek antiquities. This provided a closer vantage point to where the darkly dressed man had been reading. He was gone when she got there, his books abandoned on the table. She went by, glanced around to make sure the man was nowhere in sight, then examined the titles. All books involving European folklore and superstitions. One was even written in German.

Grabbing two random books off a nearby shelf, Helen hurried toward the special-collections room. From there she heard the voice of the head librarian in the same area where she had seen the intruder two nights earlier. Helen strode across to the reference desk and glanced down at the registry. The last signature was that of Perceval Grey. She repeated the name twice under her breath as she sat down at the desk and waited.

A short while later, Grey appeared and walked past with only the quickest glance at Helen. She collected her coat and bag from the third floor while giving a hasty, jumbled excuse to Mr Meserve. After hurrying back downstairs, she dashed out the front door and caught sight of Perceval Grey moving east. She followed behind as he entered the busy square where Free Street angled in to meet the juncture of High and Congress. Helen hurried in and out of shadows cast by the tall spires of Plymouth Congregational, First Universalist, and then the Free Street

Baptist Church, all of which sat in a cluster, looming over the congested intersection.

A bit farther on, Grey stopped for a moment and glanced about. Helen feigned interest in the sidewalk displays of the Congress Fish Market. After one of the Portland Railroad's horse cars rumbled past, moving down the rails in the middle of the stone-paved street, Helen continued her pursuit. The powerful scent of the day's catch gave way to the sweet smell of sugar from the massive Hudson's candy works across the street.

Grey turned in to a doorway just ahead. Helen slowed her pace as she passed the entrance. Gilded letters arching across the upper limits of the large plate-glass window announced the Western Union Telegraph Co. She did her best to glance casually into the branch office and watched Grey take a pad from the man at the first of three telegraph windows. Grey dashed out his message. After only two lines, he snapped the tip of the pencil, and the clerk handed him a new one.

An idea sprang into Helen's mind, and she felt a devious smile creeping across her face. She watched Grey hand the pad back to the man along with the payment. Helen took several steps back in the direction she'd come and made an earnest effort to study the pastries on display in the window of Calderwood Brothers bakery. Grey exited and continued along Congress Street. Helen took several steps after him, then stopped in her tracks, unsure of whether to abandon her plan for the telegraph office. To her great relief, Grey went only another block before crossing Monument Square and heading into the four-story Preble House, one of Portland's finest hotels.

Helen hurried into the telegraph office and approached the clerk who had served Grey, cutting off a man heading for that same window. She made a show of apologizing breathlessly before turning to the clerk. 'I beg your pardon, but my employer was just here, Mr Perceval Grey. He was in such a rush he thinks he may have accidentally sent his telegraph to the wrong party. Could you please check for me? Was it directed for a Mr Charles Andrews?'

'Just a moment, ma'am, I'll check.' As the clerk turned away to retrieve Grey's message, Helen reached through the service window for the pad of paper and quietly tore off the top sheet.

The clerk returned to the window. 'No, ma'am, sent to a Mr Walter McCutcheon.'

'Oh, thank heavens. He'll be so relieved. That could have been quite embarrassing.' She gave a broad smile of relief, and the clerk nodded at her. With the sheet of paper tucked into her handbag, she hurried back onto the sidewalk. Helen made her way down the block, under the stately elms that lined the front of the Preble House. She had to walk just past where Grey had entered, one door farther down to the ladies' entrance to the hotel.

Inside, she circled around to the main lobby, looking over the bustle of guests, porters, and the lunchtime crowd mingling near the doors of the hotel restaurant. She focused on taller men in dark suits, but it was no use; Grey had disappeared. She stood for a moment planning her next step. As she prepared to head for the front desk, a loud squeak from the door to a public telephone booth drew her attention. She was startled to recognize Grey's sharp features as he exited from the cramped space. Helen took a roundabout route to the booth, allowing Grey time to exit the hotel. She pressed the call button twice, turned the lever and latched it before picking up the receiver. When the operator came on, Helen read the four numbers printed below the phone.

'Requested number?' asked the tinny voice through the receiver.

'Could you please place the last call again?'

Helen waited anxiously until the operator came back on the line. 'Yes, ma'am. It will be just a minute while we ring through to the Harvard switchboard.'

Helen hung up the receiver and glanced out the glass of the phone booth. Through the large front windows, she could still see Perceval Grey lingering on the sidewalk. She guessed he was waiting for the next horse car. Helen stared at the receiver, willing it to ring. Eventually her mental efforts were rewarded with a loud clanging. She snatched the receiver off its hook.

'Hello.'

'Go ahead, sir,' said the operator.

'Professor Newell Scribner speaking.'

Helen suddenly realized that she had not thought of what to say if her plan to reconnect Grey's call actually succeeded. She managed nothing better than a few confused stammers along the lines of an apology before hanging up. She fumbled her way out of the booth's folding door and scanned the windows for any sign of Grey. He was gone. Helen strode to the exit, where the white-gloved attendant in his gray coat with burnished brass buttons held the door for her.

The commotion of Monument Square washed over her. The scene was not as active as it had been when the area had been accurately titled Market Square. While most of the stalls and vendors had vanished since the square was reconfigured a year prior and the massive war monument erected, the space was still home to all manner of commercial endeavors. She scanned the square to see if Grey was heading into any of the businesses. Apart from the Preble House, the square was also home to the grand United States Hotel, as well as dozens of restaurants, halls, shops, and offices for such disparate enterprises as the *Evening Express* newspaper and the Portland Theatre, as well as the Portland Plasterers' Union, the Phoenix Crayon Company, and the Imperial Banjo, Guitar and Mandolin Club. But for sheer motion, none could compare with the offices of the Portland Rail Road Company as well as its streetcar depot. The ebb and flow of activity surrounding that hub of the city's horse rail lines caused pedestrians to alternately stroll or dash to safety across the triangular square and the various streets that emptied into the plaza.

All this movement, like a series of massive brick-fronted anthills, was set under the watchful gaze of a towering bronze Athena-like figure. *Our Lady of Victories* stood atop an ornate twenty-foot-tall pedestal bearing bronze reliefs of Civil War sailors and soldiers and this inscription: TO HER SONS WHO DIED FOR THE UNION. Helen stared up at the helmeted and laurel-crowned goddess, so sure and regal in her contemplative gaze. *If you're so wise*, she thought, *then tell me where he's gone.* As if by divine intervention, a horse car pulled past her. At the rear, in plain view, stood Perceval Grey.

Helen hailed a hansom cab and followed Grey the length of Congress Street past City Hall, Lincoln Park, and the Eastern Cemetery. Per her instructions, the driver momentarily delayed the pursuit of the trolley car when it stopped at the base of Munjoy Hill. A second horse was hitched to haul the car up the steady quarter-mile slope. She kept her eyes locked on Grey as people hurried aboard and settled themselves. After a minute the car lurched forward on its slow ascent. Helen let her mind wander, and her eyes landed on the Portland Observatory ahead on the right. The brown wooden tower was domed and octagonal, giving it the appearance of a hilltop lighthouse. The observatory was actually a maritime signal tower, built eighty-five years earlier, when Munjoy Hill was nothing more than an empty cow pasture.

As the car approached the summit, it slowed in preparation for detaching one of the draft horses. Grey dismounted at the base of the observatory. A man waited for him at the bottom of the staircase leading to the second-floor entrance. Helen stared for several seconds before realizing she knew the man. Her carriage pulled close, and he glanced in her direction. Helen whipped her head around to avoid making eye contact with Deputy Archie Lean.

20

Lean waited at the bottom of the wooden staircase leading to the front door of the observatory. At his left was a large fenced-in yard. To his right, at the peak of the hill, was the Fire Department Engine No. 2. 'So just what is it you wanted to see?'

Grey pointed past Lean, his finger angled into the air. Lean looked up, his eyes following the line of the structure's octagonal sides. The tower slanted inward, starting from a base diameter of thirty-two feet and narrowing to less than half that six stories up at the observation deck. The observatory was capped by a white, canvas-covered dome that was topped with a metal ball. It was a striking building, visible from most of the city and all of Portland Harbor.

Grey was already on the stairs, and Lean took the steps two at a time to catch up. The front door was a full story above the street, since the bottom level of the observatory held 120 tons of rubble that served as ballast for the structure. The building's plan, designed by a sea captain, had allowed it to stand firm against a dozen hurricanes and countless winter northeasters. The first floor was a large, empty octagonal room with exposed beams, including the eight colossal white pine support timbers that ran the entire height of the tower. A circular staircase hugged the outside wall. Each side held several narrow windows on alternating levels, so that every floor had enough daylight to allow people to see the way along the stairs.

The next-to-last floor housed large shelves that stored the various flags and pennants used on the observatory's three flagpoles to relay messages to the waterfront and signal the approach of specific vessels so owners and dockhands could prepare for the arrivals. The two men moved up the last of the 102 steps from the street to the top of the tower. The stairs were capped with a trapdoor that formed part of a small raised platform inside the top level, called the lantern. Inside, they were greeted by the young man on duty, who informed them that all visible ships had already been signaled. At the sight of Lean's badge, the young man gladly agreed to give them a few minutes' privacy by stretching his legs and going down to the market across the street.

The lantern was a window-encased room eight feet across. Immediately to the side of the trapdoor was the narrow exit out to the open-air walkway that encircled the lantern. A painted black bench ran along the remainder of the interior wall. Hanging from an iron rod in the center of the ceiling was a London-made, five-foot-long achromatic refracting telescope. The scope could swivel 360 degrees from Casco Bay to the White

Mountains of New Hampshire seventy miles to the west. On clear days the telescope's sixty-five-times magnification was enough to spot ships as far as thirty miles out. Closer to home, the city's rooftops were spread out below, interrupted by occasional spaces of green growth and a maze of narrow, twisting streets intersecting at irregular angles, like a web of paving stones spun by a gigantic, crazed spider.

'My father used to bring me up here when I was a boy,' Lean said as he caught his breath. 'He thought it was a nice little mix of navigation, history, and geography. Of course, the old man could never resist a bit of the fanciful.'

'So that's where you get it,' Grey replied.

'He'd always comment on the number of steeples and tell me of the old English folktale about how when a young boy and his sister climb a hilltop searching for lost sheep but instead see seven church spires in the setting sun, then would King Arthur rise again to save England once more.'

'Touching. Of course, I prefer the tale of the grown man with an annoying habit of waxing poetic about childhood fables when he should be concentrating on a murder inquiry. Father never mentioned anything along those lines, did he? No?'

Lean grinned. 'Doesn't ring any bells, I'm afraid.' He stepped up to the telescope eyepiece and turned his sights on the immediate harbor. There was Portland Head Light, commissioned 101 years earlier by George Washington, jutting out at the edge of Cape Elizabeth, near the main harbor entrance. Halfway Rock Light was close to that, a stone tower lighthouse on a short stretch of exposed ledge rising out of the bay. Standing more than two hundred feet above sea level, Lean could see the dozens of islands in Casco Bay and all the channels and passages.

'Certainly is a whole new perspective,' he said as he stepped away from the telescope. 'Quite a magnificent tool. This scope, and Polaris to steer by. That's all you would need.'

'North's that way.' Grey pointed a bit to Lean's left.

'Are you sure?'

Grey motioned upward, where a compass rose was painted on the ceiling.

'Forgot about that,' said Lean as he reoriented himself. 'Well, who needs Polaris anyhow? Your good cheer is as constant as the North Star.'

Grey smirked in response as he stepped out the narrow door, down onto the railed-in walk that encircled the lantern. The walkway was three feet wide and slanted just a bit down and away from the tower. Lean followed and rested against the waist-high railing as he stared out past the Eastern Cemetery, toward the waterfront where the Portland Company stood.

'We know that the killer was observing the watchman on multiple past occasions. Even if the killer hadn't been interrupted, he would have been quite a sight after the murder. He likely planned to clean himself or hide his appearance. In either case it would have been prudent for him to have shelter nearby,' Grey said.

'That fits with the watchman's report that he never heard any carriage fleeing the area,' Lean said.

'In his drug-induced stupor and the panic of the moment, he probably wouldn't have noticed anyway. The ears are surpassed only by the eyes for unreliability in times of duress.' Grey continued to scan the buildings visible on the hillside. 'But I agree that the killer likely escaped on foot to some nearby refuge. He can't go south into the Atlantic. He would have been seen if he fled west into the open space before reaching the Grand Trunk Station.'

'Plenty of moonlight that night. Just a few days past full.'

'So he came uphill, north or east. Somewhat sparse that way.' Grey motioned to the open grassy ground leading east up Munjoy Hill that dominated the eastern end of Portland. 'A man who spent so much time in planning surely contemplated a quick and easy departure. More cover straight ahead north. And plenty of tenements and boardinghouses within a quick dash uphill here.'

Lean sighed and rubbed his neck. 'There's a fair piece of ground that will have to be canvassed.'

'From Freeman Lane to Munjoy Street, one block deep from the waterfront, the city directory lists seventeen boarding rooms,' Grey said, 'though there's probably twice that number when you include those who let rooms on the side, whenever the space is available. If necessary, we can expand our search to include Mountfort to the Eastern Promenade.'

21

On June 21, a full week after the murder, Lean sat at the table in Dr Steig's study, his notebook open before him. 'There are thirty-one rooms to let in the four blocks immediately fronting the Portland Company. Nineteen were occupied by single male boarders at points during the week before the murder. We were able to see or get reasonable descriptions of all but three.'

Grey smiled. 'Excellent.'

'One of our patrolmen, McDonough, boards on Waterville

himself and knows most of the folks. No real trouble getting most of them to talk. Of those sixteen boarders, six were described as short. Four have dark hair. One was questioned already, and his alibi for June fourteenth was confirmed – out of town that night. The three others have left their rooms and are not available. Their names are: Harvey Farr, a mariner; James Alexander, whose trade was unknown; and John Willard, a traveling salesman.'

Lean flipped the page. 'Now, get this. Alexander wasn't there long but quickly earned a reputation for quarreling. On multiple occasions he denounced people in the street, making all sorts of accusations as to sinful conduct of his neighbors. It's got to be him. A religious zealot. He fits perfectly.'

Grey held up a cautioning finger. 'He warrants further interest, to be sure. But again, I must warn you. A preconceived theory is an even greater liability in those cases involving the most extraordinary circumstances.'

'How so?'

'It's an unfortunate facet of human nature that a man's mind will seize on any element of a story that hints at the unusual or strange while utterly neglecting those aspects most familiar to us in our everyday lives. Yet experience proves that it is most likely to be those commonplace, overlooked details that reveal the identity of the criminal. A quick survey of the lurid stories screaming from the front pages confirms that mankind has a natural inclination toward discovering sensational or fantastical features where they do not exist.'

Lean answered, 'And thank God for that. If there were no natural desire for the spectacular and the grand, then we'd still be in the Dark Ages. No art, or music, or poetry.'

'Well and good for the poet. But for the criminalist, everything bearing the least mark of exaggeration must be purged, and he must guard against it with the strictest discipline. That being said ...' Grey drew a thin book from an interior pocket of his frock coat.

'What's that?' Dr Steig asked.

'This, gentlemen, compliments of a professor friend at Harvard, is a rare little volume that proves, despite everything I've just said, there are occasions where a case does indeed seem to hinge on the most sensational and fantastic of circumstances.'

He handed the book to Lean, who glanced at the cover and read aloud, "*Strange Tales of Warwickshire* by F. Bertram Clapp, 1889."

'Be prepared to be pleasantly surprised that your own theory of a religious zealot was actually flawed by virtue of not being fanciful enough. Go on – there where I've marked it.'

Lean let the text fall open to a bookmarked page. His eyes settled on the heading of a new chapter: 'Meon Hill.'

'"Close by the Rollright Stones, overlooking the villages of Upper and Lower Quinton, lies Meon Hill. This is yet another ancient site reputed to have long associations with dark forces. Legend has it that in Anglo-Saxon times pagan rituals were performed atop Meon Hill, and even in recent years many townsfolk have heard whispers that the hill remains a meeting place for covens of witches. An eerie howling is said to be common about the hill on foggy nights, and more than one frightened soul has reported encounters with a black dog said to haunt the hill. As is often the case in villages throughout the country, superstitions abound of such spectral black hounds as harbingers of death.

'"About 1869, a farmer named Donald Whitten reported

seeing the dog on his way home past the hill. Although he was a hale and hearty fellow, two nights later he died in his sleep. In 1885, it is told that a young plough boy named Charlie Walton met a great black dog on Meon Hill three nights in a row. On the final night, the dog was followed after by the shape of a headless woman in a white dress. Within a week, the boy's sister took ill and died."'

'Grey, this makes for some wonderful ghost stories, but—'

'Please,' Grey said with mock plaintiveness. 'Indulge me just one paragraph further.'

Lean sighed and returned his attention to the page. '"By far the most chilling episode thereabouts happened several years earlier, in 1875, when the body of a woman named Ann Turner was found murdered in the village of Long Compton. John Haywood, who was described as being a rather feeble-minded young man, was soon after found guilty and hanged. Haywood confessed that he had pinned Ann Turner to the ground with a hay fork before using a billhook to slash her throat and carve the shape of a cross into her neck and body."'

'My God, this is uncanny.' Dr Steig's eyes had grown wide.

'Is this true?' Lean asked Grey, who responded by rolling his hand forward in a circle, motioning Lean to read on.

'"At his trial, Haywood repeatedly asserted his earnest defense that he had done the act to save not just himself but the whole village. He swore that Ann Turner had not only bewitched him but had also put a curse on the land of many of the local farmers, fouling several wells and springs to poison the cattle. This manner of death, the 'sticking' of the body with a hay fork, was an ancient and traditional way to kill a witch, according to folk-lore dating back hundreds of years. John Haywood confirmed this superstitious belief in his own testimony, stating that the carving of the cross and pinning her to the ground was the only way to stop a witch from once more rising from her grave."' Lean closed the book. 'Maggie Keene was killed over witchcraft?'

'Helen!' Dr Steig blurted out. 'That man at the library was looking for some old volume on witchcraft. That's our man.'

Grey shook his head. 'She reported the man as blond; our killer has black hair. But I agree there appears to be some connection between the two events. Unfortunately, unless Mrs Prescott can identify the man, there's little chance of progress along that avenue. I suggest we focus our attention on the role witchcraft plays in the death of Maggie Keene. Did our man truly believe her to be a witch?'

'Not necessarily,' Dr Steig said, trying to regain his composure. 'He could simply be delusional and applying the term "witch" loosely to mean a sinful woman.'

'So he is on a religious crusade of some sort,' Lean said.

Grey rolled his eyes. 'You're like a dog with a meat bone.'

'Perhaps, like this fellow in the book, he thought himself bewitched by her.' Dr Steig waved his pipe about like a magic wand. 'Of course, not in the sense of poisoned cattle and all that. But in his own unbalanced view of the world, he's tormented by her, having shameful desires, such as the suckling. Unable to control these feelings, he blames his own weakness on her conduct. She has caused his problems – bewitched him. He must rid himself of her.'

In the silence that followed, Lean contemplated the doctor's theory. It had the distinct advantage of being much more fleshed out than his own simple explanation of religious fervor. 'Well, Grey? You haven't said what you make of it.'

'We can safely assume that, in our man's mind, Maggie Keene deserved a witch's death. As to why ... mere speculation. We need more facts. There must be some link, something about the victim that marked her for death in this manner. We need to know more about the unfortunate Maggie Keene.'

22

Two mornings later, Lean passed the intersection of Gorham's Corner with Dr Steig beside him. This was the most densely populated, and the most Irish, section of town. A few blocks on and they turned down a thin alleyway littered with trash and puddles of what Lean optimistically thought of as muddied rainwater. Ahead of them some street kids quit whatever they were doing, took stock of the approaching men, and scattered. Lean and the doctor moved farther down the alley of grime-covered brick walls streaked chalky white by old water stains. Overhead, staggered rows of dingy laundry hung out to languish in the fusty air. There was the occasional flapping sound from linens so thin from long use that they barely offered any resistance to the puffs of wind.

They turned down a staircase and headed into the dark confines of the underground barroom. It took a moment for Lean's eyes and nose to adjust. There was little light, except for two candles on a couple of the slanted, poorly cobbled tables. The atmosphere inside was thick and stifling, as if the rank air from the entire space of the alleyway outside had somehow been condensed into the small barroom and held captive for weeks on end.

The bartender reached below, grabbing hold of something hidden from view. Lean slipped his left hand into his pants pocket, the motion causing the lapel of his suit coat to shift aside and reveal his badge. The man tensed behind the bar, returning the unseen weapon to its resting place.

It wasn't hard to spot Boxcar Annie. There were only two women in the room, one so old they might have raised the building around her. Boxcar Annie was sitting alone at a table. Lean had never arrested her before but thought he recognized her face. Although she'd earned her moniker for her habit of working, when need be, near or in empty rail cars, this was one of those arguably fortuitous occasions when the title fit the person's actions as perfectly as it fit her appearance. Her flat face was set into a square head that was itself hunkered down on her shoulders like a stone gargoyle squatting atop a condemned building.

There were a half dozen men scattered about, but it was early enough that they weren't yet bothering her, each man instead focusing his attention on his mug. They all looked up at the new-comers with varying degrees of concern. Most merely spared a glance before returning to the pressing business of dulling the world. One man took on a nervous air, drained his cup, and left without making eye contact. On the other end of the spectrum was a grizzled old soaker who was propped up at a table in the shady corner past Boxcar Annie. He barely moved his head from where it hovered just inches over his mug.

'Annie Gordon,' Lean said.

She had cheeks of a dull scarlet tint and a rum-blossom nose to match. When she turned her head with the least amount of effort needed to take them in, Lean noticed how the red of her face highlighted the sickly yellow of her eyes. The woman didn't respond. Lean could tell she was still guessing at what they wanted.

'Boxcar Annie?'

The use of her professional name caused her face to relax. 'Not often I get two such fine gents as yourselves come around. All the same, I can't accommodate you right now.'

'We need a few minutes of your time.'

'Only a few minutes? Well, at least you're honest, but I'm not working that way right now. Why don't you go down to Haskell's and ask for Big Kate. She's enough for the two of ya. Or is it just you alone, and yer da likes to watch?'

Her words were slurred; Lean thought at first that it was just the drink. Then he noticed that even when she wasn't talking, her jaw was slack, hanging open a touch to reveal a semitoothless set of gums. He remembered hearing that Boxcar Annie had been in and out of work at the Portland Star Match Company over the past fifteen years, often during the winters, when her usual work on the streets became even less accommodating. She had phossy jaw. He'd seen even worse cases of it among the Irishwomen who started young and then spent too many years bunching and bundling up the phosphorus-tipped matches, the dust from it eventually eating away at their teeth and jawbones.

'This is about Maggie Keene.' Lean showed his badge.

'I don't 'afta talk to you.' There seemed a touch of authority in her answer, a sureness that exceeded the regular obstinacy that veteran prostitutes often displayed when dealing with police.

'Says who?'

Boxcar Annie didn't answer, but for a second, Lean thought she might, that somebody had actually told her not to talk to the police.

127

She gave a defiant glance toward Dr Steig. 'He don't look like no cop.'

Lean thought about it and decided she might respond best to an honest approach. 'That's Dr Steig. He examined the body.'

Boxcar Annie pondered this for a moment, then took another swig. 'Before or after she was buried?'

'Before,' interjected Dr Steig with a curtness that betrayed sensitivity to allegations of that type of corpse procurement that had lent the medical profession something of a ghoulish reputation in recent decades.

'Wouldn't be the first time I heard of the other. 'Specially for one of us girls. Dug up and landing up on some doctor's platter even after she's had prayers over her grave. Like they ain't been poked and prodded right enough while they was living! Downright sinful.'

'He performed the postmortem on Maggie as part of the investigation into her murder.'

'You mean he's the one what cut her up more after she was dead already.'

Lean nodded.

'He's not much better'n that other gent that did her first.'

'I know this isn't pleasant – that Maggie was a good friend of yours.' Lean watched her lower her cup an inch, a touch less hostility in her eyes. 'But we still need to get a few answers to help with the investigation.'

She laughed in harsh snorts, then wiped her nose on her sleeve. 'Investigation? You mean where you pick some witless stiff and beat a confession out of him.'

Lean ignored the woman's bitterness. 'We need a few details about what Maggie was doing in the week or two before she was killed. Who she was seeing. If any fellows were coming around more often, looking for her in particular. If anyone was acting strange.'

'Ha! A man's looking for a bit of the old trip up the alley and acting strange, is he?' She waved about at the assortment of men in the room. 'Show me one of these dirty stiffs what ain't acting strange.'

'Fair enough. Anyone acting worse than usual. A man that stood out, did or said anything that worried her,' Lean said.

'Didn't mention any stiffs bothering her more than usual, OK? Now, I ain't got nothing more to say about Maggie. Except she didn't deserve what he did to her.'

'Of course not, and that's why we need your help, Annie. To see that this fellow swings for what he's done. To make sure he'll never do this to another girl who doesn't deserve it any more than Maggie did.'

Boxcar Annie drained the last of her drink just as Lean finished talking.

'There ain't no other girl deserved it less than Maggie – what that gent did to her. All the same, I know damn well he won't ever meet the noose for it. They never do. You gents will never let him.' Her cheeks turned a more violent shade of red, her voice rising to a hoarse shout.

Lean could tell they weren't going to get much from her in this state, and the other bar patrons were growing agitated as well. There was no use in pressing on. 'All right, Annie. We'll be going, so calm yourself. But we may need to speak to you again about all this.'

'Don't bother coming back. I got nothing more to say to the likes of you!'

As they left, Lean could feel Annie's red-hot stare burning into him. Back on the street, he paused for a moment to collect his thoughts. In his head he ran over his questions to Boxcar Annie once again, thinking hard about her responses. Something about what she'd said nagged at him, and for a moment he was reluctant to walk on.

'She knows something more.'

'Maybe we'd have better luck earlier in the day,' grumbled Dr Steig. 'Before she's had the chance to climb so far into her bottle.'

They walked down the alley. Lean didn't look back, so he didn't see the boy who slipped out the door to McGrath's place and dashed off in the opposite direction. Nor did Lean see the old drunkard emerge and follow after the boy at a pace quicker than a man of his age and condition should have been able to manage.

Two hours later Lean brushed aside the curtain and peered out into the dusky street from Dr Steig's front parlor at the Soldiers' Home. 'Where the blazes is Grey?'

'Patience,' said the doctor. 'I'm sure there's a reason for keeping us waiting.'

He handed Lean a healthy pour of whiskey. For half a second, Lean contemplated objecting, citing his duty to enforce, or at least pay a nominal amount of respect to, the Maine Liquor Law.

'I have a license, of course,' said the doctor. 'If it'll make you feel better, I can formally prescribe it for your nerves.'

Lean smiled and downed half his tumbler. Just then there came a soft rapping at the front door. He didn't bother waiting for the doctor's servant. Instead, he rushed into the hall and whipped the door open himself. He stepped back in surprise when he saw the old soaker from McGrath's place standing on the front step. His right hand instinctively curled into a fist at the sight of the surprise visitor.

The man flashed a smile at Lean, then said, in a voice much firmer than expected, 'Come now, Lean, threatening the downtrodden.'

Recognizing the voice, Lean stepped back and released his fist. The ragged man shuffled into the hall, closed the door, and stood up to his full height, slightly taller than Lean. Then he doffed his tattered gray cap, revealing black hair.

'Grey? What the devil?' His voice drifted off as he watched Perceval Grey tug off his white eyebrows and rub his face with a handkerchief, erasing two decades of apparent age.

'I assume that your disguise has accomplished something even more useful than causing our good deputy's mouth to drop.' Dr Steig had appeared in the hallway and beckoned both the younger men back into his private study.

'I have indeed turned up a rather puzzling connection, which certainly bears closer consideration. And I will explain myself in due course, but first let me hear your impressions from speaking with our dear Lady of the Rail Cars.'

'I believe she may have seen our man,' Lean said.

'What makes you suspect that?' Grey asked.

'The way she spoke about him. Never "that man" or "the killer" or even "that bastard." Nothing broad, like she was talking about just anyone. Always "he" or "him," someone in particular.'

'The papers have painted quite a graphic portrait of an insane, bloodthirsty Indian,' Dr Steig said. 'Perhaps she has some phantom image specifically in mind.'

Grey shrugged. 'Your point is quite perceptive, Lean, but there's something else about her description of the killer. Think back to the specific phrases she used. Several times she referred to the pair of you as "gents." Other men, her regular customers or those in Farrell's club, were always "stiffs." But not the killer; he too was always a gent. Even if she didn't mean it in a kind way. If she was only speaking of the killer as described in the papers, such a creature would surely be classified with the stiffs. She would never call him a gent.'

Lean shot a glance at Dr Steig, who nodded.

'Now that I hear you say it, I do believe that's true. I mean about her choice of words.' The doctor ruminated on the observation for a few moments, then gave a soft chuckle. 'Fascinating.'

'For now we'll take it as only a theory,' Grey said, 'that our man is not some street tough or outwardly deranged drifter, but rather a man of means. Someone that a woman of Boxcar Annie's ilk would consider respectable. This may well make my other discovery more meaningful.'

'Yes, getting back to all that,' said Lean with an exaggerated wave toward Grey's tattered costume. 'I suppose there's some reason we needed to be kept in the dark about your efforts.'

'I couldn't risk any unintentional show of recognition. I assumed, correctly, that Boxcar Annie's sudden relocation to McGrath's establishment, just after the murder of her dear friend, was more than coincidental. If there was something of value at stake with this woman, we wouldn't be the only ones interested in what she has to say. My efforts were rewarded; immediately after you left, the bartender sent a boy to carry the news of your visit to Maple Street.'

'McGrath's house,' Lean said.

Grey smiled. 'And ten minutes later that same boy reappeared and ran over to 53 Temple.'

'What's there?'

'The headquarters of Colonel Blanchard's Maine Temperance Union.'

Dr Steig stopped in the middle of lighting a cigarette. 'You don't honestly believe that any one of Colonel Blanchard's associates have something to do with Maggie Keene's murder?'

'"Believe" is a dangerous word. So no, I do not yet believe that Colonel Blanchard or any person in his employ is actively involved in the murder of Maggie Keene. But the facts do allow us to at least begin to craft a working theory.' Grey rose and started to pace as his explanation continued.

'My observations of Boxcar Annie reveal she is a rather typical example of her peers. She displays less-than-average intellect, perception, or ambition. Like the vast majority of mankind, these women tend to act primarily for one of two reasons: personal gain or self-preservation. In light of the fact that her good friend has just been murdered, one would assume that her sudden departure from Munjoy Hill and reappearance at Gorham's Corner was prompted solely by an interest in her own safety. But her revelation that she was not currently plying her trade, coupled with the fact that she obviously had coins enough to pay for several drinks, shows that she has seen a significant improvement in her financial situation.

'I suspect that the new asset she has to her name is information concerning the identity of Maggie Keene's murderer. She has found shelter with McGrath, who is offering her protection and money so long as her information remains valuable.'

Lean rapped his knuckles on Dr Steig's desk. 'And when

questions start getting asked, especially by the police, the price of him continuing to protect Boxcar Annie's silence goes up for whoever stands to lose if it became public knowledge,' Lean said.

Dr Steig pointed his pipe at Grey. 'Really, though, to think that someone in the hierarchy of the temperance union has any involvement in such a heinous murder ...'

Lean exhaled deeply, then pursed his lips while he let all this information seep into his mind. Finally he announced with a hint of reluctance, 'We're going to have to arrange a meeting with Colonel Blanchard.'

'Agreed.' Grey held up a finger in warning. 'But not until we strengthen our hand. It will take some careful doing, but I'll make inquiries into whether the colonel and McGrath have had any recent financial dealings. Also, we need to speak to that woman once more to find out exactly what she knows about the killer.'

'Perhaps not too soon,' suggested Dr Steig. 'Assuming she remembers us in the morning, I think it's safe to say she may need to cool her head before she sees us again.'

'Very well. We can let her be for a few days; we have another piece of pressing business to attend to in the meanwhile.' Grey drew a telegram from his pocket. 'I assume you've heard nothing from your inquiries to other police departments regarding our missing first murder.'

Lean shook his head. 'One stabbing in Bath. But it was between sailors.'

Grey set his telegram down. 'I've received an interesting response to our inquiry from an old colleague in Boston.'

Dr Steig pulled his desk chair closer, while Lean stepped forward to read over the doctor's shoulder.

Grey, glad to hear your break from this type of work is going so well. Asked around. Boston last week woman multiple stabs to chest and abdomen recovering in hospital. No arrest. Malden three weeks ago man with wooden leg shot. Prostitute arrested. Scituate month ago woman throat cut disemboweled. No arrest. Last month in Boston woman assaulted cuts to face neck. Gang of three awaiting trial. Lowell three months ago woman decapitated. Accident? Near rail lines.

Here if needed.
Regards,
Walt

'Man with a wooden leg?' Lean glanced up at Grey with a dubious grin.

'The inquiry was for wounds to the throat or abdomen and severed body parts. Apparently I should have been more specific as to the age of the wounds.'

Lean perused the options once more. 'Maybe this Scituate one.'

'I thought the same and sent another query.' Grey pulled a second telegram from his pocket and read aloud. '"Scituate – Hannah Easler young woman not prostitute – good family churchgoers. Found in woods. No weapon at scene. Great violence to the body but nothing missing. Police mum just rumors. Spurned man? No known suitors. No arrest or suspects. Rail not far – possible vagrant. Walt."'

Lean read the telegram a second time, again pausing over the words that sent the message veering off on a new course. 'Scituate's a small town. They'd know if she had a fellow at all. So what makes them think a spurned lover?'

'Too soon to say. But if her character and background don't

suggest some manner of sexual speculation . . .' Grey let the infer-
ence hang in the air.

'The nature of the killing must. Still, no pitchfork mentioned.
No missing body parts.'

'He could have taken the fork with him,' Grey said. 'We don't
know for certain that our man meant to leave it stuck in Maggie
Keene. He was startled away by the watchman.'

'If there was serious damage to the body, it's possible that slim,
piercing wounds from a pitchfork could have been missed on
examination,' noted Dr Steig.

'So, Lean?' Grey was peering at him like a hawk. 'The first
train for Boston leaves at half past five in the morning.'

Lean bobbed his head slightly from side to side as if he were
actually weighing scales in his mind. 'I can ask my wife's sister to
come help her out for a day.' He nodded, trying to rally himself
to the cause. 'Yeah, fair enough. Scituate it is.'

23

The next morning, Helen took a detour on her way to the historical society and made an unannounced visit to her uncle's
house. She sipped her tea and looked across the table in the
sunlit dining room of his home. Dr Steig was finishing off his
breakfast of eggs and sausage. He made some comment about
plans later that summer for them to take Delia farther up the
coast for a vacation, but he seemed distracted. Helen just smiled
and said the idea sounded nice. Her thoughts were elsewhere
as well.

On the ride to her uncle's that morning, she had once again studied the telegraph paper she'd taken while tailing Perceval Grey a week earlier. A pencil back-and-forth across the page revealed a partial impression of the note Grey had sent to a man named McCutcheon at the Boston office of the Pinkerton Detective Agency. No matter how intently she had stared at the page, she could make out only a few of the words: 'months . . . cases in Mass . . . death . . . mutilation . . . stab or pierce . . . neck. Urgent.' She didn't know what to make of the gruesome message, and her efforts to learn more about its author had been equally frustrating.

'Has Deputy Lean said anything further to you about his investigation?'

Dr Steig looked at her in surprise.

'The strange man at the library,' she explained.

'Oh.' Dr Steig's face relaxed. 'No, nothing further, I'm afraid.'

'Deputy Lean, he was in the paper last week for that murder at the Portland Company.'

'Yes. A horrible business.'

Helen noticed that her uncle's eating had ceased. She took another sip of tea and asked, as casually as she could, 'And who's Perceval Grey? Haven't I heard you mention him before? Some sort of detective, isn't he?'

Dr Steig looked at her for a long moment, and she knew he was trying to guess her intent.

'A former student of mine, yes. Why do you ask?'

'He came to the library last week. I think he's investigating our intruder with Deputy Lean. I passed the two of them talking on the street.'

Helen saw her uncle smile; he looked relieved. That meant he did know what Deputy Lean and Perceval Grey were investigating, and she had guessed wrong. It was something much more serious than the man at the library. Her thoughts returned to the words in Grey's telegram. They certainly could be related to the recent murder of Maggie Keene.

'Grey is a detective, actually, but I don't think he'd have any interest in your mysterious library man. Probably just a coincidence. They must have been discussing some other matter.'

'Something like that murder at the Portland Company,' Helen suggested.

Dr Steig wiped his lips and set his napkin on the table. 'Perhaps.' He stood and walked over to collect his jacket.

'I wonder what in the world that murder has to do with witchcraft.'

Her uncle turned toward her, his expression like stone. 'What are you getting at?'

'I want you to tell me what's going on. Why are the police consulting with Grey, and what does it have to do with that man who chased me? Why were he and this Grey fellow both looking for books on witchcraft? I think I have the right to know what this is all about.'

'It's not about anything. It has nothing to do with you. There's no need for you to worry about any other incidents at the library.'

'I don't need to worry? That man could have killed me.'

Dr Steig came over and put a hand on her shoulder. 'Deputy Lean assures me you are not in any danger. So I must insist that you put all this aside. No good can come of your being foolish and sticking your nose in where it ought not to be. Leave the detectives to their work. You have a daughter to worry about. You can't be rushing off, leaping into things. That's how you get into trouble.'

She stared at him for a moment, her mouth slightly open as she struggled for a response.

'That's what you really think, isn't it? That I'm some foolish woman who can't take care of herself. That Delia is just some trouble that I got into.'

Dr Steig straightened up, looking embarrassed. 'That is not at all what I said.' He cleared his throat. 'I adore the child, and you know it. Not at all what I said.'

He walked toward the hall and picked up his hat from a side table. 'I have to go; I'm already late for an appointment.'

After her uncle left, Helen finished her tea in silence, then sat thinking for several more minutes before making her way toward the front hall. One of the servants was there, holding her coat ready. She glanced at the closed door to her uncle's study, then back at the servant. Helen smiled and mentioned how her uncle had meant to lend her a book. She was in rather a hurry, so surely he wouldn't mind if she found it in his study, since he was out and she wouldn't be disturbing his work.

Once alone in the study, Helen made straight for her uncle's work desk. She knew he always kept his pressing files in the top right-hand drawer, and within a minute she held a black leather writing journal that contained anatomical sketches of Maggie Keene in its front pages. The details of that poor woman's demise turned her stomach, so Helen flipped through the pages until the notes moved to other matters. She stopped at the sight of the names of Perceval Grey and Deputy Archie Lean.

The notes were jumbled, but as she scanned over them, the picture began to emerge as to the theories of the manner, location, and motive related to Maggie Keene's murder. Helen's attention lingered on the final note addressing someone named Boxcar

Annie. 'Has vital knowledge of a recent male client – a person of great interest. Gorham's Corner, basement at the rear of the Portland Fenian League. Reticent – suspicious of our motive. Belligerent when drinking. Need second interview: new approach required.'

Helen heard movement in the hallway. She tore a blank page from the end of the journal and scribbled a note, which she slipped into a fold in her dress. She returned the journal and closed the drawer. After pulling a random text from a bookshelf, she composed herself and left the room, striding to the front door. She made her way to Congress Street and waited for the next passing horse car. She got on and found a seat. Her heart raced as she retrieved the note. Her hand shook, and only partly due to the trolley's bumpy ride. She stared at the page as she passed beneath the long shadow of the Portland Observatory and committed to memory the address where she could find Boxcar Annie.

24

Lean stared out the small rail car window, watching the trees slip by. He squinted and let the scene melt into a pale green blur. Soon the woods gave way to scattered farmhouses and fields aglow in the morning light. He glanced at Grey, who sat across from him taking notes from some dusty old tome.

Lean tipped his hat down over his eyes and tried to clear his mind so he could catch up on some sleep. It was useless, the same as the night before, when everything he knew about this case kept racing through his mind. He tried to organize the facts to see if there was any sense to all this. The whole thing seemed a maze with no beginning and no end, and him standing there playing Theseus but with no ball of thread. He didn't know what to expect from this trip to Scituate; the report had been so vague. He decided that the odds of finding any proof, over a month after the fact, to conclusively tie their killer to Scituate weren't good. The resulting uncertainty would be the worst possible scenario. They'd be forced to wait, dreading the news of another murder, maybe in another town where no one had the slightest inkling that a devil walked among them.

He tried to force his mind from the subject and focused instead on his pregnant wife, but even that image turned sour for him. He saw her standing in their cramped kitchen that morning, a doubtful look in her eye as Lean assured her that his travel expenses were being paid by the city. Furthermore, if he solved this case, it would go a long way toward ensuring his continued higher salary as a deputy marshal. Portland's mayor made those appointments, and there was no guarantee that Ingraham, the only Democrat to hold the post since the Civil War, would win reelection next year. Even if he did, Lean couldn't be sure his position was safe. After all, it was something of a mystery as to why Mayor Ingraham had appointed him as one of Portland's three deputies in the first place.

Emma was growing more concerned about their situation with every passing week. Lean couldn't believe that July was just two days away. She hadn't yet reminded him of his promise that they would buy a house soon, a few months after the baby was born at the latest. Then they could get out of their small apartment and have a separate nursery and more room for the kids. Despite their best efforts, they had not saved as much as they'd hoped. He tipped his hat back and stared out the window as they passed through some small Massachusetts town he couldn't name. His mind felt drained by his various worries, and soon his eyes began to flutter.

From the connection in Boston, Lean and Grey had taken the Greenbush Line south along its winding coastal route, through Braintree, Weymouth, and Hingham. They exited at Egypt Station in Scituate to be met by Grey's old colleague Walt McCutcheon. He was of average height, with a new bowler set atop his dark, wavy hair. A full handlebar mustache sat above a wide grin as he greeted them. He had a hearty handshake but seemed unwilling to meet Lean eye to eye. For a brief moment, Lean was suspicious, until he realized that McCutcheon was simply stealing glances behind him at a fine-drawn blonde who was waiting with her baggage.

Lean guessed that McCutcheon had been a fit enough fellow in his younger days, but he was now red in the face and a bit thick through the midsection. He wore a stylish cutaway suit of blue wide-wale diagonals with ivory buttons, a crimson silk vest, and a dark checked bow tie. There was a gleam in his eye that Lean read as the sign of a man who thoroughly savored life and did not suffer much guilt about enjoying whatever pleasures the world had to offer.

McCutcheon gave Grey a friendly slap on the shoulder. He welcomed them to Scituate, a town that, after having spent twenty-four hours there, he could declare to be about as entertaining and useful as the small end of nothing. 'Though not without the occasional bit of savory to recommend it, eh?'

Following McCutcheon's wandering gaze, Lean's eyes landed

on the attractive young woman who had exited the train and was greeting family members nearby.

'Wouldn't mind turning a short stroll into a long walk with her,' McCutcheon said.

He then suggested they go to the hotel to refresh themselves, which Lean thought was a brilliant idea. Grey was adamant, however, that they proceed to the scene of Hannah Easler's murder while there was still some good daylight. McCutcheon had their bags sent ahead to the Gannett House, where they had rooms reserved, then led them to the carriage he'd rented. The young driver looked skeptically at the newcomers.

'On, boy. I'm not paying you so well to gawk at my friends,' McCutcheon boomed.

As they moved through town, McCutcheon apprised them of the situation as he had found it in the past day. He'd asked around at the hotel but was met only with embarrassed looks or mumbled claims of ignorance. Eventually he'd located an older boy hanging around in the street who was happy to earn fifty cents by showing McCutcheon exactly where the girl's body was discovered. The boy hadn't actually seen the corpse, but he'd been to the site the day after the discovery, when blood was still visible upon the path through the woods where Hannah Easler had met her fate. McCutcheon had then tried gathering information from some fellows at a dockside pub, but with no more luck than at the hotel.

'No one's talking. They won't even listen to my questions. The whole lot of 'em won't even meet your eye once you mention the girl's name.'

McCutcheon's questions were not entirely in vain. They gained him an escorted trip down to the sheriff's station, where he had to explain himself as a stranger asking untoward questions about a murdered woman. The sheriff made it clear he was handling the matter and didn't need any city detective sticking his nose in. As far as he was concerned, the killer was from outside the town, likely passing through on the train to or from Boston.

'And, as the sheriff was all too happy to point out,' McCutcheon said with a grin, 'we all know the type of vermin that can arrive on the train out of Boston. After he got done puffing himself up in front of his pals, this other old-timer hands me back my piece and shows me the door. He says not to waste my breath around here. And I tell him, "I get it – no one in this town wants to answer my questions." He just looks me clear in the eye and shakes his head, all sorry like. And he says, "No one in this town even wants to *ask* your questions, let alone answer them."

'So I wait around outside until dinner and tail him to a place a few blocks away. I let him have a couple of stiff ones before I amble over. At first he wants none of it, but soon enough he's talking.'

The carriage arrived at the start of a wooded trail, where the three men disembarked. McCutcheon ordered the driver to wait, then led the way along the narrow footpath.

'The girl, Easler, worked as a seamstress at a dressmaker's closer to the harbor. Lived on the southwestern side of town, Greenbush area. So her way home shouldn't have taken her anywhere near that path through the woods. No one knows what she was doing up north of the town center. Her parents went out looking just before nightfall. Pretty soon half the town was at it. Found her just after dawn.

'It wasn't pretty. Her throat was slit. Some other cuts on her, but mostly the guy had split her open. Sliced her from Cupid's alley right up to her ribs.' McCutcheon thrust out a thumb and mocked gutting himself. 'The parents went out of their heads, as much over people in town seeing her that way as about the fact that someone had done this to her in the first place. They raised such a stink over the whole bit – her being looked on like that – that the doctor never did get a chance for a postmortem. They wouldn't allow it. No photographs, either.'

'We'll need to talk to them,' Grey said. 'Convince them to change their minds.'

'You'll get as skinny as an almshouse dog waiting for that.' McCutcheon stopped on the path and took a deep pull on his cigarette while they waited for an explanation.

'They were so mortified by the whole affair, they couldn't bear to show their faces. Packed up and moved. Took the girl's remains with them. Wouldn't let her be put in the ground here, where people would see her stone and talk about the way she'd been found.' He had another drag. 'That's just about the end of it all. And now here we are.'

They entered a small clearing. This was the murder site, little more than a widening in the dirt path. The ground was littered with leaves. Lean's heart had been slowly sinking throughout the story, though he desperately clung to the hope that McCutcheon was merely spinning out his tale and waiting to reveal some lead at the end. It never came. What Lean had feared now seemed painfully obvious: They were not going to find any conclusive proof here one way or another as to whether Hannah Easler had been killed by their man.

'They didn't bring anyone in? They must have questioned someone. How the hell else does the sheriff spend his days around here?' Lean asked.

'They made the rounds down by the harbor. No one had been seen acting suspicious or with a drop of blood on him. They reckoned the fellow must have gotten plenty bloody in all this. Besides, we're not far from the tracks. They think maybe some tramp skipped off the train, then hopped back on later that night and was gone.'

Grey gave a crooked smile. 'Local people simply don't do this kind of thing.'

Lean glanced up through the treetops to the dimming sky. 'This is giving me a headache.'

'Well, that's one matter I can solve,' McCutcheon said, 'as soon as we get back to the hotel bar.'

'One moment.' Grey was studying the ground. 'There's something missing here.'

Our entire case, thought Lean. He said nothing, not wanting to advertise his sense of failure at their trip. Perhaps a nice drop of whiskey or two would be just the thing to grease the wheels and set his mind back on track. It was a good enough excuse for a strong drink, anyway.

25

'It'll be the same mess of trees, leaves, and dirt, Grey.' McCutcheon's jaws eagerly worked over his after-breakfast cigar. 'Just what do you expect to see that you couldn't last night?'

'You never know what may appear when you observe matters in a new light,' Grey replied.

They were standing in the narrow street behind the Gannett

House. Lean glanced up at the pale blue sky. It was going to be a fine morning, but he couldn't wholeheartedly agree with Perceval Grey. His mood was no better than when he'd gone to sleep the night before. With no body to examine and no one willing to speak, their trip had proved to be in vain.

There was nothing else to do but wait and see if this devil was going to strike again in Portland, here in Scituate, or somewhere entirely new.

His eyes settled on a plain-faced woman in her early twenties who had just stepped out of a house nearby. She was a bit stocky, with a bulging belly. Her dress was nothing fancy, a simple cambric jersey wrapper; she was probably a farmer's wife, or maybe a grocery clerk. She spoke a few quiet words to a matronly-looking woman who patted the younger lady on the arm, then closed the door.

Lean felt an elbow nudge him in the ribs, followed by McCutcheon's voice, in an enthusiastic whisper. 'She could keep a calf well enough, eh?'

The younger woman glanced over and saw the two men staring in her direction. She looked surprised to be the subject of their attention, and her pale face blushed before she quickly turned away.

'Coming?' Grey had already set off along the street in the direction of the path through the woods where young Hannah Easler had met her horrid fate.

Lean followed after the others, kicking at the ground as he went. This was the same route taken by the Easler girl. McCutcheon had mentioned the night before that the girl's parents lived a mile south from the far end of the path. That's where she was going. But where was she coming from? Her parents hadn't known where to look for her that night. That meant she'd likely been somewhere she wasn't supposed to be.

Lean stopped in his tracks. 'Hold up a moment!' The others stared at him. He looked back the way they'd come. 'There's something I want to check into. You can manage without me, I assume.'

'By all means. We'll meet you back at the hotel,' Grey said.

'Just a . . . strange thought that's occurred to me.'

Grey gave him an understanding nod, and they parted company. Lean strode back toward the hotel. The image of the thin, pale-faced woman he'd seen in the street minutes earlier now flooded back into his mind. McCutcheon's observation about keeping a calf aside, it had not been the woman's bosom that had caught Lean's eye. The young woman at the house was pregnant. His mind flashed back to their supper at the hotel last evening. From his seat by the window, he'd seen another woman pass by who was with child. She too had exited a nearby building. Was it the same house? He ran the images through his mind. It very well could have been. Those two young women he'd noticed had been drawn there for a reason. Any number of other young women could come from all around town if they had that same reason. A reason that would be a joy for most but, for someone like unmarried Hannah Easler, one that would have been kept secret.

He rapped on the door, a bit more loudly than he had intended. The stout, matronly woman answered. The friendly glint in her eye vanished the moment she saw him.

'Yes? Can I help you?'

'Sorry to bother you, but please, can you tell me . . . are you a midwife, ma'am?'

'I am.' She was regarding him with even closer scrutiny.

'I'm Deputy Lean, and I have to ask you a few questions.'

'I don't know what you've heard, but I do not do that kind of work. Good day to you!' She slammed the door closed.

Lean rapped on the door again; he could hear her thudding away inside the house. 'I've come about Hannah Easler.' He heard her feet stop. 'I need your help. She needs your help.'

The door creaked open a few inches. 'What's this about?'

'Hannah had been to see you, hadn't she?'

'I don't know you from Adam. She told me the father was a sailor.'

'I'm not him, I assure you. In fact, I'd never even met Miss Easler. But I've come a long way to find out what happened to her.'

'I told the sheriff what I know. Why don't you ask him?'

'Because he's not talking. And I need to know the truth of what happened to her.'

The woman's gaze dropped to the floor. Her hands were clenched. 'Some things should never happen to no one, and when they do, they should never be spoken of.'

'What happened to her – I think it's happened again, to another girl. And if I can't find the man who did this . . .'

'Oh, dear God.' The woman's eyes welled up as she took several slow steps back into the parlor.

The midwife began to recite everything she knew about the small, lonely life of Hannah Easler. She rambled on until her telling drew near to the girl's last day.

'Did she mention anything unusual that evening?' Lean asked. 'Talk about anyone she had met or seen? Anything that had made her nervous or scared?'

149

'No, nothing. In fact, she was a bit happier than usual. She lived in fear of her parents finding out about it all. But she said that her fellow was coming back in a few weeks. They planned to run off and get married. He had prospects in New York, an uncle in Albany who had work for him. She just had to make it a little while longer without her folks knowing.'

'Did her parents say anything to you after? About her being in a family way and all?'

'No. Of course, I'm not sure they ever did find out.'

Lean gave her a puzzled look.

'Well,' she explained, 'the sheriff swore he never told them or anyone else that she'd been here to see me that night.'

Lean nodded. 'But they took her body. You said she was four months along. And from what I understand, she was cut open.' He motioned with his hand from his pelvis up to his rib cage. 'Wouldn't they have seen the ... evidence of how she was?'

'You said this same thing happened to another girl.' Now it was her turn to give Lean a puzzled look. 'The same ... so I thought you meant. That is, I thought you knew.'

'Knew what? What are you saying?'

'He took it.' Tears leaked out of her eyes, and then she began to sob. 'He cut the baby out of her, and he took it.'

Minutes later Lean stepped outside the midwife's house and began pacing as he came to grips with the revelations about Hannah Easler's death. He fought the urge to run madly out to the woods to tell Grey the news. Instead he went back to the hotel, where the landlord only denied his prenoon request for a bottle of whiskey once. Reclaiming the window seat from last night's dinner, he glanced out at the midwife's door before staring in the other direction, toward the path where young Hannah Easler had met her vicious end. When Grey and McCutcheon returned, the midwife's news spilled out of him.

Grey stared through the window toward the midwife's house. 'And you discovered this connection upon seeing the pregnant woman this morning?'

'Putting that together with the other woman who came by the window last night.'

'Very perceptive. I didn't notice a thing.'

'Why *would* you notice 'em?' asked McCutcheon. 'They're all got up already. No use looking for a ticket to a sold-out show.'

'Suppose I only noticed on account of my own wife, being "all got up" herself. When you have it on your mind, you'd be a bit surprised how often you notice pregnant women.'

Grey peered out the window again, studying the midwife's house. 'It seems we occupy a uniquely good vantage point. That is, for a visitor in town who had it in mind to watch for a pregnant woman.'

Later, after hasty travel arrangements and a quick farewell to McCutcheon at the rail station, Lean and Grey retreated to a private compartment, where Lean again repeated the midwife's entire story.

'Something else?' Grey asked.

'Hmm? No. It's only ... I've been so excited about the discovery of this new evidence that I almost forgot just what it is we've discovered. That poor girl. So afraid. So hopeful of a very different life.' Lean closed his eyes. '"For I have heard a voice as of a woman in travail, and the anguish as of her that bringeth forth her first child, the voice of the daughter of Zion, that bewaileth herself, that spreadeth her hands, saying, Woe is me now! For my soul is wearied because of murderers.'"

'Longfellow?' asked Grey.

'Jeremiah.' Unsure of whether he was being mocked, Lean threw a questioning glance at his traveling companion.

Grey shrugged. 'American?'

'Israelite.'

'Hmm. Not familiar with his work.'

'That doesn't surprise me, actually,' Lean said.

A quick smirk slid across Grey's face.

'So there it is.' Lean dug out a folded sheet of paper from his pocket and read over the short list that Grey had obtained from the hotel landlord. It held the names of men who had stayed alone at the Gannett House in the nights just prior to the murder. 'J. Trefethan, Arthur Cummings, Hollis Lancy, John Proctor, or Peter Flaherty. One of these is our man.'

'One of those is, at least, the name our man used while in Scituate,' Grey said.

'We're sure of that, right? That this is the work of the same man.'

Grey slipped a hand into his coat pocket and retrieved a small lump of dull, waxy material. 'In my excitement over your discovery, I nearly forgot my own. It was there at the murder site.' He handed it to Lean, who pondered the object for a moment, then lifted it up for a closer look. The faint scent of bayberry reached his nostrils.

'A single candle. The first. It matches the two he left at the Portland Company.'

26

'Who are you with again?' Boxcar Annie asked.

'The Women's Civil League,' Helen said.

'Ain't heard of them. That like some temperance lot?'

From the way the woman was slurring her words, Helen guessed nothing would draw Annie's ire quicker than any mention of a temperance union.

'Heavens no. Quite the contrary. We're not interested in telling women what they can't do. Rather, we want to show what women *can* do, if given the chance. Equal treatment and protection for women under the law.'

Boxcar Annie's face still showed a fair share of skepticism. Helen turned away for a moment, taking in the scenery. It was insanity for her to be here among the dark walls, crooked tables, and stools where men slouched like sacks of potatoes dropped on the sidewalk by a passing delivery cart. Nervous energy began to well up in Helen, threatening to overwhelm her senses. She took a breath and continued.

'After all, you shouldn't have to be a wealthy man, or married to one, to be treated fairly. It's practically the twentieth century, time society stopped treating women like we lived in the Dark Ages.'

'And what's this got to do with Maggie?'

'Everything,' Helen said. 'You know as well as any that she wasn't given much chance in this life. Never had anything handed to her. Not like some people.'

'Aye, that's true enough. No more than most of us.'

'Exactly. I'm not saying that the world owes us much of

anything. But we do have the right to live our lives as best we can. It's not like she was hurting anybody.'

'That's true too. She was a kind girl,' said Boxcar Annie.

'Certainly deserved better than she got.'

'A lot better. He should swing for it.' Boxcar Annie took a full swig of beer and slammed her mug down.

Helen stared into the drunken face opposite her. 'But will the man who did that to her pay for his crimes?'

Boxcar Annie threw glances to each side. 'What are you on about?'

'Why haven't the police found her killer yet? If a rich girl had been killed, I bet they'd have found him already.' Helen saw she had Annie's attention and pressed on. 'We've been making inquiries. More than the police have bothered to do. And we have reason to believe that Maggie's killer wasn't some drunk or some savage Indian. He may have been a respectable gent. Someone she'd met recently. Maybe a man with dark hair. Rather short.'

'The devil's breath.' Boxcar Annie crossed herself. 'How do you know all that?'

'We've heard some talk. But it's not enough. We can't afford to be wrong if we're going to bring pressure to bear on the police.'

'I'm not s'posed to tell anyone anything 'bout this.'

'You wouldn't be telling me. We've already heard. You'd just let me know that we're right in pushing ahead, demanding justice for Maggie Keene. We owe her that much.'

'You're going to the police, though.'

'Not with names. Just with as much of the truth as we can get.'

Annie finished her drink. Helen slid her own, still untouched, across the table.

'All right, then, for Maggie's sake. I'll tell you what I know, the truth about it. That's what she said too, you know – the truth. *This* gent was going to show her the truth of all things. That's a new one.'

'You'd seen her recently?'

'The day before. She looked worn to a shadow. Been fussing over stomach pains for about a week. Having trouble keeping food down.'

'This new man. What was he like?' Helen asked.

'Paid well enough. A right big talker – when he *could* talk, that is. Something wrong with him, had trouble getting his words out. Anyway, I think she might have believed him some. She took part of that money he'd paid her and spent it trying to look a little better for him. Bought a new hat the day before she died. Had enough money left over to buy a pair of shoes, good enough to get her through a night on the old cobblestones. The fellow was going to bring her some medicine for the pains. He had a room over on St Lawrence. She'd spent a few nights there with him before she died.'

'She mention his name?' Helen asked.

'Just John. He wouldn't say his last name no matter how much she asked. She was such a believing fool sometimes. Said he was here for only a few weeks on business.' Boxcar Annie treated her hoarse voice with another gulp of beer.

'I told her how he sounded all froth and frizz. Mind, I weren't mean about it, but she didn't always have the most sense in her head. She was an all-right-looking girl, but even a few years at this work is enough to take the shine off ya. If he was being straight with her, I mean, why would such a man, as wealthy as he claimed to be, take a fancy to *her*? He hadn't even yet bothered to have his money's worth.'

'But he'd been seeing her several nights that week?' Helen said.

'Do you believe that? Had her strip bare on the first two nights and groped at her all over.' Annie gestured to the side of her rib cage. 'She had a little bump there, always shy of it. Anyway, he flat-out bit her there. Let loose a shriek, didn't she? That made him mad, though, all worried that someone around had heard. He never regained his enthusiasm that night. Sails at half mast and the winds all still. The second night more of the same, though she were ready for it. Bit her own knuckle to keep off from yelping.'

'He sounds like a peculiar one. And that was all?'

Annie nodded and took a swig. 'Always kept his own shirt and trousers on. She offered herself up a number of times, reminding him he'd paid good money for her company. But nothing doing. Course, that happens, though usually with them that's had too much, or older gents.' She grinned at some private memory. 'This one, though, was only interested in talking. Going on about all the beautiful things he could show her. Every night he's whispering a string of grand promises in her ear.' Boxcar Annie's voice was trembling, and her eyes threatened to overflow. 'Such a fool she could be.'

Helen dug in her handbag and found a handkerchief.

Helen exited McGrath's place, and even though the few steps up brought her back into the dingy, litter-strewn alley, she filled her lungs as if she had emerged onto a pristine mountaintop. It was later than she had planned, and she needed to hurry home to pick up Delia from her neighbor. But she paused to take more deep breaths, her eyes closed, trying to acclimate herself back to the outside world, so very far from the miserable existence on the far side of the barroom door.

'That's her!'

Fifty yards away, at the mouth of the alley, Helen saw a grubby-looking boy and two men in dark coats and hats. They started to move toward her.

Helen thought for a second about retreating into McGrath's but immediately realized she'd be trapped down there with little hope for assistance from that lot. She looked in the other direction. It was almost a hundred yards to the next street. She could hear the men behind her, running now. Immediately to her right was another alley. It was dark, but she could see several doorways close by. Maybe one would be open.

A few quick steps brought her to the first recessed doorway. It wasn't until she turned into it that she saw the huge, dark figure standing there. Helen let out a small shriek. The man grabbed her arm and yanked her into the shadows. Before she could scream again, he clamped a massive, callused hand over her mouth.

She thought about biting, but then she heard his low voice.

'Keep quiet and don't let them see you. Understand?' His tone was urgent, bordering on furious, but Helen sensed that the threat in his voice was not directed at her. When she finally took in the giant man's features, she recognized something. So she simply nodded her head silently, her lips pursed to keep herself from screaming.

The man reached down and grabbed a long ax handle with the head missing and moved out of the doorway. Helen heard the running footsteps of her pursuers enter the alley. She crouched back, not daring to look. There were curses, then scuffling feet and a horrible sound that she knew was the wooden shaft meeting flesh and bone, followed by a terrible shriek. Helen leaned forward and peeked out of the doorway. The giant man was upon her again. He took her by the wrist and yanked her after him down the alley.

'Hurry along now, miss,' he said, panting heavily. He wiped his mouth with his free hand. Helen saw blood there.

Glancing back over her shoulder, she could make out the two men lying in jumbled heaps. Helen hurried to keep pace with the man, her apparent rescuer. She wasn't entirely sure what to make of him. As she stared sideways at the man's sweating face and his bushy reddish mustache, Helen realized where she'd seen him before. He was one of her uncle's former patients.

27

The day after their return from Scituate, Lean and Grey shared a carriage, answering Dr Steig's frantic summons to the Soldiers' Home. Dr Steig's housekeeper led them to the study door. They could hear raised voices inside the room.

'You're just being stubborn, Helen.'

'And you're overreacting.'

The housekeeper knocked, which produced silence, and then she opened the door. Lean saw that Dr Steig was red in the face. He recognized Helen Prescott as the doctor's niece who had reported the late-night intruder at the public library.

'Gentlemen, please come in. I believe introductions may be in order.' The doctor tugged on the bottom of his waistcoat, tidying his appearance. 'And then perhaps an explanation on my part. Deputy Lean, you remember my niece.'

'Of course. I trust there has been no further trouble.'

'No. Thank heavens, though we have been more careful in our duties at closing time.'

'I'm very glad to hear that,' Lean said.

Dr Steig motioned toward Grey. 'And this—'

'Is Mr Perceval Grey. I'm Helen Prescott.'

'So nice to have a name to put with the face,' Grey said.

Helen gave him a puzzled look.

'From that morning when you followed me into the telegraph office and across half the city. I was initially flattered. Then suspicious. And now simply curious.'

'You saw me then?'

'Yes, though I must compliment you. It seems you must have followed me all the way from the library. I didn't spot you until after I'd reached the telegraph office.'

'I'm sorry. It was after the incident at the library. I was still very much distressed, and you showed such keen interest in the lecture series we have going. Asking about witchcraft and all, it just seemed too much a coincidence, being the same material that man had been after. So I followed you to see what I could learn.'

'And what did you learn?'

Helen paused and bit softly into her lower lip. Lean could tell she was considering how to answer honestly.

'You placed a call to Harvard. Then you sent a gruesome-sounding telegraph to the Pinkertons in Boston before meeting Deputy Lean at the observatory. Which showed that you weren't connected to the man who'd threatened me, though you were likely investigating him.'

Grey smiled at her. 'Well done, Mrs Prescott. Though I am unhappy with myself for leaving so clear a trail of my own activities. I'd say your investigative talents are being wasted in your present profession.'

Helen gave Dr Steig a triumphant smile.

'Unfortunately, Helen's investigative exploits don't end there,' said the doctor. 'After you left for Scituate, I was informed by the staff that Helen had borrowed the book I'd promised her. Only I didn't recall any such promise. Upon a close inspection of my shelves, the only volume missing was Kirkbride's work, *Arrangements of Hospitals for the Insane.* You can imagine how puzzled I was, being unaware that my niece was currently engaged in the construction of an outdated insane asylum.'

'There's no need for sarcasm, Uncle.'

'Knowing Helen's overly curious nature, I concluded it was not that book but access to my study that she was after. The only thing I was hiding in this room was my notes on the investigation. I assumed the worst, and it's damn lucky for her that I did. Fearing she might do something foolish, I asked Tom Doran to keep an eye on her. And sure enough, she's down to McGrath's place the very next day. If Doran hadn't been there … well, I daresay I'd be … ' Dr Steig's voice had risen, and his attention focused on Helen as he finished: 'I'd be making arrangements for the grieving, orphaned Delia to come and live here after her mother's funeral!'

'I've already apologized, Uncle. And promised not to do anything so careless again. I was wrong to go there … unaccompanied.'

Dr Steig tried to answer but couldn't manage to get out a response to such an infuriating understatement.

'But you have to admit, my visit wasn't totally in vain.' Helen then recounted her discussion with Boxcar Annie: The new man in Maggie Keene's life was named John; he was short and dark; he made references to wealth, power, and grand designs; he was secretive and showed hints of anger; and he knew something of medicine and supplied her with some.

Lean felt his excitement grow as Helen provided detail after detail that matched their suspicions about the killer, and a new thought struck him. 'Maggie Keene was having stomach problems. That could be a connection to Hannah Easler. Doctor, during your postmortem, could you tell if—'

'No. Maggie Keene was not pregnant.'

'But her pains did come on about the same time as this John appeared?' Grey asked.

Helen thought for a moment. 'Yes, both occurred in the week or so before her death.'

'This shows an even deeper level of preparation and cunning than we'd previously thought. He dosed her with something, and the resulting stomach pains provided an easy excuse to have her well drugged on the night of the murder. I daresay my estimation of this man's fiendishness continues to grow,' Grey declared.

Lean could see that Helen had something else to say, though she didn't look overly excited about it. 'Is there something more?'

After some hesitation, and several sideways efforts at easing into the matter, Helen just plunged in and described what Boxcar Annie had told her about Maggie Keene's physical relations with the man. She was red-faced by the time she ended and could not look Dr Steig in the eye as she added, 'Sorry, Uncle Virgil.'

'I'm a doctor, dear. You haven't hurt my ears any. I only regret that you were the one who had to hear all that business. It does confirm our impressions from the postmortem. He was fascinated with this excrescence of hers in life as well as at her death.'

'Excrescence?' repeated Lean.

'Her witch's tit,' Grey said, 'as you so graciously put it.'

'I've done quite a bit of reading on the Salem trials for our lecture series,' Helen said, 'and they actually would conduct searches of the accused witches' bodies. Looking for these. Could be anything really. Warts, moles, any sort of additional bit of flesh or growth that was deemed unnatural. Thought to be the devil's mark. Used as actual nipples by these witches to suckle their demonic familiars.'

'What do you mean by "familiars"?' Lean asked.

'Demonic spirits that drew nourishment from the witch. The familiar was believed to be a pet in addition to serving as some kind of bond between the witch and the devil. Could take any form; yellow birds were a common one. Cats, dogs, and toads as well.'

'It makes no sense,' Lean said. 'Is that why our man singled her out, because he thought that bump made her a witch? Then why on earth would he suckle at this thing himself?'

'It's yet another riddle. Our man is becoming not only more dangerous but an ever more challenging mystery to unravel.' Grey turned to stare out the window. 'Where are you leading us, John?'

'John,' Lean repeated, then drew a paper from his pocket and set it on the table. 'If he stuck with that name when he was in Scituate, that would make him the John Proctor from our list of Gannett House guests.'

Dr Steig went to his desk and rummaged through his notes.

'No John Proctor among the recent boarders on the east slope of Munjoy Hill.'

'Boxcar Annie mentioned that John's room was on St Lawrence Street,' Helen said.

The doctor flipped through his notes again. 'Well, look here, one of the three names on our list of short, dark-haired boarders who've gone missing: John Willard at the house of Mrs Kittredge on St Lawrence.' Dr Steig set his notebook down beside Lean's page.

Helen came close and stared at the names. 'What a strange coincidence.'

'What do you mean?' Lean asked.

'The names he chose,' Helen replied. 'John Proctor and John Willard were two of the five men hanged as Salem witches.'

28

'It's highly unusual, Mr Grey.' The owner of Harding's Oyster House and Lunch Room had come straight from the steam-filled kitchen and was still dabbing at his sweaty forehead. 'I do have my other customers to consider.' He waved his arms, indicating the wide expanse of the bustling men's dining room behind him. The man's gestures were so emphatic that Lean wouldn't have been surprised to see two hansom cabs pull up in front of the restaurant's tall street-side windows.

'Of course, Henry,' said Grey. 'I wouldn't have asked, except the young lady and her uncle, Dr Steig, were assisting me on a delicate matter. Now I've kept them from their supper.'

Henry smiled as if to say, *So unfortunate, but there's really nothing I can do.* His hand was lifted at his side, the fingers pointing up the stairway, mimicking the carved wooden sign outside with its over-size gloved hand gesturing up to the second-floor dining room for ladies.

'I feel obliged to remedy the situation but can't bring myself to take them to one of the lesser oyster rooms.' Grey rubbed his chin, his eyes lifted toward the ceiling. 'Though I've heard good things about Johnson's new place on Exchange.'

A look of disgust passed over Henry's face. Miniature shock waves rippled outward from the epicenter of his wrinkled nose, across the expanse of cheeks, before subsiding in the bright pink of his braised jowls. Grey reached out to brace the man, and Lean saw a bill disappear into the proprietor's meaty grip. Henry raised a finger, an exclamation point punctuating the revelation that had just occurred to him. He led them through the dining room, along a snaking path through the canyon of stony stares from the curious, dismissive, or even hostile crowd of napkin-necked bankers and insurance men. Lean guessed that some of the disapproving looks were aimed at the tawny skin of Grey rather than Helen's presence in the men's dining room.

They were deposited in a semiprivate booth in a back corner, facing away from the main dining room. Grey ordered for the table, then turned to Helen. 'Lost in the excitement of today's discoveries, we must remember our gratitude to Tom Doran for our being able to meet here, all in good health.'

Helen smiled. 'I tremble to think what might have happened. I must have thanked him a dozen times, but it seems so inadequate. There must be something more we can do for him, Uncle.'

Dr Steig shook his head. 'Lord knows I've offered tokens of

gratitude in the past, for lesser favors, of course. But he'll have none of it. Still thinks of himself as being indebted.'

'What is the story with our Irish giant, Doctor?' Grey asked. 'You made reference to some history, back at Maggie Keene's funeral.'

Dr Steig took a drink and considered the question. 'Tom saw a lot of fire in the war – Fifth Maine Infantry. He wasn't quite the same afterward. Some men see so much killing, it's like a part of them dies in battle too. Took to drinking and brawling. He spent some time with me at the Soldiers' Home, but I couldn't help him.' The doctor paused to light a cigarette.

'It wasn't until he met a young woman named Mary Mitchell that he pulled himself together. She was able to calm him, set his soul at ease. They were married and had a little girl. But then Mary lost a second child. She caught a fever and died. Tom started drinking again and didn't stop until the police came for him. It took six men to bring him down. He broke one man's jaw. The judge would have put him away for a good spell if I hadn't testified to Tom's army service, Mary's death, and promised to keep him confined and get him sober.'

'What about the child?' asked Helen.

'That's the indebted bit,' answered Dr Steig. 'Tom couldn't have cared less about me getting him out of jail sooner or sobering him up. But I managed to keep the girl out of the orphanage. Got her put directly with a nice, decent couple.'

'Does he see her much?' Helen asked.

'Never. Tom was unpredictable, given to rages. The new family worried what he might do, so their identity was concealed as part of the bargain, and Tom agreed to it.'

'He never asks about her?' Lean said.

Dr Steig shook his head. 'He just takes it on faith that she's been with a good family and God's watched over her. That's what he says, anyway. Though I've seen him stop in a crowd and stare at a girl who's about the age she would be now, one who maybe reminds him of his poor Mary.'

"'Such is the cross I wear upon my breast,"' Lean recited, "'These eighteen years, through all the changing scenes / And seasons, changeless since the day she died.'"

There was a short silence afterward that was cut mercifully short by several waiters, heavily burdened with oysters both fried and escalloped, turtle soup, duck and oyster croquettes, Saratoga fried potatoes, and beets stewed with onions. An hour later and the table was littered with plates, bowls, platters, and tureens, looking like a pile of bones discarded outside the den of some primitive scavenger. Lean's head was spinning trying to make sense of the web of facts, theories, and opinions that the group had chewed over during the course of their extensive lunch.

The killer was obsessed with Salem. Consumed with what Dr Steig had labeled as a fixed idea about witches. Was he killing these women as witches, or just as sinners? And why these particular women? Traveling hundreds of miles to different states seemed random and incongruous for one whose actions at the Portland Company were so elaborately planned. Maggie Keene died inside a rail-car shop. And Hannah was killed near train tracks. Both were killed on bare ground. But there was no other connection between the victims: different backgrounds, both mutilated but in different ways; there had been prior intimate contact with Maggie but not with Hannah. There were too many missing details about the Scituate woman to divine any motive. But his treatment of Maggie Keene's body gave a possible hint:

The pitchfork and cross cut into her chest were meant for her as an actual witch.

'"Thou shalt not suffer a witch to live." Exodus 22:18,' Lean said as he broke the surface, emerging from the depths of his contemplation to rejoin those at the table. When he saw all three pairs of eyes staring at him, he added, 'I think he's conducting an actual witch-hunt.'

'A witch-hunt?' Dr Steig set his coffee cup down and dabbed at his mouth with a napkin. 'He's two hundred years late. Real-live witches, today, in our city? Why, it's preposterous.'

Lean gave him a questioning look. 'No doubt it all sounds utterly mad. But is it any less mad to learn that someone is assuming the names of Salem witches, traveling hundreds of miles, singling out women for no reason at all, and actually murdering them as witches? Just like in the Salem trials.'

'Mrs Prescott,' Grey said, 'you are our resident expert on the Salem witch trials. Please confirm for the deputy that those Salem victims, like ours, were not in fact real witches.'

'Of course not. At least not in the common understanding of witchcraft – standing around the kettle casting spells and all that. That's not to say that people back then weren't engaged in certain activities that were considered witchcraft at the time. Things that today we view as harmless superstitions, charms and such.'

'That's more of what I was getting at,' Lean said. 'I'm not suggesting Maggie Keene spent her nights flying about on a broomstick.'

'We know for a fact that is not how she spent her nights,' Grey said.

'But she may have been involved in something, some occult group or activity that could have gotten her named as a witch and killed for it. After all, those Salem witches didn't need to be casting real black-magic spells, yet how many of them died?' He turned to Helen and shrugged, showing that his question was more than rhetorical.

'Nineteen hanged, one pressed to death, and some others died in jail during the months of waiting for trials,' she said.

'See?' Lean wagged a finger. 'Nearly two dozen dead all the same, because they were thought to be witches. And now our man apparently believes the same of these women. Why?'

Grey pondered this for a moment, while his right eyebrow arched upward, like the hammer of a rifle being drawn back. 'What do you think, Mrs Prescott? Is it plausible that Maggie Keene could have been involved in something perceived as the practice of witchcraft?'

'I'm certainly not an expert on modern witchcraft,' Helen protested, 'although while gathering materials for our Salem lectures I did speak with some of the women around town who work as spiritualist mediums. So yes, I would have to say that there are people, even today, who are actively interested in ideas such as black magic.'

PART II

July 4, 1892

So it is with all human actions; not one of them happens by pure chance unconnected with other happenings ... They are the fruits which must of necessity develop under the influence of nature and individual culture, fruits whose formation is explained by the organism producing them ... We do not look to gather grapes from thorns or figs from thistles.

Dr Hans Gross, Criminal Investigation

29

Helen unlocked her front door and entered, followed by Dr Steig and her daughter, who was still waving the small flag from the earlier Independence Day celebrations. Helen glanced at the clock and saw it was half past seven.

'Oh my, Mr Grey will be here in thirty minutes. Hurry upstairs, Delia. You can help me get changed into something for the evening.'

'Can't I come too, Mother? I'm old enough to stay up and see the fireworks.'

'Not tonight, dear. This isn't to see the fireworks. This is some business we're working on. Next year I promise to take you. Now, hurry on. I'll be right up.'

The girl pounded her way upstairs with heavy steps to emphasize her disappointment. Dr Steig glanced out the curtains and lit a cigarette.

'Are you certain about that? This is just business?'

Helen stared at her uncle. 'Whatever do you mean?'

'You've had a spring in your step all day. Now you're practically beaming about Grey's arrival.'

'Certainly it's business. Of course, it *will* be rather nice to spend an evening out, see the fireworks, with music and dancing and all. Heaven knows it's been an awfully long time since I've done that.'

'So your excitement isn't caused by Grey himself.'

Helen's cheeks reddened a bit. 'It should be quite an enjoyable evening to be escorted out by such a cultured, intelligent gentleman. Do you think otherwise? You've always spoken highly of him.'

Dr Steig waved away the idea. 'It's not that. He's a perfect gentleman, of course. A brilliant man. It's just, well ... ' The doctor began to pace as he struggled with a tactful choice of words. 'He's just quite different from other men.'

'Then he's to be congratulated.'

'Don't be glib, Helen. I can assure you that whatever your interests and expectations are for this evening, they bear little resemblance to his.'

Helen studied her uncle's face for a moment, noting a mix of warning and discomfort in his eyes. 'Is this because he's Indian? Are you embarrassed to have me seen with him?'

'What? Of course not. I only mean to say that there is a single-mindedness to him. He's not one to be overly concerned for the feelings of others.'

'I think you underestimate him. After all, we're going there tonight to see if I can identify those men who chased me in the alleyway. I believe that Mr Grey has a genuine interest in apprehending those brutes who meant to harm me.'

'He thinks the men who chased you outside of McGrath's place came from the Temperance Union. They're likely some of Colonel Blanchard's old soldiers, acting on his orders. There's a connection between the Temperance Union and what Boxcar Annie knows of the murder at the Portland Company. Grey wants you to identify those men so he can use that information as leverage against Colonel Blanchard, find out his connection to Maggie Keene's death. That's his only interest.'

Helen waited, making sure her uncle had stated his piece. 'Of course we're doing this for the murder investigation, Uncle. I'm perfectly aware of that. Now, if you'll excuse me.' She moved to the stairs. 'I have to get ready.'

The crowds of pedestrians and carriages on Congress Street blocked any further progress toward the Eastern Promenade, so Rasmus Hansen dropped Grey and Helen at the corner of Vesper Street and arranged to wait for them a block east. From there the pair walked the final two blocks arm in arm. Grey was sharply attired in his full-dress evening suit, silk-faced to the edge, and double-breasted tattersall white vest. Helen looked dazzling in a blue suit of plain material trimmed with lace. The skirt had three rows of lace flouncing and puffed back drapery. She had looped the short front drapery at the side with white ribbon bows. The night was hot, so she had forgone a hat in favor of an elaborate ribbon wound through her plaited hair, the red silk completing her patriotic color scheme.

Congress Street ended at the Cleeve and Tucker Memorial, a granite pillar erected in honor of the 1632 arrival on the peninsula of the first two English settlers. Each of the square-based monument's four sides was engraved with one of the names the city had held in its history, from the original Indian title of Machigonne to Casco, Falmouth, and finally Portland. Normally an expanse of green park space, over half a mile long and five hundred feet deep, sloping sharply down toward Casco Bay, would be visible before them. Tonight, however, there were almost ten thousand people crowded into the area. The sun was setting behind them as Helen and Grey made their way toward the eastern terminus of the Promenade, where the old site of Fort Allen's earthworks battery was now marked by a large bandstand. For the Fourth of

July festivities, a long white tent had been raised to house a temporary wooden dance floor.

Nearby was a platform and podium, decorated with red, white, and blue bunting, where Colonel Blanchard was to give his temperance speech. A line of chairs set at the back of the platform was occupied by various civic and business leaders who, publicly at least, supported the Maine Temperance Union. The site of the colonel's speech had been well selected; Fort Allen Park recalled his military service while also being located within eyeshot of Fish Point. That easternmost corner of Portland Neck was a favorite locale of vagrants and drunken tramps and would highlight the immediacy of the colonel's message.

Blanchard walked onstage and exchanged pleasantries with several of the seated men. These weren't the ones Grey wanted Helen to get a look at. The men they sought would likely be in their old uniforms in one of the ceremonial guard formations positioned around the grounds of the park. Or they might be lingering in plain clothes at the sides and front of the platform, ready to break up any trouble or roust any drunks. The colonel's views on drinking were not appreciated by a significant share of the city, and his speeches brought a good chance of getting one or two men well into a bottle and itching for a livelier debate on abstinence and the evils of alcohol.

A wave of applause greeted Colonel Blanchard as he stepped to the podium. The colonel held up his hands, gesturing at the crowd to ease its volume. He was a tall man with a stern face, heavily lined, that looked like it could have been chiseled from a block of New Hampshire granite.

'My dear friends, I know that most of you already enjoy the blessings of sobriety. But today, on this Day of Independence, I come here to see if I can add but one more person, one father, one mother, or even one child, to the rolls of those who already bask in the glorious freedom of temperance.

'Those of you who know me know that I have borne witness to that glorious terrible conflict wherein our generation was called upon to honor the laws of heaven and be our brothers' keepers. To free our fellow men from the unholy yoke of servitude. And yet I declare that all the pain I saw inflicted in my three years of war is but a cup when measured against the ocean of suffering which deluges our communities every day.'

From where they stood on the Promenade, slightly above the speaking platform, Helen and Grey had difficulty identifying anyone in the crowd. Daylight was fast fading, and most of the people below wore hats that shaded their faces. Grey took Helen's elbow to assist her as they moved down the grassy hillside and worked through the crowd to observe the area surrounding the platform. Helen hoped he was getting a decent view, since her shorter vantage point was useless in the sea of feathered bonnets and top hats. Many of the men in the crowd smoked cigars or cigarettes, but past those hazy covers Helen detected whiffs of whiskey and rum.

They slowly maneuvered around in a circle, heading to the side of the stage where Colonel Blanchard had entered. When the two of them had woven their way close to the left front of the stage, Grey started pointing out possible suspects, some of whom he recognized and others he was simply guessing at, from their bearing and location, as being the colonel's men. Helen repeatedly denied recognizing anyone, noting that it had been rather dim and hectic in the alleyway, so she hadn't gotten a good look at her pursuers.

As the colonel's speech neared its conclusion, his voice continued to boom out over the heads of the crowd. 'The hard facts support us in showing that the practice of drinking spirits, thought by so many to be a harmless indulgence, results in greater misery to more individuals than any other custom or event that has ever existed or occurred in the history of man. By comparison, war is the cause of but little misery, especially as the combatants have nobly sacrificed their lives for the sake of their country. The true War for Independence, the war for our nation's very soul, is still being fought, and you are all called to be soldiers in this righteous army.'

The colonel waved to the crowd and left the stage to a roar of applause, as well as a decent chorus from those offering their sincerest wishes that he spend a long time as a houseguest of the devil. Blanchard, followed by his retinue, made his way from the stage area to the nearby tent, shaking hands and offering thanks to his supporters.

After casually strolling around the grounds, past several groups of uniformed veterans, Helen and Grey came to the edge of the great white tent that housed the temporary dance floor. Many of the side flaps were removed, allowing breezes and enabling the dancers to hear the music from the adjacent bandstand. Gaslights attached to the support poles lit the interior.

'There, in the corner,' Grey said, and motioned with a tilt of his head.

Helen glanced into the tent, past the twirling figures of waltzing couples. On the far side, she spotted Colonel Blanchard engaged in conversation with a circle of men. The bandleader announced there was time for one more song before the fireworks were scheduled to begin.

'May I have the honor of this dance?' Grey said.

Helen let him take her hand. 'You may.'

The band launched into Sousa's most popular dance song, 'The Washington Post March,' and Grey led the two-step, slowly maneuvering Helen into the middle of the floor. She smiled at him. 'I think the last time I danced like this, I was still in school. But you're rather clever on your feet, Mr Grey.'

'I don't have much call to practice these days either, but when I was a young man, my education was certainly varied and thorough.' Grey continued to guide Helen toward the far side of the tent, to within twenty feet of the colonel.

Helen studied the men standing alongside Blanchard and shook her head. They two-stepped along until Helen was positioned to see the faces of the men who stood opposite the colonel. Her eyes darted over all the surrounding faces, locking onto a strongly built man with short-cropped blond hair. He wore a black patch over his left eye. She felt the surprise spread across her face as she blurted out, 'It's him!'

All of Blanchard's group, and several dancing couples, looked in Helen's direction. Grey spun her around quickly so that she faced away from their scrutiny.

'The blond hair and the eye patch,' she whispered. Helen watched Grey's face as he stared at the colonel and his men for a few seconds before casually leading her back across the floor to where they had entered the tent. They stepped out under the night sky as the music faded behind them. Grey kept hold of Helen's hand.

'Let's move along. We'll have a better view for the festivities.'

It wasn't exactly the sort of comment Helen was expecting after having just identified the colonel's associate, but she let Grey lead her away from Fort Allen Park, weaving among the crowds of spectators standing on the hillside or else spread out on picnic blankets, all awaiting the aerial display.

'I shouldn't have cried out like that,' she said. 'Do you think he suspects us?'

'I don't believe he saw your face.'

They continued on along the grassy slope, Grey leading at a casual pace, shooting glances behind them. Helen looked back toward the tent as well, but it was too dark to make out anyone in particular.

'Are we being followed?'

'There's nothing to worry about.'

Helen only half believed him, noting the way that Grey hunched his shoulders, making himself shorter and less noticeable among the crowds. A sharp whistling sound rose from the waterfront at the base of the hill, where the fireworks were being staged. The crowd offered up a collective cheer. Grey and Helen paused to watch the flare rise into the sky and burst into a shower of blue and white directly over the crowd. Several more bursts followed. As soon as there was a lull and the sky grew dim again, Grey guided Helen farther uphill toward the street. Each time a new flare sounded, they would pause and await the explosions. Helen was so amazed at how close the bursts were, nearly filling her entire field of vision, that she forgot all her thoughts of Colonel Blanchard and the blond man. After several rockets combined for a particularly dazzling burst, she said, 'Isn't this spectacular?'

'Yes.' Grey's uninterested tone caused her to look sideways at him, and she realized that he was paying no heed to the fireworks. He was instead using their illuminating effect to scan the faces in the crowd.

'What's wrong?'

'We should be going.' The sky began to darken again, and Grey reached out to guide Helen up the last stretch of hillside. As they stepped onto the pavement of the Eastern Promenade, Helen turned and saw a soldier following after them. He motioned to some unseen comrade, then pointed in their direction. Grey urged her forward to one of the carriages that sat in a row, awaiting fares at the end of the fireworks show. He helped her up into the enclosed four-wheeler.

As Grey climbed in, the driver called out, 'It'll be a bit of a wait, sir. Packed in here tight until them in front of us move out.'

'Yes, thank you,' Grey said. Inside, he did not take a seat but moved directly across to exit the opposite door, then assisted Helen down on the street side of the carriage. Her choice of shoes, bowed Dieppe ties with Louis XV heels, was not conducive to flight, so Grey held on to her as they hurried over the Promenade's uneven paving stones. Once across the wide avenue, they turned in to the corner of Moody Street to escape from view.

Helen glanced back and didn't see anyone following them, but Grey pressed her along the sidewalk, moving up Munjoy Hill to where Rasmus waited with Dr Steig's carriage. Between the excitement and the slope they were facing, Helen's breathing became quick.

'Are you all right, Mrs Prescott?'

'Perfectly fine, thank you. An evening of dancing, fireworks, fleeing from angry soldiers – what more could a lady ask for?'

'I do apologize. This was needlessly risky on my part.'

'Oh, I'm just having you on a bit. I'm fine. Truly.'

'Shh!' Grey held a finger to his lips as he pulled Helen toward

179

a recessed doorway. She glanced about as she stepped in but didn't see or hear anything that would cause alarm.

'What is it?' she whispered.

Grey waited, then leaned forward several inches and peered down toward the boulevard. Helen risked a peek. Two men, silhouetted against a streetlamp and wearing army hats, were standing in the middle of the street, one block away. They looked all around, then moved on toward the next side street.

'That was him with the blond hair,' Helen said.

'His name is Simon Gould. He's one of the men who chased you in the alley?'

'Not the alley – the library. He was the man in the lobby.'

'But is he the man who actually pursued you in the library later that night?' Grey asked.

'Maybe. He might have been.'

'Could you swear it to the police? Or a judge?'

Helen sighed. The rush of excitement drained out of her. She couldn't honestly swear that Simon Gould was anything other than an unnerving man who had asked about books on witchcraft. If she accused him now, the authorities would dismiss her as quickly as Archie Lean had the morning after that incident. No one would arrest one of Colonel Blanchard's close associates on the uncertain word of a nervous woman, frightened out of her wits in the dark, rushing through the library at night in fear for her life, after spending the evening listening to a lecture on witchcraft.

'I'd like to get home to Delia now.'

Grey nodded and took Helen's hand as they hurried along the rough sidewalk toward the waiting carriage.

30

A week had passed since the return from Scituate and the subsequent revelation by Helen Prescott that the killer was using aliases drawn from Salem's male witch-trial victims. July's arrival had broken a long pattern of rainy weather. More important, the Independence Day weekend had brought Lean some welcome time with his family and a respite from the mayor's requests for updates. When he saw Grey waiting by the steps to the public library and historical society, all such pleasant thoughts faded.

As they made their way to the top floor to meet Helen, Grey relayed her identification of Simon Gould as the man in the library, further solidifying the theory of a connection between the Portland Company murder and the temperance union. When they reached the third floor, Helen was sitting at the reference desk. Only one other person occupied the room – a thin, scholarly man who looked as if he were intentionally ignoring the newcomers.

'Is there somewhere we could talk in private?' Lean asked.

Helen glanced at the wall clock. 'We close in another fifteen minutes. Though, I suppose once the last visitor leaves, I could shut the doors early.'

Grey sauntered over to where the visitor, a mousy-faced man with a twitchy mustache, was perusing a book. He studied the man as if he were an amateurish painting hanging in a gallery that ought to show better. Eventually the man acknowledged his discomfort by asking if there was some way he could help Grey.

'No. But aren't you running late for your birching?' Grey flicked his arm, mimicking a whipping motion.

'I beg your pardon.' The man drew himself up to his full, but still unimpressive, height.

'Keeping that burly woman in high leather boots waiting isn't going to improve her mood any. Or is that the whole point?'

Helen's face turned a violent shade of red reserved for occasions of deep personal embarrassment. Lean bit his lip to keep from laughing as Grey followed the nervous man to the exit and shut the doors behind him.

After Grey rejoined them, no one spoke for several moments until a stunned Helen uttered, 'Was that really called for?'

'I certainly hope so,' Grey said. 'It depends on how rewarding your research has been.'

'Yes, well . . .' was all that Helen managed as she led them into the back room of the historical society. The space, used for storage and organization of archived documents and material, was an eruption of books and stacks of papers. Small wooden crates dotted the floor, some with lids off, revealing their cargoes of texts like recently unearthed treasure chests left by long-dead, and strangely erudite, pirates. Stuffed bookshelves lined the walls, and a few pitiful tables sagged under their loads.

Lean surveyed the random stacks of bound and loose pages. 'Looks like the devil's been holding a rummage sale. This isn't all for us, I trust.'

'No, we're just a bit behind in our cataloging. I've set aside a work area for materials from the two hundred years since the witch trials.'

Helen stepped toward a small desk that held her notes. 'I assume you know the basic facts from 1692. Salem was rife with factions and long-running disputes over land, religious matters, and anything else they could think of. Not exactly the type of great city on a hill envisioned by the Puritans. In the winter some of the village girls had gathered together and done a bit of fortune-telling. Shortly afterward some of them started having spasms and writhing in agony, contorting into unnatural postures, uttering all sorts of nonsense. The village physician examined them and concluded they were "under an evil hand." Salem's minister, the Reverend Parris, called the neighboring ministers to his house, and they all agreed the devil was conducting an unholy assault upon their community.

'You must bear in mind,' Helen said, 'it was an established doctrine that the devil could not interfere directly against humans, except through other human beings acting in confederacy with him – that is, witches. The question on everyone's mind was, who were the agents of the devil that were afflicting the girls? I call them girls, though some adult women soon joined their ranks. Anyway, the constant pressure to identify their tormentors finally became too great. One after another, the girls cried out the names of the Reverend Parris's Caribbean servant, Tituba, along with Sarah Good and Sarah Osborne.'

'What about the accused men?' Lean asked.

'It was popularly known that women were much more likely than men to be witches. But it was also thought that people closely related to witches were themselves in danger of becoming witches. So, soon after the next group of women was accused, two of their husbands, John Proctor and the very elderly Giles Corey, were also named. The afflicted girls would normally be at the bottom of the legal and social hierarchy. Some of them were servants in others' households. The fact that they became such important and powerful figures in the witchcraft crisis was a remarkable event. It turned the social order on its head. Despite the afflicted girls' newfound influence, they were not always able to formally bring charges against accused witches. Often that task would fall upon the male head of the household.

'Some men, such as John Proctor, were openly skeptical of the accusing girls' fits and their claims of being tormented by witches' specters. His servant was among the afflicted girls, but he refused to support charges made by her, instead threatening to beat the fits out of her. Not surprisingly, John Proctor's defense of his own wife's innocence and his hostile attitude toward the accusers soon earned him a place among the accused witches.

'As for Giles Corey, he was called up for trial, pleaded not guilty, then refused to answer the required question of whether he would be tried by God and country. The traditional punishment for failure to agree to trial was to lay the prisoner down with a wooden board atop his chest. He would be pressed with stones until he either agreed to a trial or died. Despite the mounting weight, the eighty-year-old only uttered, "More weight," when his compliance was demanded. It was a slow death, with one witness recalling that Corey's tongue was forced out of his mouth from the pressure, only to have the sheriff push it back in with his cane.'

'Just so you know,' Lean said with mock sincerity, 'I'd do you the same favor. If it ever came to that.'

Grey nodded. 'Thank you. It had been preying on my mind.'

Helen cleared her throat. 'The old and infirm George Jacobs was accused by a servant as well as by his own granddaughter. His body was searched and revealed several apparent witch's tits. The servant had accused Jacobs of wickedness and failing to pray. Jacobs responded that this was because he could not read. When instructed to recite the Lord's Prayer, he made several errors and could not repeat it correctly despite numerous attempts. This inability to recite the Lord's Prayer perfectly was considered a sure sign of guilt.'

Lean started to fidget as his old questions on the subject resurfaced. 'Our man is quoting the Lord's Prayer as well, only in Abenaki. There must be a connection. Hardly anyone alive, other than an Abenaki, knows that tongue today.'

Helen nodded. 'The same was true back then. English colonists typically considered the Indian language, as well as their culture, to be crude and savage, even satanic.'

'Is that it?' Lean gave Grey an elbow nudge. 'Is he conducting some sham ritual? Reciting the prayer in the devilish language of Satan's Indian allies?'

Grey refused to match Lean's outburst of enthusiasm. 'It's a plausible theory.' He eased a step further from the deputy and addressed Helen again. 'There were other accused male witches?'

'Yes. John Willard was one. Accused by Ann Putnam as well as Susannah Sheldon, who had been a young child in Maine during the first Indian war when several of her relatives were killed. Susannah reported visions of four dead people who claimed Willard had murdered them. She also saw his specter suckling two black pigs at his breast and kneeling in prayer before the black man.

'Another was George Burroughs, a minister who'd lived here in Portland and was suspected of working in league with the Abenakis. After successfully accusing such a prominent man, the girls became bolder, and the number of accusations increased dramatically. Documents don't survive for all of them. Many of the newly accused were men, though some were never formally charged due to a lack of credible evidence. Others, such as John

Alden, simply fled the area or escaped from jail rather than await trial. Like Burroughs, Alden seems to have been named due to the belief that he had allied himself with the Abenakis and the French, and so was in league with the devil. Alden was a wealthy shipowner and merchant who was active in trading along the Maine coast. He was well known as an Indian trader, and there were rumors of his supplying provisions to the French and Indians in return for lucrative beaver pelts, even during periods of hostilities.' Helen set her notes down on the table. 'I'm afraid that's about the sum of my investigation.'

'Don't be disappointed, Mrs Prescott,' Grey said. 'It's all very informative. You've unearthed connections between Portland and some of the accused men, as well as the past use of the Lord's Prayer. But the link to the present remains uncertain, which returns us to your other generous offer of research: the status of witchcraft today.'

'Yes,' said Lean, eagerly taking up the scent again, 'are there people here in Portland today who are practicing witches?'

'Certainly some who claim to be,' Helen said.

'Did any of them know Maggie Keene?' Grey asked.

'I don't think so. Once I steered conversations in that direction, they were all very eager to talk about her, but none of it struck me as genuine.'

'Did you hear, during your talks, that there had been acts of violence against any of these occult mediums?' Lean asked.

'Just minor incidents from time to time,' Helen answered.

Lean thought for a moment. 'Did any of them mention a supposed witch called something like . . . Old Stitches? She's one that may have had some troubles.'

'I don't recall hearing her name,' Helen answered.

'She's the woman mentioned by the Abenakis. Does it mean something to you?' Grey asked Lean. 'Did she die here in Portland?'

'No. East Deering, across Tukey's Bridge, out along Back Cove. So it wasn't our case. I never heard any details.'

Grey thought for a moment. 'Perhaps you should canvass some of these spiritualists, Lean. Our man's interests lie within their sphere. He may have been making the rounds with them, seeking information about occult matters, witches and such. Maybe one will remember something that will help us identify him.'

31

'This is probably a waste of time,' Lean said over the noise of the carriage wheels as they rumbled across the wooden planks of Tukey's Bridge, leaving Portland behind. Red, white, and blue streamers, left over from the Independence Day celebrations several days earlier, still hung from the posts along the bridge. 'Fake mediums and spirits and dead witches.'

'Not necessarily. The belief that a charlatan, preying upon desperate people, can reveal the secrets of the dead is utter foolishness.' Grey raised his index finger. 'This, however, involves an actual dead body. That fact alone makes it of interest. And while I don't believe in any aspect of witchcraft, I accept that our killer appears to. This Old Stitch character, by virtue of her reputation and her recent death, warrants at least a cursory review.'

They left the bridge and turned onto Main Street. A half mile farther and Grey rapped at the roof with his walking stick. The driver deposited them by the side of the road, and Grey made arrangements for the man to collect them in an hour. Lean looked around. The side of the street away from Back Cove was sparsely populated with houses, while the area closer to the water was wooded.

'Our guide will be along shortly,' Grey said. 'Tell me again about the police report.'

'The body was found by a customer on February fifth. The coroner ruled she'd been dead a few days. No external injuries, but traces of vomit in her mouth and blood in her nostrils.'

Grey nodded. 'Nothing was taken. No signs of robbery.'

'The customer had been there before. She didn't notice anything missing, but then there wasn't much of value in the place to begin with.'

'And the constable reported signs of some séance?' Grey said.

'A deck of fortune-telling cards on the table, spread out, as if the woman was in the middle of a reading. It was thought she died from a sort of seizure.'

'Brought on by the shocking appearance of some otherworldly specter, no doubt.'

'Do you really not believe in spirits?' Lean asked. 'The possibility of communicating with some eternal soul in the afterlife?'

Grey looked at him with one eyebrow pointing up to heaven. 'The overwhelming majority of people in the world are unimaginative dullards who, in their three score and ten allotted years, manage to divine no purpose for their being other than to chase money, seize what moments of physical pleasure they can, and to create new, largely unimproved versions of themselves, whom they raise with the same mindless disregard they have applied to their own lives. Tell me, please, what use would such beings have for an afterlife? Whatever would they do with an eternity?' Grey motioned down the street. 'Ah, here we are.'

Lean turned to see their guide approaching. The scrawny boy couldn't have been more than thirteen, though he tried squinting and affecting a slight sneer in an effort to look serious. The boy tipped his cap and addressed Mr Grey with a tone of respect before leading the men along the edge of the woods. At some inconspicuous landmark, the boy turned and led them into the trees. Fifty paces in, he stopped and pointed.

'Path picks up again right ahead. Just keep on there and you can't miss it.' The words shot out of the boy's mouth. Lean could tell he was spooked to be so close to what must have been a cursed place in the lore of the local children. He handed over some coins, and the boy vanished into the brush, scurrying uphill, back toward his idea of civilization. Looking toward the dim, murky woods, Lean felt less than enthusiastic. He drew his revolver and rechecked that it was fully loaded.

'I assume the Deering police report noted that the woman is already dead,' Grey said.

'It's not her that worries me. Who knows what else is slithering around in there?' Lean holstered his weapon again. 'I don't see anything resembling a path here.'

'Well, I guess we just push on, then. I'll take the flank.' Grey moved off to the right as Lean pushed forward, shouldering aside low-hanging branches and plowing through the underbrush that had overtaken any old path. The land sloped down, and the ground became increasingly damp. He picked his way along several small stepping-stones across a miniature creek and sank a half inch deep with each step across the boglike ground, so that the water seeped in at the seams of his shoes.

The overhead foliage was sparse enough to let in patches of light. Lean saw an angular shape looming about twenty yards ahead, and he recognized it as a slanted roof. He let out three quick, sharp whistle bursts, then continued forward slowly, giving Grey time to find him.

'What was that supposed to be?'

'That was a legitimate bird call,' Lean said.

'Ah, the elusive Presbyterian warbler.'

Lean chuckled. 'Fine, I'll send up smoke signals next time.' He motioned with his head. 'There – straight through.'

The two detectives pushed by the last bit of brush and emerged into a soggy clearing. A small structure, which could not honestly claim any title grander than hovel, squatted before them. At one time it had a window on the front side, but the glass was broken out, and the primitive plank door had come off its hinges. The roof was made of loosely fitted wooden boards of various sizes, through which a rusty stovepipe protruded. Lean stood silent for a moment searching for the words he needed, then recited:

> 'There, in a gloomy hollow glen, she found
> A little cottage built of sticks and reeds,
> In homely wise, and walled with sods around,
> In which a witch did dwell in loathly weeds.'

Lean glanced to his side to see Grey standing nearby, peering at him with an arched eyebrow. 'Spenser,' announced the deputy. 'You're not the only bloke around here who's ever opened a book.'

They stepped over the rotting door and entered the shack. At their approach, several small things scurried. Crooked beams of

190

daylight sifted down through cracks and holes in the bare roof, displaying thin pillars of swirling dust. The smell of decaying plants outside the hovel had been replaced by a more putrid smell, smoke combined with the stale odor of human presence and waste. Lingering above it all, Lean thought he could detect the scent of death, though perhaps, knowing that the woman's body had lain there undiscovered for some time, his mind simply expected the smell.

The shack seemed even smaller inside. A dingy, stained blanket had been strung up to cordon off a third of the room. It hung half off its line now, revealing a flimsy, tattered mattress on the floor, well stained with every shade of human usage. The larger portion of the room held a rickety bench, a small circular table, and a thick chair painted black and covered with etchings and strange designs. From an exposed beam above hung a series of strings on which dangled a variety of small animal bones. There was a second window on the south side of the shack that still held its grimy pane of glass. Set there, upon a wooden crate, were four potted plants, only one of which clung to life.

While Lean knocked about the small room, Grey went over to peer at the plants. He plucked something from the last living one. After a few moments, he moved across the room to a shelf near the fireplace that held a variety of glass and earthenware jars. He began to examine the contents of each container and sniffed at a few of the selections, one of which turned his head. He dumped the offending brown powder onto the floor.

'Anything interesting?' Lean asked.

Grey pointed to the surviving potted plant. Lean examined the specimen, a woody, prickly, twining, herblike plant with numerous slender, smooth-textured branches. A few of the branches had sprouted a dozen pairs of leaflets, which looked to be dying before having reached their peak. Pinkish flowers that had faded to near white were on the branches' swollen nodes or else had dropped off and withered in the pot. Many of the branches had been snipped.

'Looks bare, like it's dead. But it's really been trimmed down to nothing.'

'Exactly,' Grey said.

'So?'

'So where are the rest of the seeds? There's not a single specimen in all these jars. They're all gone except for this single bit, which, judging from the small size, may have sprouted after the plant was trimmed.' Grey held up a sprig whose tip bore a cluster of pods, which had opened and curled back to reveal small, oval-shaped seeds of a glossy scarlet.

Lean looked a bit closer and saw that the bright red only covered the bottom two-thirds of each of the quarter-inch-long seeds. The top third of each was black.

'So she trimmed them and sold them all to her customers.'

'Perhaps. Odd, though – every container here but one holding something. One jar emptied. And just this one plant that she valued highly enough to care for more than the others. Perhaps she wasn't the only one who valued this plant.'

Lean shrugged. It was a long bit of speculation about some old plant seeds when what they were there to investigate was a question of murder. 'There were no signs of violence. No struggle, if it's a robbery and murder you're getting at. There was just her body sprawled out there by the hearth.'

Lean went and stood before the chimney, which was of a crude design: wood, plastered over with a heavy clay-based mud mixed with hay and twigs that had then been baked hard. He looked down between his feet. For all the other aesthetic and structural failings of the dismal little dwelling, the hearth actually showed some signs of skilled workmanship. A rough area of about four by six feet had been covered with large, irregular fieldstones. The mortar between the stones had gone black with age but was still set firmly in place to fashion a solid hearth of bluish gray rock.

'Peculiar,' said Grey after turning to examine the area. He knelt down and ran his finger along the edge of a small and shallow but perfectly round hole in the mortar joining two of the flat stones.

'There's more,' noted Lean. 'There and there. Five of them around in a circle.'

'A pentagram,' said Grey.

Lean's mind flashed back to the image of Maggie Keene, her body splayed out to make five points.

Grey stepped back over to the shelf and returned with a thin candle, which he fitted into one of the holes. 'I imagine this is where she put on her displays. Candles at her feet, but otherwise in darkness, with a fire behind her. Tossing in her magic powders. Sleights of hand while the flashes of color distracted the customers. Pulling who knows what from hidden pockets in her skirts.'

Lean knelt down on the hearth and craned his neck to look up the chimney. He stuck his hand up and ran it around, feeling for any secret hiding spots. The reward was nothing but a palmful of slick soot.

'A show like that would have been a sight more interesting than what she's left behind – which is nothing.' Lean placed his hands on the hearth to steady himself as he rose. The fingers of his left hand poked into a seam of grime between two of the stones, and he quickly pulled out his handkerchief to wipe at the ooze. He was about to stuff the handkerchief back into his pocket when the thought hit him.

'There's no mortar around this one stone. Just wet mud.'

Lean found a broad-bladed knife in an old washbasin and used it to pry the stone up enough to get a fingerhold and lift it out of the way. On top of the soil lay the flattened remains of a small animal. It was not yet completely decomposed, and though worm-eaten, its skeletal wing frames, pointed beak, and some matted feathers revealed that it had been a bird. Lean flicked it aside with the tip of the knife. The dirt beneath proved to be more loosely packed than it should have been under the pressure of the hearth. He used the knife to dig away the soil, and within a minute the blade made contact, scraping on some still-hidden object. Abandoning the knife, Lean scooped away the dirt with his hands.

'Glass. Some type of jar.'

He locked a finger around the small handle and freed the wine jug from its grave. Lean brushed off the damp earth that clung to the outside and sloshed the two inches of dirty liquid at the bottom of the glass jug. There came a faint metallic rattling from inside the jar. After a series of tugs, the stopper came loose. Lean peered in at the yellowish brown liquid before the stench hit him.

'Ugh!' His wide eyes shot from the bottle to Grey and back again. 'It's piss!'

With the jar at arm's length, Lean hurried outside, stooped closer to the ground to minimize splashing, and poured the contents onto a flat patch of earth. Several long, rusted nails and pins landed amid the foul froth pooling in the dirt.

'Well?' Grey stepped outside and nodded toward the puddle of fermented urine. 'Aren't you going to collect the evidence?'

Lean smiled, glanced at the bits of metal on the ground, then moved on into the small clearing that surrounded the shack. He glanced around at the murky setting once more. They were only a hundred feet or so from Back Cove. The mudflats were exposed at low tide, and a gentle southerly wind was wafting up the potent scent of tidal decay.

'This Stitch woman certainly had an eye for locales,' Lean said. 'I suppose you don't attract much business if you're a witch living in a well-kept home on the West End. Customers have expectations, after all. With these types of services, they're paying for what they want to believe in.'

'Still, the thought that she actually raised children here ...' Lean returned his attention to the shack and kicked around the perimeter. His eyes wandered over the ground once more, making sure there was nothing else to see in that dismal spot. He noticed a black seam running along the base of the wall, maybe a foot off the ground. He knelt for a closer inspection and saw that the wood was charred.

'The bottom wood's still blackened from when it was burned down. She built it back up again after.'

Grey approached and studied the wood. He crumbled some of the charred fibers between his finger and thumb.

'I'm beginning to think that this has been a fool's errand,' Lean said.

'Perhaps,' answered Grey in a distant voice, 'or maybe the things that were seen here years ago, the things that matter, simply remain hidden from us.'

32

'It's protection, a countercharm.' Helen's voice was tinny coming through the telephone receiver. 'Boiling a bewitched person's urine in a pot with iron nails would not only break the spell but cause it to return and injure its creator. In fact, there was even an instance at Salem involving Dr Roger Toothaker. Women with medical knowledge were definitely open to suspicion; he was the only male medical practitioner to be named. Toothaker was accused mostly because he told people that his daughter had killed a witch using such a technique that he'd shown her – baking an afflicted person's urine in a clay pot overnight.'

Lean made sure Emma was still sitting in the kitchen. Then, in a hushed voice, he asked, 'And what about burying a jug of urine like that?'

'I've read of burying these pots outside a doorway to keep a witch from entering a house.'

'Ever hear of burying one on the spot where someone died?' Lean asked.

'Bury one with a witch and it was said to keep her from rising again after her death.'

Lean thanked Helen and hung the receiver back on its stand. He grabbed a bottle of whiskey that he kept stashed at the back of the top shelf in the kitchen. He poured a drink tall enough that it would fall in that thin strip of ground between setting his mind at ease and making him just not care at all about witches and murders for the rest of the night. Half the whiskey went down to fulfill its destiny while Lean wandered over and stopped in his son's bedroom doorway. The light from the hall slanted across the dark room to reveal the boy curled up in his bed.

Emma came up beside him and slid her arm around his waist. Lean rested his hand on her far shoulder and gave her a peck on the forehead. Her familiar mix of scented powders and creams made him smile.

'Do you hear that?' he asked. There was a pause followed by a harsh clicking noise. Owen was grinding his teeth.

'He's a worrier. Like his father.'

'What's a five-year-old boy got to worry about these days?'

'Well, his wooden soldiers had a rough go of it today. Heavy losses suffered on the march across the kitchen. I think the burden of command is beginning to weigh on him.'

'He'll be bitter and toothless, but at least it was for a good cause. God and country. Once more into the breach.' Lean pulled the door nearly closed, then went and sat down at the kitchen table. Emma went to the sink and started in on the dishes.

'And what's weighing on you?' she asked.

'Nothing.' Lean took a drink. 'Not a single thing that I can find.'

'Still with the Portland Company murder?'

'The man who did it might have been visiting mediums. He's got some serious interest in hocus-pocus. But as soon as they see what I'm after, they start coming up with everything under the sun. Hoping to guess right and earn a couple dollars.'

'They've told you nothing at all?'

'Well, I wouldn't say nothing. The last one was in contact with Uncle Michael. Says he forgives my dad for not coming to see him on his deathbed.'

'Michael? You never had an Uncle Michael.'

Lean stroked his chin, as if contemplating a new twist. 'Well, that explains why Dad was so callous toward him at the end.'

Emma laughed. 'Now see, you learned something today after all.'

'I'm beginning to think Grey's right. The whole lot of them are nothing but charlatans.'

'I have a confession.'

'Finally.' Lean sat back and folded his hands across his midsection. 'You're secretly the daughter of royalty, and you've just come into a massive inheritance?'

'Well, yes, there's that. But I'm talking about something else. About ten years ago, shortly after Father passed, Mother had an idea.'

Lean raised an eyebrow at her.

'Fine. It was my idea. Mother and I went to see a woman. She didn't advertise for it. It was just known that she had the talent. She told us some things that day that no one else could ever have known. Things Father had said to each of us alone. Years earlier. Some things I barely remembered myself until she said them. It was like he was there in the room with us. I know you think we heard what we wanted.' She leaned in and rested her hand on top of his. 'But I swear it was real. I still see her on the street once in a while.'

'I don't need a genuine medium, Emma. I need to find one that this man has been to and who's honest enough to tell me what she remembers about him, instead of what she thinks I want to hear.'

'Her name is Amelia Porter. You should go see her.'

It took two days and a trip to an old friend at the post office before Lean was able to track down Amelia Porter. She had moved several times in the decade since Emma's visit, never leaving word of her next address. Her last neighbors knew her by sight but had never spoken to the woman and were unaware of any supposed powers to speak with the spirits of the dead. Her current address on Mayo Street was a nondescript apartment house. There was no sign advertising any sort of business, and the name on the mailbox read 'Mr T. Porter'.

She appeared on her front steps in a plain dress and bonnet, looking every bit the part of a seamstress or music teacher. There was nothing about her mannerisms that gave any hint of the powers Emma had described. His interest piqued, Lean followed the woman as she strolled toward the waterfront, stopping at a few shops along the way. He trailed her across Commercial Street to a fish market at the top of the Custom House Wharf. He let her complete her purchase of cod and move away from the din of the fishmongers' calls before he finally addressed the woman.

'Amelia Porter?'

She turned, her package clutched to her chest like a threatened child. 'Yes?'

'My name is Archie Lean. I was wondering if I could have a moment of your time?' From the look on her face, Lean knew she'd played out this scene countless times over the years.

'I'm sorry, I no longer – I can't help you.'

She started past Lean, and he instinctively reached out for her free hand. Mrs Porter lurched backward, her hand still in Lean's. He stared into her eyes. There was an emptiness there, something deep and vague he couldn't focus on. The color drained from Mrs Porter's face, leaving her with a blank look. Her hand turned cold, and Lean released his grasp, taken aback at the thought that he had so alarmed her as to induce some sort of malady.

199

Mrs Porter continued to regard him with her frozen stare for a moment longer. When she finally opened her mouth to speak, Lean half expected to see the vapor of her breath, despite the warmth of the summer morning.

'Come at four tomorrow, Mr Lean.' She started to move past him, then, with her voice in a sharp whisper, said, 'And bring the others.'

33

At ten minutes to four the next day, Lean, Dr Steig, and Helen stood in the dim, heavily curtained parlor of Mrs Porter. Marks on the rug showed that the table had been dragged in from the kitchen for the occasion. Four straight-backed wooden chairs and a rocking chair were arranged around the table. Mrs Porter looked surprised when they entered her home, glancing past Dr Steig as if looking for an additional visitor. Grey had decided not to come, since Lean was perfectly capable of discovering whether Mrs Porter had been visited by a client who fit what they knew of the killer. Grey declared that anything else the spiritualist had to say would amount to nothing more than an exercise in mutually agreed-upon gullibility.

Mr Porter, a bald, meek-looking man, was visibly agitated by their visit. His wife had him remove the extra chair as she herded him off to a back room. Mrs Porter gave the group a tepid smile. Lean noticed her eyes lingering on the bony, slightly withered right hand of Dr Steig. She then arranged the visitors so that Lean was to her left. If form held from other recent séances, he would be holding her left hand, the same as in the fish market the day before. Helen was to sit opposite Mrs Porter, and Dr Steig was on the medium's right. Lean wondered whether this was a kindness to the doctor, to spare him any discomfort at the need to share his damaged hand with a stranger, or if it was for her own benefit. He glanced up from the doctor's hand and saw that Mrs Porter was watching him.

'I don't know why you're here. But I have the sense that it's a recent occurrence. A new loss. Sometimes old wounds have a way of becoming tangled up in the present. It confuses things. Makes things difficult to discern.' Mrs Porter leaned forward to light a new candle in a silver holder in the center of the table. Then she sat back and laid her hands flat on the table in front of her, fingers fanned out as wide as they would stretch. She directed the others to do likewise, so that each person's fingers overlapped both neighbors'.

'I can't promise anything,' she said. 'I can't make the spirits come if they aren't willing. And I'm not going to tell you things for the sake of you hearing something. I still feel things sometimes, but I will be honest with you. It's been years since I've seen clearly into the Other. I don't hold out much hope for you today.'

'But you've agreed to try,' said Helen with an encouraging smile.

'Yes.' Mrs Porter looked at her with a certain sadness, then turned to Lean, her fingers closing a bit tighter on his. 'We can try. But I will need help. My abilities have faded with age. I think the dead prefer the young. More full of life, perhaps.' She took a deep breath and closed her eyes. 'Tell me who you are searching for.'

Dr Steig and Helen both looked at Lean, who weighed his options before answering.

'A killer,' said Lean, and he watched Mrs Porter's eyes flicker open in surprise, then close again. 'A killer of young women.'

There was silence. Mrs Porter's chair began to rock, slowly, barely making a sound on the thin carpet beneath them. More than ten minutes crept past with nothing more than all of their breaths disturbing the stillness of the room. Lean's back was growing stiff from sitting motionless in the hard wooden chair. He tried to stretch without altering the position of his hands. It was then that he noticed Mrs Porter's touch growing cold. Her rocking chair slowed and was still.

'A tower standing in a pool of darkness. It's thick like blood. It's filling with darkness. There's a spark there. A flame? I can see a flame. There's still time. Dear God, please hurry.'

There was silence. Lean exchanged glances with the others as they waited for something further. Another minute passed.

'Floating. In darkness.' Mrs Porter's voice began as a whisper, then grew, but was still soft enough that each of the observers leaned forward to hear better. 'It's tight here. The stones were rough, but now I'm floating.' Her neck arched, and Lean could see her eyes rolling back into her head. 'Stars. So many.' The words drifted out of her mouth. She gripped Lean's hand.

'A little farther, dear,' she said in a lower voice, pleasant still, but urgent. 'Look at the lights, John. Do you see them there? Like little halos. He can't hear me. My mouth is so ... ' Mrs Porter pulled her right hand away from Dr Steig, and her fingertips fumbled about her lips. 'That sound – like starlight breaking, icicles falling. What is it?' She answered herself in her second, lower voice. 'Nothing, love. Come in now. I've got you.'

Her head swung a bit to each side. 'It's dark here. Twisted shapes. Sharp metal. I can't see, John. Hold the candle higher. Stopped. Funny.' Mrs Porter's head flopped forward onto her chest. 'Dirt? Where have we gotten to?' Her hand shot up to her face. She was clawing at something near her mouth. Her body jerked, and she released a pained gasp, as if the wind had been knocked from her.

Lean rose from his chair. 'Mrs Porter!'

Dr Steig also stood and reached across with his left hand to keep Lean from interfering with the woman. Amelia Porter was now still and silent, her eyes shut. Her husband came rushing into the room. His gaze went from his wife's motionless form to the faces of the visitors. He stared at his wife and took a step backward, eyes widened in fear.

'Black.' The word escaped from Mrs Porter's lips like a drip from a leaking faucet. 'Floating. Nothing in the world touches me.' Her eyes flicked open for just a second, and then her head fell to her chest again. 'I'm down below. How? What are you . . . ? What have you got?'

Mrs Porter's head craned upward, as if she was desperate to look away from the table. 'A giant metal circle. Little teeth, minutes on a clock, but pointing out. A cold, dead clock.'

Her body convulsed in a sudden shock of pain. She slumped forward. Lean grabbed hold of her, cradling her close as he lowered her to the carpet. He was near enough to hear her voice.

'I know the truth of all things,' she whispered.

Within a minute, Lean and the others were ushered out of the apartment by an agitated Mr Porter. They found Rasmus Hansen outside, atop the doctor's cab, waiting to take them to Grey's rooms on High Street as previously arranged. Along the way they went over their precise memories of everything Mrs Porter had said, Lean copying it all down in his notebook.

On High Street, the landlady, Mrs Philbrick, told them to go right up, they were expected. Lean took the stairs two at a time and rapped at Grey's door.

'Enter . . . ' Grey's voice boomed out. Lean pushed in through the door as Grey completed his greeting: ' . . . all those who seek truth from the spirits of the dead!'

Lean froze in midstep. Grey's apartment was dark. The curtains were closed, and no lamp or any other light source could be seen. But there was Grey, seated at his desk, arms spread out before him in greeting, enveloped in an eerie yellow light.

'Who dares disturb the thoughts of the Great Spirit Guide Professor Mallephisto?' Grey's voice thundered across the room.

Lean heard Dr Steig chuckling behind him and went to turn up the gas lamp. When he faced Grey again, he could see that two small glass bottles had been placed atop the desk. Grey removed the thin white fabric that had been covering each, revealing the dirty yellow-brown liquid contents.

'What's that, then?' Lean said.

'Phosphorous,' Grey said. 'Dissolved match heads. It was a bit tedious preparing the concoction, but I hope the effect was worthwhile.'

'What effect is that?'

'To demonstrate that whatever displays you think you witnessed at your séance are easily explained and replicated. It's all common knowledge.' Grey handed over a book to Lean, who glanced at the title: *Revelations of a Spirit Medium*, by A. Medium.

'For your information, there were no such displays at all. Simply Mrs Porter going into a trance and making some rather uncanny statements.' Seeing the doubt in Grey's eyes, Lean added, 'And I completely vouch for the validity of the woman's abilities.'

Helen nodded. 'She was thoroughly credible. Gave me shivers down my spine, in fact.'

'It certainly appeared to be an authentic trance.' Dr Steig's head tilted slightly, as if his mind were a scale actually weighing the evidence. 'Though I didn't physically examine her.'

Grey sat back with fingers folded in front of him and said, 'Fine. Let's have it; the identity of the murderer has been unveiled from the beyond. And here we were wasting all our time with an actual investigation. What a fool I've been.'

'She didn't actually reveal a suspect. Although she did call him by his Christian name.'

Grey arched an eyebrow. 'From the beginning. What information did you give her?'

'I did say we were searching for a killer,' Lean said.

'Of young women,' added Dr Steig.

Grey slapped his own forehead in disbelief. 'And you had already identified yourself as a police deputy?'

'No. But I *had* given her my name,' Lean said.

'Then it's no large feat for her to determine where your interests lie. And how many murders of young women have been in the newspapers in the past few months? Easy enough for this Porter woman to sniff out the trail. Continue.'

Lean sat down while he read his notes aloud, then announced, 'I don't know what the whole business is with the dark tower and blood and a fire.'

'Meaningless imagery to set the mood and capture your imagination,' Grey said.

'Maybe. But the rest of it – I think she's describing Maggie Keene's last minutes alive.'

'Interesting. Your analysis.'

'First she's floating, in darkness. It's tight, and the stones were rough, but then she can't feel them. We know that the killer led Maggie Keene to the site through a dark, narrow alley, where cobblestones gave way to earth.'

'That could describe a hundred places in this city. But go on.'

'Then she calls him by name: John. Our man was using the alias John Proctor at the boardinghouse on St Lawrence Street.'

'Also the most common male name in the English language, and the one most likely to be offered by a client who doesn't wish to reveal his true name to a prostitute,' Grey answered.

'She notices lights, like halos. Not a light up close, because the streetlamp near the door to the machine shop had been busted. She only sees the gaslights in the distance. Little halos.'

'An imaginative stretch, but I'm following you.'

'Next she implied difficulty talking; her mouth or lips seemed affected. She touched them like so.' Lean repeated the gestures.

'That could well be a sign of having been drugged. The entire narrative had that tone to it. An affect of the voice similar to one who was heavily sedated,' said Dr Steig.

Lean nodded. 'Then there's a breaking sound. Like starlight or icicles falling. Our man punched in the glass to unlock the door. They're inside now. It's dark, she sees twisted metal shapes, and this man John has a candle. Then she stops, she looks down and is surprised to be standing on dirt. After all, she's inside the building now. Then she gasps, suddenly, like she's been struck.'

'Yes. That is how it sounded.' Helen's wide eyes showed

that her mind was still afire with the memory of the bizarre encounter.

'Next, she was trying to pull something away from her face. You yourself suspected that Maggie had been chloroformed. He must have held a cloth to her lips. At this point, Mrs Porter's body was violently struggling. Then went deathly still. When she spoke again, she says she's floating, and then it's like she's looking down on Maggie Keene.'

'Chloroform has been known to produce an effect in some of a sensation of floating outside one's own body,' said Dr Steig.

Grey shrugged. 'An external perspective would also be naturally adopted by a complete stranger trying to describe an event as she imagined it to have happened.'

Lean continued. 'Then she asks what the man is holding. Mrs Porter's head turned away, not wanting to look, and she starts talking about a metal circle above her. It has little teeth pointing out from the center. The description fits: that giant gear that was suspended above Maggie Keene's body on the crane in the machine shop. Then her body shook, and it was like she was dead. It's the very portrait we've constructed of Maggie Keene's death.'

'Yes, and it's all explainable – Amelia Porter could have learned or guessed all this from newspaper accounts, a visit to the Portland Company, and a few well-placed questions,' Grey said.

'Tell him what she said at the end,' prompted Helen.

'Right. Before Mrs Porter came to, she said, "I know the truth of all things."'

'The same comment that Boxcar Annie reported from Maggie Keene,' Helen explained. 'This man said he would show her the truth of all things.'

'And the same comment that Boxcar Annie, or another of

Maggie Keene's business associates, could have repeated to Amelia Porter. An explanation wholly more plausible than the belief that Mrs Porter actually channeled the spirit of our murder victim from beyond the grave.'

Helen stared at Grey. 'Do you simply refuse to even consider the possibility that someone like Amelia Porter has powers that you or I cannot explain?'

'Oh, I can explain her powers rather easily. Her power lies in the need of others to believe in something inexplicable. People pay good money to have that belief confirmed, that there really is something more out there.'

Helen peered at Grey again, a deeply perplexed look on her face. 'I for one refuse to believe that everything we experience in this life can be observed and measured and explained. That's not life at all. Don't you agree, Mr Grey?'

Grey responded with a weary smile.

'You weren't there,' Lean said. 'We all felt something extraordinary while in Mrs Porter's presence. And I do choose to believe it, whether or not there's any earthly explanation.'

'Believe what you will, but tell me, what have you learned? Are you any closer to the killer?'

'I don't know. But it's a piece of information. Another view of the killing. Something we didn't have before.'

34

On the evening of July 14, Grey pushed through the wrought-iron gate on Danforth Street and climbed the steps to Cyrus

Grey's house. His grandfather's middle-aged butler, Herrick, greeted him with a look of surprise before allowing himself a smile.

'Is the old man at home?' Grey asked.

'I'm afraid not.' Inside the grand entrance hall, with its electric-light chandelier hanging from the ornately paneled ceiling, the paunchy man took Grey's stick and hat. 'Would you care to wait in the living room?'

'The attic, actually.'

'Of course, sir. How foolish of me to ask.'

The pair made their way up two flights of stairs with dark handrails over gleaming white balusters, the treads laid with thick carpet. Portraits of stern-faced men and dour-looking women stared down on them from within large gilded frames.

'Tell me, Herrick, are my mother's old boxes still up there?'

'I believe they've been left as they were.'

Grey took the last flight alone and stooped as he entered the cramped space. Fifteen years had passed since Grey had been in there; it was even smaller and more cluttered than he remembered it. The air was still and twenty degrees hotter than outside, so he hung his coat on a nail and loosened his tie.

The unfinished room, with its exposed wood beams, slanting walls, and rough floorboards cluttered with boxes and junk, was the opposite of every other immaculate, manicured room in the building. It had been Grey's boyhood sanctuary in the first unfamiliar months that he'd lived in the Grey house, the one room that felt like home. It was the only spot where he could hear raindrops on the roof above him rather than the footsteps of some servant milling about, something he'd never experienced when living among his father's people.

Grey inched his way through the room, peeking into boxes of clothes, old place settings, and household records. The attic could never lay claim to being the heart of the house, but in a way it was the soul. The dining room and parlors held portraits and decorations meant to greet the outside world. It was the dusty corners of the attic, however, that harbored the unimportant paper records, mementos, and tokens of small moments that held meaning for only a person or two in the entire world.

After ten minutes, Grey found a box set aside after his mother's death. There were pieces of jewelry, a few letters from friends, and several small advertisements for various stage shows, performances by his mother after she'd first left home to pursue a theatrical life. There was a picture of his father that Grey stared at for a long moment. Beside it was a pipe with a long stem of sumac and a bowl carved from a reddish soapstone. Grey slipped it into his pocket and turned his attention to some books at the bottom of the box. One well-thumbed text caught his eye and he flipped through the pages as he moved to the pale light by the window.

The voices of two boys passing in the street caused him to gaze out through the dingy glass. A faint memory of other boys came to him, accompanied by the echoes of mocked war whoops. Those boys patted their fingers against their howling lips and waved imaginary tomahawks in the air, their war dance directed toward Grey's usual perch, high above in the window.

Grey looked at the frontispiece of the book in his hands. His name was written there in his mother's graceful hand. Violent pencil marks had slashed through the name, and he recalled the incident with a flicker of shame at his childhood rage.

'That's not my name!'

'It's your new name,' his mother said. 'It's a good name. Sir Perceval.'

'A good name? You mean an English one.'

'Things change in life, you know that. This is where we live now, and we have to make do. Things will get better. Soon it will be as if you've been here all your life.'

He could see the sadness at the edge of her eyes, lingering there as it always did in those days, some predator just beyond the campfire, wary but desperate with hunger. 'No matter what my name is, they'll still look at me funny, like I don't belong here. I'll never be the same as them.'

'That's true,' said his mother. 'You will always be different. And that frightens people. But don't let it frighten you. I don't ever want you to be the same as all of them. But you will need to understand their ways to get along in life. It's just something new for you to learn. Why they act the way they do and what they really mean when they speak. So study them, but that doesn't mean you have to be like them. Who you are inside will never change, so long as you live.'

The memory faded, drummed away by a heavy tread on the attic stairs.

'Your grandfather has returned and requests your company,' Herrick said.

Grey handed the box to Herrick. 'Please have this brought around to High Street.'

He started down the stairs. 'By any chance, Herrick, do you recall when my mother and I first arrived here?'

'Of course, sir.' Herrick had been employed by Grey's grandfather all his adult life, working his way up to his present position.

211

'I mean specifically,' Grey said. 'The time of year, the circumstances?'

'It was early spring. A Sunday morning.'

'Really? A rather impressive memory, Herrick.'

'It was Easter Sunday. You were expected, and there was much discussion down below as to whether your grandfather would let the household go off to church or whether we'd all stay and wait. In the end I stayed home, and, sure enough, you arrived while everyone else was at the service.'

'Was there much work required before our arrival?'

'A couple of days' worth of work, I suppose.'

'Interesting. Thank you, Herrick.' Grey moved on to meet his grandfather.

Cyrus Grey sat stiffly in a tall-backed chair at the far end of the massive living room. Near him was a brick-faced fireplace topped with a broad landscape oil painting. Large Oriental rugs filled the floor between him and Grey. Tall windows with floral-printed curtains faced south, while glass-fronted bookcases lined the opposite wall. The old man checked his pocketwatch against a nearby clock, then rose in slow, wooden movements. A strip of white hair circled from one temple to the other, laying siege to Cyrus's bald dome. Long sideburns framed a parched face that looked to have never tolerated a drop of perspiration in its eighty years of life.

'And what have I done to warrant the honor of a visit by my only grandson?'

'Just come to pay my respects.'

'To the dead, as always, not the living. Rummaging around up there, stirring up dust and memories. Find what you were looking for?'

'Yes, actually.' Grey took a seat at the grand piano.

'Damn thing's out of tune,' said his grandfather.

Grey lifted the fallboard and let his fingers hover over the keys. They began to slide back and forth, darting here and there in a silent performance.

Cyrus Grey poured himself a glass of brandy from a crystal decanter. 'The only things up there that would interest you are your mother's old belongings and that old Indian stuff. Things from before.' He waved his arm as if dismissing some unruly child. 'So it's this business with the Indian killing that woman, isn't it? I should have known you'd be involved. Suppose I ought to be grateful I haven't seen your name in the local newspapers yet.'

'I didn't realize you followed my work so closely.'

'Bah! Herrick has a most annoying habit of scouring the Boston papers. I sit for breakfast and there they are, folded out to one gruesome business or another with your name tucked away in there. I'll never understand it. All this fascination with murder and crime. Such a morbid disposition.'

'We don't need to dig up this subject again. It is my profession. There's no point holding out hope that I'll suddenly turn to medicine or the law.'

'You could have, very easily.' Cyrus's age-dulled gaze bored into Grey, as if he were actually trying to see into his grandson's soul. 'I provided every advantage for you. You'd have a more-than-respectable practice by now, in spite of everything.'

'Everything?'

'You know what I mean.'

'I always have,' Grey said.

The old man turned away, fumbled briefly with the crystal

decanter, then tipped a bit more brandy into his glass. 'I can't believe you find it so much better, what you have. A life spent among thieves and killers and policemen.' His tone revealed no more leniency toward the latter than the rest of the disreputable classes.

'It has its interesting moments.'

'Throwing away your life for the sake of interesting moments. That's a poison in the blood you get from your mother.'

'Unlike speaking in the bluntest of terms. Which apparently skipped a generation.' Grey took a step toward the door. 'I really should be off. There are matters to attend to.'

'Of course.' The old man followed toward the hall. 'You could stay for dinner?'

'I have things to see to.' Grey collected his hat from a side table.

'Just one more of my dwindling hours won't ruin you. We can talk of other things. Things that aren't at all interesting, and you can pretend to enjoy yourself.'

Grey smirked and set his hat down again. '*Now* who's guilty of stirring up old memories?'

35

There was a tangle of early-morning delivery wagons ahead on Commercial Street, so the driver pulled up short of the Maine Central Rail Road depot, leaving plenty of room to wheel about and head back into the heart of the city. Lean handed over his coins, then walked ahead and cut through the empty station.

On the other side, he entered into a sort of wasteland, several acres of open space crisscrossed by rails leading to the depot, the rail houses, and other branch lines heading off toward the waterfront. Much of the view of the actual water was blocked by the row of buildings comprising the International Steamship Company as well as the Portland, Bangor and Machias Steamship Company. Still, Lean took some comfort in the sight of the tall masts just to the left of the steamship buildings. Portland's deepwater wharves began there. More than two dozen of them, some close to a thousand feet long, jutted out in a series spanning more than a mile to the east. He was glad to taste the salt on the air; it helped clear his head for what he knew was awaiting him.

He stepped across the tracks and wandered over the dirt and gravel, past sporadic outgrowths of knee-high weeds, kicking aside bits of trash as he went. It was past sunrise, but the sky held a thick cover of gray clouds, rendering the scene even bleaker. A patrolman was approaching, coming from the raised wooden trestle that connected the base of Clark Street to the bridge leading to Cape Elizabeth. They met a hundred yards shy of the overpass.

'She's down close to the trestle. There's a few empty rail cars there.' The patrolman pointed back in the direction he'd come.

'How's it look?'

He shrugged. 'Nothing like that last one up to the Portland Company.'

'Stabbed?' Lean asked.

'Nope. Deputy LeGage says strangled.'

Lean could tell that the patrolman was at the end of his shift and eager to be going, so he nodded and continued on. As he drew closer, Lean saw the shapes of rail cars in the shadows of the

215

trestle with a few people milling about. Directly beyond was the gasworks, dark smoke rising from its stacks. Behind that, even greater amounts of sooty filth were spewing forth from the Portland Star Match Company and the towering stacks rising up above the five-story behemoth of the Forest City Sugar Refinery. He walked on, the last traces of sea salt drifting away from him, overpowered by the combined might of oil, phosphorous, and burned sugar.

At the first of the rail cars, he saw two patrolmen with an old sheet they would use to wrap the body and toss it into the waiting wagon. Deputy LeGage stood nearby and greeted Lean with a thin, tobacco-stained smile.

'What's the matter, Lean, afraid you won't get your name in the papers on this one?'

Lean moved toward the open rail car, not sparing a glance at LeGage. Four weeks had passed since Maggie Keene's murder. Lean still had no suspect, nor any idea of where to find the man. He was beginning to fear he never would, but he mentioned none of this. He smiled and said, 'Just thought I'd take a look before you got around to ignoring the last of the evidence.'

The woman was at the edge of the open rail car, her right arm dangling out from the door. A trickle of dried blood stained the corner of her mouth. Lean bent forward and saw she had bitten her own tongue. There were clear bruises on either side of her neck. Two hands, with thumbs overlapping, had crushed the windpipe. Lean studied the face, noting the differences that death produced: the waxy look of her skin and the drooping of the flesh around her jawbone. The jaundiced eyes still held a look of dull indifference, but now the fierceness had dissipated. It wasn't that she looked peaceful, far from it. It was only that the fight had so completely and horribly gone out of Boxcar Annie's eyes.

Lean stood in Grey's study, glancing about at the clutter of papers, books, and stacks of newspapers that dominated every available work surface.

'Strangled. No sign of any mutilation of the body, so I don't think it's our man. Course, it can't just be a coincidence, either. What I can't figure is, if she was concerned for her safety and McGrath's being paid to protect her, how does she end up by the waterfront to begin with?'

Grey considered the question. 'And as is often the case, the same facts contained in a puzzling question will, when inverted, reveal the likely answer. You misstated one vital element. McGrath wasn't actually being paid to protect her, but rather to protect what she knew about the murder of Maggie Keene. She'd be alive now if McGrath were still being paid to ensure that. Which leads me to suspect that he was finally paid off to achieve the opposite result.' Grey motioned Lean to come closer and held up a document from his desk.

'Records from the Maine Savings Bank show a transfer of two thousand dollars in the week after Maggie Keene's murder, from the temperance union to the personal account of Simon Gould.'

'The colonel's right hand,' Lean said, recalling the man's scarred visage. 'The one with the—'

'The very unfortunate face, yes. As well as an avid interest in library books on witchcraft. Gould withdraws three hundred. One week later three hundred again. Two days ago another cash withdrawal. This time it's one thousand. Within twenty-four hours, Boxcar Annie is roaming free and is murdered.'

Lean studied the paper. 'Gould was paying McGrath off to keep Boxcar Annie quiet. But then they figured it was cheaper to take care of the problem once and for all.'

'McGrath probably knew he couldn't control the woman much longer. She's not the type to stay in one place for any length of time, or to keep quiet, especially when she's drinking. If whatever she knew got out, she wouldn't be worth a dime.'

'He cashed in while he could,' Lean said. 'Took the thousand and put her out on the street. Gould or some other of the colonel's old soldiers was waiting.'

'It's the most plausible theory,' Grey said. 'But we still don't know why the colonel's people were so interested in Boxcar Annie. What did she know about Maggie Keene and her killer that was such a threat to the temperance union?'

While Lean pondered this, his eyes fell on Grey's mantelpiece, which held the long-stemmed pipe he had recovered from his grandfather's attic. 'I didn't think you were so interested in your Indian heritage.'

'It belonged to my father,' Grey said.

Lean nodded. He recalled the mention at the Indian fairgrounds of Grey's father's death and was prepared to let the subject drop.

'It may be of interest to our inquiry, actually.' Grey approached and picked up the pipe, cupping the bowl with his fingers. 'Would you mind having a cigarette?'

Lean smiled. 'If you insist.' He drew one and lit it.

'I noticed something while you were enjoying a smoke with the Abenakis at Camp Ellis. Compare our grips,' Grey said.

Lean held his cigarette between the top joints of his index and middle fingers. 'You hold a pipe different from a cigarette. What of it?'

'I observed that some of the Abenakis held their cigarettes like so.' He took the cigarette from Lean and held it with his thumb and index finger more toward the middle than usual, and the top of his hand facing out. 'It must be force of habit, but they would actually hold the cigarettes in the same manner as a pipe.'

Lean gave him a puzzled look.

'Remember the cigarette butts I recovered outside at the Portland Company? It was damp that night, so the paper held impressions from the killer's fingers. He held the first sample the way you do. Like a white man. The last cigarette, the one he didn't have time to finish, showed imprints from being held in the old-fashioned Indian manner.'

'Which means what, exactly?' Lean smirked at Grey. 'He's only half Indian?'

'If he had Indian blood, Maggie Keene would have mentioned it, and you can be certain Boxcar Annie would have been screaming about it. No, he's a white man. But he displays some connection to Indians. The tobacco in the cigarettes, the mangled quote from the Lord's Prayer, the contemptuous references to Indians in his letter to the mayor. It's an odd mixture of incorporating Indian elements while also professing his disdain for them.'

Lean snapped his fingers. 'That sounds just like the witches. Gives Maggie Keene a witch's death yet calls himself by names of falsely accused witches, but then he goes and suckles at that witch's tit on her side. As if he doesn't know what side of the fence he's on.' He threw his dwindling cigarette into the fireplace. 'Witches and sinners I understand. But what's his obsession with Indians?'

'When we catch this man, we may find that he has spent time among the Indians. He learned some rudimentary speech and writing, adopted some habits, but maybe the experience was unpleasant and left him with contempt for them.' Grey replaced the pipe on the mantelpiece.

Lean's eyes lingered on the pipe. 'Indians have a strong reputation for drunkenness. Among white people, anyway.'

'Hence the liquor-agent ordinance.'

Lean knew the reference. The Portland city ordinance, premised on state law, prohibited anyone from providing liquor, even medicinally, to classes of people to whom it would be dangerous: children, drunkards, others requiring guardianship, and Indians. 'Deserved or not, the reputation exists. So I wonder if Colonel Blanchard has ever spent time among them, preaching sobriety and seeking converts. We need to speak with him.'

36

'I'm sorry, gentlemen,' Simon Gould said, 'but the colonel's schedule is quite full. Perhaps you could call again in a few weeks.'

'If that's how the colonel sees it, then that's how it is.' Lean shrugged. 'Well, we've got some time now. Could head right over to the *Argus* and see Dizzy Bragdon, drop him the story of how the temperance union is in business with McGrath. I mean, since the colonel doesn't have the time to meet with us.'

Gould's lips pursed. His jaw seized up, and the right side of his face, marred by burn marks suffered in the war, trembled. Gould had one of the servant girls bring Lean and Grey to the colonel's study while he went to find the man. The room was an unabashed testament to a view of life as man's contest against all creatures. Sheathed sabers and crossed rifles adorned the walls. A black bear's head, teeth bared, was mounted above the stone fireplace. The only painting on the wall depicted St George slaying the dragon. Other hangings took the form of framed temperance broadsides and annotated maps detailing the actions and troop movements at Gettysburg, Antietam, and Petersburg. There was a wide expanse of windows across the room from the colonel's desk. Nearby, a slender bookcase held texts on military history and a few small framed photographs. Grey studied the contents of the shelves. He picked up one of the framed pictures and peered at it. Lean glanced in that direction long enough to see what appeared to be an old family portrait: the colonel, his wife, a son and daughter. Grey set the frame down as soon as Colonel Blanchard entered the room.

He was not a large man, but he had a commanding presence. His stern, angular face held deep fissures rather than mere wrinkles. The colonel's thick white hair was parted to one side, his coif angling upward like the windswept cap of a snow-covered mountain. His voice matched his face in every way.

'What's all this rubbish about? Coming here, threatening me with lies and accusations. I should have you both bound and dragged. You ought to mind yourselves and be on your way.'

Lean fought back the urge to smile. It was clear that Colonel Blanchard was used to being in command. 'And good morning to you, Colonel. I'm afraid we can't do that quite yet. You see, we've looked into some matters at the Maine Savings Bank. And there's reason to believe that some parties associated with your union have provided funds for the benefit of a Mr McGrath. He's rumored to run some illegal drinking establishments.' Lean threw a look at Simon Gould. 'Which, we can all agree, would be very perplexing to members of the public, especially those who provide financial support for your efforts.' Lean paused, offering the colonel the chance to bluster, but the man didn't take it. He simply stood there staring at Lean with ice in his eyes.

'Furthermore,' Lean said, 'we have information which seems to indicate an interest being taken in the whereabouts of a woman commonly known as Boxcar Annie.' Lean thought he detected the briefest crack in the frozen gaze of the colonel. 'She was a prostitute who had found her way into McGrath's . . . care. That is, until she turned up dead.'

'What do I care about a dead whore?'

'You tell me.'

The colonel's hands balled into fists. 'I could have your job, Deputy.'

Grey cleared his throat. 'Yes, but not before your supporters hear about all this. And by the way, I don't work for the city. Someone here was paying McGrath to keep him informed about this woman and what she knew about the death of Maggie Keene. Perhaps you heard about that one. It was in all the papers.'

'What's your name again?' Simon Gould asked.

'Perceval Grey.'

'I've heard of you.' Gould's milky right eye seemed to linger on Grey while his good one shot an unspoken warning toward the colonel. 'That Keene woman was killed by a degenerate drunk. Two more victims of the demon alcohol.'

'There was probably a nice rise in donations to the cause after that,' Lean said.

'There are always casualties in war,' said the colonel. 'Her death, though brutal, at least served to remind the public of just what's at stake and why the tolerance of liquor must be abolished. Maybe in dying she lit the path to abstinence for a few other young women. If so, her death was probably the most honorable thing she ever accomplished. It teaches a lesson too valuable to be lost. That was my only interest in that matter.'

'Which doesn't explain the later interest in Boxcar Annie, or money heading from here to McGrath, a known whiskey smuggler.'

'I do not associate with either of those types of individuals. No society can prosper in which the ignorant, the depraved, and the vicious associate on equal terms with the sober, the virtuous, and the learned. I associate strictly with a distinct class in society to which neither McGrath nor those women belong.'

'All men are equal under the law, Colonel,' Grey said.

'The laws of man are written by men beholden to the politics of the day. But there is a deeper truth, a law beyond any authored by man.'

'Gentlemen, you must remember. Some of our soldiers for temperance are just that, soldiers.' Simon Gould's one living eye flashed between the detectives' faces. 'They are not saints. So it is not outside the imagination to think that one of our men, in a moment of weakness, acting as soldiers do, might have shown some personal interest in this Annie woman. A soldier's simple indiscretion. There may have been some action taken to keep the embarrassing episode quiet. Colonel Blanchard would know nothing about that, of course.'

Lean looked at the colonel and watched the internal struggle play out for a few seconds. It was distasteful to admit such conduct by one of his men; it reflected directly on him as the commanding officer, a role he was unable to abdicate. Finally, however, Blanchard concluded that it was less damning than whatever the truth was, and he nodded his agreement.

'If there was some type of indiscretion, I don't see why it needs to be made public. I would find the man out myself and deal with him personally. A bit of military justice is much more efficient than that offered by the demands of a misinformed public.'

'I must say it sounds as if you have taken a more militaristic tone than many of the temperance speakers I've heard,' Grey said.

'Make no mistake, Mr Grey, there is a war on, and the stakes are the greatest imaginable: the souls of our children and the fabric of our country.'

'Your own son assists in your work, I take it,' Grey said.

The colonel folded his arms across his chest, his chin pointing at Grey. 'I have no son.'

'Then who's the young man in the photographs?' Grey picked up one of the framed pictures on the shelf in which the colonel and a boy displayed poles and hooked fish.

'He is no longer with us.' Colonel Blanchard walked over to the shelves, took the picture, and set it facedown without looking at it.

'I'm sorry to hear that. How did he die?' Lean asked.

Simon Gould started to object, but the colonel silenced him with a raised finger. 'My son suffered from a weakness of character. He was given to flights of fancy, unwilling to accept certain difficult realities. Let's just say that this inability to bear up against the hard truths of life proved his undoing.'

'With all due respect,' Grey said, 'you display a less-than-sympathetic regard for the boy.'

'It is the nature of things. I take it you are of a scientific bent, Mr Grey.'

Grey nodded.

'Well then, you will be glad to hear that I share an appreciation for the theories of Mr Darwin. Nature's promulgation of those most worthy to carry on the species and all that. The weak are necessarily culled from the herd. This is a point where science and faith need not argue; the theory applies to the slow of foot and also to the morally unfit. Unpleasant to hear, perhaps, but vital to the continuation of our race.' He looked at Grey with a smile. 'By which I mean the civilized races of mankind, of course.'

Grey returned the smile.

'As a gangrenous foot must be taken to save a leg, so must degenerates be removed from society. And so it is true of the political body – the cancer of slavery, that moral blight that so tormented our nation's very soul. There was no alternative to war if our country was to be saved. And thus it is now with liquor, the greatest threat our society has ever faced.'

Grey selected a text from the shelf. 'Then you agree with Mr Darwin's cousin as well. Galton's ideas about the inherent deficiencies of certain peoples. Some have argued in favor of the forced sterilization of habitual drunkards, imbeciles, and the like. I've even heard the argument advanced in the case of certain races – say, American Indians.'

'The developments out west over the past fifteen years lend credence to Mr Galton's theory on the ultimate fate of the Indian. Of course, that destiny need not apply to every individual. Take you, Mr Grey. You obviously have been blessed to inherit the stronger traits of your white ancestry and would clearly fall within that class of Indians who are properly integrated into the civilized population.'

'How kind of you to say.'

'Colonel?' Simon Gould held his pocketwatch in his hand.

'Yes, thank you, Gould.' Blanchard turned his attention back to the detectives. 'If you'll excuse me, gentlemen. I have important matters to attend to. And an hour's idleness is as bad as an hour's drunkenness.'

As they went downstairs to the exit, Lean asked, 'What was all that about Indians?'

Grey waved his walking stick in the air. 'Just a sample of the unchecked idiocy common to parlor philosophers. Those who have trouble distinguishing between windows and mirrors.'

'Ahh,' said Lean with a nod that gave no hint of understanding but indicated an agreement to move on. 'What do you make of the colonel's explanations?'

'For such a sober man, he can lie as well as any drinker I've ever questioned.'

'You know, Grey, it's just that sort of keen perception that warrants your inclusion in the civilized population.'

Grey chuckled. 'Do *I* have a say in the matter?'

37

Lean sat with his son on the parlor floor. He could hear his wife talking to someone at the front door, but any details were lost in the explosions issuing from Owen as his troop of blue-coated wooden soldiers proceeded to massacre Lean's line of red-coated ruffians.

'Archie' – Emma leaned in through the doorway – 'there's a woman here to see you. She won't come in.' Then she added in a whisper, 'Amelia Porter.'

Lean threw on a waistcoat and buttoned up as he made his way to the door.

'Mrs Porter. What a surprise,' he said with complete honesty. He hadn't expected to see the medium again so soon after the séance. 'Would you like to come in?'

The woman shook her head, though by the way she glanced about, Lean could tell she was not altogether comfortable outside the door either.

'Is there something I can do for you?' he asked.

'Yes. That matter you came to see me about.'

'We're still investigating.'

'I know. You see, I ... I haven't been sleeping well since you came. There are' – she gave a little shrug – 'things that remain unresolved, that have not been allowed to rest.'

'Have you seen anything else? Anything you think might help us?'

'Nothing specific. Just a feeling, a sort of dread.' Her gaze dropped to the floor, and Lean suspected she was holding something back. 'It's like ... have you ever knocked on a door and no one comes to answer? But you stand there because you know they're just inside, waiting for you to go away. That's sort of how it is for me. Only in reverse. I'm the one inside the door, waiting for the person outside to knock. And afraid of opening the door when they do.'

'Mrs Porter, are you sure you won't come inside? Have a cup of tea or something?'

'No. I've only come to give you this.' She pulled a folded paper from her coat pocket but did not yet hand it over. 'I was at my kitchen table this afternoon, had just put the kettle on and was making my shopping list. The next thing, the kettle's steamed itself dry and I'd written this. Maybe it will mean something to you.' She forced the note into his hand, then turned away. She made it five steps before he called to her. He saw her shoulders hunch together slightly, tensing for his question.

'Yes, Mr Lean?'

'I know you're not active as a medium. But in the past year or so, have you been visited by a man, maybe smallish with dark hair, wanting to learn about occult matters, witchcraft? Maybe the Salem witches in particular?'

Mrs Porter thought a moment. 'No, I'm sorry.'

'That's quite all right. Thank you anyway. You've been most helpful.'

Mrs Porter retreated several more steps, then stopped again, not turning back to face Lean.

'I'm sorry. I lied earlier.'

Lean said nothing, and the night stretched out between them, silent and empty.

'I *have* seen something else. I've seen *you*, Mr Lean. And there's death all around you. Promise me to God you'll be careful.'

Lean set Mrs Porter's paper on a table in Dr Steig's study, and the others gathered around.

'"The darkness rising beware the Good woman and her child,"' read the doctor. 'What do you suppose it means?'

'I don't know,' answered Helen, 'but it certainly is disturbing.'

'I'll say,' added Grey as he pointed above the cryptic message to where Amelia Porter had begun to write her shopping list.

'"Five pounds of parsnips." I mean, honestly, how many parsnips can two people eat?'

Helen's head sagged toward her shoulder. 'They could be having people for dinner. People do that sometimes – socialize, talk about things other than murder and dismemberment.'

'Ghastly business,' said Grey.

'Returning to the note,' Dr Steig said. 'She was unaware what she had written?'

'Automatic writing. Some mediums do it while in a trance,' Helen said.

'Still doesn't explain all those parsnips. It's not as of you can serve them as an entrée.'

'Can you please be serious for a moment, Grey?' Lean said. 'I find this message, and the obvious concern displayed by Mrs Porter, alarming.'

Grey nodded, and Lean took this as the closest he would receive to an acknowledgment of his concern.

'The "darkness rising" bit. She mentioned that in the séance,' said Dr Steig.

'It's vague. So is the part about the good woman and her child. Why "beware"? Does this "good woman" pose some threat?' asked Helen.

Grey glanced at the note again. 'Good is capitalized. Perhaps it's not a description but a name.'

Dr Steig went to his bookshelf and pulled down the 1892 Directory of Portland and Vicinity. He flipped through the pages. 'Here we go. There's only one woman by that name, Miss Nellie, a laundress boarding at 56 Maple, which appears to be the home of her father, William, a shoemaker. And the last name is spelled with an "e" on the end.'

'Wait just a minute.' Helen bolted up from her seat and moved to the table. She began riffling through pages of stacked research. 'Given that the killer enjoys using names of Salem victims, it just seems a bit of coincidence that . . . Here we are. Sarah Good. No "e" on the end. She was in the first group of women accused as witches. Hanged on July nineteenth, 1692.'

'Does it say there if she had a child?' Lean asked.

'That's why I remembered her. Dorcas Good. Four years old. Also accused of witchcraft.'

38

Lean sat at his kitchen table, the pages Helen had assembled spread out before him like some oversize game of solitaire. Most of the passages had been copied from the texts of the Reverend Charles Upham and George Lincoln Burr, referencing the actual transcripts from Salem as well as contemporaneous witnesses and writers like Deodat Lawson, Cotton Mather, and Robert Calef, the last a rare voice of reason amid the collective Salem delusion.

He had gone through a larger stack of writings, boiling them down to the handful of pages that remained under his nose. This reflected the sum of Sarah and Dorcas Good's role in the Salem tragedy. A mother and her very young daughter, singled out for accusation and condemnation for an illusory crime against God and their fellow colonists. Lean tried to think of the Puritans as mere human beings: flawed, imperfect, reacting to the fears and prejudices of their own ignorant age. But each time he read through the notes, his anger grew.

He closed his eyes and reminded himself of his goal, the connection he had to find. 'The darkness rising beware the Good woman and her child.' He picked up a page and started to read once more the story of the arrest and trial of the first of those accused as Salem witches.

Salem Village, 1st of March, 1692. After prayer, the constables produced Sarah Good, Sarah Osburn, and Tituba. Sarah Good was first examined. In bringing her forward first, the prosecutors showed that they were well advised. There was a general readiness to receive the charge against her, as she was evidently the object of much prejudice in the neighborhood. The family was very poor; and she and her children had sometimes been left to wander from door to door for relief. Probably there was no one in the country around against whom popular suspicion could have been more readily directed. She was a forlorn, friendless, and forsaken creature, broken down by wretchedness of condition and ill-repute.

Next Lean took up the transcript from the hearing where Sarah Good was first charged. It was a transcript in the loosest sense only, capturing not so much the exact words spoken two hundred years ago, but rather the impressions of a prejudiced and convinced recorder, concerned primarily with justifying a result that was never in doubt.

Examination of Sarah Good before the Worshipful Esqrs. Jn. Hathorne & Jn. Corwin.
Sarah Good, what evil spirit have you familiarity with? – None.
Have you made no contracts with the Devil? – No.

Why do you hurt these children? – I do not hurt them. I scorn it.

What creature do you employ, then? – No creature: but I am falsely accused.

Have you made no contract with the Devil? – No.

Sarah Good, why do you not tell us the truth? Why do you thus torment these poor children? – I do not torment them.

How came they thus tormented? – What do I know? You bring others here, and now you charge me with it.

We brought you into the meeting-house. – But you brought in two more.

Who was it, then, that tormented the children? – It was Osburn.

Lean took a cigarette from his coat and glanced down the hall at the bedroom door. Emma would be sound asleep. He moved a chair to the window, lit the cigarette, and blew a deep chestful of frustration and doubt, about two centuries' worth, out into the dark night. The examination of Sarah Good gnawed at him. The magistrate, Hathorne, an ancestor to the author Nathaniel, conducted the judicial proceeding more like a police interrogation. Reading over the record of the hearings and the trials, Lean could not escape the sense of wrongdoing.

The Puritan judges and magistrates set verbal traps for the accused, ambushing them with leading and disingenuous questions, browbeating them with unconcealed incredulity and animosity. They assumed guilt from the first and sought nothing other than to coerce anything that could be perceived as a confession. As Upham's treatise had noted, every kind of irregularity was permitted. Accusers were allowed to make private communications to the magistrates and judges before or during the hearings. In some instances, as in the case of Sarah Good, the magistrate endeavored to deceive the accused by representing falsely the testimony given by another. The people in and around the courtroom were allowed to play a role, by clamors and threatening outcries; and juries were overawed to bring in verdicts of conviction and rebuked from the bench if they exercised their right to do otherwise.

Lean flicked the cigarette butt out the window, then watched it plummet and strike the paved alleyway below in a pathetic burst of sparks that flickered and vanished. He dragged the chair back to the kitchen table and flipped through the pages to find what he considered the most flummoxing event in the whole of the Salem witch trials, an incident at the trial of Sarah Good as reported by a skeptical Robert Calef.

One of the afflicted fell in a fit; and, after coming out of it, cried out at the prisoner for stabbing her in the breast with a knife, and that she had broken the knife in stabbing of her. Accordingly, a piece of the blade of a knife was found about her. Immediately, information being given to the Court, a young man was called, who produced a haft and part of the blade, which the Court, having viewed and compared, saw it to be the same; and, upon inquiry, the young man affirmed that yesterday he happened to break that knife, and that he cast away the upper part, – this afflicted person being then present. The young man was dismissed and she was bidden by the Court not to tell lies; and was employed after to give evidence against the prisoners.

Lean reread the passage, and his mind struggled against the impossibly flawed words on the page. A witness, testifying about an invisible specter supposedly sent forth by the accused, was caught red-handed before the judges maliciously attempting to plant the sole piece of physical evidence from a witchcraft attack. The only response of the judges was to tell her not to lie again before she continued testifying against the prisoner in a matter punishable by death.

He took up another page and began the far more depressing portion of his search for a clue to Mrs Porter's warning.

Dorcas, a daughter of Sarah Good, was brought before the magistrates on March 24. She was between four and five years old. When led in to be examined, Ann Putnam, Mary Walcot, and Mercy Lewis all charged her with biting, pinching, and choking them. The afflicted girls showed the marks of her little teeth on their arms. The evidence was considered overwhelming; Dorcas was committed to the jail, where she joined her mother and an infant sibling who would die before its mother was hung that summer.

On the 26th of March, the magistrates were at the Prison-Keepers House, to examine the Child, and it told them it had a little Snake that used to Suck on the lowest Joint of its Fore-Finger; where they Observed a deep Red Spot, about the Bigness of a Fleabite, they asked who gave it that Snake? Whether the great Black man, it said no, its Mother gave it.

By the account of the Boston jailer, it appears that they both were later confined there: as they were too poor to provide for themselves, the country was charged ten shillings for two blankets for Sarah Good's child as well as the following charges: 'May 9th, Chains for Sarah Good and Sarah Osborn, 14s. May 23d, Shackles for 10 Prisoners. May 29th, 1 pair Irons.' Even little Dorcas Good was put into chains, based on the belief that extraordinary fastenings were necessary to hold a witch, along with the assertion of the 'afflicted' that their sufferings did not cease till the accused were in fetters.

Little Dorcas Good, thus sent to prison, lay there chained in the dark, dank cells for seven or eight months. The permanent effect on her mental condition is reported eighteen years later in her father's petition for damages resulting from the expense of looking after her. Dorcas Good's father alleged that, 'being chain'd in the dungeon was so hardly used and terrified that she hath ever since little or no reason to govern herself.' He was allowed thirty pounds in restitution.

Lean rested his head in his hands and muttered, "'The darkness rising beware the Good woman and her child.'" If there was some connection between Sarah Good and the current killings, he just couldn't see it. All he could see was a five-year-old shackled to a stone wall in an unlit cell, screaming in fear, all because of some fantastical ramblings about a pet snake. Lean considered the unfathomable and often absurd statements that his own son's imagination produced every day and shook his held in disbelief at it all.

There was a sound from the back of the apartment, a moan coming from Owen's room. Lean took a lamp and walked back down the hallway, where he eased open his son's door. The flame guttered for a moment. It was a humid July night, and the window was propped open with a foot-long scrap of wood.

Owen let out another low moan that sounded almost like a protest. Lean peered in the direction of the boy. There was something different. He held the lamp high and moved a step closer. Then he saw it: a dark shape squatting on the sleeping boy's chest. Lean took two quick steps forward and swung at it.

The back of his hand connected with a dense, furry mass. The thing sprang from the bed. It hissed, and Lean caught the glare of its eyes. He waved the lamp, and the cat leaped to the sill, then darted out beneath the open window.

Owen stirred at the commotion. Lean bent and kissed the boy's head. 'It's all right. Back to sleep now.'

He lifted the window higher and stuck his head out. The peak of the small roof above the side entrance to the building was less than three feet below. A nearby tree branch would have let the cat jump to the roof and make its way in. Satisfied, Lean was about to pull his head back into the room when he caught sight of a dark shape. He looked down the alley where something, or someone, had definitely moved.

He closed the window and returned to the hallway, leaving the boy's door ajar. By the time he retrieved his pistol and made it outside to the alleyway, there was not a living creature to be seen. He heard several voices passing a block over, but a trip up and down the alley and around the corner showed no trace of any dark shadows, human or feline.

39

Lizzie Madson tromped up the last dark flight toward her third-floor apartment, one hand on the loose rail, the other halfheartedly holding up the hem of her brown linsey dress. There was the faint rumble of a trolley car moving away in the street below, but otherwise the building was still. Each stair creaked out its lonely objection. She knew that the neighbors were out; the telltale mix of loud voices was absent from the hall-way. She reached the top step and took her key from a pocket sewn inside her short jacket. Peering closely in the dim hallway light, she worked it into the lock, then closed the door behind her. The apartment was not fitted for either gas or electricity. She drew a packet of wooden matches, broke one off, and struck it to light the candle she kept on a small stand just inside the door.

'You here?' There was no answer to her call.

Lizzie stepped around the corner into the parlor and stopped short. She gasped and took a half step back before she realized her error. Surprise gave way to curiosity. Across the room, near the doorway to the kitchen, a white dress was hanging from a peg. For an instant, Lizzie had thought a person was standing there. She crossed over, her eyes fixed on the long-sleeved dress with a sweeping skirt and white lace trimming around the neck. She set her candle down on a table; only then did she see the coiled rope that was set there. Beside the rope was a long filleting knife, the kind used in the fish stalls. Lizzie's brow furrowed at the sight of the strange items on the table. They definitely hadn't been there when she left earlier in the afternoon.

'Hello? You home?'

With her mind still mulling over the puzzle, she turned back again to look at the white dress. Out of the corner of one eye, she saw a flash of blackness – a shadow cast by the flickering candle-light – only too solid, too real.

Before she could look, a hand was over her mouth. A weight pinned her left arm to her side, and she felt her chest being compressed, the air squeezed from her body. She was spun around and slammed face-first into a wall. Lizzie squirmed and flailed, but the body behind her was strong, pinning her up against the wall so that only the tips of her toes touched the floor. She reached out with her right hand, trying to shove away from the wall, but couldn't find the leverage to force her attacker backward. Lizzie's right hand went up to her face. She clawed at the hand that held a rag to her mouth, gagging her. Only now was she aware of an odor stinging her nostrils. Her eyes began to well up.

'Sorry, love . . .' His voice paused in silent struggle.

She could feel his lips brushing against her ear. The voice had been low, with an undercurrent of animal rage, but she recognized it as his. Lizzie's stinging eyes blurred further, and then the tears slipped down her cheeks. For a few seconds, she could hear only the rush of blood pounding in her ears and her own muffled cries, sounding far away as if chained down deep in the pit of her stomach.

' . . . but you haven't been true. Have you?'

Lean sat at a small table behind the front desk of the patrol station. Before him on the table were calendar pages for May, June, and July. His eyes focused on today's date, July 18, then slid over the surrounding squares. Soon one would be marked with an X as the next murder date. Beside the calendar pages was the patrol house's logbook for the previous week. Each entry recorded, using the fewest words possible, all complaints actually lodged with the police. Shorthand notations conveyed names, addresses, the gist of the problem, which officer had responded, and whether anyone had been taken into custody.

Set out in small hills, forming a defensive perimeter around Lean's research, were stacks of recent newspapers. One pile was dedicated to each of the city's four dailies: the *Eastern Argus*, the *Portland Daily Press*, the *Evening Express*, and the *Daily Advertiser*.

A final stack encompassed the latest editions of each of a dozen different weeklies. He was working his way forward in time, toward today's editions. He'd been through nearly all of them and found nothing. From Hannah Easler's murder to Maggie Keene's had been just over a month: Wednesday, May 11, to Tuesday, June 14. It wasn't much, certainly not enough to show a pattern of behavior by the killer. Still, if the killer stuck to this schedule, another body would be discovered any day now. He stared at the calendar pages, willing them one last time to divulge what they knew.

'Where's the body?' He hadn't meant to speak aloud and earned a quizzical look from Officer Bushey.

'Beg pardon, sir?'

'Just something I'm thinking on.' Lean stood and walked past the front desk.

'Oh,' said Bushey, not even trying to fake an air of understanding. 'Well, if it's any comfort, you're not the only one looking for a body.'

Lean glanced over to see Bushey holding a newspaper in his hand. Lean shook his head. 'What've you got?'

'Morning edition, just arrived. Someone saw a dead woman on the side of the road, out in Berwick two nights ago. But by the time he got back with the sheriff, the woman's body was gone.' Bushey shrugged. 'She ain't turned up yet.'

'Let's have the details,' Lean said. Then he listened as Bushey repeated the story's salient points.

A man riding the Berwick Road saw a woman laid out just off the side. She looked so peaceful that he thought she was just asleep or passed out. Her face had a strange reddish color, but there were no signs of injury. Her skin was chilled, and he couldn't wake her. He didn't get a chance to do anything more before he heard a

239

gunshot and saw a man coming toward him out of the woods. He hopped aboard his wagon and didn't look back until he reached town. When questioned further, the man confirmed he didn't recognize the woman. He described her as in her mid-thirties, dark hair, with a plain face, and wearing a fancy white dress.

'Odd,' Lean said.

'York County sheriff's stumped. Putting it down to some kind of hoax.'

She wasn't the next one. The killer never would have left intact the peaceful-looking face and left no sign of injury. A more likely explanation would be that the man with the gun was traveling through when the woman died. Natural causes or otherwise. Too poor to afford a proper burial, or else afraid of being blamed, he found a spot by the side of the road and dug a grave in the woods. Panicking when he saw the good Samaritan stop by the road, he fired a shot to scare the man off. Lean felt a mixture of relief and disappointment.

'Just in case, do you know of any other reports of women gone missing lately?'

'Let's see,' Bushey said. He proceeded to spend a minute looking through a stack of papers. 'Two teenage girls gone and one Chinaman's wife. Our mystery woman's too old for them first two and too pale for the other.'

Lean started away, then paused. 'This was in Berwick, right?'

Bushey glanced at the paper. 'Not quite to town, but on the Berwick Road.' The officer glanced at the paper once more. 'Right on top of Witchtrot Hill.'

Lean gave a slight tip of his hat to Mrs Philbrick, then bounded up the stairs, knocking on Grey's door even as he turned the handle. At the sight of Grey sitting behind his desk reviewing a stack of papers, Lean smiled. He'd found it first. Lean held up the morning newspaper clipping.

'I think I've got her. Two nights ago, on the road just outside of Berwick. And here's the good part, the spot where she was found is called—'

'Witchtrot Hill,' Grey stated. He held up his own newspaper. 'I've already sent word to Mrs Prescott to research the origin of that name.'

Lean's arm dropped to his side, the clipping crumpled in his left hand. 'I assume you've made travel arrangements.'

Grey shook his head. 'No need. We'll learn nothing at Witchtrot Hill.'

'You don't think this is our victim?'

'On the contrary, I'm sure the mysterious woman in white is our number three.'

'And she was found at Witchtrot Hill,' Lean said.

'Correction,' said Grey as he stood and put on his coat, 'she was *seen* at Witchtrot Hill. She was not *found*. The article is quite clear on that point. No body was discovered there, despite a thorough search of the area all around. Which means, of course, that whatever clues might have been left behind have been ground into the dirt by the party of bumbling searchers.'

'Then where are you going?'

'The woman in white was seen at ten o'clock on Witchtrot Hill; then she vanished. It appears this same woman was spotted again, just before sunrise yesterday, less than a mile from here.' Grey handed a second newspaper clipping to Lean, who read it aloud.

241

'Mrs Celia Darton of Winter Street summoned police to her home in the early-morning hours of July 18. Mrs Darton, who lives alone on the second floor, reported being awoken in the dead of night by a disturbance. Fearing a burglar, she peered out her window into the courtyard and alleyway behind her residence. She reported a man in a dark coat and hat moving a woman along the alleyway. A second man from the property next door joined them, and they all departed in a waiting hansom cab. Mrs Darton described the woman as wearing a white dress and appearing to be dead drunk. In her statement to the police, Mrs Darton asserted her strong belief that the unidentified woman had been the victim of some criminal mischief or assault.

'Upon further investigation, the officer at the scene discovered no evidence to confirm the report. No other neighbors witnessed or heard any such activity that night. Of note, this is the fourth time this year that Mrs Darton has reported to the police various instances of disturbances or suspicious behavior at the property next to hers. That is the residence and offices of Dr Jotham Marsh and also serves as the headquarters of his Thaumaturgic Society. Dr Marsh was not at home for comment, and none present at that address were aware of any such conduct as reported by Mrs Darton.'

Lean set the clipping back on the desk. 'What's a thaumaturgic society?'

'The formal name. Known to its members as the O.S.L. – the Order of the Silver Lance.'

'Which is what?'

'Reportedly it's your standard, run-of-the-mill magical society,' Grey said. 'Sort of a poor man's Hermetic Order of the Golden Dawn.'

Lean shook his head.

'Spiritualists and would-be magicians tapping into the mystical wisdom of the ancients and all that. And the head of the order is one Dr Jotham Marsh.'

'Never heard of him,' Lean said.

'I've heard a few vague rumblings. At some point, I may have to devote some further research to the man.'

Lean rubbed his jaw. 'What makes you so certain these two incidents are related? White dresses are not so rare.'

'An unconscious, possibly dead, woman in a white dress is spotted on Witchtrot Hill, attended by an unknown man so desperate to avoid investigation that he starts shooting. Her body then disappears into the night, shepherded away by the unseen man. Several hours later an unconscious, possibly dead, woman in a white dress is spirited away, by unknown men, from the property of a magical society. If it's not the same woman, then you're proposing what?'

'It could be a coincidence,' Lean said.

'Coincidences are only the observations of those too lazy to puzzle out the connections and consequences hidden from casual view.'

Lean and Grey moved down the front walk and left Celia Darton standing in her doorway, her voice creeping up in volume with each step they took away from her.

'There's goings-on next door. And whatever it is, it's against God. I know it.'

Glancing back over his shoulder, Lean gave the woman a brief smile, just enough to assure her that he would treat her fevered ranting with the utmost seriousness.

Lean muttered, 'That woman is—'

'Enthusiastic in her many opinions,' Grey said.

'To say the least.' Lean glanced at his notebook one last time. There, among the details provided in the interview, was the name Lizzie. Mrs Darton was sure she recognized the young woman who used to frequent Dr Marsh's society but whom she hadn't seen come around recently. 'In any event, we now have a possible name.'

They went around the side of the house, up a narrow paved walkway, into a fenced-in courtyard infested with weeds. There was a gate at the back, which opened up into another alleyway. Grey proceeded to make a detailed study of the ground by the fence. After several minutes he stood and brushed himself off.

'There's too much foot traffic to be certain of exactly what transpired. However, it does appear some heavy load lay here along the fencing. The ground all around is damp. The area was washed down. The fencing just above there has been scrubbed. The paint is damaged, and the wood is still wet.'

Lean considered the implications. His mind flashed back to the Portland Company and the message written there. 'It could have been another message. Another line from the Lord's Prayer that someone felt the need to dispose of.'

Grey nodded, then pointed at the ground. 'Leading away toward the front gate, there are numerous tracks. But look here: two straight lines. She was held up and her shoe tips scraped along when she was removed from the courtyard. She was not stumbling, being helped along in a drunken stupor. Her feet were not moving at all. She was unconscious or dead. This yard will tell us no more.'

Lean glanced around at the small, enclosed piece of land. 'Maybe Jotham Marsh will.'

40

The library of the Order of the Silver Lance was a hexagonal room with a floor of black and white tiles. A tall, red-curtained window faced the door, the inside of which was decorated with an embroidered silk scroll. The other walls held broad sets of shelves. The top levels were devoted to various figurines of mythical entities. The Egyptian pantheon was well represented, interspersed with a variety of East Asian gods or demons carved in jade. Above the shelves the white walls extended up two stories to a skylight.

'There was a report filed by one of your neighbors.' Lean reached across the circular table, inlaid with a five-pointed silver star, offering the newspaper clipping with its allegations of a woman spirited away in the night. Dr Jotham Marsh did not move to accept it.

'I never read the newspapers. Nothing but canned bleating. People read the papers to learn what is happening in the world. You couldn't find a lazier and more misdirected guide if you tried. Even when there is no deliberate deception, the accounts either wildly exaggerate or else completely underestimate the actual importance of the events described. No event can be accurately judged unless it is considered with adequate background and perspective, both of which newspapers ignore and the reading public disdains.'

'There is an element of truth to your observation, Doctor,' Grey said, 'especially when it comes to efforts by newspapermen to interpret facts. But as to the simple facts themselves: Mrs Darton witnessed a distressed woman being taken away down the alley.'

'It's not the first time she's complained,' Lean added as he studied the man.

Dr Jotham Marsh was in his middle forties. His dark hair had gone gray at the temples and had started to recede, leaving a sharp widow's peak. His mouth hinted at a bemused smile, but his eyes did not agree. Lean found the man's gaze to be uncomfortable, and after a moment he noticed that Marsh rarely blinked.

'Of course Mrs Darton cries wolf at me. She is an ignorant, uneducated woman. I, on the other hand, am an independent thinker. I do not act in accordance with those beliefs that others cling to, not because they are wise or beneficial to humanity but because they are merely customary. I offer something new and unheard of, and so I am despised, cursed at, declared a rebel. And when I offer these new ideas, and a few others are seen to agree . . . well then, to the unthinking herd, I become something akin to the devil.'

'The devil?' Lean sat up straighter. 'Do your ideas involve the devil?'

'I've encountered few meaningful ideas in my life that didn't.' Dr Marsh grinned, then shook his head. 'Not in the manner you mean, Deputy. The Christian ideas of the devil and hell hold no meaning for me; they are utterly false moral concepts, created by man as a means of deifying his own fears and weaknesses.'

'So you're not a Christian, then?'

'Don't take me the wrong way; Christianity certainly incorporates some valid ancient wisdoms and universal truths, which I acknowledge. But as a religion – no. Like all religions, it teaches that my beliefs are right and yours are wrong; think as I do, speak as I do, act as I do, or you should be struck down and your soul be damned.'

Marsh removed a small penknife from his pocket and, without glancing down, began to scrape and clean his untrimmed nails. Lean noticed that the man had strong-looking hands. Overall, he had the appearance of one who had led a vigorous, active life as a younger man, although the skin had since started to sag a bit on his face.

'Are there many who are active here at your Thaumaturgic Society?' Grey asked.

'Numbers vary and are irrelevant. I would rather have two devoted students than a hundred dilettantes.'

'Speaking of your followers' – Lean fixed Marsh's eyes with his own – 'you had one recently by the name of Lizzie.'

'So we come to the heart of the matter at last. Lizzie ... Madson. I wouldn't really call her one of my followers. She never progressed beyond Adept, Second Degree, before she left us a few months ago.'

'And why did she leave?' Lean asked.

'Students leave for many reasons.' Marsh shrugged. 'Unrealistic expectations are one reason. People think they can simply walk through the door, learn an incantation, and that's that. They do not understand that the key to attaining magical power is in the training of the psyche, freeing and perfecting the will and the imagination. To master both these components of the mind is an extremely daunting challenge. And when these students realize that they prefer to daydream rather than work to develop their abilities, they quickly become disenchanted.'

Grey raised a finger. He was staring intently at Marsh's face. 'You said that was one reason. Is that why Lizzie Madson left?'

Marsh returned the stare, his face revealing no inkling of his thoughts. 'Some students simply come to us for the wrong reasons to begin with. You see, gentlemen, I've devoted myself utterly to the Great Work of Attainment, of becoming an entirely spiritual being, free from the constraints, accidents, and deceptions of a material existence on this plane. The Great Work is the supreme state of the human mind and the single main object of all high-magic rituals. The unification of the microcosm and the macrocosm, the one and the all. Attaining unity of the human soul with the divine spirit. The use of magic for any other purpose, undertaken only for immediate worldly uses, is black magic. Those who come here looking for that path will be disappointed.'

'You don't practice black magic?' Lean asked.

'I have been accused of being a black magician. A great insult. To practice black magic is to violate every principle of science, decency, and intelligence in the delusional pursuit of the petty objects of one's selfish worldly desires.'

'You describe your magic as part of a spiritual journey, yet, if I understand correctly, those seeking less noble goals can wield this same magic to serve their ends?' Grey said.

'Magic has been called a science, an art, and a philosophy. But I prefer to think of it as a discipline. It essentially consists of imagining change, then causing change to occur in conformity with one's true will. But, as in any discipline, progress is not premised upon adherence to society's moral codes or religious tenets. Magic will yield its secrets to the heathen or the saint. Just as you need not be a preacher to discover a new comet or to paint a masterpiece. An unscrupulous person with enough desire and emotion can be quite powerful magically.'

'Why emotion?' Grey asked.

'All magic deliberately intensifies, through rituals, the force of emotion. There is a danger, of course, because those emotions which are the most easy to arouse – hatred, fear, greed – can be among the most powerful. Failing to channel them appropriately can have dangerous results.'

'For someone who doesn't practice it, you know a lot about black magic,' Lean said.

'The way to beat an enemy is to define him clearly, analyze and comprehend him. Once an idea is intelligently grasped, it ceases to threaten the mind. Wouldn't you agree, Mr Grey?'

Grey nodded, as if put out with even having to answer such an obvious question.

'We've gotten rather far afield from Mrs Darton's story,' Lean said, 'that an unconscious woman was taken from here and disappeared.'

'I'm not aware of any disappearing woman. Stage magic is not my area of expertise. Probably a student, or some acquaintance, had too much to drink and a kind gentleman saw to it that she arrived home safely. Mrs Darton's imagination has gotten the best of her.'

'A perfectly reasonable explanation,' Lean said.

'Of course it is, when you consider the facts. But people are mostly immune to the facts.' Dr Marsh lit a cigarette. 'They prefer ideas that inflame the imagination, no matter how preposterous.'

249

'Of course, Doctor. Well, it seems we've come on a fool's errand. Thank you ever so much for enlightening us. We can show ourselves out.' Grey stood and started for the door, then paused. 'Oh, yes, Dr Marsh, if I can trouble you with one more question. Did Lizzie have any particular' – he paused, making a show of choosing the correct word – 'gentleman friend?'

'I'm afraid I can't help you. But as I said, she wasn't connected with the order very deeply, or for very long.'

41

Minutes later, standing outside on Winter Street, Lean looked over the neighborhood of well-kept two- and three-story brick town houses.

Grey approached the waiting carriage they had once more borrowed from Dr Steig. 'Rasmus, the neighbor woman mentioned seeing a brougham with red trim about the doors and wheels. Pulled by a sorrel with a distinctive white patch on its rump.'

The driver's head bobbed up and down. 'Sounds like Noddy Oakes's rig.'

'Any idea where to find him?' Grey asked.

'He works the hospital and Western Prom loop. We'll see what we can see.'

Two loops around the Promenade and half a dozen inquiries of other drivers eventually led Rasmus Hansen down and around the base of Bramhall Hill. There, on St John Street, he spotted Noddy Oakes parked outside Union Station. Completed fours years earlier, the long stone rail station, topped with a series of second-story dormers and fronted with two short circular towers, was by far the grandest of Portland's rail depots. Noddy's cab was sitting in the shadow of Union Station's five-story-tall clock tower, a structure that lent an ecclesiastical air to the depot.

Lean and Grey listened as Rasmus quickly explained the situation to the other driver.

'Sure, I remember it,' said Noddy Oakes, 'on account of that woman they loaded in here. She was in sorry-looking shape.'

'Can you describe her?'

'Couldn't see her face. Had a big-brimmed hat and a dark shawl wrapped about her shoulders. One of the fellows was bringing her along but having a bit of a time with it. Another guy comes running out. You know I don't go poking into others' business, but this second fellow's crying, "I got it! I got it!" Course, with all the hullabaloo, I look and see him holding up a key. A big one – on a ring, like the kind you'd see a guard locking up a prisoner with or some such.'

'So where'd you take them?' Grey asked.

'Over to Spring Street.'

'Do you remember the number?'

'I remember only 'cause I asked, but they didn't give me none. Just told me Spring Street, on toward the end.'

'We'd like to see the spot.'

Noddy protested; he was waiting for a fare. Grey handed him several dollars, and the cabbie gave a tip of his battered hat before leading the way back up Bramhall Hill to the city's fashionable West End. 'Dropped 'em here. They paid well and didn't say another word.'

'What of the woman? Was she moving about yet?' Lean asked.

251

'Nah. The whole ride here, she was about as still as a cemetery in winter.'

'Then you proceeded on ahead,' Grey said.

'Nope. Turned about right here in the street.'

'Because ...' Grey raised a sharp eyebrow at Noddy.

'On account of the boneyard being right there.' The driver jerked a thumb toward the end of Spring Street and the Western Cemetery. 'These wheels on the cobblestones – loud enough to wake the dead.'

'So you sat here a bit longer.' Lean motioned to the closest residence. 'And did you happen to see whether they went into this house?'

'I did take a gander, on account of the woman didn't seem well at all. But they weren't moving neither. Just watching me. Sort of like they were waiting for me to go. I suppose they were embarrassed by the state she was in, trying to get her home on the quiet and all.'

'And you let it go at that. Not curious enough for another look back?'

The cabbie smiled. 'Maybe one last peek.'

'And?'

'They were walking down yonder.' Noddy stretched out his hand; a block away, Spring Street ended where it met Vaughan. Visible directly across the intersection were the iron fence and stone archway at the entrance to the Western Cemetery.

A minute later, Noddy was on his way while Lean and Grey stood just inside the cemetery. Looking in from the gates, they could see the fifteen-acre grounds sloped gently toward the back and to the left. A short distance in front of them was the small receiving house. It wasn't used much anymore, since there were only occasional new burials, those being limited to persons who already had family members in the grounds and in plots with enough space to allow for additional interments. The area just past the receiving house was a wide-open circle that held no gravestones. It provided a peaceful space for quiet contemplation or picnicking.

Trees dotted the perimeter of the cemetery. Beyond the edge of the grounds, there was a drop of about five feet to where the Western Promenade ran past. Another row of trees on the far side of the Prom helped envelop the cemetery, providing only partial scenic views of the Fore River and Cape Elizabeth. The effect was one of pleasant isolation, being above and separated from the outside world. The detectives moved forward, drifting away from each other as they went. The tombstones were generally from the 1830s through the 1870s, mostly small with rounded tops, not particularly ornate. A few pedestals were spread among the grounds, as were some stones decorated with urns or with weeping-willow leaves etched into polished areas above the names.

Lean looked up to see that Grey was in front of him, facing back the way they had come.

'The men in question had a key. The kind you might use to a prison cell – or a tomb.' Grey motioned to the left of the front gate.

Eighty paces to the side of the gate was a row of eleven short, brick-walled tombs set into a short, brush-covered hill. The two men walked past the first in the row. It was smaller and set apart from the rest, which were all spaced at more regular intervals. The main series of tombs were each nearly identical in appearance, arched and slanted upward to a short peak. The brick structures were narrow, and the faces were only seven feet at the height of the gables. Above the family names, most of the tombs were dated in the mid-1850s. The metal doors were only about five feet in height. The keyholes on the massive locks were large, and Lean imagined that a prison-size key would fit perfectly.

Several doors down, Grey stopped. 'The Longfellow tomb.'

'You think they may have hidden the body here?'

'No, I just thought you might feel the urge to recite some more poetry.'

Lean held up a finger and cocked his head, trying to recall some lines. Grey turned his back and moved on. Undeterred, Lean recited, '"Life is real! Life is earnest! / And the grave is not its goal; / Dust thou art, to dust returnest, / Was not spoken of the soul."'

Grey pretended not to hear and looked up at the next tomb's inscription. 'Ingraham.'

'The mayor's family, I suppose.'

'If it is,' Grey said, 'they're going to need a wider door.'

At the third-to-last tomb, Grey stopped again. Lean joined him and glanced at the name engraved in the granite slab above the door. 'Well, what do you know?'

'I don't suppose we can simply go ask Dr Jotham Marsh if we can borrow the key to the family tomb.'

42

'Are you serious?' Mayor Ingraham's face recoiled, setting his multiple chins atremble. 'You want the city's master keys for the

Western Cemetery tombs. My approval to invade the final resting place of Portland's most prominent families. My own family's buried there, for God's sake.'

'Only one tomb.'

'Do you have any idea of the public outcry that would result from the desecration of even one tomb? I'm the first Democrat to win this office since the Civil War. I let you do this, and it will be another thirty years before we're allowed back in.'

'We'd be very discreet, of course,' Lean said. 'Before dawn or after sunset if need be. We could disguise it as routine maintenance. Masonry work, perhaps.'

'Have you completely lost your mind?'

'When that tongue arrived on your doorstep, you wanted me to do whatever it took to catch this killer.'

'Yes. And in the shock of the moment, I meant it. But a month has passed, and I, for one, have regained my senses. Clearly you have not. First I hear that you're harassing Colonel Blanchard, looking into his private financial affairs. And now this: you want to disinter some of our most prestigious citizens. The very thought is positively ghoulish. And why? Because of some daft old lady's story and some hack driver who saw a drunken woman being helped down the street near the cemetery. This is what your investigation has come to – it's insanity.'

'Grey and I believe that this could be the key to our investigation.'

'This was your investigation alone, Deputy Lean. And it has been an utter failure. You've failed me and the good people of this city. You are obviously not up to the task of solving the murder of Maggie Keene. I'll speak to the marshal this afternoon; you'll no longer be associated with this matter.'

'Sooner or later there will be another victim,' Lean said.

'Despite the theories of your insufferable Indian cohort, there has never been any conclusive proof that Maggie Keene's death was anything more than an isolated incident. If there is another murder, Deputy LeGage will handle that investigation. In the meantime, street patrols will increase.'

'That won't stop him.'

'There is nothing more to be done, Deputy. Certainly not by you. If I learn that you've acted otherwise, you will be removed from your post.'

Congress Street was the backbone of Portland Neck, running along the ridge between the high points of Bramhall Hill to the west and Munjoy Hill at the east. It served as a divide, not only topographically but also in a commercial and social sense. Pearl Street, which ran perpendicular, exemplified this. To the south of Congress Street, Pearl was home to the full gamut of commercial enterprises as it ran down toward where the Fore River met Portland Harbor. To the north of Congress, Pearl became residential, and increasingly squalid as it descended to the perpetually rancid tidal mudflats of Back Cove.

A day after their discovery in the Western Cemetery, Lean and Grey stood beside a set of tall front steps on a still-respectable block of Pearl Street.

'What's so important that I had to rush my dinner?' Lean asked.

'In the next few minutes, we will be gaining access to the Marsh tomb.'

Lean glanced about. 'Of course. Why didn't I see it sooner?'

'All we need do is wait.'

'For what?'

'It's who,' Grey said. 'Stackpole's his name. Portland's super-intendent of burials lives at number 67. He should be arriving home shortly. An ideal time: end of the workday, senses dulled, within steps of his own front door. His guard will be down. Everything is in place.' Grey nodded his head across the street. Lean peered in that direction and caught sight of a petty thief named Sam Guen standing in a shaded doorway a block down the street.

'How do you know Guen?' Lean asked.

'I get my supplies at his uncle's Chinese tea shop on Congress. Top quality. On my first visit, Sam tried to pick my pocket on the way out. I paid him to teach me how he operates. Also top qual-ity.'

Sam Guen raised his left hand and tipped his hat. Lean noticed that the man's right arm was at his side, the bottom half of his coat sleeve folded up and pinned to the upper arm to give the appearance of one who has lost a limb.

'There's our man. Don't follow me too close,' whispered Grey as he started off at a casual stride across the street. He fell in ten paces behind Stackpole. Lean followed farther back. He was surprised to hear Grey call out to the man they were trailing.

'I say, good fellow, here now, that won't do at all.'

Stackpole glanced back and saw that Grey was motioning toward him. He stopped in his tracks and took an unsure step backward as Grey closed the distance to him.

'I fear you've stepped in a bit of filth. All them trolley-car horses about and such. That won't do at all if you're heading to meet with anyone. I've been behind you for two blocks and smelled the offending matter the whole way.'

'What? Oh, shit.' Stackpole staggered a bit as he picked up his right foot and glanced at the clean sole. He was lifting his left foot when Grey took hold of his elbow.

'Steady, now,' Grey cautioned. 'You were about to tumble over.'

At that instant, Lean saw Guen brush up against Stackpole, breaking stride for the briefest of moments, and then he walked on toward where Lean had stopped to watch the whole proceeding. The superintendent of burials completed his check of his left sole, then proudly announced that he hadn't stepped in anything after all.

'Well then.' Grey released the man's elbow and lifted his own sole, which was heavily soiled. 'For heaven's sake! There I was heaping it on you, when all along it was me who'd stepped in it. Please forgive my mistake.'

Stackpole smirked, tipped his hat, and admonished Grey to watch his step, then turned and went on his way. Guen approached Lean, brushing past with a smile. Lean's brow wrinkled. He slipped his hand into his own coat pocket and felt a metal key ring there.

43

Lean's eyes settled on the high stone archway of the Western Cemetery gate. From there, his eyes shot left, then right, tracing the four-foot-high wrought-iron fence that ran along Vaughan Street. Cooler air had swept into the area during the day, prompting a dreary evening. While it hadn't properly rained, a thick mist persisted, forming halos around the gas lamps that dotted the sidewalk. He could see no one moving along the street. Lean crossed over and walked along the fence.

'Psst.' Grey stood up from his concealment near the bushes on the inside of the cemetery fence.

Lean carried a shuttered bull's-eye lamp, which he handed over to Grey. Then he stepped onto the lower crossbar of the iron fence, planted his hands between pairs of the ornate wrought-iron spikes, and heaved himself up and over. Grey caught him as he came down on the inside of the cemetery. The pair of them hurried along to the right, toward the tombs and away from the gaslights on Vaughan Street.

'Any problem getting the tomb key?' Grey asked.

It had been no problem at all, since one of the keys stolen from the superintendent of burials unlocked a drawer in the city clerk's office just two floors up from the police headquarters. Like all the surrounding offices, that section of City Hall was empty by half past five. The drawer in question held a variety of labeled keys from the various city cemeteries. Lean had lifted the Marsh tomb key and placed Stackpole's personal key ring under his desk, as if the man had dropped it there himself. Lean held up a large metal key, and Grey gave the smallest of nods.

'See anybody poking about tonight?' Lean asked.

Grey shook his head. 'It's been four days since the last murder. If victim number three is still in there, they're probably never planning to move her.'

Lean threw several glances back toward the street, although there was no need. It would be almost impossible for any unsuspecting pedestrians to catch sight of the detectives as they passed through the dark grounds of the cemetery. They moved ahead with a thin layer of ground fog swirling about their shins. Before them, through the mist, a row of dark shapes appeared. Lean counted to himself as they passed by the tombs. When they reached the ninth structure, both men stopped. Out behind the tombs was a small rise of land that stretched along the northern side of the Western Cemetery. Further above this tangled mass of brush and trees was Bowdoin Street. The houses there announced their presence through a few distant flickers of their interior lights. Otherwise, the cemetery was black. Lean opened the shutter on his lamp for just a second to read the name of Marsh above the tomb's door. He glanced back one last time in the direction of their approach. He could see the small receiving house silhouetted against the faint glow of Vaughan Street's gas lamps.

'Hear something?'

Lean shook his head, and Grey motioned him forward to unlock the Marsh tomb. Lean struggled with the key in the darkness. Grey opened the lamp a sliver, angling the light toward Lean's hands. The key slipped into the lock. There was some initial resistance, but Lean doubled his effort and the tumblers clicked. He glanced over and saw Grey searching for something in his kit.

'Here goes.'

'One moment, Lean. Open it just a touch –'

Lean had already put his weight into it, and the door began to move, slowly at first until its own weight took over. It swung in on its rusty hinges, the loud screech reverberating inside the tomb.

' – so I can oil the hinges first.' Grey fixed an unimpressed stare on Lean. 'The idea was to sneak into the tomb.'

'Night like this, the neighbors will just think it was a banshee,' Lean said.

Grey stepped to the doorway with a dropper in hand and squeezed a bit of oil onto the hinges. Lean moved into the vault. Grey followed with the lamp held high, illuminating the brick-lined interior of the tomb. The whole space was no more than twelve feet wide by eighteen feet long. Lean quickly took in the scene, counting nine coffins stacked in columns. The late-July days had been hot, and the air inside the brick tomb was thick with the unmistakable stench of death.

'I think she's still here,' Lean said. 'Could be hidden behind the coffins.'

Grey aimed the light to peer along the side of the stacked boxes. 'Not behind. She's inside one of them.' He moved alongside the coffins with the lamp held close. 'Here. This one. The nail heads aren't fully set; it's been opened recently.'

The two of them placed the suspect coffin down on the floor of the tomb, closer to the door. Grey took a short crowbar from a deep pocket in the interior of his long coat. He pried open the lid and slid it halfway aside. Grey paused for a moment at what he saw and then let the cover fall open the rest of the way.

Lean took up the lamp for a better look. 'I think we've found Lizzie Madson.' The putrid smell hit him like a wave, and he gasped. His stomach muscles clenched, and he put the back of his hand over his mouth and nose. His eyes watered as hot bile came up in his throat.

Grey pressed a handkerchief into Lean's hand. 'It's been treated.'

Lean clamped the cloth to his face and breathed deeply. A strong medicinal smell filled his nostrils, and after several breaths he was able to turn back and face the coffin once more. Each man tied his handkerchief about his lower face in order to free his hands.

'Good, now we definitely look like grave robbers,' Lean said.

Inside was a body wrapped in a white sheet. It had been dumped into the casket on top of the skeletal remains of the original occupant. The mud-caked tips of a woman's shoes poked out from the bottom of the sheet.

They lifted the shroud at either end and placed the body alongside the coffin. Lean couldn't resist a glance inside at the casket's original tenant. He saw a man dressed in a light gray wool suit, his bone-thin hands crossed on his chest. A ring of scraggly white hair stretched around the head connecting the temples. Dark, vacant sockets gazed up from a face of dried, leathery-looking skin that had gone terribly yellow and was stretched taut over the bones. It looked as fragile as some ancient papyrus scroll.

By the time Lean returned his attention to the more recent corpse, Grey had managed to unfold the sheet to reveal the body of a woman in a long white dress. Her wiry brown hair, tinged with flecks of gray, was matted down over her forehead. The face was blanched, the flesh hollow and sunken against the skull. Lean thought the drooping features gave the sense that the corpse was singularly unimpressed with both her current situation and the answers to whatever mysteries she had discovered upon her departure from this world. Her neck was hidden by the high-collared white dress. The material appeared undisturbed: no cuts, tears, stains, or marks of any kind.

Grey tugged the collar as he bent forward to peek down at the skin. 'No visible marks on the neck.' He rolled the body up on its side. 'Dirt on her back, but no bloodstains.'

'Maybe she's not our third victim. Maybe this Lizzie Madson simply died at Marsh's place and they wanted to hide the body. She drank something wrong. Or just up and died for no good reason.'

'There's always a reason – good or not.' Grey moved away from the woman's head and bent down to peer at her hands, the only other exposed part of her body.

'Suppose there's no need to bother with searching the clothing for hairs and whatnot.'

Grey looked like someone had just stolen his Christmas goose. 'We can rest assured that any relevant evidence has long since been thoroughly compromised by all the post-death man-handling. No, we shall need to rely solely on the corpse itself to reveal any evidence.' He finished looking into the woman's ears and turned his attention to the inside of her mouth. 'We'll need to get her undressed and examine the entire body.'

'Of course,' Lean said, though his jaw clenched at the idea.

After some awkward maneuvering, they managed to get Lizzie Madson's multiple layers off, leaving the body naked except for her panties and knee-high stockings. Once laid out, the body was something of a disappointment. An old scar marred the left arm, but otherwise she had suffered no injuries worth mention. She simply didn't fit with the pattern of the two prior victims. Lean was struck by the sense of the body's frailty. The woman was thin, remarkably so, though he thought that it was in part due to her being dead. People always seemed to him to be perceptibly smaller, entirely less substantial, after dying.

'There just isn't much to her, is there?'

Grey was gently pressing the meatier parts of the palm just at the base of her wrist. 'True enough. There is something rather . . .

263

ethereal to the body.' He took her by the shoulders and rolled her onto her side again. 'And most peculiar is the complete lack of discoloration anywhere on the body.'

'What do you mean?'

'You've seen when a dead person lies in one position, how the blood naturally pools at the low point and the skin there becomes discolored, bruised-looking. If left in that position for long enough, the discoloration will remain even if the body's position is subsequently altered. Yet her skin is absolutely blanched all over.'

'The man who saw the body at Witchtrot Hill said she was very red in the face.'

Grey peered close at Lizzie Madson's ashen face. Then he lurched toward her feet and yanked off her stockings.

'What are you doing?'

Grey didn't answer. 'The lamp, Lean.'

Lean picked up the lamp and held it near the corpse's feet. Grey was holding up one ankle for close inspection. The deep imprint of rope marks was visible, circling around the lower calf several times.

'How did you know?'

'She was red in the face because her blood had rushed to her head. She'd been hung upside down, and the witness at Witchtrot Hill saw her shortly after.' Grey paused, his eyes running over the corpse once more. 'That explains why no discoloration.'

Lean arched an eyebrow in puzzlement as he waited for further explanation.

'She's suffered no injury of the extent that it would take. But if I didn't know better, I'd say she was near wholly exsanguinated. Drained of blood.'

'I know what it means,' Lean said. 'But how?'

'That is the mystery.'

Lean watched the progress as Grey began at the toes, searching between them for any cuts, bruising, discoloration, or even traces of needle marks. He continued upward, checking closely all the creases and wrinkles in the skin around the backs of the knees and elbows. When Grey reached the shoulder area, he let out a quick gasp. 'What have we here?'

Lean moved in for a clearer view at her left underarm, where Grey pointed toward what looked like a sizable yellow spot.

'What is that?' asked Lean.

'Sealing wax.' Grey pried and scraped away the dried, putty-like substance. Beneath it was a jagged tear in the flesh, the edges of which were crusted with blood gone black. 'He hung her upside down, then must have managed to puncture the heart or the subclavian artery. Dr Steig can tell us more after a post-mortem.'

They set about dressing the body again.

'Now we just need to explain how and where we found the body. Any mention of these tombs and we'll both be jailed,' Lean said.

'I'll claim to have discovered her at some hidden location, away from here. An anonymous tip. The mayor will have nothing to complain about.'

Lean opened his mouth to comment but stopped at the sound of a dog's bark, not too far off. He hurried to the door and stepped outside. Vague, dark shapes of tall grave markers were visible for a short distance before all was lost in the thick, misty air. Normally Lean would have looked out and seen a smattering of distant lights peeking from the thick, forested shores of Cape

Elizabeth in the distance, across the Fore River. Tonight, however, there was only the gray shroud of fog and mist. A slight movement to his side caught Lean's eye. He looked left and homed in on the gas lamps that dotted Vaughan Street. There, at the edge of a misty cone of light beneath one of the lampposts, he saw a figure in white, standing deathly still and seeming to stare back in his direction. In another second the figure slipped away, vanishing into the dark.

'Grey!' He glanced into the tomb and saw Grey examining Lizzie Madson's fingernails.

There was another bark. Lean was sure it was close enough that the hound had to be within the cemetery. He hurried back to the coffin.

'Shutter the lamp. Someone's out there in the light – watching us.'

Grey was peering at some smudges on the fingertips of his gloves. He glanced up at Lean's news, weighed it for a moment, then frowned. 'Are you sure?'

'No. But in either case, we've lingered too long.'

Grey wrapped the sheet over her again, and the two men hefted her up at either end. Once outside, Lean pushed on the tomb door a touch harder than he meant to. It closed like a cannon shot, reverberating against the cavernous walls of fog that surrounded them. A dog answered in the distance, three angry barks echoing through the misty air of the burial ground.

'Damn!' Lean managed to get the key into the lock and secured the door.

'Over the hill.' Grey motioned up the rise at the back of the row of tombs. 'If there's a night watchman with that dog, he'll be coming from the gate.'

With the wrapped body of Lizzie Madson stretched out between them, the detectives struggled up to the top of the rise that encased the tombs, then fought their way through a stretch of gnarled, scraggly brush. Several more angry barks sounded out behind them. They rushed across the open ground to where the black wrought-iron fence separated the cemetery from the rear of several houses lining Bowdoin Street. Lean saw no one in the backyards or on the street beyond, which was unlit and scarcely populated.

'Heave her over,' Lean said.

Grey shook his head. 'Leave her here. The watchman will find her in the next few minutes and save us the problem of reporting the body.'

Lean was unsure of the plan, but Grey had already dropped his end of the winding sheet and was in the process of rolling the corpse out onto the ground. Grey then bundled up the shroud to take with him. Both men took hold between the metal spikes that decorated the top of the fence and heaved themselves over.

Once they were past the houses and out to the street, the only thing visible nearby was Bramhall, the sprawling mansion built by the sugar magnate John Brown. The grand edifice was lit up like a fairground, sitting alone in the midst of sweeping lawns that were roughly the size of the entire Western Cemetery. They continued to where Bowdoin Street crossed Vaughan and turned right, heading back toward the front gate.

'She was right up ahead,' Lean said. He saw Grey's dubious look and added, 'The woman that I saw looking down toward us.'

'It was a woman?'

Lean nodded. 'Yes, a woman in a long white dress. Right under this lamp. She was staring right toward me.'

Grey stopped near the stone archway of the entrance and regarded Lean. 'And this mystery woman, in the long white dress, just vanished into the mist. You saw her right after we had discovered the body of our murdered woman, also wearing a long white dress.'

'I know what I saw.'

'I have no doubt that you are sure of that.'

A low growl rose through the fog. It was coming from inside the cemetery. Lean peered toward the fence but could see nothing. They crossed the street and walked along. Rasmus would be waiting for them two blocks ahead. Lean looked back toward the cemetery and squinted, making out a low, black form prowling back and forth inside the fence. A high whistle sounded in the distance, and the shape disappeared back into the darkness and fog.

Once they reached the carriage, Rasmus Hansen flicked his switch and the cab started forward, clattering over the pavement stones. The sound was lonely and angry among the quiet streets of the West End.

44

Lizzie Madson's body lay upon the examination table in the morgue. Dr Steig used a thin metal probe to indicate the wound in the underarm. 'Obviously, the puncture to the subclavian is what killed her. It wasn't a surgically precise wound. I'd guess the killer knew enough anatomy to accomplish his task, but he's not highly skilled. The wound's somewhat ragged, and that's what your colleague, Deputy LeGage, seized on.'

'He's definitely calling it accidental?' Grey asked.

Lean nodded. 'He's chalking it up to the woman's being drunk and foolishly trying to climb over the spiked fence. She slipped and suffered the wound on one of the sharp iron tops. Bled to death there, just inside the cemetery grounds.'

'He's not troubled by the total absence of blood at the scene?'

Lean shook his head. 'He's not the type to let the smaller details worry him. Rain washed away the blood.'

'We haven't had the kind of prolonged torrent that would be required to rinse all visible traces of blood from her white dress after so violent an end.'

'True enough,' Lean said, 'but he has his explanation and considers the case solved. Doctor, I saw you checking her fingernails. Did she scratch him?'

'No flesh under her fingernails,' Dr Steig said. 'Some plaster, actually.'

Grey peered at the right hand. 'She was likely attacked indoors and didn't have a chance to fight him off.'

Dr Steig nodded. 'There's a clean slit on one fingertip. Enough to bleed, but not at all serious. Otherwise, only some mild premortem bruising to the face and on her right wrist.'

Lean said, 'He could have taken her by surprise.'

'Perhaps,' Grey replied.

'Or do you wager she knew the man, trusted him?' Lean said.

'I won't wager.'

Lean waited for him to elaborate, but Grey showed no signs of cooperating.

269

'Because it's a sin?' Lean ventured with a smirk.

'In the intellectual sense anyway. Guessing or gambling is the last resort of the desperate and the foolish. Why trust blindly to chance when a valid solution is perfectly discernible?' Grey drummed his fingers on the examination table. 'We just need to know more about this woman. And, more important, who her associates were.'

'Once news of the body reaches the papers, someone will come forward,' Lean said. 'Then I can charge Marsh and his cronies.'

'I don't think that's a realistic option,' Grey said.

'He meddled with a murder investigation and disturbed that poor woman's body.'

'How would you ever explain everything? Due to your secret knowledge of other unreported murders, you had reason to suspect that a new murder victim had appeared behind Marsh's property. Two of his society members, rather than calling the police, had covertly moved the body to Marsh's tomb. And you knew this because you employed a pickpocket to steal the key ring from the superintendent of burials. Then you broke into a city office to get the tomb keys so you could illegally enter a family's burial tomb to discover a mutilated body.'

Frustration began to mount in Lean as Grey continued.

'And when you somehow manage to convince Mayor Ingraham not to fire you, then what? There's no evidence that Marsh was involved in the actual murder, only that his people moved an already dead body and interred it illegally. A crime, certainly, but no worse than our own actions.'

'So we do nothing about victim three,' Lean said.

'On the contrary, we do everything we can about her. Same as the first two. We find our man and stop the next one.'

'That plan hasn't worked so well yet.' Lean knew that it made sense, but knowing it did little to take the sting out of the situation. He felt like he'd been punched in the gut, then told he couldn't hit back.

'No, it hasn't.'

They all turned at the voice and saw Mayor Ingraham standing in the doorway.

'I suspected I might find the two of you here. I'm not a fool, Deputy. A dead woman just outside the tombs you wanted to open. And now I have your confession. It's enough to discharge you' – the mayor pointed an accusing finger – 'and see the both of you before a judge.'

'Where I, for one, will gladly testify as to what we found in the Marsh tomb,' Grey said. 'Exactly what your deputy told you we would find. A murdered woman, whom you refused to search for, out of fear of outraging the city's most prominent families. I'll also mention this is the work of the same man who killed Maggie Keene. A man whose description we've had for over a month, resulting from an investigation which you demanded we keep secret from the public – out of fear of causing a panic, and being ridiculed for involving an Indian in the matter.'

'You're twisting the facts!'

'Not nearly as much as the papers will,' Grey countered, 'once they get a whiff of you placing your political standing ahead of finding a murderer who is stalking Portland's streets.'

'There's no firm proof of any of that,' Mayor Ingraham said.

Lean took a step forward, his palms out, pleading for reasonable minds to agree. 'But you've heard what we found. You know we're right about this.'

'I know no such thing.'

'You know the man who came to your door and left that tongue is still out there.' Lean said with quiet urgency. 'Ready to kill again if he's not found.'

The fervent look on Ingraham's face wavered for the first time since entering the morgue.

Dr Steig set down his probe and approached the mayor. 'You risk a debacle if he strikes again and the truth comes out. What will you lose by letting the investigation continue?'

'If they're wrong, and it gets out that I was complicit in all this – searching citizens' bank records, defiling tombs – I'll be finished.'

'You needn't be complicit,' Lean said. 'This doesn't have to be an official investigation. Just let us proceed without interference.'

'And if you fail – and this becomes public?' A look of desperation entered the mayor's eyes. 'I'll need your solemn word that neither of you will ever bring my name into this.'

'Done.'

'Agreed,' Grey said.

The mayor's doubt was still clear upon his face. He looked to Dr Steig, who nodded.

'There's no other choice. Lives are at stake.'

The mayor nodded back. As he turned to exit the morgue, Mayor Ingraham's hand gripped the door frame. 'Good luck, gentlemen.'

It seemed that he wanted to say something more, but those words had ended his involvement. The mayor was left with nothing else but to hurry away down the hall.

'I almost feel sorry for him,' Dr Steig said. 'If we make him

272

reverse course on this investigation one more time, he might keel over.'

'He's a politician,' Grey said with a wave of his hand, 'he'll be just fine.'

'So where does that leave us?' Lean asked.

'There's some connection between the killer, the victim, and Jotham Marsh. I'll make inquiries. See what I can find out about this Lizzie Madson,' Grey said. 'If you can spare time from your regular duties, it may still be worthwhile looking into the circumstances of the fire at Old Stitch's. Something about that story still intrigues me.'

'I'll see what I can do.' Lean looked out the window. Disappointment settled onto him. They had just discovered the third victim, yet all it seemed to gain them were more random threads in this jumbled web of murder, witches, Indians, and black magic. 'But first I'm going to have a word with Marsh. No matter what I can or can't prove.'

Lean and Grey stood in the long entry hall to Jotham Marsh's Thaumaturgic Society. The interior door opened, and Marsh appeared, accompanied by a younger man with dark, slicked hair and a fine worsted sack suit.

'Gentlemen, I am in rather a hurry. Is there something important enough to demand immediate attention?'

'How about the dead body of Lizzie Madson? She was found murdered inside the Western Cemetery fence last night. It appears from new information that it was Lizzie Madson who was seen leaving these premises several nights ago.'

'Well, that is something. Of course, I've heard otherwise – that the police are treating this as an unfortunate injury, not a murder.'

Lean frowned at how quickly Marsh had come by that information. 'In any event, she was here that night, and I want to know everything about it.'

'Do you know anything about this, Jerome?' Marsh asked.

The younger man nodded toward Marsh with a hungry, almost desperate look in his eyes. 'There must be a misunderstanding. Lizzie was not here that night. I was in the cab that left here. We were only escorting another young lady who'd had too much to drink. Certainly no crime in that.'

'Your neighbor and the carriage driver will be able to confirm that the woman they saw that evening was Lizzie.'

'What about it, Jerome?' Marsh said.

'Oh, that's right, it was Lizzie in the cab that night.' The man's mouth formed contemptuous shapes when he talked. 'We got as far as Spring Street. She was going to stay with some friends there. But she became most agitated and refused any further assistance. Ordered us off in no uncertain words, and we left. She must have suffered her accident shortly thereafter.'

'There wasn't enough blood on the ground thereabouts. There was no accident at that location. Lizzie Madson had already bled to death before arriving at the cemetery.'

'If that was proved true, I'm utterly puzzled how it could be,' Marsh said.

'Oh, that's right,' Jerome said in a matter-of-fact tone, not caring whether he was believed. 'Forgive me, so absentminded. I found her dead in the backyard. No idea how she got there. In any event, I simply panicked. I didn't want the society to be associated with such an ugly tragedy. So I moved her to the cemetery. It seemed for the best – so she could be found by the right people and given a proper burial.'

'Well, there you have it, gentlemen. No matter what peculiar ideas you may have in mind about Lizzie Madson – who she was, how she may have died, where she was found, lying on the ground by the cemetery fence, you say. All certainly peculiar. But she was a troubled young woman, with no current connection to this society. And even if she was here that night, you said yourself that she'd already met her tragic end. My associate would be found guilty of nothing more than a youthful indiscretion, occasioned by his utter dismay at discovering a dead body.'

Lean stared hard at Marsh. 'You know what really happened to Lizzie Madson.'

'The first I've heard of it, and I can't imagine how you would ever establish otherwise.' Marsh gave them a smile. 'I believe there's nothing more to discuss, gentlemen. Jerome will show you out.'

Jerome approached the detectives. He placed his hand on Lean's upper arm, but Lean shrugged him off.

Lean pointed a finger at Marsh. 'I know you people are up to something here. I'm not finished with you.'

Marsh didn't answer. He barely acknowledged Lean's comments, focusing instead on the still-silent Grey.

'On the contrary,' Jerome hissed at Lean, 'if you're not more careful, you'll be the one praying that *we're* finished with *you*. You haven't the slightest idea of what we're accomplishing here.'

'There is one thing I'm pretty damned sure of,' Lean said.

'What's that?'

Lean's right fist shot up, snapping Jerome's head back. The man stumbled, then dropped to the floor, his oiled hair knocked out of place and blood flowing from his broken nose. He reached for his face, then cast a wounded look at Marsh.

'Thought so,' Lean said with a nod.

'Quite unnecessary,' Jotham Marsh said. 'Mr Grey, I suggest you keep that bulldog of yours on a tighter chain. Best for all, I do believe.'

Grey gave Marsh a tip of his hat before turning to follow Lean out the door.

45

Lean held the key to Lizzie Madson's apartment. He had commandeered it the day before from the building's owner, a disinterested man who lived and worked comfortably far away from this run-down building on Oxford Street. The owner told them that Lizzie Madson had paid three months in advance and lived alone. Any other facts were more likely to come from the neighbor, who at that very moment was hovering over Lean's shoulder as if the deputy were reading a copy of the only newspaper printed in the past twenty years. The lock twisted hard, and Lean lowered his shoulder to budge the door open.

'No, like I said, I ain't ever seen a man with her,' said the neighbor. ''Course, these walls being thin as they are, I could hear when a fellow was in there with her, plenty of times.'

'Lots of different men?' asked Grey.

'She weren't like that. I don't know if she were all right, but she weren't no peddler's trull neither. Besides which,' added the man, 'I could always hear it was this same one guy on account of he sometimes had a hard time talking.'

'What's that mean? Drunk?' Lean held the door just an inch

ajar, unwilling to give the gawking neighbor any more of a view.

'Nah, just not talking good. You know, couldn't get the words out of his mouth. Especially when the two of 'em were getting into it over something or another.'

That bit matched Boxcar Annie's description of Maggie Keene's last customer. Lean shot a look at Grey, who nodded at the connection. The two of them stepped into the room.

'Thank you. We'll let you know if we have any further questions.' Lean closed the door as the neighbor craned his neck, trying to see into the apartment.

Lizzie Madson's rooms were plain and simple. The parlor held a small square table with two mismatched wooden chairs. Off that room was a small kitchen, and the back held an equally unadorned bedroom. Lean and Grey went through the parlor thoroughly, working their way toward the back bedroom, which held only a narrow dresser and a bed.

'Interesting,' announced Grey.

'What? There's nothing here. No trace.'

'Don't you find that peculiar? Lizzie Madson lived here for two months with a frequent, but unseen, male guest with whom she had loud rows in the time before her murder. And yet this place is devoid of any indications of the sort of person she was. A few implements and scraps of cloth show she earned a bit as a seamstress. But that's it. It's hardly lived in.'

Lean shrugged. 'She didn't have much to her name.'

'Yet she's paid up months in advance.'

'Apparently our marble-mouthed killer has money enough.' Lean glanced into the tiny kitchen without bothering to step in. 'Did he plan to kill her this whole time, the two months he's been renting this place for her? All that planning, and all the effort he took with the body, yet he's left us nothing.' Lean could feel confusion spread over his face.

Grey held up a cautionary finger. 'Nothing can be learned if nothing has happened. That is true. But much has happened here, in a manner of speaking. Consider the victim. She was brought to Witchtrot Hill, murdered, and then brought back to Portland again. Clearly he places some distinct importance on specific sites. Yet she is different from the two prior victims. It's the first time he hasn't simply selected a victim who was convenient to the location. And also she is the first that he moved after the fact. The first two were mutilated and left as they lay.'

'But here,' Lean finished the thought, 'he hid the wound, redressed her in unsoiled clothes.'

'Why is she different? Why, after the murder, does he treat this body with greater care?'

'He cared for her in some way?' Lean waved off this idea. 'You can't attach human emotions to such a beast.'

Grey shook his head. 'It's a mistake to view him so. However ghastly his deeds, we must remember he's just a man. Granted, he killed her in a most gruesome manner, but perhaps our killer really was Lizzie's tongue-tied beau. It's not inconceivable that in some way he felt a reluctance, if not genuine remorse, about killing her.'

'I don't know about remorse.' Lean spit out the last word. 'Certainly less violence against the body. Not even signs of a struggle.'

'Until now.' Grey moved over to a wall beside the doorway to the small kitchen. Lean joined him and saw three scratches dug into the wall about five feet off the floor.

Grey held his own hand up and fitted three fingers into the

grooves gouged into the wall. 'The plaster under her fingernails. This is where he attacked her. She was pressed up against the wall until she was subdued. Perhaps chloroform again. Took her by surprise.' Grey glanced around the room. 'She was coming through from the front door. He came up from behind, around the corner.' Grey motioned to the kitchen doorway a few feet off.

Lean stepped in to inspect the kitchen. A brick chimney ran up one wall, and a small cast-iron woodstove stood at the base. The two detectives started toward the counter and the few spare furnishings that occupied the space near the chimney. Passing through the center of the room, Lean noticed some small dark spots splattered underfoot. 'What's that on the floor?' He knelt down for a closer look.

'Lean.'

He looked up at Grey, who was rubbing his right hand with the fingers of his left, his eyes fixed instead on the ceiling. It took Lean a moment to grasp what he was seeing. Letters were scrawled there, thick and crude, like finger painting: AMANTA PATCHI WAWITTA SPEMKIK DALI O NOBI DALI KIK.

'"May it please the Creator there in the above land here the same on earth,"' Grey recited the passage. 'Line three of the Lord's Prayer. But once again queerly worded.'

Lean drew out his handkerchief, dabbed it on his tongue, then rubbed at one of the stains on the floor. Grey opened the curtains above the sink. With the improved light, Lean could see a reddish-brown smudge on the cloth.

'Blood.'

'The message explains the cut Dr Steig noted on Lizzie's fingertip. He bled her enough here to spell out his message.' Grey was still massaging his right hand.

'You all right?'

Grey seemed confused by the question, then glanced at his hand. He stopped rubbing it, although he continued to flex the fingers as if they ached. He then peered at the floor, his gaze moving outward in concentric circles. It stopped at the wood-stove. He leaned forward and ran his finger along the floor where a thread of ashes had fallen in front of the grate. He studied the ashes, then rubbed them between his fingers. 'Someone's been burning papers.'

Grey took the handle to the woodstove's grate and eased it down. The two men peered into the opening. Inside was a short stack of burned and blackened papers. Grey reached in very gently and tried to ease out the twisted, carbonized top sheet. It crumbled in his hands, the small black shards falling in wisps to the floor.

'I'm going to need very thin tracing paper, several boards, pins, a solution of gum arabic – fairly clear – a razor blade, some cloth rags, a wide cooking pan with a bit of water. And, just in case, about a dozen small panes of glass. Eight by ten.'

46

The next afternoon, Grey sat at his work desk. He ignored the six panes of glass set atop the black rectangles he had reconstructed from fragments of burned pages. Instead he focused on a single sheet of white paper that held two separate lines of his own handwriting: '*Kia K'tabaldamwogan paiomwiji. Amanta patchi wawitta spemkik dali o nobi dali kik.*' The words left above Maggie Keene and at Lizzie Madson's apartment were the killer's attempt to render the second and third lines of the Lord's Prayer in Abenaki. Grey closed his eyes and let his mind stare into the darkness. The lines were simply wrong. He felt his hands sliding along the edge of the desk, and he gripped the sides.

He saw a man standing before him, old and pale, with a stern face behind round spectacles. It was Mr Copeland, his first tutor in his grandfather's house. The man stared at him, arms crossed, one hand holding a long wooden pointer. Grey was seated, with his hands pressed flat against the top of his child's desk

"'Our Father in the above land sitting, made glorious like a great chief is thy name. May it be pleasing to you, give us today our everyday bread.'"

'No, no, no!' Mr Copeland's eyes widened in exasperation. "'Our Father which art in heaven, hallowed be thy name." Your translation is wretched enough. But then you're skipping lines. Now, listen.' He whacked the desktop with his pointer. "'Thy kingdom come"!' The tutor struck again. "'Thy will be done, in earth as it is in heaven"!'

Grey stared into the pale, watery eyes of this man who would have him pray to God as the white men did, not as his own father had taught him. "'Our Father in the above land sitting, made glorious like a chief is thy name. May it be pleasing to you, give us today our everyday bread.'"

He heard the tutor's stick cutting through the air, then felt his right hand burst with pain. He clenched his teeth and sucked in his breath.

'Correctly, now! "Thy kingdom come. Thy will be done, in earth as it is in heaven."'

"'Our Father in the above land sitting, made glorious like a chief is thy name. May it be pleasing to you, give us today our everyday bread.'"

The stick came whipping down again.

Lean rapped at the door, then stepped into Grey's parlor. The shades on the right side of the room were open. The long table near those windows, normally a mess of equipment and papers, had been organized with everything stacked in small piles close to the perimeter. Grey was seated, holding the edges of his desktop. He released his grip and began to rub at his right hand again, the way he had at the apartment the day before.

"'Dead he lay among his books! / The Peace of God was in his looks,'" Lean said with a smile that faded as soon as Grey peered up from the table where he was working. He was still in yesterday's clothes, eyes glazed, dark circles hanging beneath like anchors. 'Have you slept at all?'

He was swamped with regret over his failure to assist Grey. The day before, Lean had observed the start of the laborious process of retrieving each burned page from the stove, moistening the page by close exposure to a damp cloth, so that it would be less brittle and less likely to disintegrate when gently pressed into place on tracing paper covered with a thin layer of gum arabic. Sheets that had broken apart involved a much more delicate and lengthy reassembly process. Finding that he was of little use in the endeavor, Lean had excused himself and started to make inquiries on a long-neglected task. It was a side note at best, but still Grey had seemed interested and there might be something to it.

Grey waved off Lean's remark and, with a satisfied smile, motioned toward the table. 'Come, see what I've done.'

Lean moved closer. In the dim light, it was impossible to read the carbonized papers. They looked like nothing more than black rectangles. 'Remarkable. But what do they say?'

'I have no idea. The ink on the page is practically invisible to the human eye.'

'Then why—' Lean stopped himself as it occurred to him that Grey had just completed some massive waste of time and the man's smile was the result not of success but rather a mild delirium caused by lack of sleep.

'To the human eye. Fortunately, modern technology has given us something better: the camera. I'm hopeful that the ink on the pages will be discernible in the photographic images. I had pictures taken of each an hour ago. Now we must wait.'

'So you're free this afternoon,' Lean said.

'What do you have in mind?'

'I have a lead on the fire at Old Stitch's place over at Back Cove.'

'Yeah, I remember it. That was back ... oh, early seventies maybe. We took the engine across Tukey's Bridge, but the place was down in a little hollow in through the woods. Couldn't reach it with the truck hoses.' Noah Cobb, captain of Casco Engine No. 5, had a far-off look in his eyes as he stood in the broad doorway to the engine bay. It was like he was back there again on that day, every detail still perfectly captured in his mind.

Lean wondered if he would be the same in twenty years, every thief's name entered on the docket of his mind, every confidence man's face plain as a photograph. The memories of his own life blurred with time, but the details of all his cases burned clear into him.

'We were going to try pumping water out of Back Cove, but by then the fire burnt itself out. That little shack was a real tinderbox. No wind that day, else it might've spread into the brush all around there. Why are you asking?'

'Just trying to figure what happened,' Lean said.

Cobb snorted his laughter. Somewhere beneath the massive expanse of his gray handlebar mustache, a wide grin was enjoying life. 'I know you boys can get busy sometimes, but coming round twenty-odd years later is a bit much.'

'Better late than never,' Lean responded.

Cobb laughed again, and the effort rippled through his lungs, setting him to coughing. He took a few steps out and hawked a gob of phlegm onto the grass. The fire captain turned back toward them, wiping his mouth with a shabby handkerchief that looked as if it should have started drawing a pension years ago. Lean saw that the man's face was two shades redder than his normal ruddy tone and his eyes were watering from the coughing fit.

'Well, that fire was set, all right. From all the talk, it came out there was some old hag what lived there. She spooked the neighbors something awful. So a bunch went and smoked her right out.'

'But no one died in the fire?'

'Don't think so. Maybe some talk of someone hurt or missing. Don't remember a body being found, but then we weren't the first ones there, and we didn't stay too long neither.'

'Odd you don't remember a detail like that. Whether someone died in a fire,' Grey said.

'You know, Lean, your friend here's even funnier than you. And you're about as funny as having a bad case of the shits in church. It weren't even our fire, and what you're talking about is a police matter anyhow. Now that I'm thinking on it, maybe you guys aren't so late after all. Some copper did come around asking about it. What was his name?' He thought on it a moment, then shook his head. He let fly another lung deposit and called out to a fireman busy inside the bay, polishing the engine. 'Hey, Moran, remember back about twenty years ago that fire across the bridge? Little shack round by the creek down to Back Cove. What was the name of the cop who came around after investigating that?'

Moran stomped over. He was a stocky man, a few years younger than Cobb, judging by the scattered specks of black that remained in his own full face of hair. A well-chewed stub of a cigar worked its way to the corner of his mouth. 'Cap Tolman. A real prick.'

'Don't know him,' said Lean.

'Before your time, probably,' Moran said.

'Cap? He was a captain?'

'Nah.' Moran grabbed a hold of his cigar and gestured with it as he spoke. 'He took a bullet in his kneecap. Ate him up pretty good. Got to where he couldn't talk about nothing else. He was done not long after.'

'Still around?' Lean asked.

'Used to see him sometimes down around Gorham's Corner in the whiskey shops.'

Cobb issued another productive clearing of his throat. 'Last I heard, he was taking his time dying down at some Chinaman's place by the wharves.'

'Yengee Lee's opium den,' Grey said.

Lean knew the place, and the proprietor. Decades ago the Asian man's youthful passion for the American ideal of liberty and his dread at sharing a name with the Confederate commander had prompted frequent and heavily accented proclamations of his support for the Union. Thirty years later he was still known as Yengee Lee.

'We'll try there tonight,' Lean said.

'For what it's worth, Lean, maybe you'd better go by yourself.' Cobb nodded in Grey's direction. 'Nothing against yourself, mind you, but he doesn't care much for other races. Only goes down to the Chinaman's place because they take care of him on the cheap.'

Lean saw a flash of annoyance on Grey's face, and he thanked Cobb for the information. At the corner of Congress Street, they waited for a rail car to pass.

'We'll both go all the same,' Lean suggested.

'Information is the only thing that's important, not any imagined slight to me. If he'll speak more freely to you alone – so be it.'

'Fair enough, if it doesn't bother you,' Lean said.

'Yes, how I cringe at the thought of missing what is sure to be a brilliant conversation with some opium-addled bigot.'

Lean tried to suppress a smile. 'Like I said, so long as you're not bitter about it.'

47

Later that night, Archie Lean spent several minutes repeating his promises that he was only looking to speak with Cap Tolman and had no business with, or plans to arrest, any other customers on the premises. Only then did the panel at the rear of the apothecary slide back to reveal a door that led down a short flight of stairs. His guide let him into Yengee Lee's opium den and pointed toward a vague figure huddled near one corner of the room.

It was a poorly lit space with no visible windows. Some candles were set in sconces along the walls. There were a few mirrors and several other decorations, mostly hanging rolls of pale yellowish rice paper, with simple strokes depicting birds or the outlines of misty mountains or green-lined hillsides with Chinese characters running down the side. There were close to twenty habitués, some alone, others in small groups. These customers came from every corner of the city, every station in life. Lean passed a ruined man in a tattered suit sitting just feet away from a banker in a finely tailored morning coat.

Each layout had all the smoker's needs: a foot-and-a-half-long pipe, a bowl, spoon, dross box, and tray. Small, elaborate oil lamps with glass chimneys burned at each layout. Most of the patrons were lying on their sides on woven bamboo mats set atop the low bunks, wide benchlike platforms that lined the walls. A few more bunks, littered with large square pillows, were set in the middle of the room.

Lean settled onto a low stool across from Cap Tolman, who was half reclining on a padded bench against the wall. His unfitted sack suit was missing a button and showed signs of excessive wear. Lean garnered something resembling a smile of recognition when he mentioned he was a police deputy. He spoke quietly, trying not to be overheard. The closest habitué was a thin man with graying hair who had passed out facedown on his own bunk. A gold watch had slipped from the man's pocket and dangled from its chain. Lean knew that the man's property was safe among this morally vague collection of souls. Despite the sundry vices the others might practice in the outside world, there was an unspoken code of honor, a mutual amnesty, that governed their conduct within these hazy confines.

'I'll cut right to it, Tolman. I need to know about a woman called Old Stitch.'

After a minute Tolman's jaundiced eyes focused, and he gave a shake of his head. 'I've cooked up the card. How 'bout you get him to roll up some pills for me, and we'll have ourselves a talk.'

'Fair enough. I'll spot you the next bit of dope.'

'Hey, Yengee,' called Tolman, 'another quarter for me.'

Through the haze of blue-gray smoke, Lean watched the house cook at work. The deputy had a basic understanding of the process. The raw opium was already prepared, the cook having shredded it, then boiled it down to separate out the pure opium. The essence obtained, the cook then kneaded that residue in a shallow pan, and the resulting concoction, thick and black, was a fermented pastelike substance known to the users as dope.

'The witch woman who lived on the East Deering side of the cove, not far from Tukey's. They burnt her out back in '71.' Lean saw a glimmer of recognition in Tolman's eyes. 'What was her real name?'

'Dunno. Black Lucy, she was called then. But even in those days, her hair was going white. She weren't even that old to look at her. And not a bad bit of mutton – worth the dollar, anyway. I had a taste of that once or twice myself. A good ride too, if you didn't mind her two little shit-heel runts peeking through the cracks in the walls the whole time.'

Tolman smacked his parched lips, then reached for a small porcelain cup of tea on the layout in front of him. He grimaced after taking a sip. 'Don't know how these pigtails drink that piss water.'

'What happened? The fire,' Lean said.

Tolman's eyes moved to the steady light of the oil lamp. He picked up his spoon, using it to scrape at the resin inside the bowl. He dumped the resulting dross out into a little box that sat on top of the polished teak tray.

'Smoke. I could see it coming cross Tukey's. Nothing like the Great One in '66, mind you. You could see that forever and a mile.'

'What did you see there at Black Lucy's?'

'Dying down to the wisps by the time I got there.'

'But what about her? You see her after the fire?'

'Not for a long time. She showed up later a couple other places, but she'd never last long afore they'd run her off again. I even heard she joined up with one of those red-Indian shows. Ended up back there, rebuilding that old shack by the cove.'

The proprietor appeared with two small black pellets presented in a lichee nutshell, which he set down after collecting Lean's money.

'What for? Why'd they run her off?'

'Why? She was a damned witch. Why the hell wouldn't they? Hell, that old whore's lucky they never did worse after what she did.'

'What did she do?'

'Killed a woman with her medicines. She peddled all sorts of poisons. For getting men, getting babies, getting rid of 'em. Woman died. Baby she was carrying too. That's why they went down there with fire. Eye for an eye.'

'Who burned her out?'

Tolman shrugged. He set one of the pellets atop the knoblike bowl, where it settled into place in an indentation at the center of which was a small hole.

'No one was ever arrested?'

'Hah! There were whispers, but no one would ever talk. And we didn't ask too hard either. She was no use to no one. And her boys, neither.' Tolman leaned forward, holding his bamboo pipe at an angle and just far enough over the oil lamp so that the heat wouldn't be too great, igniting the opium, burning it away. Instead the low, steady flame vaporized the drug into a dense blue-white cloud. There was a sizzling gurgle as Tolman drew the smoke into his lungs. After a moment he sat back, and his eyelids began to droop.

'What about the boys?' Lean asked.

'What about 'em?'

'Ever see them around after?'

'They never found the second one.'

Lean sat up straighter. 'You mean they really did kill one of her boys? There was never a report.'

Tolman shrugged again. 'No one ever complained. Not even her. Besides, that fire burnt fast and real hot. No body left to raise a stink over.'

'Still,' said Lean, 'murdering a child ...'

'Only a kid for a few more years. He'd have been a whore's son and a thief forever after that.'

There was a long lapse in the conversation, and Lean started to wonder whether Tolman had drifted off. 'What about the other one? There were two boys.'

'Hmm? Oh, we found him later, hiding in the woods. One of the orphanages claimed him.' Tolman's eyes opened again, but his voice was starting to fade, the words coming more slowly on each other's heels.

Lean bent forward, his head hovering over the lamp, rich with the scent of sesame oil. Tolman's words filtered through his mind, spinning all around like silt from a sandy lake bottom that, once stirred up, refuses to settle back into place. 'Has someone gone out and killed Old Stitch,' Lean whispered to himself, 'for revenge – even after twenty years?'

'Twenty years?' Tolman's eyes had gone wide. He was suddenly seized with a look of intense purpose. 'It's no more'n a day when you've got that pain inside you. Gripping so tight you can't think of nothing else.'

'This woman,' Lean said in a low, calming voice, 'the one who died from Black Lucy's medicines. What was her name?'

'No.' Tolman shook his head. 'A moment can ruin you right down to the bone. Years slip by while the pain eats its way down into you. Him that did this to me' – he nodded toward his wasted leg – 'if he was here now, I'd kill him with my bare hands. Tear him away like he tore me.'

'Her name,' Lean urged.

The color went out of Tolman's face, as though his last rant had drained him down to nothing. The old veteran's eyes flickered, and the lids sank almost shut, leaving two slits of white like twin crescent moons lying on their backs.

'Tolman! What was the woman's name?' Lean shook him by

the shoulders. 'Look at me. Come on, man! What was her name?'

A hand, firm but not threatening, took hold of Lean's arm. 'Come along, Deputy. You risk a spectacle. And no amount of pleading will raise this Lazarus from his opium tomb.'

Lean stared into the aged face. It took a moment to recognize him as the passed-out man who had been laid out in the nearby bunk with his gold watch dangling. As Lean stared, the man's stooped shoulders straightened slightly and the squinting eyes relaxed. The man's dull expression sparkled with a renewed vitality. He winked at Lean, turned, and exited the room. Lean hurried after him, through the curtained entry, up the narrow staircase to the pharmacy, then out into the steamy July night.

He caught up with the man in an alley around the corner. 'Damn it, Grey! These masquerades of yours are giving me fits.'

'No time for hysterics, my good man. Tolman has laid our work out for us.'

'You heard well enough, I assume, that he never revealed any names.'

'Exactly. And so we must attach the name ourselves.'

Lean followed him to a waiting hansom cab. 'And how do you plan to do that?'

'Your excitement, or the opium smoke, clouds your mind, Lean. We live in a city still gripped by the memory of its own near death. Fires in Portland do not escape mention in newspapers. The same is true of pregnant ladies who die under mysterious circumstances.'

48

Lean closed his eyes and listened to the clock in the parlor finish chiming seven. He thought back over the day. A visit to the records room at City Hall, followed by two hours thumbing through dusty fire-department reports, provided the date of August 8, 1871. The brief entry held little else of use. No name was attached to the property at Back Cove. There was only a mention of two engines dispatched from Portland, one building lost, and no surrounding damage. After verifying the date of the fire at Old Stitch's place, he'd telephoned the information to Grey, who undertook the next stop in their search: the newspaper morgue of the *Eastern Argus*. That had been lunchtime, and Lean was beginning to fixate on the clock. Each minute that ticked by was like the gentle strike of a small hammer, tapping a coffin nail into his hopes that their efforts would prove worthwhile.

Lean reached across the table for the packet that had arrived in the evening post. He slid out a single page. On top was a brief note from Grey:

> *For your consideration. Only three photographs produced legible views of documents from Lizzie Madson's stove. Copies also sent to Dr Steig and Mrs Prescott. Thought best to review separately, then compare interpretation. Rather an interesting puzzle.*
>
> G.

The photograph showed a single page of elegant handwriting that had the appearance of an antique journal or manuscript. Lean picked up the photograph and read:

For every dark spirit summoned, every spirit commanded, a dark soul offered. In the first month of my travels in service of the ascension of my Master, James, did I come to Roma the place of my Master's birth. There one night I saw full the sister of the mad king father, the sister who would not bleed. Beneath the sign of the Soldier's Boot she came to know the Master. She bade me await the fullness for her offering. But I could not, and so the first offering was taken from her. There the brimming cup was readied.

In the second month of my travels, I came to Constantinople, where the Master first took life and did there himself accept the Lord of the Air. There still clearly did I see the man who was nomine tenus the greatest among men. He bade me record my sins and ask forgiveness. But I would not, and so the second offering was taken from him. On that very ground, the libation was poured to the Master.

In the third month of my travels, I came to Tridentum, where the Master's powers were beheld, the skies were made to tremble, and the Master compelled the hosts of the air. There in the half-light did I see the child Zealot at the home of the Wanderers. He begged me to save him, but I would not. So the third offering was taken from him. There the Master –

That was it. The document ended there – the meaning still completely hidden and any possible resolution left dangling. That more or less summarized Lean's view of the entire inquiry. The whole investigation was like trying to cross a river at night: a matter of finding stepping-stones where none could be seen.

His wife peeked in from the kitchen, where she was busy making supper. She whispered something, and a moment later

Owen came thumping into the room. He plopped down on the chair next to his father. The two of them sat for a long while, each silently taking the other's measure.

'Are you in a dark place, Daddy?'

Lean sat up straight. It was not a question he ever expected from his five-year-old. 'I think I am. But just a little bit.'

'One time before, when Tiger died, I cried because I loved him. Mommy said I wouldn't have to be sad if I loved God.'

Lean's memory was that the boy had hardly ever acknowledged their old cat when it was alive, but he nodded and said, 'You should listen to Mommy.'

'Do you love God?'

'Yes,' Lean said with a smile.

'How do you? What do you do?'

Lean considered this for a moment, how to most simply explain the concept. 'You try to live like God would want you to. Try to help people. Doing right by your family and others. Doing right, period.'

'That's it?'

Lean bent his shoulders forward, bringing himself down closer to his son's face. 'No, I suppose there's more to it. I'd say loving God means trusting him. Opening your heart to him, so you can be saved. It means you let his love into your heart.'

'Inside you?' Owen giggled with delight and clutched at his shirt like he was having himself a friendly little heart attack. 'Can you feel God's love when it's inside you?'

Lean smiled and nodded.

'What's it feel like?'

'I guess it feels like hope.' Lean reached over and pulled Owen close. The boy giggled again and tried to squirm away, but Lean held on. 'Hope that everyone else loves him too. No matter what your eyes tell you.'

A sharp knock at the door announced Grey's arrival. Emma took his hat and walking stick before trying to excuse herself from the room with Owen, a process delayed by the boy's interest in, and obvious disapproval of, the visitor. Grey seated himself at the table, placed his bag on the table, and revealed a satisfied smile.

'I was beginning to think you weren't coming. That we'd hit a dead end,' Lean said.

'Sorry. I had a few other matters to check on at the *Argus*.'

'So? You found something.'

'Indeed.' Grey set out a handwritten page. 'I took the liberty of copying the original.'

Lean read it aloud, careful to not let his voice carry. '"Agnes Blanchard, formerly Millner, devoted wife and mother, went home to the Lord after a brief illness. She was buried in Evergreen Cemetery on August seventh."' He looked up. 'That's the day before Old Stitch was burned out.'

'Read on,' said Grey.

'"The daughter of Clement and Adele Millner, she was married on June twenty-third, 1857, to Ambrose Blanchard."' Lean stared at the page for a moment. 'The colonel?'

'Our very own war hero, crusader for temperance, and secret correspondent with rum smuggler McGrath on subjects related to the death of Maggie Keene.'

'This isn't good.'

'On the contrary,' Grey said, 'it's excellent news. Finally we see a connection. Colonel Blanchard is our first solid link in this muddled picture of murder and witchery.' There was a sound from the parlor, and Grey lowered his voice. 'The colonel's wife dies. Reportedly of some concoction made by this Old Stitch, or Black Lucy, or whatever nom de guerre she was employing at the time.' Grey slid the paper back into his bag. 'Two days later, Old Stitch's family was attacked, one son killed, and their home burned to the ground in apparent retribution for the death of Mrs Blanchard. Twenty years later, Stitch, who is a reputed witch, is dead and Maggie Keene's pinned to the earth. A gruesome death that her killer thought uniquely suited to a witch.'

As Grey paused to draw a breath, Lean picked up the thread. 'And McGrath was taking payments to protect Boxcar Annie because she knew something about the murder of Maggie Keene. Whose death is linked in a chain with those of Hannah Easler of Scituate and Lizzie Madson.'

Grey smiled. 'The colonel and his temperance union have just assumed primary importance in our investigation of all three murders. How Old Stitch's own death, in February, fits into this equation remains unclear.'

49

The next day, while the two detectives waited for Helen, Grey fixed himself a cup of tea. Lean wandered across the consulting room to Grey's desk. There were various pages and books on Salem and on temperance movements. A small, yellowed article, set aside from the others, caught Lean's eye. The headline read DROWNED MAN PULLED FROM RIVER. The story related that Joseph Poulin, an Indian, was found by searchers combing the riverbank. He had been missing for a day, and it was supposed that he accidentally fell into the waters. Lean glanced at the date: April 22, 1867. He recalled Grey's mentioning his father by name when they visited with Chief White Eagle after the brawl at Camp Ellis. Embarrassed to be snooping into Grey's personal affairs, Lean moved away.

He busied himself with studying the titles on the bookshelves lining the wall. Lean noticed a volume of collected essays by the English scientist Francis Galton. Recognizing the name from their meeting with Colonel Blanchard, he flipped through the pages.

Then he glanced at the clock. 'She's late.'

'The cemetery will wait for us,' answered Grey as he returned to his desk. 'The people we're looking for there certainly aren't going anywhere. Besides, Mrs Prescott's message indicated some urgency. I think her ongoing research has finally revealed something.'

Lean returned his attention to an essay titled 'Hereditary Character and Talent' and smiled. 'I think Colonel Blanchard may have been onto something with all his talk about Galton's theories on Indians.'

That was enough to grab Grey's attention.

Lean cleared his throat. 'On Indians he writes, "The men, and in a less degree the women, are naturally cold, melancholic, patient, and taciturn ... The American Indians are eminently non-gregarious. They nourish a sullen reserve ..."' Lean paused and looked directly at Grey, then slowly repeated the words: '"A sullen reserve."'

He tried to keep a straight face as he read on. '"... and show little sympathy with each other, even when in great distress ...

They are strangely taciturn. When not engaged in action they will sit whole days in one posture without opening their lips, and wrapped up in their narrow thoughts."

'Ah, but don't despair, Grey, here's a good bit.' Lean grinned and raised a finger. '"On the other hand, their patriotism and local attachments are strong, and they have an astonishing sense of personal dignity." Unfortunately, it's not enough to save you. Mr Galton advises that "the nature of the American Indians appears to contain the minimum of affectionate and social qualities compatible with the continuance of their race."' He slammed the cover closed.

Grey regarded him, expressionless, for a moment. 'The character of an entire continent of people capable of summary in a single paragraph. Further proof of Galton's myopic views. Utter nonsense.' He shook his head and tried, unsuccessfully, to return his attention to his papers before adding, 'A man will always be defined by his choices; that will always be the final truth of the matter, regardless of his ancestry.'

Lean opened his mouth but heard the sound of the front door closing downstairs before he could speak. He shelved Galton and hurried across the room to open the door just as Helen came rushing in, carrying a bag overstuffed with papers.

'Welcome, Helen; good to see you again.' Lean said. 'And now that we're all here, I can call to order this first official meeting of the Salem Witch Society.'

Helen placed her hat on the rack by the door. 'Oh, I like that. A nice ring to it.'

'Yes, and very timely as well.' Grey craned his neck and contemplated the ceiling. 'Only just this morning I was despairing of our investigative prospects and our inability to adequately title our collective effort to find this homicidal madman. But now that you've provided the clever sobriquet that we have been so sorely lacking, we might actually be able to solve this matter. Thank you, Deputy. '

'Please, think nothing of it,' Lean said, clearly pleased to have annoyed Grey.

'Mrs Prescott, I pray you at least have something that might actually contribute to our inquiry.'

'Your question about Witchtrot Hill. The answer is the Reverend George Burroughs.' She brushed past Lean with a distracted smile and set her bag on the table.

'Reverend?' Lean said.

'Yes. Shocking, isn't it? That they would go and hang a minister. One of their own, actually; he preached in Salem Village for a short while, back before the witchcraft trials.'

'And all of that?' Grey pointed at the stacks of paper that Helen had settled into piles on the table.

'Everything there is to know about George Burroughs. Every mention made of him from every available source in the library. It's really a most fascinating story.'

Lean stared at the assortment of pages; Helen had obviously put a great deal of work into the matter of George Burroughs. 'Before we're forced to wade through that whole pile, you're certain that this Burroughs warrants all that effort?'

Helen's eyes lit up. 'Let's see what you think.' She pulled a page from the top of her stack. 'This is my copy of the deposition of Ann Putnam, testifying on May fifth, 1692, against George Burroughs:

"I saw the apparition of Mr George Burroughs, who grievously tortured me and urged me to write in his book, which I refused, and

he told me that he was above a witch, for he was a conjurer. Then he told me that his two first wives would appear and tell me a great many lies but I should not believe them. Then immediately appeared the forms of two women in winding-sheets, and napkins about their heads, at which I was greatly affrighted. They turned their faces towards Mr Burroughs and looked very red and angry and told him that he had been a cruel man to them, and that their blood did cry for vengeance against him, and also told him that they should be clothed with white robes in Heaven when he should be cast into Hell. And immediately he vanished away. The two pale women told me that they were Mr Burroughs' two first wives and that he had murdered them. One told me that he stabbed her under the left arm and put a piece of sealing-wax on the wound. And she pulled aside the winding-sheet and showed me the place."'

'My God ... Lizzie Madson,' Lean said.

'I know we'll have to read the whole lot, but perhaps you could give us a quick overview,' Grey said to Helen.

Helen sighed and retrieved a page of notes. 'Graduated from Harvard in 1670. He lived and preached in Maine both before and after his time in Salem, though he was never actually ordained as a minister.'

'Was he from here?' Lean asked.

Helen shook her head. 'Upham reports him as born in Scituate.'

'Scituate? Really?' Lean threw a surprised glance in Grey's direction. 'What are the chances?'

'He was preaching here in 1676 and seems to have been highly regarded. It was still called Casco, just a frontier outpost, when the entire settlement was overrun by an Indian assault. Thirty-two inhabitants were killed or carried into captivity. Mr Burroughs led a party that escaped to one of the islands.'

Grey went to a bookcase and began examining the contents. Helen paused, but Lean shrugged and motioned for her to continue.

'In 1680, Burroughs preached at Salem Village, where he inherited a contentious parish quarrel. Just two years later, discord and financial issues caused him to give up on his position there and return to Maine. Seems he preferred the Indians at Casco Bay to the litigious people in Salem.'

'Smart man,' Grey said without bothering to look up from the book he'd selected.

'Burroughs remained here at Casco until 1690. Apart from surviving the first destruction in 1676, he also had the foresight to leave Portland again just before the town was overrun by the Indians and French in 1690. Hundreds of other residents later surrendered after being promised safe passage, only to be massacred outside the fort walls by the Abenakis. Burroughs's ability to continually escape the Indians unharmed was viewed with great suspicion, especially by those, like Mercy Lewis, whose own families suffered repeated losses.

'He relocated to Wells, where he preached until his accusation by the afflicted girls at Salem led to his arrest. On May fourth, 1692, unaware of any allegations of wrongdoing, he was seized from his family's dinner table and hurried down to Salem Village to face the charges against him.' Helen flipped ahead through the papers.

'And here is where the story leads us: that trip down to Salem. After the arrest, the constables led him through the woods, and a terrible storm blew up. Lightning smashed right down on the treetops, casting an eerie glow with electricity dancing all around them. The constables felt their horses lifted up by the swirling winds so that their hooves no longer touched the ground. Yet the horses never bolted, just kept on at their same old trot, carried along in the very air. The jailers feared for their lives, but Burroughs never flinched. Upon reaching Salem, the constables reported that the wizard's spell had called the fiends of the air to his aid and they had an army of devils at their backs the entire way. The hill where the storm occurred is still known today as Witchtrot Hill.'

Lean considered this for a moment. 'So what does that give us? We already knew our man is obsessed with Salem witch-trial victims. The male ones anyway. First he's using their names as aliases, now he's placed a body at a site named after Burroughs. It's almost like he's paying some manner of tribute to them all.'

'Scituate and Witchtrot Hill are both connected with Burroughs,' Grey said. 'He's the focal point.'

'It makes sense, as far as a Salem connection,' Helen said. 'He was in some ways the central character in the accusations. He was the alleged ringleader of the witches. The one who supposedly turned all the others into witches in the first place. The afflicted girls get the attention, and we always think of the witches as women, but to the Puritans' narrow-minded view of the world there had to be a man behind it all. The danger was so great, the damage to the community so severe, it made sense to them that the corruption had to have been on a grand scale. And what betrayal could be worse? The devil had turned one of their own ministers against them.'

Grey nodded. 'Mrs Prescott, would you be so kind as to bring my copy of Cram's 1890 Atlas. It's there on the table by you.'

Lean joined Grey by the desk and glanced down to see that he was studying a map entitled 'Plan of Falmouth Neck, Now Portland, 1690.' The image on the desk showed a much thinner version of Portland Neck, heavily wooded and spotted with several areas of marsh and wetlands. Three dozen houses were marked, along with various numbered reference points, including two garrisons, Fort Loyal, the burying ground that was now the Eastern Cemetery, and George Bramhall's farm below the Western Promenade.

'What do you see?'

'Nothing yet,' Grey said, 'but I hope to see the Reverend George Burroughs.'

'I don't think the map is quite to that scale,' Lean said with a smirk. 'Out with it, Grey.'

'Your comment just now. The body on Witchtrot Hill as a "tribute" to Burroughs. What if each murder was some sort of tribute?'

'What makes you think—'

'Consider. Hannah Easler murdered in Scituate. The birthplace of George Burroughs.'

'I have seen other references saying he was born in London,' Helen said.

Grey waved the argument away. 'We are dealing with a man willing to kill for some reason connected to the two-hundred-year-old trials of witches. What matters to him is what he believes in that twisted mind of his. And he's read that Burroughs was born in Scituate.'

'Fair enough,' Lean said.

'Now, we know murder victim three was subsequently moved to Marsh's house and then the family tomb. But it appears she was actually killed at a site made notorious by Burroughs's presence.'

'Fair enough again,' said Lean. 'But Maggie Keene? The Portland Company wasn't there two hundred years ago.'

'Which brings us full circle to one of the original questions posed in this case. Why did the killer remove the floorboards, setting the body directly upon the earth beneath? He was never interested in killing her inside the Portland Company. It was always the ground underneath that was important.'

'Here you are.' Helen handed over the atlas and set it on the desk. Grey flipped ahead until he located the city of Portland, Maine. He set his right index finger on the 1890 map in a blank space at the East End below Fore Street, where the Portland Company now stood. Then he pointed with his left index finger to the 1690 map.

'The early settlement was concentrated here, at the water-front near the East End. Notice the only four streets in the town are clustered there. A very short Queen Street, which is now Congress, forms the upper boundary. Broad, now India Street, joins this to the waterfront. Running along the shore, we have Fore Street until it crosses Broad and becomes Thames. That continues east and ends at . . .' Grey ran his finger an inch along the map to where Thames Street ended.

Lean's eyes darted back and forth between the identical locations. On the 1890 map, it was the Portland Company. The same site on the 1690 map was marked with the number '2.' He glanced down to the reference key at the lower left corner of the 1690 map.

'Number 2. The Meeting House.' He looked at Helen, then met Grey's eyes. 'The town minister.'

Grey nodded at Lean. 'The Reverend George Burroughs. Our man is committing murders in a pattern derived from the life of George Burroughs.'

50

The carriage, borrowed once again from Dr Steig, rolled downhill on Green Street, past the smokestacks of the Casco Tanning Company, where the wide expanse of Deering Oaks Park came into view. Grey seemed lost in thought, and Lean's eye was drawn to the park. Midday strollers dotted the carriage paths winding among the tall trees. In the large duck pond, couples in swan-shaped paddleboats steered around the spray of the fountain. Grassy fingertips of land along the pond were crowded with picnickers. A sudden regret gripped Lean as doubt over this seemingly endless investigation came creeping along the edges of his mind. He wished he were in the park now, watching Owen throw bits of bread over the heads of the greedy duck vanguard, to the hungry stragglers. Instead, he was on his way to a cemetery, looking to the dead for a clue, some thin thread connected to the live phantom they were chasing.

As they passed the border of the park, marking the city line where Green Street in Portland became the town of Deering's Forest Avenue, Grey finally spoke.

'You understand that there is no one else.'

Lean stared back at him, unwilling to admit he had no inkling of the man's meaning.

'To the rest of the city, the tale of this crime begins and ends with Maggie Keene's murder. They can even forgive that it remains unsolved. In time, those who remember the murder will even revel in that fact. There's something very appealing to the common man about an unsolved mystery. And even if someone else had been willing to take up this inquiry, they wouldn't have gotten as far as we have.'

He knew that Grey was trying to encourage him, but Lean felt cold pincers gripping deep inside his chest. 'As far as we have.' When Lean repeated the words, they carried more of a sting of bitterness than he'd intended.

The cab hurried along, running parallel to the Portland & Rochester line. Grey returned to some private train of thought, and Lean was grateful for the renewed silence. Another mile and they passed into the sprawling suburban neighborhood of Woodford's Corner, traveling over the unpaved road and bumping across multiple sets of rails. Dr Steig's driver steered them past the raucous cheers emanating from the half-mile racing track of the Presumpscot Trotting Park. The cab proceeded along unpaved Stevens Plains Avenue, past the grand residences of newly moneyed merchants and professionals escaping from the city.

Massive granite posts and a trolley waiting room marked the entrance to Evergreen Cemetery. Broad canopied elms, maples, and arborvitae hedges lined the main avenue, reminding visitors that this was a different space from the two older cemeteries on the eastern and western edges of the Neck. Unlike those constricted fields of granite headstones, bookends bounding in the life of the city, Evergreen was a sweeping, parklike cemetery. It was the last day of July, a Sunday, so the cemetery was alive with parasol-wielding couples on parade and groups lolling on blankets under shade trees. A half mile in from Stevens Plains Avenue, the grounds became slightly hilly. The carriage passed by wide, grassy plots dedicated to single families who sat atop a series of hillocks.

'This will do, Rasmus,' Grey called out.

They climbed down and surveyed the scene. Lean moved forward and stood up on a short, two-foot-wide granite border that surrounded a small, houselike burial vault, while Grey consulted his notebook, then peered about the manicured landscape.

'Over there.' Grey pointed to the right and led Lean across the short, plush grass. He wandered up and down rows of grave markers.

'We're looking for Mrs Blanchard, I take it,' Lean said.

'We are indeed.'

'And to what end?'

'After meeting her charming husband, I'm curious to see if she has improved the company she keeps. Ah, here we are.'

Lean stepped forward to see the resting place of Agnes Blanchard. Cut flowers, now dead, were set upon the ground just below the headstone. It was a simple inscription on a plain-faced rectangle of granite: BELOVED WIFE AND MOTHER. NOVEMBER 29, 1836–AUGUST 5, 1871.

'The anniversary of her death is next week,' noted Lean. He looked up to see Grey examining the nearby markers. 'Find someone interesting?'

'On the contrary. I don't see a single name of interest.'

'The son?'

'Notable by his absence. There are plenty of burial lots free and others nearby buried in recent years,' Grey said.

'He might simply be buried elsewhere.'

'Or nowhere at all.'

'Why would the colonel lie about such a thing?' Lean asked.

'The same reason he lied about everything else. To protect himself and his movement. So the interesting question becomes, does this missing son have any bearing on our inquiry? I suppose we shall have to ask the colonel's daughter on Friday.'

Lean stared at Grey. 'You've already located that daughter and scheduled an appointment with her for next Friday?'

'Not that she's aware of. But she should be here' – Grey motioned to the week-old flowers resting by Mrs Blanchard's headstone – 'with a fresh bouquet on the anniversary of her mother's death.'

51

Lean and Grey stood in Helen's parlor, awaiting her return from upstairs. There was a tall bookcase along one wall, and Lean perused the titles. One of the lower shelves held Delia's primers and stories. Grey approached, bent down toward the young girl's shelf, and retrieved a small, pewter-framed photograph. Lean glanced at it and saw a younger Helen Prescott with a handsome man beside her.

'Dr Steig mentioned he died not long after Delia was born,' Lean said.

Grey, still holding the picture, moved along the perimeter of the room, taking in a few paintings and a couple of other photographs of Helen and Delia. Lean heard Helen coming down the stairs, and a moment later she entered from the kitchen.

'She's all tucked in. Now, gentlemen. What a pleasant surprise. If I'd known you were coming, I could have fixed something to eat.'

'No need, Mrs Prescott.'

'We're sorry to impose on you unannounced, Helen,' Lean added.

Helen saw what Grey was holding. She stepped forward and took it from his hand.

'Sorry. It's just that Delia is very attached to this picture of her father.' Helen strode to the bookcase and set the picture back in its spot.

'It must be trying for a girl to not have her father around. Difficult to explain, I imagine. Questions that need to be answered and such.'

'Yes, it is difficult. Very much so.' Helen's face was flushed, her hands clasped before her. 'I don't think you can imagine, Mr Grey. But I've done all that I can to shelter Delia from the unpleasantness of his death. And I think I've done as well as could be expected in the circumstances.'

'Yes, I would say you've done a commendable job.' He offered a quick smile, some veiled sort of truce offering.

Lean glanced back and forth between the two of them, trying to pick up the thread of the conversation that he had somehow missed.

Helen gave a little nod and walked around her visitors. 'Have you made some discovery? I was just getting ready to have another look at that page you sent.'

'Any luck so far?' Lean asked.

She led them over to a rolltop desk, where three pages lay side by side. Lean recognized the page salvaged from the woodstove in Lizzie Madson's rooms.

'I have a thought about the first line, but after that it has me utterly confounded,' Helen said.

The men stood looking over her shoulder as she read, '"For every dark spirit summoned, every spirit commanded, a dark soul offered." He's killing women he views as sinners – dark souls that he is sacrificing for some diabolical reason.'

Lean nodded. 'I thought the same. He's not a religious fanatic after all. He's pursuing some type of black-magic ritual.'

'It explains the puzzle of why he killed Maggie Keene as a witch, then suckled at her molelike protuberance,' Grey said.

'Like a witch's familiar,' Helen said. 'Drawing power from her, serving as some link between the witch and the devil.'

Lean shook his head. 'He's really seeking some connection with the devil?'

'"For every dark spirit summoned,"' she said. 'It's essentially the same crime George Burroughs was accused of in Salem. He was the one charged with originally converting the others to witches. He'd have them sign their names in blood or red ink in his devil's book.'

Lean snapped to attention. 'Maggie Keene's postmortem – the red ink that stained the inside of her right glove. Our man actually had her sign his devil's book or some such.' He looked to Grey, whose head was bent in deep concentration. 'What do you think, Grey?'

Grey ignored the question and addressed himself to Helen instead. 'There's another book mentioned in the trial material you provided to us on the Reverend Burroughs. A book mentioned by one of the afflicted girls. She'd been a servant in his household here in Maine.'

'Mercy Lewis,' Helen said as she started to search through her research files. Soon she pulled out a sheet of paper and held it up in triumph. Grey motioned her on and she read the page aloud. 'The deposition of Mercy Lewis, who testifies that: "At evening I saw the apparition of Mr George Burroughs whom I very well knew which did grievously torture me and urged me to write in his book and then he brought to me a new fashion book which he did not use to bring and told me I might write in that book: for that was a book that was in his study when I lived with them. But I told him I did not believe him for I had been often in his study, but I never saw that book there. But he told me that he had several books in his study which I never saw in his study and he could raise the devil."'

Grey smiled. 'Our killer is obsessed with George Burroughs; he's aware of this supposed book of black magic that the reverend could use to raise the dead. He must think this is it, that these burned pages are from Burroughs's witch book and he too can use it to summon some dark spirit.'

Lean pounded the side of his fist onto the desk. 'He's not the only one thinking that. Helen's scare in the library that night – Simon Gould was sent to look for an old book on magic. It can't be a coincidence. He was after these same pages. Hopefully we've found them before Colonel Blanchard.'

'Not that finding them has helped us any. It's all a muddle,' Helen said.

Lean sat down and weighed an idea in his head for a moment before speaking. 'You know, sometimes I don't truly grasp the depths of a poem's meanings until I've spoken the words. Lifted them off the page and breathed a bit of life into them.'

Helen picked up the page and read it out loud. She looked up at Lean, awaiting some response. His mind raced. Hearing the words spoken had provided no new sudden lightning flash of understanding. He was left with the same general conclusions he had reached when reading the page himself earlier. 'There is a pattern in the paragraphs. A repeating rhythm to the entries.'

'An order of months,' Grey said. 'Then a location, a city, is identified, followed by an action by this master. A reference to visibility and seeing a person who makes a request, which is denied. An offering is taken, and then mention is made of a drink being prepared.'

'The murders have occurred every month,' Lean said, 'though not exactly a month apart.' Grey knew his thoughts on this already, so Lean glanced at Helen and explained. 'I've been poring over the calendar, trying to find some pattern – number of days, days of the week, full moons. There was a full moon when Hannah Easler was killed in Scituate. But nothing else fits.'

'Full moon,' Helen repeated. She glanced back at the page. 'The first month mentions "full" twice. It says: "I saw full the sister ... " and then, "She bade me await the fullness for her offering." I suppose it could mean something.'

Grey stepped forward to look at Helen's page. He ran a finger down through the lines. 'In the second month ... "There still clearly did I see the man ..."' His finger swept on down the page. 'Then, "In the third month of my travels ... There in the half-light did I see the child Zealot."'

'Full moon, to still clear, then to half-light. What were the moon phases on the nights of the other murders?' Lean asked.

'I have an almanac,' Helen volunteered. She moved to her

bookshelf and searched for a moment before seizing the thin volume.

'June fourteenth for Maggie Keene,' Lean announced.

Helen began to flip through the pages as she wandered back toward them. 'That would have been just four days past full.'

'And July sixteenth for Lizzie Madson.'

Helen's face wrinkled up in disagreement. 'It says that was the last quarter. Not half.'

'The lunar cycle is measured from new moon to full and back again, so the full moon is halfway through the cycle,' Grey explained. 'What's called a quarter is actually a moon that's half lit.'

'So far we've had full moon to about three-fourths lit to a half moon,' Lean said.

'Now we're looking for August.' Helen turned the page and studied the almanac. 'When the moon's midway between half lit and new. That would be maybe August nineteenth, or the twentieth. It's hard to be exact.'

'We have a few weeks, but no idea where he'll strike.' Lean picked up the page containing the riddle. 'He mentions Rome and Constantinople and Tridentum, wherever that is.'

'The cities are distractions,' Grey said, 'but he also mentions another location – the place of his master's birth. The first murder was in Scituate.'

'George Burroughs's birthplace,' Lean said, and then he stared down at the page. 'Second month is the place where the master first took life and himself accepted the Lord of the Air. An old name for the devil, eh? Well, Maggie Keene was killed on the old site of Burroughs's meeting house.'

Helen said, 'There were several allegations at Salem that

Burroughs murdered two of his wives, one in the town of Wells, and also the wife and child of another Salem minister. And that he caused the deaths of many soldiers at the hands of Indians to the eastward, meaning Maine. But I don't recall anything specific to the meeting-house area.'

Lean let out a disappointed grumble. 'The third month – "where the Master's powers were beheld, the skies made to tremble, and the Master compelled the hosts of the air." A perfect match for Witchtrot Hill!'

'It doesn't help us, I'm afraid,' Grey said. 'Those cover only the first three months. We're facing the fourth month's murder now. We need to find out what book this page came from and locate a complete copy for ourselves. Without the next paragraph, we'd be guessing at what event from the reverend's life is indicated next. The site may be in Portland or Salem, but it could well be in a dozen different spots throughout New England.'

'So now what?' Lean said.

'I'll look for information on this book,' Helen said. 'My boss, Mr Meserve, is quite an expert on the colonial period in Maine. He may be able to help, if I can share the page you discovered.'

Grey nodded his assent. 'We'll also need your assistance on an additional path of inquiry.'

'Which is what exactly?' she asked.

'The one that brought us here tonight in the first place.'

PART III

August 5, 1892

But here is not a task in which one can advance little by little, along a natural and clearly demarcated route ... There is always a new problem to unravel; the investigator whose work is half done has accomplished nothing. Either he has solved the problem and quite finished the work: that means success; or he has done nothing, absolutely nothing.

Dr Hans Gross, Criminal Investigation

52

The following Friday, Helen sat on the warm grass in front of the strategically located headstone of a long-dead woman she had never known. She cast glances at another nearby visitor to the Evergreen Cemetery. That woman, Miss Rachel Blanchard, had approached almost half an hour earlier and spent several minutes removing the old flowers, pulling a few weeds, and offering prayers. She had remained sitting next to the headstone of her mother, Agnes Blanchard, ever since.

At thirty yards, Helen was far enough away to be inconspicuous but too far to hear the young woman, who appeared to be speaking in hushed tones. Rachel Blanchard was dressed in black, with her hair pulled back and hidden under a mourning bonnet, revealing a high forehead. Her face was plain, with close-set eyes and a small mouth. Helen thought the woman had the look of a stolid, dutiful daughter, but there was no keenness in her expression, no hint of particularly deep currents of thought. At last the woman rose up and rested her hands atop the gravestone, offering one last prayer. Rachel Blanchard's body began to shake slightly, and she bowed her head. She reached into her purse and removed a kerchief to dab at her eyes, then turned to go.

Helen walked after her. Rachel slowed a bit and moved to rest a hand against a tree to support herself.

Helen hurried forward. 'Here, dear, are you well?'

'Oh, thank you. Yes, I'll be fine. Just a bit overcome.'

'Don't apologize. I understand. Visiting your late husband?'

319

'Oh, no. Mother.'

'It's so difficult sometimes,' Helen said. 'Here, take my arm. We can walk together.'

'You're most kind.'

'Oh, think nothing of it. I'd prefer it myself. I always feel so lonely on the walk away. Like I've left a bit of myself down there with him, every time I visit. Isn't that terribly silly?'

'No, not at all,' Rachel Blanchard said. 'I know what you mean. Your husband, then?'

'No, my brother, actually.' Helen walked in silence for several steps. 'He was such a sweet boy when he was younger. Sadly, he was a bit troubled in later years. Of course he's gone to a much happier place now. I suppose it's just me being selfish, but I do sometimes wish he were still here with me, even if he was being a bit of trouble, as he usually could be. I suppose that's always the way with younger brothers.'

'Yes. It seems to be.'

'You have a brother, do you?'

'Yes. Geoffrey.' After a few more steps, Rachel tilted her head in toward Helen in a conspiratorial manner. 'Don't think me a terribly horrid sister to say such a thing, but sometimes I do wonder if . . . if it wouldn't have been for the best if he had died along with our mother.'

'I'd put her in her mid to late thirties and her brother, Geoffrey, several years younger. He was always his mother's child. She favored him, and he was devoted to her. When she died, Geoffrey was inconsolable with rage and grief, just couldn't let her go. When he was older, he saw every spiritualist in the state trying to contact her again.'

Lean sat up at that news, his eyes shooting over to Grey, ready to give him a triumphant, just-as-I-suspected look. But Grey's head was tilted back a bit, and he was staring at some point on the ceiling.

Helen continued. 'At some point their father would no longer tolerate his grieving. He said Geoffrey's stubborn refusal to come to terms with the loss and accept the matter as final revealed a disturbing weakness of spirit. Trips away to relatives failed to cure him. He was always shuttled back, the relations being unable to deal with the boy's morbid outbursts. He was sent to schools throughout the northeast, but never for long. There were incidents, more than one, the nature of which she wouldn't say but grave enough that the boy was sent on rather quickly. He was enrolled in the army but discharged for medical reasons. Finally, at his wits' end and thoroughly shamed by his son's behavior, Colonel Blanchard had Geoffrey committed. He's been in and out of asylums for the past ten years. The last three at the Danvers Lunatic Hospital, where he remains today.'

'Amazing, she let all that out in a half hour,' Lean said.

'Rather a sad and lonely person. I think she desperately wanted to tell it.'

'But so much family history, and to a perfect stranger?'

'Sometimes it's easier to talk to a stranger,' Dr Steig noted. 'They're usually more polite and less likely to judge.'

'We may need more details. Did you manage to leave it on terms that you might speak again?' Grey asked.

Helen pursed her lips and shook her head. 'She clearly needed to speak, but afterward she was a bit taken aback at her own openness. I think she'll be relieved not to come across me again anytime soon. I must say, that's my wish as well – I don't think I could go on with the deception.'

Grey looked at Lean. 'What do you think?'

'It's possible that Geoffrey Blanchard knows something of Old Stitch. He was in a rage at his mother's death. Perhaps he was there when the mob burned her out from Back Cove. He may have seen what happened.'

'We won't know until we question him,' Grey said.

'Perhaps,' said Dr Steig, 'but if the fixation on his mother's death is still so strong, after twenty years, and with so much time spent in asylums, who's to say what state he's in now?' He showed his palms and shrugged. 'I have a few colleagues at Danvers. I'll make some initial inquiries about this Geoffrey Blanchard.'

53

F. W. Meserve's rooms on Oak Street occupied part of the third floor of a narrow brick building that appeared to be compressed skyward by the shorter, blocky neighbors attached on either side. The exterior façade of sturdiness was immediately betrayed by the sagging and tilting steps of the inside staircase. Meserve clutched onto a handrail that gleamed from the steady polishing under his palms, always sweaty from the climb up in the summer heat. The historian ascended the stairs, with his nose peeking over a load of books carried in his free arm. Atop the stack was a thin packet that Mrs Prescott had asked him to review. He took every step with patience, double-stepping, one foot before the other onto each tread, like a toddler still learning to trust the length of his own legs. A bell tinkled as he pushed the door open and let himself in. The alarm was redundant, as any hypothetical visitor would be heralded well in advance by the tortured creaking of the staircase, each step like another turn of the wheel, stretching the wood's very fiber almost to its breaking point.

The layout of the apartment was haphazard at best, a series of halls and small rooms meandering through the building at improbable angles. It was as if some mad builder had broken through a side wall and then snaked his way along, repartitioning the closets, storerooms, and hallways of other tenants. All in all, the result was an act of architectural gerrymandering that would have made any old-time politician proud. Meserve had selected these accommodations because the various spaces allowed him to catalog and store all his diverse texts and documents according to an indecipherable system of his own design.

He heated up some leftover soup and found a stale heel of bread for his dinner, which he ate sitting behind his broad desk, glancing at research notes. The unpolished oak desktop was obscured by piles of books and papers that formed a protective phalanx around the man. He felt most at home there, temporarily shielded from the endless barbaric forces of all those things yet to be studied and learned. A few minutes later, he set the remains of his supper on the floor beside him, to let his cat, Herodotus, lick the bowl clean. Meserve was a lifelong bachelor, somewhat by choice, and now approaching fifty years. This placed him comfortably past the age when his slovenly habits concerned him in the slightest.

He took out his pocketwatch and angled his head back to peer over the tip of his nose, where his reading glasses perched: two smudged, rotund lovers clasping wire hands and contemplating a united plunge over the edge, to end it all in one grand gesture. It was twenty minutes until eight o'clock. He would allot that much time to Mrs Prescott's request. She had given him the packet days earlier, but he'd set it aside while he finished an ongoing project. Her appeal was made with urgent tones, but Meserve was always loath to alter his existing work schedule. Upon standing to get a better view of his various piles, he spotted the large envelope and searched about for his letter opener.

He was very much regretting his inability to reject the request that Mrs Prescott had put to him days ago. The problem was that Meserve was not quick on his feet when it came to unexpected situations. While not as problematic and unknowable as the future, the present was still something of a treacherous crossing for Meserve. This was the true reason he had devoted himself to historical studies. The past was set and never changing. There were no awkward shifts in conversations or people's actions. Caesar always crossed the Rubicon, Washington always crossed the Delaware. With careful examination, events could be wholly understood. New sources could be found that altered the context of one's understanding, but rarely was there any truly surprising development.

He slit the envelope and let the paper slip out onto his desk. Much to his surprise, his interest was immediately piqued. It was a picture of what appeared to be an old paper damaged by fire. The handwritten words were faint, but still legible, in the photographic image. Holding the page close to his lamp, Meserve read through as quickly as his eyes would let him. He read it a second and a third time as his mouth hung open and his throat went dry.

After retrieving his magnifying glass from a drawer, he settled into his chair and began to inspect the page in earnest. So engrossed was he by the text, Meserve failed to even notice that Herodotus had leaped into his lap and curled up after a vigorous bout of kneading. Several minutes later Meserve let out an astonished gasp. In the margin, near where the page mentioned 'the ascension of my Master, James,' a faint note had been scribbled. It was almost impossible to make out, but staring at the faded lines, he deciphered a name: James Arrelan.

Meserve bolted to his feet, sending Herodotus crashing against the desk front, then onto the floor. 'My God,' he announced his victory to the empty room, 'this is it! This is from the Black Book!'

54

The cab was open, exposing the three passengers to the midday August sun but also offering an unobstructed view of the multiple buildings of the Danvers Lunatic Hospital. Dr Steig was intent upon the scene before them during the short ride up from Asylum Station. Grey stared off at the side of the road, evidently engrossed in some internal meanderings that he had no interest in sharing, until he suddenly turned to his companions and announced, 'You know, the asylum rests atop Hathorne Hill. Named for its former owner, John Hathorne. Who just happens to have been the chief examining magistrate during the Salem witch trials.'

Lean turned his attention to the asylum, with its massive, turreted buildings, rising up like brick mountaintops from a sea of green lawns. He wondered about the thoughts of those who saw this sight for the first time when being committed against their will. He hoped such arrivals were scheduled for daylight hours. The sight of those dark spires against a night sky would have been unnerving. 'Imposing' was not a sufficient description of the place. It was like some sprawling, late-medieval fortress built to withstand a hundred-year siege. Only these walls were built to protect the outside world from the horde of mentally deranged barbarians huddled within the keep.

As they drew up to the front of the administration building, Lean decided it wasn't really so much a fortress. Instead he was put more in mind of a painting he'd seen of an immense alpine monastery tucked away in a remote corner of Europe. A half hour later, their shoes clanging on the tiled hallways as they passed rows of closed cell doors, the idea of a monastery remained in Lean's mind, refusing to be thrown aside. The image kept twisting itself into a grotesque mockery of its origins. Cloisters replaced by barred windows on cell doors. Gregorian chants supplanted by a cacophony of low, tortured groans and calls. Monks replaced in the night by lunatic doppelgängers. For these men, either God had vanished into the abyss of each one's uniquely fractured mind or else he towered over them at an incomprehensible distance, speaking in words they could no longer gather.

The hospital administrator guided them through the halls as he described for his old colleague Dr Steig, the details of the building's layout and the principles upon which the patients were categorized and located. Lean initially attempted to follow the conversation, but his mind soon wandered as he contemplated the sheer scope of the hospital. Unlike a prison, meant to confine the bodies of criminals, this place contained the suffering, damaged minds of the inmates. He struggled with the thought: brick walls intended to rein in the delusions, as if the physical barriers could somehow keep the insanity from leaking out into the world. He wondered how much had really changed in the two hundred years since little Dorcas Good had been chained to a prison wall, in the belief that the heavy manacles would keep her witch's specter from leaving the jail to torment the afflicted girls of Salem.

'Just through here,' the administrator said as he unlocked a steel door that led to a windowless hall. 'He's refused to speak to me in a month, so I won't let him see me accompanying you in there.'

'Thank you,' Dr Steig said.

Lean, Grey, and Dr Steig entered the hallway and closed the door behind them. There were four rooms in this short corridor. Only one other was occupied, and that by a withered old man who lay in a fetal position on his cot. In the last cell, Geoffrey Blanchard sat at a small wooden table pushed up against a side wall. Before him was an arrangement of small colorful feathers, some twine, and several inch-long hooks. There was a narrow bed against the other wall. In the middle of the stone floor was the faint chalk outline of a circle with miniature designs lining the outside perimeter.

Geoffrey Blanchard turned the chair to face his visitors. He was a scrawny man with dark brown hair, a long, angled nose, and deep, still eyes like murky pools of fouled water.

'What does the colonel want now?'

'We wouldn't know about that,' Dr Steig said. 'We have nothing to do with your father.'

'He's no father of mine.'

'Funny, we were led to believe you're the son of Colonel Ambrose Blanchard,' Lean said.

The man gave a slight shake of his head. 'I believe in one secret and unnameable Lord, and in one star in the vastness of the universe in whose consuming fire we are forged and to which we shall return, one Father of Life and Death eternal, Mystery of all Mystery, whose name shall be Chaos. One Earth, the Suckling Mother of us all, and in one womb wherein all men are begotten and formed and wherein they shall rest formless, Mystery of Mystery, and Her name shall be Babel.'

'I'll take that to mean that Agnes Blanchard was not your mother.' Grey continued with a casual wave of his hands. 'That is, before she was murdered by that witch. The one who lived down near the flats of Back Cove.'

Geoffrey's eyes bored into Grey, his expression a thin veil that could not mask his contempt. 'You speak of mere fragments of experience. They hold no true meaning.'

'No meaning?' Grey said. 'The death of your own mother. I find that hard to believe.'

'Your beliefs bind you as hard as manacles. The Innermost is one with the Innermost, yet the form of the One is not the form of the Other; unity requires its opposite. You must release the faith of belief and instead adopt the faith of understanding. When you free yourself of the beliefs that the weak-minded have imposed upon you, the death of your earthly mother, whether by murder or even her own hand, ceases to be of any real concern, Mr Grey.' A grin escaped from the inmate. 'Awaken. Know thyself. And take solace in that knowledge.'

Lean felt the hairs on his neck stiffen in alarm; they hadn't

328

introduced themselves by name to Geoffrey Blanchard. He glanced at Dr Steig, who frowned, clearly surprised.

Grey just smiled in response. 'And I suppose you have convinced yourself that your own actions there at Back Cove are also without meaning. Burning down that hag's cottage. The murder of her son. All of that, your own crimes that day. Your sins against the lives of others.'

Geoffrey Blanchard released a long, slow chuckle but finally regained his composure. 'Sins? You wallow in the mud of social constraints. Mastery of understanding comes by small measures to one who, with dedication, courage, and wisdom, gives over the purpose of his life to understand the universe and to surrender to it and thus prevail. So shall his understanding increase until he has attained completion. "Restriction" is the only word that is sin.'

'Are we to understand that you have turned your soul away from God?' Dr Steig said.

'My soul was in the throes of death, and all through the night I saw God and Satan fighting for my soul. When the dawn came, I felt that God had overcome, but I had only one question left that I could not answer.' A feral, catlike grin spread across Geoffrey's face. 'Which of the two was God?'

Grey held out his hand palm down, urging the doctor to desist. 'Have you been leaving the grounds of the institution, Mr Blanchard?'

'Of course.'

'How often?'

'Nightly. Why would I ever remain here?'

'And by what means?' Lean asked.

'You will never understand. You are blinded by what you

think you see: the obstacles and deceptions of the material plane and physical existence.'

'So you travel free of this cell spiritually,' Grey said.

'On the astral plane.'

'And when you are traveling in that aspect,' Grey asked, 'you can have an effect, interact with people who are themselves confined to the material plane?'

'In a manner, though it would be rather difficult for someone with your fettered perceptions to comprehend.'

'What about her?' Grey drew a photograph from the inside pocket of his coat. Lean saw that it was the close-up of Maggie Keene's face after her death inside the Portland Company. Grey slid his hands through the bars, holding the picture facedown. 'Have you ever had contact with the woman in this picture? In this plane or another?'

Geoffrey Blanchard's eyes darted back and forth between Grey's face and the hidden picture. After a minute, curiosity bested his apparent lack of interest in the lives of those restricted to the material plane. He walked across the floor of the cell. He took the photograph in his hand, but as he did, Grey refused to release it for a moment. Geoffrey's arm straightened out as he stepped back. Another moment and Grey released his own hold on the photograph. He apologized and asked Geoffrey to take a close look at the dead woman's face.

Lean saw Geoffrey's mouth curl up a bit at one corner. Finally the man said, 'One is so much like another; who can say about this woman? But I do not think I have ever had the need to address her.'

'Too bad. Not too late, though,' Grey said. 'Won't you join me in prayer for her soul?'

Lean shot a glance at Grey, wondering whether he was at all serious. Grey's head was slightly bowed, but his eyes were looking up, locked on Geoffrey Blanchard's pale face. 'Our Father which art in heaven, hallowed be thy name. Thy kingdom come. Thy will be done even in earth as it is in heaven.'

Geoffrey Blanchard dropped the photograph back through the bars and strode over to his table. As Grey continued the prayer, Geoffrey snatched up a fishhook, then moved to the center of the chalk circle drawn on the concrete floor. He crouched down in the circle, jabbed his left thumb with the hook, and then traced a thin, smudged line of blood along the outline of the circle.

'What are you doing, Geoffrey?' Dr Steig asked.

The inmate grinned at them, a self-satisfied look on his face. 'You have truly wandered into the dark with no candle to guide you.' His tone switched from condescension to that used by a teacher of young children. 'The first rule of any invocation ritual is, of course, for the Mage to make his circle completely impervious.'

Grey finished his recitation: 'For thine is the kingdom and the power and the glory for ever. Amen.'

Geoffrey Blanchard was kneeling on the floor, arms out wide, his palms upward, head tilted back slightly, and eyes closed. 'I invoke thee, the Bornless One. I invoke thee, the Deathless One. I invoke thee, the Formless One. The One who was always, the One who will ever be, that in Chaos did create the Heavens and the Earth, that did from the ether shape all space and time. From the Immortal Fire drew breath that was the Bornless Spirit, did seize the spear and pierce the veil of the universe, from the blood of the creation did form the shape of Woman and Man.'

The man's hands fell forward onto his lap, and his voice slowed into a hushed, steady droning. 'I become thee who art truth. I become thee who art love. I become thee who art hate. I am he that is the Grace of the Universe. I am he that holds the fire. I am he that brings the night. The Heart Consumed by the Serpent is my name; I am the Bornless One.'

Geoffrey's eyes fluttered, showing the whites, and then his head slumped forward to rest, motionless, upon his chest. The visitors watched him for a minute, trying to decide whether or not the man truly was in a trance or just faking. Either way, Geoffrey Blanchard had clearly ended the interview.

Lean and Grey stood outside on the gravel driveway, waiting for Dr Steig to complete his social obligations inside. 'Psychosis. Grand delusions. Fixed ideas. I don't care what the doctor calls it, the man's a lunatic. And a dangerous one at that.' Lean dropped his cigarette and ground it out underfoot. 'How does he end up like that? His own mother was killed by a witch woman's potion, so why on earth would he take up the occult?'

'His sister reported that he was desperate to contact his mother after her death. From séances to black magic, it could be a slippery slope for an unsound mind,' Grey said. 'But I'm more intrigued by his claims of leaving the building. Interacting with others on the outside.'

'What, because he knew your name?'

Grey dismissed that notion with a wave. 'I've never met the man. He does not know me personally. His little attempt to impress us with his claims of some sort of supernatural knowledge or vision revealed one of two things. Either he has some connection in the outside world who is communicating with him

332

regarding our inquiry into this matter or else he is, in fact, making trips outside the hospital.'

'The hospital boss confirmed he leaves only twice a year for a day out with his sister. And even then they have an attendant who accompanies them.'

Grey shrugged. 'Somebody is being paid well to lie and protect Geoffrey Blanchard. Did you notice what he was working on at his little table?'

'Some sort of sewing. Probably a hobby to keep his mind pre-occupied. I've heard Dr Steig mention such things.'

'Not sewing, exactly. He was tying flies. For fishing.'

'Fishing?' Lean said. 'That's a bit optimistic.'

'Maybe not. Did you notice anything else peculiar about the man?' Grey asked.

'Peculiar? Him?'

'I meant his appearance.'

Lean shrugged and awaited the answer.

'His hands were tanned. I noticed it when he reached for the photograph. His sleeve raised; his wrist was pale by comparison. The last time out with his sister was on April twenty-seventh. And supposedly he's been refusing all outdoor exercise.'

'But he did have a small window. Perhaps he sits by it to tie his fishing flies.'

'It's noontime,' Grey said, 'and you couldn't cast a shadow from that window if you tried. It faces directly north.'

Lean lit another cigarette. 'So he's definitely getting outside of the hospital somehow.' He pondered the implications. 'Is it possible? Twenty years later.'

'Lean?'

'Thinking about what Cap Tolman said in the opium den.

Twenty years could be nothing to a man driven mad for vengeance. Geoffrey Blanchard is somehow removing himself from the asylum. He could have had something to do with Old Stitch's death – poisoning her the same way his own mother was poisoned. If he waited so long to kill Old Stitch, what about the other boy, her son that lived? He's the only witness to that burning who wasn't part of Blanchard's mob. The only one who might tell us who murdered his brother and maybe confirm if there is a link to his mother's recent death. He could still be in danger.'

'An excellent thought, Lean. Whether the motive for killing Old Stitch was revenge, disposal of a witness, or some other cause related to her witchcraft, we should find her surviving son before he ends up like our last known witness.'

The image of Boxcar Annie's swollen, lifeless face flashed in Lean's mind. 'Tolman said the boy was taken to one of the orphanages.'

'The search will be a tedious one,' Grey said. 'In the meantime, I think our new friend Geoffrey Blanchard bears a bit closer watching. It's only ten days to the crescent moon. I'll telegraph McCutcheon for assistance.'

'You think he's up to keeping a hawk's eye on this place?'

'Have you formed so low an opinion of McCutcheon's detective skills?'

'Not that. It's just, Geoffrey Blanchard doesn't exactly have flowing locks and an ample bosom. I wonder if he'll keep McCutcheon's attention for more than a few minutes.'

Grey chuckled. 'Yes. He does seem to devote a bit more of his observational talents to that half of the population. But I think he'll manage. For all his idiosyncrasies and dubious social behavior, the man is an extremely competent and conscientious investigator.'

'Of course,' agreed Lean. It struck him then that this assessment of McCutcheon revealed the true reason Grey continued to associate with the uncouth Pinkerton: He was useful during investigations. That was the solitary consideration by which every living person, apart from clients, victims, and criminals, was to be judged by Perceval Grey. Lean wondered, when this whole affair was over, would the two of them ever have reason to speak again?

55

Lean slid the box of papers back into place on the loaded shelf and took hold of its dust-covered neighbor. After returning down the narrow aisle, he rejoined Grey at the small table borrowed from the city clerk. Two stacks of papers were set before Grey. He quickly finished taking some notes on his pad and stuck a sheet of paper back into place.

'Find something?' Lean asked as he put the box down and took his seat opposite.

'An unrelated matter.'

'A piece of business on the side? You've got quite a nerve, Grey, considering the princely sum you're receiving from the city for your energies.'

Grey smirked.

'The truth is,' Lean said, 'I hope whoever else you're working for is paying enough to keep you in tea and newspapers.'

'Actually, no. He's not even aware of my efforts on his behalf.

In fact, the task hadn't even occurred to me until last night, when I was contemplating our work here.'

'A friend, then?'

'An acquaintance. One who may prove useful in the future,' answered Grey.

'Well, I can see you're not disposed to share the details, and I'm content to deal with only a single mystery in this dark little dust mine.'

Lean returned his attention to the yellowed sheets of paper that filled the boxes. Each listed the known facts surrounding the life and circumstances of a child born in the city of Portland. The current box contained notices of births for the period from May 1871 through January 1873. The record-keeping effort produced imperfect results. Official notices were sometimes lacking for those who had entered the world in less-than-ideal circumstances or were, for whatever reason, given up by their mothers. Children who were delivered to the various orphanages or other custodial agencies were also filed among the birth records. When birth dates were unknown, they were recorded chronologically among the live births according to the date that they were handed over to the orphanage. Most of the orphans' forms were largely blank. Some had notes reflecting their adoption into new families. Others, typically those who were older when they first arrived, showed no such arrangement. They gave a date only when the child left, often at age sixteen, sometimes noting placement at a factory or workhouse.

Lean's concentration was just starting to wander when he caught sight of a name that made him snap to attention. 'Lucy,' he muttered. He looked up and saw Grey staring at him. 'This boy, Jack Whitten, his mother is listed as Lucy. Lucy Whitten.

August ninth, 1871. The date fits. He's listed as thirteen years old when he's placed with the Catholic orphanage.'

'We don't know for certain that her true name was Lucy.'

'No, but it all fits. Even the note here at the bottom – says he was brought in by the police. No further explanation.'

Grey had come around the table and was reading the sheet over Lean's shoulder. 'Father: unknown. Mother: Lucy Whitten. Age: 35? Her place of birth: Whitchurch, England. Whereabouts: unknown.'

'It all fits,' Lean repeated.

'Perfectly.'

'He was discharged April of '74. No indication of where he went.'

Grey grabbed his notepad and started copying the information. 'No, but someone at the cathedral might know something about him.'

Lean cut across Lincoln Park, then rounded onto Franklin Street. The tall, tapering spire of the Roman Catholic cathedral was visible ahead, looming over the skyline. It rivaled the observatory for the honor of highest point in the city, losing only due to the fact that the latter was set atop Munjoy Hill. Lean spotted Grey across the street, bent forward and talking to a little girl of about eight. As Lean approached, he heard the girl laugh, then watched as she ran away, pausing briefly to wave at Grey and giggle once more.

'Tormenting small children, Grey?'

'Quite the opposite, I assure you.'

'Who's your new friend?'

'She proudly informs me that she is Rose Cleary. Though don't let the Irish surname and blond pigtails fool you. She's plainly descended from Arab street traders. A full dollar it cost me to get this off her.'

Grey held up a necklace of a dozen shiny red beads, each one tipped with a black spot, threaded into a thin leather string.

'There's no way her parents will believe someone actually paid a dollar for that. They'll probably tan her backside for stealing.'

'More likely congratulate her and take the money.' Grey handed the necklace to Lean, who let it hang from his fingers.

'Very fetching, though I'm not sure when you'll have occasion to wear it.'

'I noticed it while she was playing in the yard. Look again.' Grey pointed at the shiny red circles. 'Do the seeds remind you of anything?'

'Seeds?' Lean studied the necklace a moment before he remembered. 'The ones you found at Old Stitch's hovel.'

'Precisely.'

'Well, they make pretty beads. Common enough, I suppose.'

'I don't recall ever seeing them before,' Grey said.

'Did the girl say where she got them?'

'A man gave them to her sometime ago, along with fifty cents. She couldn't describe him in any detail. He asked her to watch the cathedral for him while he waited at a serving house down the street. Funny how even small children know where liquor is sold, yet somehow the police remain puzzled. The man wanted to know when a certain priest came out.'

Lean grinned. 'That must be some sort of sin to confess, where a man waits for the priest outside to see him on the sly. So do you have a plan to track down this man?'

Grey shook his head. 'Not enough details to investigate the man. The seeds are a different story.'

They headed up the steps and toward the broad doors of the cathedral. It was a massive brick structure topped with two black-shingled spires like jousting lances raised in salute to heaven. As did many of the city's Protestants, Lean thought the building an ostentatious eyesore. For that reason, he was surprised by the unassuming office of Portland's Catholic bishop, James Healy. The room suited the man behind the desk – straightforward, plain in appearance and manner. Bishop Healy himself was on the back side of middle age. He was a mulatto, with light brown skin and short, tightly curled hair speckled with gray. Lean had seen the man plenty of times but had never actually met him. It took only the brief introduction in the office for Lean to decide he liked the man. The bishop exuded a quiet confidence; he struck Lean as being completely comfortable, and his gentle manner imposed itself on the room's atmosphere.

'So then, Deputy Lean, how can I be of assistance?'

'We're hoping you might have information on a boy who came through the orphanage about twenty years ago.'

The bishop smiled. 'A boy from twenty years ago? Hundreds upon hundreds of boys have passed through those doors over the years.'

'He was an older boy by the name of Jack Whitten.'

'Jack Whitten? My goodness.' The bishop let out a chuckle. 'How many people has he gone and killed now?'

A glance at Grey showed surprise even on his normally imperturbable features. Lean opened his mouth to ask a question, but too many thoughts were fighting to escape, causing a mental logjam.

'You'll have to forgive me,' Bishop Healy said. 'It's just, I suppose I always expected to get a visit about that boy.'

'What did you mean about him going and killing now? Has he killed someone before?'

'No, of course not. Though not necessarily due to a lack of effort on his part. You see, the reason I remember him so clearly is that he nearly did in a dozen of the other boys. Slipped something into the dinner one night. They all got violently ill.' The bishop removed his small, round spectacles and cleaned them on a handkerchief. 'Of course he denied it, and we could never figure how he managed it, but I have no doubt it was him.'

Lean took out his notebook. 'Tell me about him.'

'Jack Whitten was a quiet boy when he came to us. Tremulous, even. Though that was understandable.'

Lean nodded. 'It was reported that a younger brother had died.'

'That's what I was told. There were rumors, but the police had simply said that it was an unpleasant situation, and we more or less left it at that. Tragic upbringings can be the norm here. But Jack was particularly awkward. There was almost a feral quality to him. He didn't fit in with the other boys; they taunted him mercilessly. He was very small for his age, but he'd get into a scrape with any of them.'

Bishop Healy cleared his throat, as if it had just occurred to him that he was painting a needlessly unflattering picture of the orphans who had been entrusted to the church's care.

'For all that, he was a smart boy. Would read anything he could get a hold of. Must have read the Bible a dozen times over, though if I had to guess, I'd say he'd heard not a single verse of it before he set foot in here.'

'He was here for about three years, wasn't he?' Lean asked.

The bishop squinted as if he were actually attempting to peer into the distant past. 'Not that long. There was another incident. Jack's presence became . . . a problem.'

'What happened?' asked Grey.

'To be quite honest, I don't remember all the details now. Trying to steal something, perhaps. It was a very sensitive matter, because he'd gotten another boy involved. Son of a well-respected family. Quite an uproar – corrupting influence and all that. Jack was relocated over to the state reform school. We thought the change might be best for him.'

'Sounds like it was good for the other boys as well,' Grey said.

Bishop Healy allowed himself a bit of a smile. 'True enough, but Jack took it hard.'

'What about speaking?' Grey asked. 'Can you describe for us his stammer or his struggles with speech?'

'Not sure I follow you. A quiet boy, all right. But I don't recall he had any physical difficulties with speaking.'

'He was a dark-haired boy, correct?' Grey said.

'No. Light-haired. Quite pale, actually. You could almost see right through him. Had that sort of air about him, just not very remarkable.'

Lean sank back into his chair. He had been thinking the same thing as Grey. Jack Whitten sounded very much like the sort of person they were looking for. He'd been an angry boy, ill used by society, with a vengeful streak. There was a strong familiarity with the Bible, though coupled with an apparent hostility toward Christian institutions. But all that was tossed aside now.

'And he never spoke of his family?' Grey asked.

'Not to me, but then I never had much of a connection to the boy. The man you really should have talked to was Father Coyne.

341

He was active with the orphanage in those days. Took Jack under his wing. Until the boy was sent off, that is.'

'"Should have talked to"? Has he passed on?' Grey asked.

'No, just on sabbatical. His health has taken a rather serious downturn recently. A shame, really. I mean, he's still rather a young man, all in all.'

'Could we speak with Father Coyne?' Lean asked.

'I'm afraid not. He's not accepting visitors. Doctor's orders.'

'What, may I ask, is wrong with him?' Grey inquired.

'Nobody knows, though he never had the strongest constitution to begin with. Then, about six months ago, he began complaining of body aches, cramps, and then his eyesight began to fail.'

'What do the doctors say?' Grey asked.

'They're baffled. They thought he'd recover quickly at first. But he didn't. He saw specialists and tried all sorts of remedies. Some, to be honest, seemed to be little more than doses of hoping for the best. Fortunately, we're long on faith here.'

'Nothing helped?'

Bishop Healy shook his head. 'The final opinion was that the best thing for him was total rest. He's retreated to the Stroudwater area. His family had a little cottage out that way.'

'No visitors at all?' Grey asked.

'Not even myself. Though he's got Peter Chapman with him.'

Lean started to ask the question, but the bishop quickly added, 'Just a man who used to do odd jobs around here. Now he helps with Father Coyne's daily tasks. But apart from Peter, he lives in complete solitude. Good for the soul and hopefully the body as well. He does write when he can, and occasionally he reports days of feeling better, but it never lasts.' Bishop Healy opened a desk drawer, rummaged a bit, and pulled out an envelope. 'Received this just the other day. You can see by the address that his hand is weak.'

'I'm sorry to hear that,' Lean said. 'But are you quite sure there's no way we could speak to him, even briefly?'

'I don't think it's advisable to disturb the poor man just to ask about a boy from two decades ago. Is there something particular you would wish to speak with Father Coyne about? Maybe it's something I could answer for you.'

'Your Excellency,' Grey said, 'I do not mean any disrespect, but can we be assured that what we speak of here will not pass beyond these walls?'

'Mr Grey, I do know a thing or two about honoring confidential discussions.'

'Of course.' Grey acknowledged his faux pas with a nod. 'There was a certain act of violence against the Whitten family that precipitated Jack's arrival at the orphanage. We have reason to believe that the boy's mother may have recently been murdered, for reasons which remain unclear but which may be linked to the events of twenty years ago. We believe that Jack Whitten is the sole witness to those earlier events and, as such, the same party who had reason to kill his mother might have it in mind to seek out Jack. We need to find him before anybody else does.'

Bishop Healy's eyebrows had arched up during the explanation, and he now shot an incredulous glance at Lean, who nodded in agreement. 'I see. This sounds most serious. I must say that, despite what the doctors think, given the circumstances, I'm sure Father Coyne would wish to speak to you. I know you're anxious, but I must insist that you let me write to him and ask when he might meet with you, so as to spare him any undue surprises. I could send you a note when I get his response.'

They took their leave of the bishop and exited the cathedral. Lean glanced at the sky. It had rained earlier, and now thunderheads were visible off to the southwest.

'Pinning down this Jack Whitten is turning into quite an assignment,' Lean said.

'Speaking of assignments.' Grey drew a telegram from his coat pocket and handed it to Lean. 'McCutcheon's watch on Geoffrey Blanchard.'

Lean saw that it was dated August 12, that morning. He paused at the bottom of the steps and read in a low voice, '"Grey – G.B. left hospital. Didn't go very far. Just into Danvers proper. Room at Greenbriar Inn. Collected one letter on arrival. Ate alone. Strolled through town, bought nothing. No contacts. Note – you're not the only one interested in our man's movements. Another fellow shadowing G.B. At inn before us. Never spoke to Blanchard, but clearly marking him. Will continue observation – Walt."'

56

With a certain reluctance, Mrs Porter released Helen's hands. She leaned forward, across her kitchen table, and gave the younger woman a reassuring smile.

'I'm sorry, dear. Don't take it to mean he doesn't want to reach out to you. My abilities are not what they were. And sometimes the barriers are just too great.'

'No need to apologize. Thank you for trying,' Helen said.

'Would you like some tea?'

'That would be lovely.'

As they waited for the kettle to boil, Helen broke the silence.

'When you were active as a medium – years ago and all – did you know a woman who they called Old Stitches? She died this past year.'

'Old Stitch,' Mrs Porter corrected her. 'Yes, I knew her, years ago. Not well, mind you, but I'd hear things from customers and whatnot. Bits of news and gossip.'

'We've heard there was a fire at her house. Set on purpose, actually, maybe on account of one of her customers dying. A well-to-do customer at that.'

'Yes, plenty of the richer ladies in town would go to her in those days.'

'Must have been a peculiar sight. All those well-fixed ladies trudging down to some dank little shack by the cove.'

Mrs Porter smiled. 'Later, when she was Old Stitch. But before that, at first, she was just Lucy, the servant girl, who was able to know things.'

'A servant for whom?'

'I don't recall. But yes, when she came over, she was a domestic for some family on the West End. Soon enough all the ladies in those circles were coming round to see her. She moved on later, fell out of favor with her employers over something. But still, plenty of the women kept on going to her. You'd be surprised how attached they can get. People get so turned about in their lives, they think you'll have the answers for them. Some folks so desperately need to make sense of it all.'

'And did you ever happen to hear what happened to her after the fire? What happened to her sons?'

'Sorry, I've no idea.'

*

'You went there to ask her about Old Stitch?' Grey said.

'No, actually ... something different.' Helen diverted her attention to the makeshift laboratory set up on the corner table in Grey's study.

'I see. And did you make contact with the other side?'

'No.' Helen blushed in mild embarrassment but obscured the fact by focusing on the chemistry equipment.

'Perhaps the spirit was otherwise occupied. Or not actually dead yet.'

Helen froze. After a long silence, she readied her voice and answered, 'He's dead to me.'

'And yet you—'

'I was curious for Delia's sake. Only for Delia.'

'I see.'

'Do you? You think me foolish, that all of this is absurd. Don't you ever wonder in the slightest? Surely there is somebody – a loved one, perhaps – you'd wish to speak with again. If it were possible?'

'That's your answer,' Grey said. 'It's not possible.'

Helen moved back toward the center of the room. 'But if it were. If there was the slightest chance to say something. Or to hear something, words that a departed soul might wish to tell you now.'

'People live as they will, and they have their whole lifetime to say what they will. To hope you will receive from someone, once dead, more than he or she managed to give you while alive – it defies all reason. You may as well wish on stars.'

She took another step closer and studied Grey's face, looking for some small fissure in his cool demeanor. 'But surely you feel something for them. All the time you spend with dead bodies, thinking about them, the work you do on behalf of murder victims. Avenging their deaths. You must feel something.'

'The work I do is not for the dead. I can't give them vengeance. Perhaps it feels like that for their loved ones, when a criminal is brought to justice. But rest assured there is nothing, absolutely nothing, I can do to help the dead. The dead are the dead, and life is left only to the living.'

57

A loud thump stirred McCutcheon from his stupor. It took a moment for him to gain his bearings; he was still dressed, shoes on, sitting up in his hotel bed. The gas lamp was lit. He had no idea what time it was. He swung his legs over the side and then reached out for the nightstand to retrieve, and finish off, a tumbler of whiskey. There was movement overhead in the room above his: third floor, Geoffrey Blanchard's room. He glanced toward the ceiling after another thud, and then something crashed to the floor. McCutcheon grabbed his coat, then snatched his gun from the nightstand and slipped it into his pocket as he headed out the door.

There were sets of stairs at either end of the hallway, and McCutcheon moved to his right, hurrying while trying not to make too much of a commotion. He took the stairs two at a time, right hand gripping the gun in his pocket, while he steadied himself against the wall with his left. The third-floor hallway was dimly lit. A man in dark clothing stepped out from a door halfway down the hall. It was about the same location as McCutcheon's room on the floor below.

'You there!'

The man threw a glance at him, but it was too dark for McCutcheon to make out his face. The shadowy figure turned and fled toward the stairwell at the other end of the hall. McCutcheon sped after him but stopped at the open doorway and looked into Geoffrey Blanchard's room. A man was lying face-down just inside the doorway. A glance was enough to see that it wasn't Blanchard himself, but the blond man who'd been tailing Blanchard. There was a nasty bump on the back of the man's skull and a trickle of blood flowing from it.

McCutcheon dashed away, chasing the fleeing man, who had already disappeared down the stairs. He followed the sounds ahead of him, making his way to the ground floor and out through a side door of the Greenbriar Inn. McCutcheon saw a swatch of black streaking across the hotel's back lawn, and he started to reach for his gun, but the man was already heading into an alleyway between two neighboring buildings. He leaped down the three steps to the ground and broke into a run, threading through a labyrinth of back passages that zigzagged between shops and houses. McCutcheon dashed through murky puddles and over one drunken body sprawled on the ground as he dodged and twisted past trash bins and discarded boxes. He thrust himself over the short fence, then through more alleys and across several avenues. There were only a few souls left on the streets at that late hour, though at one intersection McCutcheon almost collided with a couple who staggered aside, cursing at him as he rushed past.

His leg muscles burned and his breath came harder as he followed after the man. Entering a wide-open street, McCutcheon saw the man's long coat flapping behind as he disappeared into a lumberyard. McCutcheon chased him past a heaping stack of logs and sawed planks, then in and out of two rows of long, open-sided sheds where huge quantities of boards were stacked in varying heights. Off to his left, and over the sounds of his own gasping breaths, McCutcheon heard a loud rumbling sound. As he scaled a smaller pile to get out the far side of the shed, a shot rang out and a piece of wood exploded, showering him with splinters. He jumped down, took cover behind a small pile of planks, and peeked around the corner. Behind the lumberyard was a field of grass with some woods looming in the distance.

There was movement ahead and a bright light, and then McCutcheon heard the whistle. The low rumbling sound he'd heard moments earlier was a cargo train coming in from the left at fifteen miles per hour. The headlight revealed the man standing still in the field, right next to the tracks. In just seconds he would meet the train, hop aboard, and make his escape.

McCutcheon stepped clear of the lumber stacks, dropped to one knee, and steadied his pistol. He fired three times. The man grabbed his leg and stumbled ahead onto the tracks. McCutcheon watched as the train reached the man, who at the last possible second vaulted out of the engine's path.

McCutcheon bolted up and ran into the field, keeping his eyes glued to the spot where the man had disappeared. Once he reached the tracks, he crouched and peered under as the wheels rumbled by. He couldn't see anyone on the far side. The last of the rail cars passed him, and McCutcheon hurried across the tracks. His eyes swept over the wide expanse of fields on the other side. There was no sign of the man.

'Beat the devil,' McCutcheon muttered as he struggled to catch his breath. He bent close to the ground again and struck a wooden match. Within a few feet, he found blood splatters. He followed alongside the tracks, lighting two more matches before the trail of blood drops ended. McCutcheon stepped onto the tracks, watching the lamp at the rear of the train recede into the night.

58

The next afternoon, Lean held on to Owen's hand as they moved through the confines of the alley below Fore Street. He guided the boy around puddles of rainwater and the city's other runoff that pooled among the uneven paving stones. They passed windows covered with steel shutters, remnants from half a century earlier, when Fore Street had snaked along the waterfront and the buildings facing the wharves were protected with steel shutters against the prows of ships docked too close. That was before the massive filling-in of the waterfront to create Commercial Street and link the railroad terminals at the western and eastern ends of town.

Father and son went around a corner and slid past the few outside tables of Ruby's Café. The large front windows were open, and Lean saw Grey seated inside, far enough back so the sun reached his tabletop but left him shaded. Lean steered Owen over to Grey's table. The boy's eyes moved from Grey to the untouched slice of blueberry pie on the table, apprehension turning to curiosity.

'Hope you don't mind.' Lean nodded toward his son. 'Emma needed a rest.'

Grey shook his head. 'Not at all.'

Lean ordered coffee for himself, milk and a ginger cookie for Owen. 'Why the change of scenery?'

'My charming landlady, Mrs Philbrick, insisted I leave so she could clean the premises.'

'There must have been threats of bodily harm.'

'On both sides,' Grey said.

Next to Grey's coffee, Lean saw a thin volume opened to an article entitled 'Properties of the Proteids of Abrus Precaratorius Seeds.' 'What's that book?'

Grey held it up so that Lean could see the cover of the May 1889 *New England Pharmacological Journal.*

'How long until she allows you back in?'

'Three o'clock,' Grey said. 'Though I doubt she'll need even half that time. Just kept yammering on about me getting some fresh air and sunlight.'

'You do look pale.'

'You probably consider that a compliment.'

'Have you been sleeping at all?' Lean asked.

'Enough.'

'Well, I hope your deprivations are at least proving worthwhile.'

'They are indeed.' Grey held up his hand, from which dangled the red-and-black seed necklace he'd purchased from the little girl outside the cathedral.

'Is that a magic necklace?' Owen asked, his eyes fixated on the shiny seeds.

'Perhaps,' Grey answered, 'if you consider poisoning someone to be magic.'

Owen's expression turned to a dubious glare. 'Are you going to poison someone?'

'Of course not, Owen. Mr Grey is just teasing,' Lean said. 'So what is that?'

'*Abrus precatorius.* Also known as Indian licorice, the rosary pea, or jequirity bean. Native to India, where it is used in decorative necklaces. It's also boiled and eaten – cooking destroys the toxins. It's poisonous only if the seeds are broken and ingested raw. They're used medicinally for everything from a contraceptive to an aphrodisiac, emetic to laxative. Also said to cure snakebites, gonorrhea, malaria, and night blindness. The root is used to induce abortion, while the juice from a paste of the leaves and seeds can treat the graying of your hair.'

'The original Indian cure-all. Explains why Old Stitch kept it around,' Lean said.

'And why someone else bothered to collect her seeds.'

Owen finished his cookie, then dug two wooden soldiers from his pocket. 'Agghh! Poison necklace, I'm dying.'

'Not at the table, Owen.' Lean turned his attention back to Grey. 'Do you suppose those seeds are what killed Stitch herself?'

'Possibly. The effects are evident within hours to days. Abdominal pain, nausea, burning of the throat, lesions of the mouth and esophagus. The worst dangers are severe vomiting and diarrhea, which lead to dehydration, convulsions, and shock that can be fatal. The toxin, abrin, can also have a direct toxic effect on the kidneys and liver. An infusion of the seeds can cause conjunctivitis by contact. Ingestion of just one or two seeds can be fatal.'

'Mom said I could have pie,' Owen informed the table.

'No she didn't. You had a cookie. You don't need pie, too.' Grey slid the plate toward Owen.

The boy reached for it, but Lean's hand landed atop Owen's before the pudgy fingers could seize the edge of the plate.

'But he said I could have it,' the boy whined.

'Yes he did. But I'm your father. You get permission from me.' The two of them stared at each other until Owen looked away, resentment clear upon his face.

'All this over pie,' Lean said. 'Why'd you even order the blasted thing?'

'Mrs Philbrick seems to think I'm rather sickly. Made me swear on her Bible I would get some fresh air and order something to eat.'

'And you actually stuck to your oath and ordered, even though you have no intention of eating the pie. Never figured you for a Bible pounder. Pegged you as an atheist.'

'Does it matter?'

Owen knocked one of his soldiers off the table. The boy slipped out of his chair and disappeared under the table.

'Owen, come out from under there. Owen, do you hear me?' Lean glanced about to see if anyone was watching. He cast his eyes skyward. 'A girl. Please let the next one be a girl. Two boys will be the death of me.'

Lean noticed Grey smirking at him and decided to ignore the boy under the table. 'Let's return to the business at hand.'

'Of course,' said Grey. He reached into a coat pocket and retrieved a letter. 'Arrived by courier this morning from Boston.'

Lean glanced at the opened envelope. 'McCutcheon. More news of the colonel's son – what's he say?' He glanced about to make sure no one would overhear as Grey read the summary of the struggle in Geoffrey Blanchard's hotel room and McCutcheon's pursuit to the railroad tracks.

'On my return to hotel, Blanchard's room empty. Never returned, never checked out. No sign of the blond man either until I boarded the train for Boston after lunch. He was aboard and only left his compartment once – didn't look well. I tailed him after we pulled in. He took the 2:15 B&M north. He's yours to worry about now. Take care with that one.

Happy Hunting,
Walt'

'A blond-haired man following the colonel's son. Simon Gould?' Lean said.

'Quite possible. First he's ransacking the library in search of an old tome on witchcraft. Intent enough to find it that he was ready to employ violence against our intrepid Mrs Prescott. Now he's monitoring our favorite lunatic inmate's whereabouts.'

'Geoffrey Blanchard is the connection between our investigation and Helen's incident at the library after all.'

'We're guilty of being so focused on our own inquiry we ignored the obvious clue as to someone else's curiosity in the same subject that now confounds us.'

'But what exactly was Gould searching for in the library that has any connection to Geoffrey Blanchard?' Lean asked.

'I'm hopeful that we'll have an answer soon. I received a note from Mrs Prescott this morning. Her boss, Meserve, has information on that mysterious page from the stove at Lizzie Madson's. He says it's from some fabled book on black magic.'

'And Gould actually thought he'd find something like that sitting on the library shelves?'

'It shows they don't know exactly what it is they're looking for. Gould sought Mrs Prescott's help in finding an old book on witchcraft. He could not offer a name, an author, or a description. They don't know the details. They know only that there is a book they must find. The temperance union's understanding of the case is less complete than our own.'

Lean shook his head. '*We're* searching for clues to when and where the killer will strike next. Why are *they* looking for it? The only clear motivation we've seen on the colonel's part has been to hide his delusional son away from the public's gaze.'

'The incident in the library was right after Maggie Keene's death. The first local murder, the first they would have heard of. Something about that murder must have alarmed them. The details were certainly distinctive enough.'

'They realize that Geoffrey is involved. They know something of his interest in the occult; perhaps he's mentioned a book on witchcraft.' Lean let the implications churn and shift in his mind.

'Are you talking about witches?' Owen's muffled voice rose up from beneath the table with great enthusiasm.

'Course not,' Lean assured him in a firm tone.

'I suspect they're not looking for the book because they want information,' Grey said. 'They want to hide it. Something about the book threatens them. It must contain some sort of incriminating evidence. Something linked to these murders.'

Lean nodded. 'The same as Boxcar Annie. They paid McGrath plenty to keep her tucked away. Perhaps her description of the killer sounded too much like Geoffrey Blanchard.'

'Gould's not the type to ever crack and confess, and Boxcar Annie will never reveal her secrets. But there's still the book. If no one could ever read it, no one could know that there's any connection between all these killings. No connection means no case to investigate, and so Geoffrey Blanchard will never be arrested or ever prosecuted unless he's caught red-handed. That's why Gould was in Danvers. Making sure Geoffrey doesn't get into trouble.'

Lean considered that for a moment. 'Do you suppose Gould was ready to silence Geoffrey for good to prevent him from committing another murder?'

Grey's head tilted as he mulled over the possibility. 'That may explain the skirmish in Blanchard's hotel room. It seems extreme, but it would ensure there was no public scandal tying Geoffrey Blanchard to the murders – and no resulting drought of donations to the temperance union's coffers.'

'If we can get evidence of Gould's involvement in any of this, we may be able to force the colonel's hand as to Geoffrey Blanchard's activities,' Lean said.

'Of course, he'll insist that nothing be made public.'

'I don't care if it's made public,' Lean said, 'so long as we can stop the killer.'

'Agreed. Though if Geoffrey Blanchard is our killer and the colonel's been concealing evidence of his son's crimes, then he's allowed additional murders to occur ... '

Lean and Grey regarded each other for a long moment. In his mind Lean was weighing what he knew against what he could possibly hope to prove if Geoffrey Blanchard or his father were ever brought before a jury.

Grey raised his cup of coffee in salute to Lean, smiled, and took a sip. 'They're waiting for us at the historical society. Perhaps it's time for you to return the boy home.'

59

Upon entering the research room of the historical society, Lean and Grey greeted Helen and her boss. 'Thank you for agreeing to help us with this matter,' Lean said to F. W. Meserve. 'I hope you've got some ideas, because the story of this burned page is a complete riddle to us.'

'A riddle?' Meserve's eyes glowed. 'Ha! Why, that's exactly what I think. A very specific riddle indeed. If my theory is correct, this is the start of what has been called the "Riddle of the Martyrs". I must say, gentlemen, the page you've sent me is the most incredible. I don't know where to begin.'

'At the outset would be fine,' Grey said.

Meserve took several deep breaths, his bulbous frame trembling with the effort to constrain his excitement. 'There is a book whose title translates to something like the "Black Book of the Secret Journeys of the Great Mage Arrelius," or just the "Black Book". It was reportedly written by a dark wizard named Jacobus Arrelius. In it, he chronicles his travels from England to the Holy Land during the Crusades. He studied magic and alchemy while in Arabian lands and supposedly died there. Tortured and killed as a heretic.'

'Do you have a copy of this Black Book?' Lean asked.

'Heavens no. It's the source of many rumors and stories, but I've never even been sure that it actually exists. I researched it a few years ago in connection with another project of mine. I've only ever found veiled references to it. Anyway, the book is not so special for what Jacobus Arrelius originally wrote. That part is said to be something of a mishmash of standard incantations and whatnot. What makes the book so infamous is an addendum from the early 1600s. A descendant of Jacobus reportedly copied the original text but made several alterations, including, some-where in the body of the work, a most dreadful and powerful spell. He called it the Riddle of the Martyrs.'

'What's so dreadful about it?' Lean asked.

'Its purpose was supposedly to raise the spirit of Jacobus, who had died four hundred years earlier. But it was not just your reg-ular séance-type spirit visit we're talking about. Legend has it the spell actually produced Jacobus into the living flesh. A full and complete conjuring of an actual live person. Literally raising the dead. And this could be accomplished only by a series of human sacrifices.'

'And you think this is it?' Grey asked.

Meserve's head bobbed up and down. 'Oh, yes, I daresay I do. Look again at the page you sent me.' He fumbled through a series of papers until he produced the photograph. 'It says here, "In the first month of my travels in service of the ascension of my Master, James ..." Given the date in the early seventeenth century, this could be taken as a reference to King James – himself a noted devotee of the study of demonology. But the clincher is here in the handwritten note to the side. Barely legible. Someone has given Master James the surname of Arrelan.'

'James Arrelan. Jacobus Arrelius.' Grey nodded. 'Similar names.'

'Very similar. Especially when you dig and find that there was an English lord who died in the Crusades named James Arrelan. Whoever had this copy thought he had finally identified the pas-sage in the book that is the Riddle of the Martyrs. The most unholy spell in the book.'

'Each paragraph does mention an offering.' Grey's eyes were fixed on the page. 'A series of human sacrifices?'

'But the rest is nonsense,' Lean said.

'The entire book is reputed to be filled with such nonsense, but don't be deceived. There are two possible explanations,' Meserve said as he pushed his dipping glasses back over the bridge of his nose. 'First, it could be genuine nonsense. An expert scholar on the subject of black magic once noted that you can often make no pretense of understanding a spell's meaning; most spells likely possess none, which is reasonable since they avail in evoking the devil, who is the sovereign unreason. Or it could be that much of the Black Book simply serves as blinds.'

'Blinds?' Lean said.

'He means intentionally obscure or misleading passages,' Helen said. 'Their only purpose is to distract and hide from the uninitiated those few significant portions of the text. If this section is indeed the riddle, it certainly is well hidden. It sounds rather innocent. You wouldn't think this is meant to raise an evil witch from the fires of hell back into human form.'

'So that leaves us with what?' Lean said. 'Part of a riddle that may just be gibberish?'

'Complete gibberish, no doubt,' Grey said. 'But our man believes he has solved this evil riddle and is acting accordingly. We must attempt to come to the same solution he has.'

'How?' Lean asked. 'By going mad, so we can think the same as him?' A dull pain was beginning to pulse in his temple. He reached for a cigarette and his matches. 'Even if we could equal his insanity, he has the complete riddle. We have only a piece of it.'

359

'Ah!' Meserve's normally molelike eyes grew wide behind his thick lenses. 'That brings me to my most important question for you. Where exactly did you find this page?'

'Within the city,' Grey said.

Meserve's hands fidgeted like those of a child ready to claw open a birthday gift.

'Good news?' Lean asked.

'It squares with another theory of mine, regarding the possible location of a copy of the Black Book.'

'Let's have it, then.' Lean took a deep drag on his cigarette.

'Bear with me. Hundreds of hours of research over the last five years deserve more than just blurting out my suspicions.'

Lean started to protest but felt Grey's hand on his arm. He shut his mouth and resigned himself to being regaled with the odd little historian's tale.

'Several years ago I came into possession of a rather unique collection of papers. Letters, diary entries, and whatnot that essentially chronicle the life of one of the earliest settlers in this area, Caleb Pierce. He was a servant to Mr Henry Jocelyn, the proprietor of Black Point, now Prout's Neck in Scarborough. Anyway, the papers recount the fascinating life of this young man who soldiered his way through forty-odd years of Indian wars here in Maine, starting with King Philip's War in 1675. I plan to edit and compile the history for publication.'

Lean raised a finger, but Meserve cut off his protest. 'Anyway, what starts to bring this all around to the business at hand are a few odd remarks and notations by Caleb Pierce that relate directly to the Salem witch trials. You see, one of his compatriots here during King Philip's War was none other than the Reverend George Burroughs.'

Lean and Grey each exchanged a quick look with Helen, who gave a conspiratorial smile.

Meserve paused, apparently expecting something more like a gasp of recognition, then continued, 'As you know, Burroughs was one of the nineteen victims hanged as witches. In fact, he was alleged to have been the ringmaster of the whole devilish conspiracy. Both before and after his time in Salem, he held posts as a minister in Maine. He was in Portland, or Casco, at the time war first broke out with the Indians. His life was at risk several times, but he always came through unscathed.'

'That was part of the evidence against him at his later trial – how he was able to survive the wars, often absenting himself just prior to the calamities that befell the colonists,' Helen said.

Meserve plucked up a paper and held it close to his face. 'This is a letter from Caleb Pierce to Mr Jocelyn, dated August thirteenth, 1676. The town of Casco had just been decimated by a surprise Indian attack. Many of the colonists were killed or captured. Pierce was with a group that escaped to one of the islands in the bay.' Meserve adjusted his glasses and squinted as he focused on the page in his hands.

'We here having little provision, the next night some men did cross back to the remains of the town and by virtue of the Lord's guiding hand, did manage to come away with provisions, including shot and powder recovered from one of the storehouses and more from Wallis' house. On our return to Andrews Isle, I was gladdened to find the Reverend Burroughs having by virtue of his own hands begun construction of a stone wall for defense. You yourself know the surprising strength in the Good Reverend's frame. The business was trying enough that all our hands were sorely cut by the jagged

rocks and work of digging out the stones for use. It is to be hoped that no more English blood shall stain that wall before the Lord sees fit to favor us with redemption.'

Meserve set the paper down and looked over the top of his spectacles. 'It goes on, but the part I read shows that Burroughs and Pierce were comrades-in-arms. Men who had placed their lives in each other's hands. Thus, when the witchcraft panic spread sixteen years later and Burroughs's life was threatened again, this time by his fellow English, it is perfectly reasonable that he turns once more to Pierce. This next bit is dated just a week before Burroughs was arrested for witchcraft.' Meserve set the letter down, took up a new page, and once again adjusted his spectacles.

'"G.B. came visiting to Black Point in a state of great distress. He delivered to me a parcel and bade me swear a great oath that I would neither destroy nor ever open it. He stated only that it had come to him under strange circumstances and there were those who would see him brought to harm by it. To reveal it could be to forfeit his life and possibly my own."'

'This next entry, by its substance, we can place in late August 1692. Pierce writes, "G.B. hanged this week past. I returned home directly and, with only my own life to risk, did break my oath and open his parcel. It is a book of foul magick. May the Good Lord forgive me that I ever held in mine own hand such a thing as this."'

Meserve's face had taken on a pinkish tinge, his growing excitement very much in evidence as he continued to read from a new page. '"I brought the book to Rev. T. today. He had scarce lifted the cover before I heard him gasp most terribly, exclaiming that it be the Devil's own. I denied all, daring not speak the truth, saying only it was left that day by a stranger at the tavern. I read the first page and knew it spoke of evil things and so brought it here. Rev. T. bade me never to speak of this. That oath I gladly swore, much relieved to be free of that cursed volume.'"

Meserve set the pages down. 'The Reverend T. refers to a Thomas, who was here in Portland in the early 1700s. I was able to track his descendants as far as 1840. If the Black Book stayed in the hands of the Thomas family, we can trace it as far as fifty years ago, with every reason to believe it has remained in the vicinity.'

Lean stared at Meserve for a minute, waiting for the payoff. 'That's an awfully long stroll of the tongue for you to tell us you don't know where it is.'

'O ye of little faith. In the course of my research, I raised some eyebrows. Because the same questions had been asked twenty years ago, by some learned-looking fellows who claimed to be private collectors but were rumored to actually be from Harvard's Divinity School. And it was said that somewhere in this city they eventually got a copy of what they were looking for.'

Lean glanced at Grey and saw a satisfied smirk appear on his face.

'Of course,' Meserve continued, 'when I took the train down to Cambridge to see about the truth of that, they wouldn't give me the time of day. Acted like they were surprised we even had books in Maine, let alone one they'd be interested in copying.'

Grey still look pleased. 'Perhaps we might have better luck.'

'If you do manage to get a copy ...'

'Agreed, Meserve. One good turn and all that.'

There were many thanks offered, and then Grey invited

Helen to step outside with him and Lean. Once on the street, free of the cloistering effect of the research room, with its imposing mounds of clutter and books, Lean took several deep breaths of fresh air. 'I didn't think the idea of Harvard Divinity School would bring such a smile to your face.'

'I was involved in a small matter at the university library a few years ago,' Grey said.

'I suppose certain unpleasant revelations came to light,' Helen said.

'They always do.'

'Are you still welcome on the grounds?' Lean asked.

'I do have one contact at Harvard who owes me a rather large favor. Unfortunately, my presence might cause him some embarrassment.'

'Would a police deputy be better?' Lean asked.

Grey considered the options for a moment. 'A historical researcher might be best. Perhaps one accompanied by her distinguished uncle.'

60

Following an early train departure the next day, Helen and Dr Steig were greeted by Newell Scribner, a Harvard professor and a scarecrow of a man. His large head was propped up on a thin neck and looked as if it might tumble aside and crash into a shoulder at any moment. He held a chair out for Helen and then gestured toward Dr Steig to take the only other seat at the table. They were in a small, private study room away from the library's public areas. The leaded windows set into the plain white walls provided ample light.

'I know that the sensitive nature of this volume has been explained, but I simply must reiterate: we were allowed to make a copy only under the strictest confidence and a personal vow of secrecy from the president of our divinity school that the book would be made available to a select few scholars. As far as the general public is concerned, Harvard University does not possess a copy of this book.'

'We understand,' Dr Steig assured him.

'So why isn't it housed at the divinity school's library?' Helen asked.

'They haven't the necessary security. Would you believe that it wasn't even fireproofed until the new building was completed five years ago? Besides which, the students practically run that place, and for them there's just the one Good Book. Apparently, every other text is free to be handled like penny serials. Here we can ensure the proper discretion and care of delicate volumes.'

'In any event, we do certainly appreciate your assistance,' Dr Steig said.

'Only the fact of a certain prior service to the university by Mr Grey – as well as your own professional reputation, Doctor – has persuaded the director to allow you this opportunity.' Scribner held out his hand palm up, looking as if he expected a gratuity. 'I hope you understand that I must ask you to relinquish any pencils, papers, or other writing implements.'

'We understood the terms, Mr Scribner. Neither of us has brought any such items.'

'Splendid. Well then, just one moment.' He passed out

through a narrow door set inconspicuously in one corner of the room. Helen heard a lock turn, and a minute later Newell Scribner returned with a dark, leather-bound book that he set on the table in front of them.

Helen stared at the volume, surprised by how thin it appeared. 'It seems so slight. I guess with all the talk it had taken on more substance in my imagination.'

'Yes, a mere eighty-seven pages. The transcription remained true to the exact pagination of the original. Though when you consider its age, and that it is essentially the travel diary of a raving lunatic, its brevity is not actually a surprise.'

'A travel diary? But I thought it was some sort of dark treatise on witchcraft,' Helen said.

'In parts, yes. Hence all the sensitivity. I must admit that this is not my area of expertise, and I have only briefly reviewed the text myself. But the bulk of the writing is, in my opinion, a rambling diatribe of nonsensical pagan claptrap. The author seems content to fill the pages with whatever random musings occur to him as he makes his way across the Holy Land in search of some mystical power.'

'If it's all just a stack of foolishness, as you say, then I fail to see why such trouble has ever been taken over the tome.'

'Well, that I can answer for you, Doctor. Two very powerful factors have worked to preserve the book and impart a heightened sense of meaning to its existence. First, there's a diabolical curse addressed to whoever would damage the book. And second, it's said to contain the promise of accomplishing, albeit in the context of black magic, the return to the flesh of the immortal soul.' Scribner smiled as he opened the book, adding, 'And all that on page one.'

Helen began to read aloud, her voice instinctively quiet in the small chamber.

'Herein, should the Servant prove unworthy, are the sacred words of the journey to the Master at the time of the fourth cycle from the betrayal by those who would not see. The summoning of the spirits of the air hastens the Master's return from the ether. The Servant is the vessel, the Servant's soul the wine of life, born in blood, in blood sustained. He is come from the void to fill the nothingness. He is called forth from the dark to draw air again and walk anew on this soil. The flesh and sinew of the emptied husk the Servant has prepared for his coming. Legion be the curses inflicted on the soul of him that would dare rend these pages or consign them to the flames. Let him know through all the days of man the endless and eternal pain, his own forfeit soul torn anew and forever. Should the Servant fail, then the Next is called as the circle again comes to round.'

'Quite an opening,' Dr Steig said.

'Most of what follows is less dramatic,' Scribner said. 'Much in the way of geographical references, astrological notes, personal observations, mad rantings against those he claims are attempting to prevent his mission. It's only later that the author actually provides examples of what some have interpreted as actual incantations and spells and whatnot. Some of them of the most sinister and godless nature. If you look further back – What . . . ?'

Scribner turned the pages, in disbelief at first, then faster, flipping through the book with far less care than he had previously displayed. Helen saw that the pages had been blotted out. It looked as if they had been soaked in water until the words had drained off the paper, leaving behind only mottled, discolored blurs of ink. Scribner stopped at a spot where only the edges of the pages closest to the binding remained. These had been cleanly cut.

'Gone.' Scribner's voice was barely audible, his thoughts still-born, the words disappearing into the air.

'How . . . I mean, who could have done this?' Dr Steig asked.

'Yes, who would have had access?' asked Helen.

'The registry.' Scribner dashed from the room.

Helen instantly produced a pencil stub and piece of notepaper from her handbag and began to transcribe the book's opening statement.

'Helen?'

'It's a clue,' she said, not looking up from the book. 'Meserve said the riddle was added four hundred years after the original. The introduction mentions the time of the fourth cycle, and if the servant fails, the next is called for as the circle comes around again. Centuries. The sacrifices have to occur on a centennial of the death of this maser wizard. It's been two hundred years since Burroughs died.'

'Well done, Helen. That's wonderful.'

'Hurry, Uncle, before he gets back. Count off the pages – which ones were cut out?'

Dr Steig fingered his way through the book, determining that pages fifty-three and fifty-four had been removed from the binding.

After another two minutes, Scribner reappeared with a red cloth-bound book. 'The registry to the reserved archives. Sign-in is required and monitored by one of the librarians on duty. There's no way to tell which volume any of the visitors used. But the Black Book is kept under lock, anyway. No one would be given permission without my knowledge.' Scribner laid the book open in front of them. 'It could take forever to question all these students and to track down any other visitors.'

'Their addresses are listed,' noted Dr Steig.

'But what are the chances he would use his proper address or his real—' Helen stopped short, then ran her finger up the names listed on the page. She reached the top line, then flipped to the previous page. Halfway up she halted.

Dr Steig read the name next to Helen's fingertip. 'George Jacobs, Salem Village. Salem, yes, but that doesn't mean—'

'The city of Salem is one thing, but Salem Village doesn't exist anymore. That area's been called Danvers for about a hundred years now. And George Jacobs was one of the five men hanged for witchcraft back in 1692, when it was still called Salem Village.'

Scribner suddenly stirred from his shock-induced trance. 'We'll simply have to request that we be allowed to produce another copy.' He stared at them, oblivious to their discussion. 'The two of you could serve as witnesses that this copy was utterly destroyed by some vandal. I could send a letter with you this afternoon and come up there to the cathedral myself at the end of the week.'

'To Portland? But why?' Helen asked.

'The original copy, of course ...' Scribner's voice trailed off, and a fevered look danced in the man's eyes as he realized the confidence he'd just revealed. 'I assumed you knew.'

61

When he first saw them, ten minutes earlier, Bishop Healy assumed that his visitors had come to confirm the August 18 meeting agreed to by Father Coyne. Now the bishop sat behind his large maple desk, his hands spread wide in a posture of utter disbelief. 'I simply don't know what to say, gentlemen. The idea has rather a fantastic ring to it. A centuries-old tome on demonology secretly handed down over the generations and hidden here in the cathedral.'

'Our sources at Harvard tell us a copy was made from the original that was housed here.' Lean absentmindedly held up the telegram he'd received from Helen in Cambridge just over an hour before.

'But that copy was destroyed?' the bishop said.

'Yes.'

'So you haven't actually seen this rumored book.' Bishop Healy raised his eyebrows but did not wait for a response. 'Gentlemen, if such a book did exist, and if Harvard had obtained a copy, then you must be misinformed. Perhaps they were not allowed to divulge the true location of the source material. I can assure you the Catholic Church does not make it a habit to secretly maintain a library of black-magic textbooks.'

'Not a habit,' Grey said, 'just this highly unusual and very singular incidence of the Black Book – which, I've noticed, you have yet to actually deny possessing.'

'A denial hardly seems required.' Bishop Healy fixed a hard stare on Grey. 'The whole story is absurd. I mean, why on earth would we keep such a text here within our walls?'

'Protection,' Lean said.

'The Church has no interest in protecting such volumes.'

'Not even as a curiosity? A point of study?'

'Witchcraft is not considered a valid intellectual pursuit by the Church.'

'Then perhaps for the opposite reason: to protect anyone else from the dangers that the book holds. It is said to contain the most vile and unholy of rituals. The invocation of demons and a method for achieving the embodiment in the flesh of some form of evil spirit or witch.'

Bishop Healy shook his head. 'And if we were holding such an evil book as you say, to keep it safely hidden away, then why would I do that very thing we are supposedly guarding against? By revealing its existence, I would be risking that the people exposed would ... what? Be corrupted, and then ... attempt to perform the diabolical rituals?' Bishop Healy released a nervous chuckle.

'With all due respect, Your Excellency, this really is a matter of the gravest concern,' Grey said. 'It cannot be taken so lightly.'

'And with all due respect to you gentlemen, I do not need to be reminded of the importance of my duties as bishop. As I'm sure you understand, Mr Grey, there have been some who have questioned my abilities rather vigorously for no other reason than my ancestry and the color of my skin. I have always taken it as a given that I had to show extra diligence in the performance of my duties. I can assure you that I have never taken my obligations lightly. And that is something that any member of my congregation would gladly confirm.'

'We're sorry, Your Excellency. There was no offense intended,' Lean said.

Grey nodded. 'I for one certainly do not doubt your commitment, Bishop Healy, or that you have completely earned your congregation's utmost affection and respect, even those who were initially skeptical because of your complexion. I suspect I am even more familiar with the issue than you. You minister to those who accept that your purpose is to guide them toward the light. I, on the other hand, serve as a guide to those dark places in this world where a soul goes only in the most dire of circumstances. Our current situation is one of those times.' Grey paused and fixed his gaze on the bishop's eyes. 'Someone has, in fact, seen this book. And that man, a deranged murderer, is actually attempting to carry out a ritual requiring multiple human sacrifices.'

Bishop Healy's body went rigid. He glanced at Lean, hoping to see that this was some bizarre jest.

Lean nodded. 'There have been three killings, Your Excellency. Maggie Keene was the second. Before that, a woman in Massachusetts was disemboweled and her unborn child cut from her womb. Most recently a woman was drained of her blood.'

The bishop was silent for a long moment. When he did speak, it was little more than a whisper. 'I haven't heard of these other murders.'

'They have been committed in such ways as to hide their true significance,' Grey said.

'What matters now is that the killer will strike again in a matter of days,' Lean added.

'Without the same book to use as a reference, we won't know where he intends to strike. We'll be helpless to stop him. Another woman will die a most gruesome death.'

'This is true?' Bishop Healy had regained most of his volume, but a vein of uncertainty had crept into his solid, confident tenor. 'There's actually someone murdering women as part of some satanic ritual?'

'Yes,' Grey said, 'and he will continue.'

Another long silence followed, and Lean watched the shocked face of Bishop Healy as the man digested it all. Lean could see he was bending under the weight of their horrific news. It was time to throw him a lifeline. The same one they were already clinging to. 'Please help us stop him. There's still time, but we need that book.'

Bishop Healy leaned back in his chair and folded his fingers in front of his chin as he considered all this. 'You must understand, if there was some book here that was being held in secrecy' – he paused, measuring his words – 'and if I had sworn to keep that evil book locked away from the world, I could not break any such solemn vow.'

'But—'

Bishop Healy held up a hand to interrupt Lean's objection. 'If any such book were held under lock and key in our library, I wouldn't simply be able to hand that over to you.' The bishop rubbed his temples and thought the matter over some more before adding, 'And I couldn't allow any such book ever to leave the premises. You understand that, don't you?'

62

Grey handed a dime to the conductor to cover both their fares on the horse car. They stood at the rear of the trolley, away from the other passengers.

'That's as close an invitation to breaking in as we're ever likely to get,' Lean said.

'It would still be against the law.'

Seconds slid by as Lean's mind navigated the shoals of Grey's unexpectedly conservative response. 'Are you serious? After all this, and knowing what's bound to happen next, you'd stand by and do nothing because it's against the law?'

'I wasn't talking about me. You, however, are an officer of the law. If I was caught, Bishop Healy would not press charges. An act of charity from an indisputably charitable man. Marshal Swett and Mayor Ingraham, on the other hand ... Your police career would be finished.'

Lean struggled for a retort, an argument in favor of his active involvement in obtaining the missing pages of the Black Book. Even as he did, thoughts of Emma slipped past the pickets in his mind to reach that place where common sense still held a piece of high ground over the bloody battlefield of this case. She was patiently, and for the most part quietly, awaiting the day they would be able to buy a house of their own. If he were suddenly sacked, or even demoted, it would be a crushing blow. Lean's blood cooled and began to flow north again, from his gut to his brain. He directed his attention outward, to the world that trickled past as the horse pulled the trolley car southwest, along Congress Street.

Lean ran the situation through his mind a half dozen times as the car trudged along. Finally he settled on a compromise. He couldn't risk being involved in the break-in at the cathedral, but he could happen to be nearby in case an alarm was sounded. That way, he could be first on the scene and assist Grey's escape, if possible.

'What's your plan, then?' Lean waited. 'Grey.'

Grey stared into the distance as the car moved on, passing by the open space of Lincoln Park, originally called Phoenix Park when it was built as a firebreak after the Great Fire of '66.

'Hmm? Oh, it would be best if you could claim total ignorance of my actions. Though a glance into the cells first thing tomorrow might be appreciated. Just in case things go awry and some Roman Catholic patrolmen decide they ought to be violently offended by my efforts.'

Before Lean could offer any further objection, Grey shifted around at the back of the car, muttered something about making preparations, then hopped down from the slow-moving trolley and made his way to the sidewalk without a glance back.

A few minutes after midnight on Thursday, August 18, Sam Guen was finally rewarded. He felt the last of the tumblers click. He opened the door to the dark walnut bookcase.

'There's nothing in here.' The disappointment had caused his voice to rise above a whisper, and he quickly corrected himself. 'Nothing but books.'

'It's a bookcase,' said Grey as he scanned the contents. 'What were you expecting?'

'Something better than books.'

Grey reached in and carefully removed a thin book of black leather. 'You can't put a price on knowledge, Guen.'

Guen moved across the floor. 'Exactly. You don't know how much to sell it for. The fence will rob you blind. Not worth the effort of stealing it in the first place.' He listened at the door for any hint of movement outside the room.

Grey chuckled. 'We're not stealing it.' He drew the curtain on the window, lit the lamp on the writing desk, and produced a blank page from his coat pocket.

'What are you doing, Mr Grey?'

'Making a copy of the information I need.'

'But we should be going. Just take the book.'

'The book is a secret. No one knows it's here, and I've been asking the priests about it recently. It wouldn't take long for the police to be at my door. I don't need to make enemies of the police or the Catholic Church.'

'Breaking in here, picking the lock, just to read a book? I don't understand why you do this.'

'But you understood how. And so long as I continue to understand why, you will always remain a very useful and well-paid man.'

Mr Grey had not bothered to look up. Guen knew he would get no more of an answer. He closed his eyes; his hearing always seemed more focused in complete darkness. It also saved him the anguish of watching Mr Grey slowly copy the page from the black leather book. Guen pressed his ear to the door again and silently willed the hallway outside to remain free of any approaching footsteps. Yes, he knew how, that was true enough. Still, if he went to jail or died for this, and had to explain himself later, it would be nice to know why.

At nine in the morning, Lean stood by the windows in Dr Steig's consultation room, his hands clutching the transcribed page behind his back, waiting as the maid set out coffee for four, then took her leave. He brought the paper around front, then glanced at the faces of the doctor and Grey, who sat waiting for him to begin. He had already pored over the page, familiarizing himself with the contents and with Grey's hurried but neat handwriting.

'"In the fourth month and the last of my travels, I came to Smyrna and the end of my journey, where on the day the Master died, where his blood flowed. There, by the light of the fire-brand, I could see the father who would not burn. He asked me would I quench the flames, and with blood I did. There the fourth, there the last offering taken. There was the cup finally emptied, and there was the vessel held ready for the Master once more."'

The silence that followed was interrupted by the sound of an arrival in the front hall. Seconds later Helen rushed into the room, dropped her handbag on the table, and let out a sigh.

'Are you all right, my dear?' Dr Steig leaned forward at his desk, studying his niece intently. 'You look rather fatigued.'

'Well, I did receive a surprisingly early note this morning requesting some immediate research.' Helen shot an accusing glance at Grey.

'I do apologize. Though I should hope if my life ever depended on it, you wouldn't mind losing a few hours of sleep.'

'We'll see,' mumbled Helen. Then, in a stronger voice, she stated, 'Here's what I found. Information on the actual Salem executions. So will he strike next in Salem? What does the next page say?'

'It provides the three crucial pieces of information we were lacking,' Grey said.

Lean handed Helen the copy and let her digest it.

'It's the end of his journey,' Dr Steig said. 'The final killing will be where the master died and his blood was shed.'

'Well, that's easy enough, then,' Helen said. 'George Burroughs died in Salem, at Gallows Hill. Though, technically speaking, his blood wasn't shed; he was hanged.'

'Fire is noted as the method in the riddle. And blood is the only thing mentioned for the part of the body. So presumably there will be wounds inflicted and the body burned,' Lean said.

'Stands to reason.' Grey nodded his agreement. 'If the worst comes to pass and we can't intercept the killer before the act, at least the fire will reveal his exact location.'

'We mustn't let it come to that. Location and method.' Lean held up two fingers. 'You said there were three bits of information to consider.'

'The date.'

'Date? The twenty-second, of course. The new moon.' Lean could feel himself frowning. It had to be the new moon. 'The last paragraph mentions no light other than the fire. It will be complete darkness out. He started on the full moon, he'll end on the new. What else could it be?'

'Look closely at the text. "In the fourth month ... where on the day the Master died." The wording's awkward, yet the reference is clear. The date of import is that of his actual death.'

Helen was working her fingers together, over and over. 'The opening of the Black Book does emphasize the hundred-year cycle of the master's death.' Her eyes shot back and forth between Lean and Grey. 'And Burroughs was hanged tomorrow, August nineteenth.'

'I don't know, Grey. You said yourself the wording is odd. How can you be sure?'

'I'm not. But we can't afford to take a risk. If I'm wrong, then we've merely wasted a night. We'll still have another chance on the new moon, three days later.' Grey dug in his pocket and took out a small sheet of paper. 'And there's something else.'

Lean recognized it as a telegram, and a stone settled into his gut. 'McCutcheon?'

Grey nodded. 'He went to check in on Geoffrey Blanchard at the lunatic hospital the day before last but was told the man was unavailable. He went back yesterday and again this morning and was turned away each time in no uncertain terms.'

Lean tapped his knuckles on the desk. Either something was wrong with Blanchard or he'd escaped or bought his way out again. 'If Blanchard managed to leave the asylum at least two days ago and hasn't returned yet,' Lean said, 'then he's had plenty of time.'

Grey nodded his agreement. 'Enough to find his victim and arrange the details of his final sacrifice.'

'They've been women so far, but we never ruled out that Blanchard may still be fixed on revenge. Old Stitch and now, maybe, her son,' Lean said.

'Father Coyne is willing to meet with us this afternoon. There's still hope that we can locate Jack Whitten if, indeed, he is the intended victim.'

63

Father Coyne's retreat was a simple clapboard structure, little more than a summer cottage, overlooking a small cove on the Stroudwater River. Grey knocked several times until the door cracked open. Above the chain lock, Lean saw a pair of squinting eyes set in a pale, homely face topped by close-cropped dirty-blond hair.

'What?'

'You must be Peter Chapman,' Lean said.

'And you must be a bloody genius,' answered the man.

'Deputy Lean, actually. This is Mr Grey.'

'And?'

'I believe that Father Coyne's expecting us.'

The man grumbled something unintelligible and closed the door.

'Did I insult the man's mother?' Lean asked.

'Someone ought to. Did you notice the way his forehead—'

The door opened again, and Peter Chapman set himself in the doorway. He was small but scrappy-looking and doing his best to show the unwelcome guests he meant business. He spoke in a sort of shouted whisper, trying to intimidate without causing a ruckus.

'He ain't well, y'know. So I won't stand for no funny business. No getting him riled. And ya can't stay long.'

The whole debate on Lombroso's theories of criminal anthropology aside, Lean couldn't shake the impression that the little troll of a man simply had a miscreant's face. Lean was sure if he dug, he'd find a history of arrests for petty crimes. But, apparently, he was one of the reformed. Sometimes even a lifer managed to find true religion. Kept his thief's sense of fellowship and loyalty but traded in his little gang for a great big one. It didn't always hold, but at least Peter Chapman seemed sincere in his concern over Father Coyne.

They followed the scrawny man through the kitchen and into the den. The drawn curtains allowed only a sliver of light.

Despite its being a warm day, there was a fire in the small woodstove. Father Coyne sat nearby with his eyes closed and his feet up on a stool. A small table, holding a closed book and a magnifying glass, straddled his outstretched legs, which were covered by a tartan throw. He wore a house robe drawn tight. His head was wrapped in white fabric rolled round and round the crown and held on with a few loops under his chin, leaving the area from forehead to bottom lip revealed. If the priest weren't so pale, Lean thought he might have passed as some type of Bedouin trader suffering a massive toothache. The floor creaked with their approach, and Father Coyne's eyes popped open.

'Father Coyne?'

'Yes, gentlemen, come in, come in.' His raspy voice hinted at a pleasant disposition. 'Forgive me if I don't rise. Peter, some chairs, please.'

The priest's assistant brought two straight-back chairs from the kitchen.

'I have Bishop Healy's letter' – Father Coyne looked under his book – 'somewhere.'

'Yes, thank you for having us,' Lean said. 'We understand it's a difficult time.'

'All this' – the priest gave a small wave around the room – 'is doctor's orders. Seem to think they can steam it out of me. Once a day with the heat, they say. Wrapped up like some dead Egyptian pharaoh.' He paused frequently to draw breath. He sounded as if he was unable to fill his lungs. 'Sweating is supposed to have a recuperative effect, invigorate the blood or some such. But enough of my troubles. You've come about Jack Whitten. What's he doing these days?'

'We were hoping you might be able to tell us,' Lean said.

'Afraid not. We haven't spoken in many years. I tried, but . . .'

'I understand there was some sort of falling-out, an incident where he stole something,' Grey said.

'He never stole anything. I'm not sure what there would have been to steal in the church library.' Father Coyne barked out a sharp cough. 'Only a bunch of old records. Nothing worthwhile.'

'Then what was the problem?' Lean asked.

'Oh, there was another boy involved.' The priest wiped spittle from his lips with a well-used handkerchief. 'Just boys being boys, really. But this other family blamed Jack for everything. He'd misled their son and all that.' He paused for another harsh cough. 'Demanded we send him to the reform school.'

'And you did?'

Father Coyne nodded. 'I should have pressed harder for him to stay.' The rasping sound of his breathing became more noticeable. 'But I was new then. It wasn't my decision. Still . . . he never forgave me his being sent away.' His throat erupted with a coughing fit. Peter came bustling into the room with a glass of water, then glared at the detectives on his way out. 'I think I was the first adult he'd ever really trusted. If I'd had more time, maybe I could have reached that boy. A failure . . . on my part. There was good in him.'

Another coughing spell shook the priest's body, and Lean moved forward to retrieve the man's glass of water for him.

'And you never heard from him again.'

Father Coyne shook his head. 'Just slipped away. For a while after, my guilty conscience would make me think I'd caught a glimpse of him here or there on the streets. Don't know what ever became of him.'

'And the other boy,' Grey said, 'do you recall his name?'

'I don't think it's my place to discredit the boy or his family now.'

'Just someone from the congregation. I see.'

'Actually, it was during a unified event. Groups from several churches coming together across the city, some gathering related to the liquor laws. A parade and speeches, lots of fanfare.'

Lean's stomach did a quick somersault. Maybe eighteen or so years ago, a teenage Jack Whitten got into trouble with a boy from a well-to-do family during a temperance meeting. Colonel Blanchard's son would be the right age. With young Blanchard acting out over the loss of his mother, the colonel would certainly be apt to cast blame for misbehavior elsewhere; lowly Jack Whitten would be an inviting scapegoat.

Father Coyne launched into another series of convulsing coughs. When the priest set his handkerchief down, Lean noticed that it was spotted with blood. 'We should let you rest, Father.'

Grey drew a notebook from his pocket. 'Father, if you wouldn't mind just a few more questions.'

Lean didn't think the priest looked enthused, but he nodded. 'Of course, if I can help.'

'We have a bit of a riddle on our hands. It may sound odd, but your being a priest, and an expert on martyrs and the like, I was wondering if you might have some insight.'

'My eyes are not what they used to be.'

'Let me read for you.' Grey took out his notes and read the first paragraph from the riddle. Father Coyne could only shake his head and profess his ignorance.

Grey continued. '"In the second month of my travels, I came to Constantinople, where the Master first took life and did there himself accept the Lord of the Air. There still clearly did I see the man who was nomine tenus the greatest among men. He bade me record my sins, and ask forgiveness. But I would not, and so the second offering was taken from him. On that very ground, the libation was poured to the Master.'"

'*Nomine tenus*,' Father Coyne repeated. 'Latin, meaning "to hold the name of the greatest among men." That name could be Maximus.'

'And is there a Catholic saint, a martyr, by that name?' Grey asked.

'Yes. What was the part about his sins?'

'"He made me record my sins, and ask forgiveness."'

'It could be St Maximus of Constantinople.' Father Coyne struggled to clear his throat. 'When he was martyred, his hand was cut off and his tongue removed so he could no longer write or speak. What a strange riddle. Wherever did you hear that?'

Lean caught Grey's glance and knew he was thinking the same thing: Maggie Keene's severed hand and her missing tongue. 'Just some old book we've come across,' Grey said before reading the third paragraph. '"In the third month of my travels, I came to Tridentum, where the Master's powers were beheld, the skies were made to tremble, and the Master compelled the hosts of the air. There in the half-light did I see the child Zealot at the home of the Wanderers. He begged me to save him, but I would not. So the third offering was taken from him. There the Master put the cup to his lips."'

'We took the reference to the Wanderers to mean the Jews, perhaps,' Lean said. 'But I've never heard of Tridentum. And a child Zealot?'

'The Zealot is usually a reference to the disciple Simon,' said the priest, 'but he obviously wasn't a child. A child named Simon, at the home of the Jews?'

'Does that have meaning, Father?' Lean asked.

'Simon of Trent, perhaps. Trent could be some sort of derivation from Tridentum.'

'And how did Simon of Trent die?' Grey asked.

'It's now known to be untrue, of course. But some ideas just refuse to die. Simon was supposedly murdered by the Jews in the Italian city of Trent.' Father Coyne paused and pressed his handkerchief to his mouth for a cough that didn't come. 'It was a persistent myth that the Jews used the blood of Christian children in their rituals. Utterly false, of course, but ignorance and prejudice can be very persistent.'

'So they drew his blood?' Lean asked.

'Drained it from his little body. As the story goes.'

Father Coyne suffered through another coughing spasm, and Lean grew uncomfortable with their prolonged questioning of the man. He tried to get Grey's attention.

'Just one more, Father. "In the fourth month and the last of my travels, I came to Smyrna and the end of my journey, where on the day the Master died, his blood flowed. There, by the light of the firebrand, I could see the father who would not burn. He asked me would I quench the flames, and with blood I did. There the fourth, there the last offering taken. There was the cup finally emptied, and there was the vessel held ready for the Master once more."'

Father Coyne nodded. 'Smyrna's famous martyr was St Polycarp. In the first century, his tormentors tried to execute him by stabbing, but he would not die. So he was bound in the center of a pyre and set aflame. He died, but not before a dove issued from his wound along with a quantity of blood enough to quench the flames.'

'Odd,' Grey said. 'I'd have thought having a live bird inside his body would have been enough to kill him.'

Father Coyne gave a puzzled look, then chuckled, and that devolved into another hacking cough. This time his manservant came close to blunt force as he ushered Lean and Grey through the kitchen and out the front door.

As they stepped onto the porch, Lean said, 'Please tell Father Coyne we're grateful—'

'Go shit in your hat!' Peter Chapman slammed the door shut.

'Damned fool,' Grey said.

'Yes, well, he seems very protective of Father Coyne.'

'Not that strange creature. Me! And you, for that matter. We've had the key to these murders right in our hands. This riddle is a map to exactly how he's committing the murders. Read the very first paragraph in light of what we now know. The event is a birth, a woman who would not bleed – she's pregnant. The fullness of her offering is a child in the womb that's taken from her. It's a description of the mutilation of Hannah Easler.'

Anger flared up in Lean at the image of that murder. He tried to funnel that emotion toward stopping this madman. 'The final sacrifice. Where the master died and his blood flowed,' Lean said. 'When do we leave for Salem?'

'Early tomorrow afternoon should give us enough time,' Grey said. 'I'll send word for McCutcheon to meet us.'

64

Shortly after noon the following day, Lean slid, dodged, and pardoned himself down the narrow aisle, past a steady flow of train travelers surging forward in search of empty compartments with the zeal of overdue trout rushing upstream. He glanced back and caught sight of Perceval Grey's dark hat jostling away in the opposite direction. Every passing man's face became a target. He moved into the next car and was halfway through when the train whistle gave two long bursts. The conductor shouted out the final call for Portsmouth, continuing to Salem, Woburn, and Worcester. Ignoring the rest of the car's inhabitants, Lean hurried forward to the next coupling. He grasped a hold bar and stuck his head out to get a good look at the platform and any last-second passengers hoping to slip aboard unnoticed. He was disappointed to see not a single soul dashing ahead through the steam as the train hissed and lurched, the wheels jerking to life with the first hints of forward motion.

A dozen people along the platform waved their last to passengers staring back through the small compartment windows. Lean's eyes settled on a solitary form, his gaze arrested by the utter stillness of a man dressed in black propped against a support pole on the platform. The man carried a newspaper in one hand and, though his felt hat was pulled low, Lean met the man's gaze for a brief moment. There was a flash of recognition before the man looked down, and his hands lifted the newspaper, obscuring his face.

The train began its slow rumble forward. Lean threw one last wild sweeping gaze up and down the length of the platform before he returned to the man in the long black overcoat. The man never moved except to cast a brief glance after the departing train. Lean wasn't sure, but he thought the man's eyes had been directed at where he stood. After completing his survey of the back half of the train, Lean returned to their compartment to find Grey waiting.

'Nothing. You?' Grey asked.

Lean shook his head, then mentioned the possible exception of the man in the black coat.

'You can't place him?' Grey asked.

'No, but I'm sure I've seen him somewhere.'

'It will come to you. Just don't be too disappointed if it's a name remembered from some other case. No shortage of men about these days anxious to avoid the gaze of a police detective. The mind can wreak havoc on a pair of eyes that are desperately searching for something.'

'That may well be,' said Lean, 'but still ... something about that fellow.'

'I suspect our man is in Salem already. And even if that *was* him back on the platform, take heart. We now have the advantage of his not having made it aboard. He'd be severely hard-pressed to get there and make whatever arrangements are necessary if he now has to wait and take the 3:40. So perhaps your brief encounter has thrown our man off track for the night and saved a life.' Grey shrugged noncommittally and glanced out the window, looking skyward. 'Barely a cloud to be seen. A fine day for traveling.'

Lean disagreed but said nothing as he unfolded his newspaper, eager to distract his thoughts. Their destination was hours away, and the mid-August sun beating down on the train's dark rooftop would soon make their compartment unbearably stuffy. The small window could be opened, but if he forgot to close it at any stop, he'd be swatting flies for thirty minutes after.

Lean tried to focus on local stories about doings at City Hall or efforts to repair damage just up the coast caused by a serious storm the previous week. After a few minutes, his natural instincts took over and he turned to the front-page article entitled INQUEST BEGINS. JUDGE BLAISDELL HEARS EVIDENCE GATH-ERED IN THE BORDEN MURDER CASE.

Like seemingly everybody in the country with access to news-papers, Lean had been following the mystery of the Borden slayings with keen interest. In the immediate wake of the double homicide of a wealthy older couple in their home two weeks ear-lier, the brutal slayings had been assumed to be the work of a bloody madman. Now, as the facts slowly came out, the evidence seemed to be mounting against Lizzie, the thirty-two-year-old daughter of Mr Borden.

'It certainly seems the daughter must be to blame for the mur-ders,' Lean said, 'but the sheer brutality of it ... There were ill feelings between the daughters and the stepmother, but so many ax blows to the head ... Then for a woman to wait another hour and repeat the deed, hacking away at her own father while he slept. It's inconceivable.'

Grey glanced at the headline of Lean's paper. 'The alternatives are even more inconceivable. All the facts point solely at that daughter. Every aspect of her account of the events has been dis-credited or is on its face suspect. Yet I fear the shoddy police work and that same resistance you displayed to believing a woman capable of the act will serve to prevent a conviction. Practically the entire community had access to the scene after the murder, and the police wasted valuable time pursuing baseless rumors. If they had simply sealed the house that very morning and searched every room minutely, I'm sure they would have discovered the bloodstained clothes belonging to Lizzie. Instead she was wit-nessed days later burning a dress in the kitchen stove. She claimed she destroyed it because it was stained with paint. Why, it's

389

nothing short of a repeat of England's infamous Road Hill murder, or a page from Wilkie Collins.'

'Oh, hell,' Lean grumbled, 'if we're going to talk about horrific murders, we may as well be speaking of Salem. Where exactly will we be looking for our man?'

'Courtesy of our indefatigable researcher, Mrs Prescott.' Grey drew some folded pages from an inside coat packet and handed them over. 'Descriptions from Upham and the other usual sources as to the execution of the Reverend George Burroughs and the location of the site where the witches were hanged.'

Lean removed his hat and coat and settled in for the long ride, before taking up the pages.

August 5, 1692. The Court again sitting, six more were tried on the same Account, viz. Mr George Burroughs, sometime minister of Wells, John Proctor, and Elizabeth Proctor his Wife, with John Willard of Salem-Village, George Jacobs Senior, of Salem, and Martha Carrier of Andover; these were all brought in Guilty and Condemned; and were all Executed Aug. 19, except Proctor's Wife, who pleaded Pregnancy.

Lean's mind turned briefly to Emma's worried face, her eyes welling up that morning as he explained nothing more than that it would all be over in the next twenty-four hours. Lean forced the image from his mind as he took up more of Helen's research entries.

Margaret Jacobs being one that had confessed her own Guilt, and testified against her Grand-Father Jacobs, Mr Burroughs, and John Willard. She, the day before Executions, came to Mr Burroughs, acknowledging that she had belied them, and begged Mr Burroughs Forgiveness, who not only forgave her, but also Prayed with and for her.

Judge Sewall's diary for Aug. 19, 1692: This day George Burroughs, John Willard, Jno. Proctor, Martha Carrier and George Jacobs were executed at Salem, a very great number of Spectators being present. All of them said they were innocent, Carrier and all. Mr Mather says they all died by a Righteous Sentence. Mr Burroughs by his Speech, Prayer, protestation of his Innocence, did much move unthinking persons, which occasions their speaking hardly concerning his being executed. [In the margin Sewall later added: Dolefull Witchcraft!]

Lean glanced up and saw Grey sitting perfectly upright, but with his eyes closed. A small smile had settled on the man's lips. 'I still think it's odd,' Lean said. 'We're just days from the new moon, and yet he's chosen to break off from the lunar cycle that he's followed all these months.'

'The bicentennial anniversary of his master's death is what is crucial to the ritual. The introductory statement of the Black Book retrieved by Mrs Prescott at Harvard spoke of the ritual being performed on the cycle of the master's betrayal and death. It is clear that, for some reason, our man has selected George Burroughs for the role of his master, and so we are heading to the very spot of that man's execution precisely two hundred years after the day of the event. Our man's grand finale.'

'I know, I know.' Lean's mind wandered back to all the writings he had examined in the past month, searching for something to solidly refute Grey's theory, but he could summon nothing. It seemed the final murder would occur tonight, far away from

Portland, in old Salem, at a place that had once served as the gallows for a deluded and merciless gathering of souls. He turned again to the page and saw that this entry contained a commentary by Helen.

Note: Robert Calef gives the more humane account of G.B.'s execution – Mr Burroughs was carried in a cart with the others, through the streets of Salem, to execution. When he was upon the ladder, he made a speech for the clearing of his innocency, with such solemn and serious expressions as were to the admiration of all present. His prayer (which he concluded by repeating the Lord's Prayer) was so well worded, and uttered with such composedness and such fervency of spirit, as was very affecting, and drew tears from many, so that it seemed to some that the spectators would hinder the execution. The accusers said the black man stood and dictated to him. As soon as he was turned off, Mr Cotton Mather, being mounted upon a horse, addressed himself to the people, partly to declare that he (Mr Burroughs) was no ordained minister and partly to possess the people of his guilt, saying that the devil often had been transformed into an angel of light; and this somewhat appeased the people, and the executions went on. When he was cut down, he was dragged by a halter to a hole, or grave, between the rocks, about two feet deep; his shirt and breeches being pulled off, and an old pair of trousers of one executed put on his lower parts, he was so put in, together with Willard and Carrier, that one of his hands, and his chin, and a foot of one of them, was left uncovered.

Lean looked up, a light dawning on him. 'Burroughs's last words were the Lord's Prayer. That's where our man is getting that bit from.'

Grey's eyes remained closed, but he nodded. 'The Puritans believed it was impossible for one in league with Satan to utter the prayer without stumbling and revealing themselves.'

'But Burroughs did recite it perfectly?'

'Only to have that fact used by Cotton Mather as the final proof of how powerfully Burroughs was aligned with the devil.' Grey opened his eyes and almost smiled. 'Damned if you do, damned if you don't.'

'So our killer sides with Mather and against reason. Burroughs's recitation is proof he exceeds the power of other witches. And our man repeats the prayer in these murders, invoking Burroughs's own last words, but he does it in Abenaki because the Indians were Burroughs's allies, in league with Satan. So he's making it a mockery of the Lord's Prayer.'

'Something like that, I suppose,' Grey said before closing his eyes again.

Lean fought off the urge to sit there contemplating the madness of the man they were chasing. It was a path that could lead him nowhere useful. He had to stay in the realm of reason and practicality, focusing only on the facts that lay in front of them.

'What about McCutcheon?' Lean asked. 'Any further contact?'

'He's already there, learning what he can of the area around this Gallows Hill and spying out the best location for our vigil. He was never able to get any explanation from the asylum staff as to Geoffrey Blanchard's sudden unavailability for visits. He'll check the local hotels.'

Lean nodded. McCutcheon gave them an extra pair of eyes and a steady hand with a gun. He was more than a little grateful for that news. It would be dark, and they'd be on treacherous, unfamiliar footing and facing a man who had already killed at least three people while leaving little trace of himself. Lean's hand slipped inside his coat and rested for a moment on the grip of his Colt. Then he focused on his final page until the words began to sink into his mind.

Gallows Hill is a part of an elevated ledge of rock on the western side of the city of Salem ... Its somber and desolate appearance admits of little variety of delineation. It is mostly a bare and naked ledge. At the top of this cliff, on the southern brow of the eminence, the executions are supposed to have taken place. The outline rises a little towards the north, but soon begins to fall off to the general level of the country. From that direction only can the spot be easily reached. It is hard to climb the western side, impossible to clamber up the southern face. Settlement creeps down from the north, and has partially ascended the eastern acclivity, but can never reach the brink. Scattered patches of soil are too thin to tempt cultivation, and the rock is too craggy and steep to allow occupation. An active and flourishing manufacturing industry crowds up to its base; but a considerable surface at the top will forever remain an open space. It is, as it were, a platform raised high in the air.

Lean looked out the window and let his eyes drift over the world. The train sped past as scenes of everyday life unfolded at their normal pace. After a few moments, he reached over and drew down the window shade.

65

Nine hours later, Lean sat pressed up against a granite out-cropping. The rumble of his stomach made him regret the way he'd forced down his supper of bangers and mash at the station when they met Walt McCutcheon to go over the plan once more. The sun was well gone, and a thin sliver of moon was just visible on the horizon. After half a minute of peering at his pocketwatch, he made out that it was almost ten o'clock. His knees ached from sitting motionless for so long, and he slowly set about stretching each leg several times. He held his revolver eight inches from his nose and checked for the third time that each round was loaded, then slipped the piece back into his coat pocket and glanced at the craggy summit of Gallows Hill. From this distance it would be almost impossible to see anyone up there. But if their theory was correct, a murder attempted there tonight would involve fire, and any flame would be visible to him the moment it was lit.

He listened in the darkness to the occasional noises that carried up from the town. In the lulls, only the sounds of night breezes and crickets reached him. Grey was somewhere off to his right, maybe a hundred yards away, also watching the hilltop. McCutcheon was posted near the bottom of the northern side of the hill, the point of easiest access or escape from the higher ground.

As he crouched, waiting for the unknown, Lean's mind began to wander, carried along on the ebb and flow of dark minutes stretching into one another, indistinguishable and endless. He thought of his wife and the little life she carried inside her.

Scrape.

His head bolted up. A definite noise on top of the hill. He squinted into the blackness. The weak crescent moon was half hidden by clouds. Lean slid his hand into his pocket and felt the cool wooden grip of his pistol. He got his feet firmly under him and listened like a robber with his ear against a safe.

Creak. A wooden noise – movement.

It was hard to judge the distance to the summit, maybe sixty yards, but it was over rocks and crags in utter darkness. Moving quickly would be dangerous, but opening his lamp would make himself a blazing target. There was still no sign of any definite motion. No light on the hill, no flame or even a spark. A loud thwack broke the stillness with no hint of regret. It was followed by three more identical sounds: something heavy striking home on wood or rock. Lean dashed forward, pistol drawn. The shuttered lamp dangled awkwardly from his left wrist as he fought to keep his balance while scrambling up the rocky slope. He tried to listen as he went, but the sounds of his own efforts made it hard to discern what was transpiring in front of him.

There was definite activity, a burst of frantic movement. He could make out at least one dark shape moving ahead. A few more strides and he came to within twenty yards of his goal. He paused, pistol aimed into the blackness. The moon came free of the clouds, and in the faint light he saw a figure before him, upright, arms outstretched.

'Move an inch and I'll scatter your brains all over this hill,' Lean warned. The figure remained still, and Lean began to move closer. 'Grey? You there?'

There was no answer.

Lean stepped to within ten yards of the figure. 'You've got it,

396

mister. Nice and still.' He slid the lantern down off his wrist so that he could hold the loop handle in his left hand. With his right, still aiming the pistol, he reached forward and flicked the shutter open. In the beam of light, he could finally see that the person before him was a dark-haired man. His arms were straight out at his sides, but the hands were empty and hanging limp. The man's head was tilted slightly to one side, as if he were awaiting further instructions.

Lean moved forward, and by the time he was ten feet away, he recognized the man: Geoffrey Blanchard.

'Grey? Where are you? I've got him. Grey!'

Lean stared at the man as the seconds passed with no answer. It dawned on him how very still his prisoner was. He moved closer, then reached forward and gave Blanchard a little shove. The man's head slipped backward and farther to the side, revealing a deep red gash that stretched full across his neck.

'Bloody hell.' Lean stepped to one side and craned his own neck, now noticing the short post to which Blanchard had been lashed and the thin crossbeam that supported the dead man's outstretched arms.

'Grey?' A burgeoning panic raised his voice to a shout.

A gunshot answered him from the bottom of the hill.

Lean bounded down the rocky slope, barely noticing how uneven the ground was. Over the sound of his own gasps, he could hear nothing other than a train whistle, still distant but drawing closer. The thought that the killer was fleeing into a populated town and that he might now manage an escape spurred Lean on. Halfway down, he found something of a path and barreled headlong the rest of the way. Once at the bottom, he dashed across a narrow field of scraggy, overgrown grass to reach the edge of the town. He passed by some small workshops and store-houses and soon had cobblestones under his feet.

He slowed his pace in order to get his bearings when another shot rang out, then a second following hard after. They were in front of him, slightly to his left. He ran forward again for a few blocks, passing into a residential neighborhood. He rounded a corner and saw two figures huddled not far from a streetlamp. With his gun lowered to his side, Lean hurried forward.

Perceval Grey glanced up at Lean's approach. Grey was supporting Walt McCutcheon's head with one arm. McCutcheon was breathing hard, almost hissing. As he moved closer, Lean saw that McCutcheon's coat was open, and the handkerchief pressed to his side didn't fully hide the dark stain on his shirt.

'How bad?'

'I don't think it's too serious,' answered Grey.

'Easy for you to say.' McCutcheon managed a smile that instantly gave way to a pained grimace. Large beads of sweat had risen on his forehead.

'We should—' Lean's suggestion was interrupted by the approaching train's whistle.

'Go after the dirty little prick? You damn well should!' Spittle flew from McCutcheon's lips. 'I'll be well enough.'

Faces had appeared in windows and doors. Lean called out, identifying himself as a police officer. He ordered one man to come attend McCutcheon while another was sent for a doctor. Then he and Grey hurried on through the streets in pursuit. Two blocks on, a voice called out to them from a second-story window.

'That way!' said a man, pointing. 'He was headed toward the station.'

They hailed a passing hansom cab. Grey thrust several dollars into the driver's hand and ordered him on to the train station with all possible speed. At that hour, the depot was well lit in comparison to the surrounding neighborhood. Lean abandoned his lamp and made for the front doors while Grey headed around the building.

As he stepped inside, Lean shot looks into every corner, taking in the entire waiting area. There was a lone ticket agent at the counter and half a dozen souls scattered about inside the small terminal, some seated on benches, others looking out the windows that faced the tracks. The killer was not there. Lean glanced about for other doors, saw only the exit to the boarding platform, and hurried out. A dozen people loitered on the hundred-foot-long platform, some with baggage, others with eyes aimed down one track. The lights of an approaching train could be seen a half mile away.

Before Lean could finish his visual sweep of the area, he heard a loud slap and a woman's shrill voice call out, 'You're a disgrace!'

He looked to his right and saw a red-haired woman in a dark coat. Most of the other people were also looking, and the woman appeared startled to be the center of attention. Her body swayed for a moment, as if she were uncertain of whether to move. Embarrassed, she raised a hand to cover her face and strode toward the doors to the terminal. As she moved away, Lean saw a small figure in black standing there.

Lean tightened his grip on his pistol. His eyes shot to the corner of the station, where Grey waited in the shadows. Lean walked toward the black-coated man. He could feel the killer's eyes burning into him from beneath the wide rim of his black hat. The man thrust his right hand into his own pocket. Lean saw the bulge there and continued to move closer, thirty feet away now.

The man took several steps back and slid behind a column. Grey ascended onto the far end of the platform. Lean noticed that Grey's arm hung inconspicuously at his side, a revolver in his hand, as he too moved toward the killer, who was now surrounded.

'You're finished!' Lean called out. 'There's nowhere to turn. Toss your gun out.'

If the killer answered, Lean didn't hear him. There was a sudden blast of the train whistle as the arriving engine drew within a few hundred yards. Grey was circling, drawing closer while improving his angle on the killer. The black-coated man noticed this and took more slow steps backward, trying to keep distance between himself and his pursuers. He quickly ran out of space, coming to within feet of the platform's edge, where it dropped away several feet to the tracks. The killer raised his arm and swung it back and forth, pointing his gun alternately at Lean and Grey like a wild clock pendulum.

'Drop your gun!' repeated Lean. He raised his left hand to the base of the pistol, steadying his right hand to fire. The approaching train was no more than thirty yards away, and Lean had no intention of letting the standoff last long enough for any passengers on that train to exit and risk getting shot. The killer threw a quick glance over his shoulder. When his head spun back around, Lean saw a look of sheer madness in the man's eyes. The man grinned, whirled, and jumped down onto the tracks.

Lean dashed forward. He saw the black figure on all fours in the middle of the tracks, the train barreling down on him – ten feet away. The man was scrambling to gain his footing, desperately trying to force his body forward, out of the way of the oncoming engine. There was the piercing squeal of the train's brakes. Lean swung his arm around, his gun coming level with the killer. Before he could pull the trigger, the killer's feet left the ground. Lean heard the sickening sound, audible even above the grinding metal brakes: the wet thud of a body giving way completely before the mass of the engine.

66

Several moments passed before the train slowed enough for Lean to jump aboard and commandeer a new lantern from a conductor who was floundering through an endless morass of half questions. Lean leaped off on the far side of the train and began to scour the ground. Grey appeared farther down alongside the train and called Lean over.

The bloodied mass on the ground was twisted about so that it took Lean a moment to make full sense of what he was seeing. Half of one leg had been ripped away, and what remained of the lower body was almost completely twisted about by the force of the blow, facing the wrong direction.

'He almost made it. Looked like he stumbled. Maybe McCutcheon's shot to the leg the other night kept him from escaping.' Lean glanced at the mangled mass of bloody flesh and exposed bones that had once been the man's legs.

'It will cheer McCutcheon's heart to know he's already gotten revenge on the man who shot him.' Grey knelt and shone his light directly onto the man's face. It was bloodied and bruised from having struck the ground several times. He took a cloth and small flask of water from his equipment pack and wiped the dirt and gore from the dead man's face. Lean recognized the features, made even more homely in the agony of death.

'The man who called himself Peter Chapman,' Grey said.

'Father Coyne's assistant?' Lean had been so focused on the man's injuries that he hadn't even noticed the color of the man's hair, his hat having been knocked away by the blow. 'He's not black-haired at all. As blond as a—'

'As blond as an undersize boy, smart and quiet. The kind who was barely worth noticing, but given to acts of vengeance. A boy familiar with Old Stitch, who also had access to the Black Book while he was at the cathedral's orphanage. Jack Whitten.'

Lean tried to process the announcement, fit it in with everything he'd learned and considered over the past three months of the investigation. But at that moment it was all too much, and his mind stubbornly returned to the dead body before him.

'But he's blond. Boxcar Annie said he was dark. And the hairs on Maggie Keene's body were black too.'

'Could have been dyed. I was a fool not to test them. Or Maggie Keene's killer could have been dark-haired after all.' Grey drew a small glass vial from his kit.

'A second killer? You mean Geoffrey Blanchard? The two of them working together?'

'We'll know soon enough.' Grey drew a pair of scissors from his pouch and snipped a pinch of hair from the dead man. He placed the hairs into the vial and secured the stopper. He then produced a small tin that contained papers and a dark ink pad and proceeded to take imprints of the dead man's thumbs. 'The local police are coming. I'll leave it to you to explain the bare facts and take care of McCutcheon. That should give me ample time to head back up the hill to secure certain evidence from that

402

body.' Grey slipped away before two Salem police officers approached from around the front of the train.

The next day Lean sank into the seat in their private compartment on the 1:25 northbound train and watched Grey reorganize all the equipment in his satchel. 'Jack Whitten. I really thought it would turn out to be Geoffrey Blanchard. He was obviously disturbed, fascinated by the occult. Figured he had a grudge against Old Stitch that he carried over to other witches or sinners.'

'I wasn't sure which of the two was the strongest suspect,' Grey said. 'Of course, now it's easy to see that Whitten had to be involved all along.'

'Why's that?' Lean asked.

'The killer had a knowledge of witchcraft generally and specific knowledge as to the location and contents of the Black Book. Jack Whitten spent time at the cathedral twenty years ago. It was during that time that the Harvard men came and copied the book. And around that time when Whitten was expelled for breaking in to the church office where the book was kept.'

'Ah, but Blanchard could well have been the other boy who was with Whitten during that incident.'

Grey held one finger up in the air and then unfurled a second. 'But our killer was also proficient with the abrus seeds kept by Old Stitch and probably used to poison her. Whitten would have been intimately familiar with his mother's ingredients.'

Lean weighed this argument before picking his counterattack. 'Perhaps the abrus seeds were the poison that killed Blanchard's mother and he knew it. Poetic justice for him to use it in exacting his revenge on Old Stitch. And Blanchard is likely the one who attacked Simon Gould and then was chased by McCutcheon.

He'd have recognized Gould as one of his father's men spying on him in Danvers. What would Whitten's motive be for attacking Gould?'

Grey didn't need any time, his own riposte already waiting. 'I checked Geoffrey Blanchard's body when I returned to Gallows Hill. There was no bullet wound on either leg. Besides, Gould wasn't spying on Geoffrey Blanchard. He was trying to protect him. Whitten needed Blanchard for the Gallows Hill sacrifice. Gould was in the way.'

'Well, in any event, a case could have been made for either man as the likely killer,' Lean said, happy to fight to a draw.

'Except for one thing,' Grey said. 'The first and most obvious clue that was left for us.'

Lean gave him a puzzled look.

'The pitchfork in Maggie Keene's neck and the billhook used to cut her chest.'

'I don't follow you,' Lean said.

'Neither of us knew what those wounds signified until I located that book on English folklore and superstitions. *Strange Tales of Warwickshire*, it was called. Only then did we realize that sticking a witch with a pitchfork and slashing the cross with a billhook was a custom for guarding against the dead witch's evil.' Grey paused, waiting for the information to sink in. 'The custom was foreign to us.'

'So?'

'Foreign to us because it isn't an American custom. It's British.'

'But Blanchard and Whitten are both as American as you or I.'

'True, but Whitten's mother wasn't. Remember his orphanage records? Old Stitch's real name was Lucy Whitten. Her birthplace was listed as some town in England. Whitechurch or something.'

'That's right. I wonder if that's anywhere near where that other woman was reported as getting the pitchfork and billhook.'

'Possibly,' Grey said. 'The village of Long Compton, 1875. That particular case would have been after Old Stitch emigrated here. But still, it shows the knowledge of that old local practice. She must have passed that useful bit of wisdom on to her sons.'

'There's a bedtime story for you,' Lean said.

'Of course, we'll know the truth soon enough.' Grey reached into his kit and held up his tin that contained the ink pad and paper. 'I have thumbprints from both Blanchard and Whitten to match against the bloody one the killer left on Maggie Keene's shoe. When we get back to Portland, we'll know for certain whether we had one killer or two.'

'Not that it matters now. They're both dead anyway.'

Grey bent forward in his seat, closer to Lean, as if they were conspirators in danger of being overheard. 'True, but after all we've discovered, the months spent on this inquiry, can you honestly say you don't need to know the whole truth of what happened here? For yourself?'

'At the moment I'm not sure what I can honestly say, or what I honestly think of all this.' Lean couldn't recall if he'd slept more than six hours in the past two days. He tried to shut his eyes, but his mind wouldn't yet allow him to close the book on this. 'You really think Whitten and Geoffrey Blanchard may have been working in concert these past few months?'

'Well, there was certainly some connection. They were both on Gallows Hill on the two hundredth anniversary of Reverend

Burroughs's hanging. They both shared a knowledge of the occult. Why not?'

'Oh, I don't know,' Lean answered, 'maybe because Whitten's mother poisoned Blanchard's. And the Blanchard family mob hanged Whitten's brother.'

'Blanchard probably had no reason to recognize Whitten. The scene at Old Stitch's hovel would have been chaos. Flames, smoke, and whatnot. She didn't even go by the name of Whitten in her work. Jack Whitten had the advantage of anonymity when they crossed paths again. Geoffrey was the boy who got into trouble with Whitten when they broke in to the church library a year or two later. But Jack Whitten learned who Blanchard was, and time passed. When the bicentennial of Salem and Burroughs's hanging approached, Whitten tracked him down again. He needed to complete his ritual and saw an opportunity to secure his final revenge against the Blanchards for his brother's death all those years ago.'

Lean stretched his legs and stuck his hand into his coat pocket. He drew out a telegraph he'd received in response to his own earlier that day and held it up as evidence.

'But if Peter Chapman really was Jack Whitten, then Father Coyne would have recognized him as the same young man he'd helped all those years ago.'

Grey shrugged. 'Almost two decades had passed. Hard years can make a young man look very different. Besides, Father Coyne's eyes were going. He couldn't see clearly enough to make the connection. A sudden onset of digestive and eye trouble about six months ago. The same time Whitten murdered Old Stitch and stole her supply of abrus seeds. Remember, the poison can cause internal problems as well as damage the eyes.'

The train's shrill whistle sounded two short blasts, and then Grey continued. 'Whitten somehow managed to poison Father Coyne. Then, not having to worry about being recognized, he ingratiated himself as some sort of handyman inside the cathedral. He worked his way into the confidence of the deteriorating Father Coyne. He wanted access to the Black Book that he'd once tried to steal from the church library twenty years earlier. The very incident that got him kicked out. But he must have been thwarted and had to get a hold of Harvard's copy instead. Took the pages he needed and covered his tracks by destroying the rest.'

'Just wish we'd have caught him alive,' Lean said. 'Could've gotten a confession.'

'Perhaps he was thinking the same thing. Jumping in front of that train was his choice as was all this. Besides, other than ourselves, who would have taken much joy in hearing that confession, having to wrestle with the realization of all that has happened here?'

'People want to know the truth,' Lean said.

The train began to move forward in lurching bursts.

'The truth?' Grey said. 'For most people the truth is more a matter of opinion than fact. No, they only want the sordid details. Preferably spun into some terrible, fascinating story they can repeat. A grisly account of sin and death, vengeance and madness is always popular. But the whole truth of it all? Good citizens hanging children. Human sacrifices going undetected by the police. War heroes paying off smugglers to keep murders quiet. No one would believe it all.'

Lean's eyelids began to sag. He opened his mouth to speak but then noticed that Grey, seated across from him in the compartment, was absolutely still, eyes shut, his breathing low and regular. Images of the past twelve hours floated through Lean's mind. After the incident at the station, the remainder of the night and the morning were all a blur of movement and questions from the Salem police. He only vaguely remembered locating McCutcheon and dealing with his medical needs. Then he'd led the Salem police up Gallows Hill and was surprised to find the body of Geoffrey Blanchard lying flat, with no evidence of the primitive cross he'd been tied to. After a moment he realized his gratitude to Grey for altering the scene. There were enough questions to answer about a dead body, even without the indications of a ritual murder.

A few hours of sleep at the police station had been followed by a trip to the telegraph office this morning, where he'd sent a note to Officer Bushey in Portland to check on Father Coyne's well-being. Another round of discussions with the police and several high-ranking administrators from Danvers Lunatic Hospital followed. They were clearly none too happy about the news, and Lean quickly figured that their displeasure had as much to do with their inability to explain how Blanchard had obtained his freedom as it did with the fact that he'd gotten his throat cut. They were gnashing their teeth over what the newspapers, Colonel Blanchard, and a potential flock of lawyers might say about the insufficient security at the asylum.

The Salem police were at something of a loss as to how to explain the entire situation any other way than how Lean had laid it out for them. He had followed Peter Chapman there from Portland in connection with the disappearance of Lizzie Madson earlier that summer. Chapman had a violent streak, and it was suspected that he and Geoffrey Blanchard had known each other in Portland years earlier. The exact nature of their relationship, and why Chapman would want to slash the man's throat, was unknown to Lean. In any event, the man was clearly deranged. McCutcheon confirmed that he was in Salem to help Lean apprehend Chapman, who had shot him during the pursuit. The statements of the other witnesses from the station confirmed that Chapman had jumped to his death before the train. In the end, the Salem police were quite happy to chalk it up to a lunatic committing suicide at the station.

As for Geoffrey Blanchard, the Danvers Lunatic Hospital officials were quite adamant in establishing that Lean had not actually seen Chapman kill Colonel Blanchard's son. So there was no actual proof of a murder. A knife had been found on the ground near Blanchard's body. It could easily have been dropped by Blanchard after he'd killed himself. And, if so, it provided a much less compelling news item. By the time Lean had been able to extract himself from the police station, it seemed in all likelihood that the police and the hospital administrators were reaching a consensus that it would be for the best if the whole event was rendered down to no story at all. It was not necessary, and could even be publicly demoralizing, to disclose the manner of Blanchard's reported suicide and the exact location. It would certainly be less problematic, and there would be fewer questions asked, if it was publicly assumed that Geoffrey Blanchard had simply died while still located properly in his cell.

After finally finishing up with the police, Lean had found Grey in attendance at the hospital bedside of Walt McCutcheon, who was looking surprisingly rosy-cheeked for a man who'd been shot the night before. As it turned out, the bullet had passed right through the ample flesh at the side of McCutcheon's midsection, striking no vital organs. While he would remain at the hospital for the next few days, there was no indication that he could expect anything other than a full recovery. Grey apologized that he would not be able to stay and look after his friend, but McCutcheon would not hear of it. In fact, he seemed quite eager for the Portland men to be on their way. He had an eye on one of the nurses and didn't need a couple of haggard, smelly detective types lurking about and interfering with whatever series of lies he intended to tell the young woman.

The thought of Walt McCutcheon's injured body failing to restrain his overly amorous sense of optimism brought a faint smile to Lean's face as his eyelids closed. His right hand slipped from his lap, landing with a soft thud on the seat. The telegraph response, which had been waiting for him at the train station, dropped from his fingers. Anyone passing by who happened to pick up the paper would have read Officer Bushey's reply to Lean's inquiry: 'Fire yesterday. Father Coyne's house destroyed. His body pulled out this morning.'

67

'Well, Grey, I'm in the awkward position of being extremely grateful for all your help in this matter, yet hoping to God I never have to see you again. Professionally, I mean.'

Grey turned away from the hackney's window and the sights of the Portland streets. The faintest of smiles threatened his face. 'It will likely be some while before we cross paths again; I still plan to return to Boston next month. I should thank you as well, though. This has certainly been an interesting summer, one of the most intriguing inquiries I've ever conducted.'

'*One* of the most intriguing?' Lean chuckled. 'I only wish we'd guessed the killer's identity sooner. Might have saved Father Coyne.'

'Yes, terribly regrettable, though I doubt we could have saved the unfortunate man. I suspect that Whitten's poison would have finished the job even if we had, as you say' – Grey cleared his throat for emphasis – '*guessed* the truth and apprehended our man earlier.'

'Maybe so.'

The carriage drew to a halt on High Street. Grey reached for the handle.

'Anyway,' Lean said, 'again I . . . that is—'

'Understood. Good day, Deputy.' Grey departed, and the carriage moved on.

Lean sat back into the seat and let his eyes close. The respite was short-lived. Not a half block on, a shriek made him bolt upright.

'Driver!'

Lean shot his head out of the open window. Back on the steps of Grey's building, the landlady, Mrs Philbrick, was standing with Grey's arms around her for support. Lean jumped down to the street and raced back. Grey had already steered the hysterical woman up the steps and inside the doorway. Lean bounded up the stairs after them. Grey was urging her to lower her voice and speak slowly, to tell him everything. She nodded but continued to rant incoherently as she fought to keep her voice at something near a hoarse, panicked whisper.

'I didn't know what else to do but pray for your swift return,' she said. 'He wouldn't leave. There was no talking to him. Of course, I didn't try much – the way he looked and all. I mentioned the police, but he looked like he'd kill me on the spot. Oh, he's horrible, something horrible has happened. I don't know what he's done, but it's terrible. Should I telephone for the police now?'

The woman's face was pale. And her eyes widened even further when she finally noticed Lean standing nearby. 'Oh, thank goodness, Deputy. You have to go up there. Arrest him. But be careful, he's all a bloody devil, he is!'

Grey took her by the shoulders. 'My good Mrs Philbrick. Everything will be perfectly fine. I want you to stand right here. The deputy and I will go upstairs and see to the man. If you hear signs of a struggle or a gunshot, you must flee at once. Run to the druggist across the street and have him telephone for the police. Do you understand me?'

She nodded and pressed her back to the doorframe as if trying to will herself into a stone pillar supporting the lintel. Lean drew his pistol and followed Grey up the stairs, each man treading lightly, although anyone waiting for them had certainly been alerted to their arrival by Mrs Philbrick's screams. Upon reaching the entry to Grey's sitting room, Lean stood back a step, facing the door with his pistol arm stretched forward. Grey turned the knob and pushed the door inward.

There was no sound from within, and everything in the room appeared in perfect order. Grey stepped into the room, looked around, and then his head jerked backward slightly in surprise. Lean hurried forward and turned to face Tom Doran, who sat motionless in a tall-backed leather chair. His coat was open, and his white shirt showed dark red smears. Recognition dawned slowly in Doran's heavy, bloodshot eyes as he stared at the two men.

'What have you done, Tom?' asked Lean as he let his pistol slowly drop to his side.

'He's dead.'

'Who?' asked Grey. 'Doran! Who is dead?'

Tom Doran just raised his massive hands and stared at the dried blood caked over his palms and fingers.

Helen sat in a chair in the corner of Dr Steig's spacious study, her puffy, red eyes turned away from the scene laid out before the heavy maple desk. Lean regretted sending for her before they had a chance to make the room more presentable. Tom Doran's huge form stood blocking the door to the hall. He had buttoned his coat high to cover the bloody stains on his shirt.

Dr Steig lay facedown on the wooden floor. The wounds were not readily apparent due to his black coat, but the blood had pooled under him. Dried stains trailed across the hardwood floor, showing his attempt to drag himself toward the door before he died. An S shape, written in blood, marked the floor just inches from his face. A larger patch of blood was smeared on the floor in front of his desk. The desktop was a mess of strewn papers, and the drawers had been pulled out and emptied.

Lean stood a few steps away. He tried to obscure from Helen the sight of Perceval Grey, down close to the floor, examining the minutest details of her dead uncle's body. Finally, Grey stood and took several steps back. He folded his left arm in front, supporting his right elbow. A fingertip moved in small circles, caressing his temple. After a few more moments, Grey crossed his arms in front of his chest.

'You've drawn your conclusions, I take it?' Lean said.

'The doctor was stabbed here, a couple of feet in front of the desk. He was facing the assailant, presumably Jack Whitten. He was in front of the desk, not taking shelter behind it. He didn't have time to react; the attack caught him off guard. He must have let Whitten into the house; the servants were off, and there were no signs of a break-in at any door or window. Whitten would have introduced himself as Peter Chapman, Father Coyne's helper. The doctor might have recognized him from our description of our earlier meeting.'

Grey stepped just in front of the desk and then bent down on one knee. 'He fell here and tried his first message. You can see there, his fingertips are stained. The doctor would have instinctively felt his wound. Then he must have thought to make some mark, perhaps an attempt to identify his killer. From the size of this smeared area of blood, I would say the first message was more complete. Whitten was distracted. Likely tearing through the doctor's desk at the time. He took the doctor's copy of the Black Book pages and whatever notes he'd made. Only after disposing of them, there in the fireplace, did he return his attention to the doctor. He destroyed the bloody message with his sole, stabbed the doctor a second time in the back—'

Helen let out a small, pitiful gasp.

'My apologies, Mrs Prescott.' Grey locked eyes with Lean for a second, then looked at Helen. 'Perhaps you would be more comfortable in the kitchen.'

Helen forced her features into some semblance of control. 'No, thank you, Mr Grey. Please, I need to know what happened.'

'Whitten then continued on his way. Note the faint portion of a bloody shoe print there as he stepped over the doctor. He must

414

have assumed that the doctor was dead at that point. Although, obviously, our good friend had a bit more sand than the killer gave him credit for. He retained enough strength to make this last mark.'

'An "S", I think. But what does it stand for?' Lean asked.

'The doctor may have been in such a poor condition at the time that he was quite unaware of exactly what mark he was leaving. He obviously died almost immediately thereafter.'

Lean looked at Helen, who was on the verge of tears again. He wished to direct her thoughts somewhere more helpful, and he was also eager to confirm her version of the prior day's events again, before she became too emotional.

'He didn't suffer long. I know this is terribly trying, but please, Helen, once more, think back. Is there anything else about what he said?'

'No,' answered Helen. 'He just said he would have to cancel our dinner plans. He'd been reviewing the riddle again and thought he'd found something. A possible error. He was planning to try to have a look at the original.'

'I doubt the bishop would have allowed that.' Lean tapped his pencil on his notepad. 'And that was at what time?'

'Just about two o'clock is when he telephoned me at the historical society.'

'And I found him lying right there this morning at half ten.' Doran's voice from the doorway startled Lean, who'd nearly forgotten that the giant was still in the room.

'So this happened after we left the station.' Lean looked at Grey. 'If only he'd come with us.'

Grey held up a finger. 'I'll need to speak to Bishop Healy, see if the doctor ever made it to the cathedral to see the original.'

'What difference does it make?' Lean stepped closer to Grey. 'The damage is done.'

'Still, in the interest of fully understanding all that has passed before us in this inquiry ...'

Lean glared at Grey, who returned his look impassively.

'My uncle,' said Helen.

Both men turned to face her. Lean's irritation at Grey's dogged pursuit of the final tragic minutiae of the case melted away when he saw the pained expression on Helen's face.

'What do we do?' she asked.

'Oh, of course,' Lean said. 'I'll have some men over immediately to take him. So you can proceed with the arrangements.'

'That's not what I meant.'

Lean gave her a puzzled look.

'He wouldn't want it known that he died like this. Murdered by some madman. My uncle always despised the way that they were treated, the insane. Feared and detested. Locked away and chained like animals, or criminals, or ...'

'Or witches,' Grey added.

'He'd hate the thought of what people would say about this. About his work. They'd use his death as another example to prove that the insane are too dangerous to treat and how they should all just be locked away.' Helen wiped the tears from her eyes. 'It was the whole reason he came here – he wanted to help the veterans, and not for just the wounds that you could see.'

'The truth of it is that your uncle was murdered,' Grey said.

'By a man who is already dead. Who cannot be prosecuted or punished in this world. Must we let that man strike out at my uncle again? He took his life. I won't have him murder his legacy as well. You owe him that at least.'

Lean exchanged a glance with Grey, who looked away after a moment.

'I can speak with the coroner,' Lean said, 'have some reliable men collect your uncle's body. Things can be arranged ... quietly.'

'Thank you, Archie.'

A short while later, Lean helped Helen into a hansom cab and paid the driver to take her home. Grey stood near, and they watched the cab turn the corner out of view.

'Do you wish to come to the cathedral with me?' Grey asked.

'No. I truly don't. Please stop, Grey. It's over. There's nothing left to answer. The inquiry is finished. It's time to let it all rest ... and bury our friend.'

68

Grey entered his study and, from force of habit, went to his cluttered worktable. The investigation had burned itself out, leaving these piles of papers and notes as worthless remnants to be swept away. He picked up a page of testimony against George Burroughs. It reminded him of a program from some momentous opera, now finished. All the glorious notes just a memory, and he was just a patron exiting into the night with nothing more than that scrap of paper clutched in his hand. The wondrous music gone, replaced by all the mundane sounds of the world.

Above the empty fireplace, his father's old pipe still sat on the mantel. The stone bowl felt cool in his palm. He never did learn if Geoffrey Blanchard had spent time among Abenakis in connection with his father's temperance activities. Instead, Grey was left with the assumption that Jack Whitten had lived among the Indians after he was released from the orphanage. He must have found his mother again while she traveled with the Indian shows. He supposed Lean was right – it simply didn't matter now. The unasked, unanswered questions would remain, themselves like dead bodies that would never be committed to the ground. It no longer mattered what had started Whitten down his murderous path. Was there any reason he chose those specific victims? Why had he bothered to kill Dr Steig? There was nothing left to gain from those questions, as frustrating as it was not to know. It was a question that he'd never left unresolved in any of his prior inquiries: Why did a certain person have to die?

Grey went to his desk and began sorting through the papers, pushing them aside until he recovered a small newspaper article: DROWNED MAN PULLED FROM RIVER.

'Last month I asked Herrick about the day my mother and I first arrived here.'

From his stuffed chair, Cyrus Grey showed no obvious sign of interest.

'Easter Sunday. He remembered it vividly,' Grey said.

'Well and good.' Cyrus returned to his newspaper.

'The year was 1867. Easter fell on April twenty-first.'

'If you say so.'

'I had occasion recently to spend some time in the basement of the *Eastern Argus* and found something that piqued my curiosity. So later I also checked the archives of the *Daily Press*, the *Express*, and the *Daily Advertiser*.' Grey drew out a small newspaper clipping from his coat pocket. 'This is the earliest report on the incident that I could find. The first mention in any Portland newspaper.'

Cyrus skimmed the article and tried to hand it back, but Grey did not accept it.

'You'll notice the date on the story,' Grey said.

'April twenty-second.'

'He died that Friday prior, April nineteenth. You couldn't have known in time. The men you sent to retrieve us arrived too quickly, before news of the death became known here.'

'Your mother must have telegraphed me.'

'She didn't leave the house after he died. Not once until those men came for us.'

'A friend of hers, then. I don't recall exactly. What are you getting at, Perceval?'

Grey sat down opposite his grandfather. 'The truth, now. Did you order them to kill my father?'

'How can you ask me that?'

'Did you?'

The old man dropped his newspaper on the side table. 'Of course not.'

'Then tell me how. Why were those men there? It would have been no later than Saturday night that they roused us from our home. What were they doing there so quickly?'

'I sent them. Is that what you want to hear? Fine. But I never told them to hurt the man. I provided money to give to him. An exchange, if you will. They were to bring your mother and you home. I never meant for that fellow to be harmed.'

'"That fellow"? You can call him my father. You can't hide the plain truth of it.' Grey held his arms out, putting himself on display. 'That was your intent? To buy us back? Give him some money and he'd just walk away?'

'Maybe it was foolishness. So I'm guilty of being a fool. But I'm

419

not a murderer. They said it was an accident. Words were exchanged; trouble started. But they swore it was an accident.'

'And that's the end of it all?' Grey slumped back in his chair. 'But why? Why send them in the first place?'

'Your mother needed to come home; she needed help. You know the way her moods were.'

'She was happy then. He made her happy.'

'You were a child. What did you understand of the world they let you see? The simple truth is she needed doctors, not medicine women or some such. Real help.'

'You still believe that? Knowing how things ended. You think the doctors helped her?'

'She couldn't be saved. I know that now. But I saved *you*.'

'From what? My family?'

'From that life. Easy enough for you to sit here now and blame me for all. But where would you be if I'd never acted?' Cyrus rose and collected himself for a moment before facing Grey again. 'Look at yourself. Look at who you've become. You can't even comprehend the life you'd be living. What would you be now? A medicine man. Some itinerant basket weaver, roaming about like a Gypsy. A drunkard working at odd jobs.'

'Not everyone in the world needs all that you have to be content.'

'Content? You'd never have been content with a simple life, full of mundane chores and accomplishments. You think me cruel, no doubt, my conduct unforgivable. But what of all these investigations of yours? All these interesting matters you devote yourself to uncovering. Because of me, you were able to pursue this strange life you've chosen. Be honest with yourself, Perceval. Deep in your heart, you don't truly regret what I did.'

Grey shot a furious look at his grandfather.

'Yes, I caused you pain, your mother, too. But I never meant to – I wanted the best for her. And I failed.' Cyrus went to the cabinet and poured himself a drink. 'Parents and children are uniquely fitted in this world; they can wound each other far deeper than God should ever allow. And there's little to be done to dull that pain. I'm sorry for your mother, more than you can know. But the past is done. Dredging it up with these questions will never make things whole.'

Grey stood. The anger drained from his eyes, and he walked to the door.

69

Bishop Healy walked up the aisle. By the light of the many flickering candles, he saw the thin, dark man seated in the final pew. In their prior meeting, he'd had the impression that Perceval Grey was not a man who placed his faith in the Lord. But now he was leaning forward, head resting on his joined fingertips, in the appearance of prayer, or at least in deep contemplation. The bishop wanted to wait for Grey to notice him, but he was busy, especially now with all the arrangements to make in the wake of Father Coyne's tragic death.

'Mr Grey?'

Grey's eyelids snapped open. He stood and reached out to take the Bishop's hand, the gesture accompanied by a tired smile.

'Thank you for taking the time to see me, Your Excellency.'

'Not at all. Would you like to come back to my office? You

seem troubled. I'd hoped that I had helped you in our previous discussion.'

'You did. Thank you again.'

'But ... ?'

'But not before another loss,' Grey said. 'A friend.'

'Not Deputy Lean?'

'Lean? No, he's fine.'

Bishop Healy expected a further word or glance that would invite another question from him on Grey's loss, but there was no such sign from the man.

'So how can I help you, Mr Grey?'

'I just have a simple question remaining. Did Dr Virgil Steig pay you a visit the night before last?'

Bishop Healy was surprised by the question. 'The same night as the fire.'

'Yes. I was sorry to hear about Father Coyne.'

'Thank you. At least his suffering is over and he is home now with God.'

'Yes.' Grey smiled, but it looked forced, and he sustained it only long enough for the gesture to be duly noted. 'And Dr Steig?'

'No. I didn't see him.'

'Not a call on the telephone or a note? Any communication at all?'

'Not that I'm aware of,' Bishop Healy answered. 'Why? Is there something the matter?'

'No. Just trying to piece some little thing together. Thank you for your time. I must be going.' Grey made to leave.

Bishop Healy had seen the strain showing through on the man's face. There was definitely something eating at him.

Though he barely knew Perceval Grey, it was not easy for him to turn away from someone in such distress. He had to at least offer the man a chance to reach out.

'Mr Grey,' he called, 'perhaps you'd care to attend the funeral masses. You might find them to be of some comfort.'

Grey's hand was on the door out to the entryway. He stopped and looked back. 'Oh, thank you, but ... masses? Father Coyne and who else?'

'His man there, Peter Chapman. You must have met him when you spoke to Father Coyne.'

'Peter Chapman? What information do you have about his death?'

Bishop Healy felt suddenly uncomfortable under Grey's piercing stare. He was not accustomed to being so regarded anywhere, let alone inside the cathedral. Grey seemed to be challenging his answer, demanding that he elaborate. 'They haven't yet recovered his body from all that rubble, but they should locate him no later than tomorrow. Both masses are scheduled for the day after.'

Grey took two steps toward Bishop Healy. 'They won't find his body. Peter Chapman died two nights ago in Salem, Massachusetts, while fleeing the scene of a crime he'd committed.'

'What?' Bishop Healy studied Grey's face; the man was completely serious. 'There must be some mistake. We can't be talking about the same man.'

'I saw the dead man's face, Your Excellency. Shortish fellow, blond hair. Gruff and rather homely, if you don't mind my saying.'

Bishop Healy felt the relief well up in him, and a smile spread over his face. 'Peter was short all right, but otherwise you couldn't be further off, I'm happy to say. Dark-haired, quite pleasant, and rather a good-looking fellow.'

Grey's eyes went cold, not far off from the look of someone who'd just learned of the death of a loved one. Bishop Healy felt the humor drain out of his own face. He knew it was his turn to be studied, with Grey reading him for some sign of a joke

'He couldn't look more different from the man I've described,' Grey said, mostly to himself.

'I suppose not.'

'This Peter Chapman of yours, with the black hair, was he ever accompanied at the cathedral by a friend or assistant? A blond man, like I described?'

'No.' Bishop Healy considered the question further. 'I never saw anyone with him other than his wife.'

'Wife? A dark-haired woman, named Lizzie?' Grey said.

'I don't recall her name, but no, she had red hair.'

'A redhead?' The perplexed look on Grey's face was overtaken by concern. 'The woman on the train platform.'

'Mr Grey, are you quite all right? You look as though you're not well.'

'I'm fine. Thank you, Bishop.' Grey began to pace. 'Something's not right here.'

'I'm afraid I don't understand, Mr Grey. Is there something else I can help you with?'

Grey stopped and stared. 'Yes, actually. Dr Steig wanted to confirm some details, but I don't know exactly what he was after. What can you tell me about the death of Saint Polycarp of Smyrna?'

Bishop Healy was so completely surprised by the question that he had no choice but to invite Grey to his office to see what they could find. Once there, Bishop Healy found a book on the lives of the saints. He flipped through the pages until he came to Saint Polycarp.

'What exactly would you like to know?'

'How did he die?'

The bishop skimmed the page, then read, '"When the funeral pyre was ready, and Polycarp was bound, he looked to heaven and prayed. The flame blazed forth in great fury, but shaped itself like the sail of a ship filled with the wind and circled around his body, so his flesh was not burnt, but rather was as gold glowing in a furnace. At length, when those wicked men saw his body could not be consumed by the fire, the executioner pierced him with a dagger. And on his doing this, there came forth a dove, and a great quantity of blood, so that the fire was extinguished.'"

'Wait. Set on fire first – then stabbed. Are you certain, Your Excellency?' Grey came closer and read the page himself.

'Why so surprised?'

Grey shook his head. 'I was told otherwise: stabbed first, then burned.'

'Well, it's just a detail. The exact order isn't the crucial element of the story, of course.'

'I'm afraid it is.' Grey rushed out the door, his final words still hanging in the air.

70

Helen stepped into Delia's room. The window was open, letting in a nice breeze. With the light from the hallway, she could make out her daughter's face as Delia lay in bed with her eyes still open.

'What is it, dear?'

'I can't sleep, Mama,' the girl said in a creaky, tear-soaked voice. 'I keep thinking of Uncle Virgil.'

'I know. I'm sad too, but it will be all right. It's been a very long day. You need to get some sleep now.'

'Will you lie with me?' Delia reached out to her mother.

Helen took her hand and sat on the edge of the bed. 'Of course.' She slipped her shoes off, settled in beside Delia, and stroked loose strands of hair away from her daughter's face.

'I'm scared,' Delia whispered.

'Of what?'

'Of how people always ... go away,' Delia said. 'Will you ever, Mama?'

'No, never. I'll never leave you,' Helen said.

'You promise?'

'Cross my heart and hope to die.'

Helen felt the girl's body tense at the final word. 'Don't say that, Mama. Not that.'

'Just cross my heart. I promise.'

Within minutes Delia's breathing became deep and untroubled. Helen could feel herself slipping away, the soft bed pulling her down into a warm, comforting darkness. She felt the weight of the past day's troubles slough off and fall from her.

When Helen stirred awake, it was to a banging sound. In that instant the noise evaporated away like the echo of a final dream. She lifted her head from the pillow, looked down at Delia's still face, and listened. She flinched when the pounding happened again. Someone was knocking on the front door. Helen wondered how long she'd been asleep and whether it was an unusual time for someone to be calling. She made her way out into the

426

hall and down the stairs. Passing through the parlor, she looked at the clock: just after ten. She reached the front door and pulled the curtain aside. It was dark, but she could make out the shape of a woman standing on the front porch. She was wearing a dark, mid-length coat over a long white dress.

Helen opened the door.

Lean dropped another stack of papers into the box. He supposed he should sort out what was worth keeping in case this matter ever came to light. He might someday be called upon to explain his role in the events surrounding the murders committed by Jack Whitten, possibly with the assistance of Geoffrey Blanchard. Much of his handwritten material was nearly indecipherable, and many of the typed pages had proved utterly irrelevant to the truth of the case.

He flipped through a chronology of the Salem trials that Helen had provided weeks earlier, tracing the dates of accusations, court hearings, and the deaths of accused witches. There were sketches of the bodies, the scenes of the murders, notes on dozens of interviews with landlords, lists of residents in the neighborhood of the Portland Company. Next came notes from his sittings with Portland's various mediums. He chuckled as he recalled the less-than-convincing accent of one woman who claimed to channel a spirit guide from ancient Egypt.

The phone rang, and his wife answered in the other room. He reached for the page of automatic writing that Amelia Porter had delivered to him at home after their séance. He smiled again, thinking of Grey's amused fascination with the Porters' grocery list.

'Archie, it's Perceval Grey,' Emma called from the kitchen. 'He says it's urgent.'

Lean strode into the kitchen and took up the receiver. 'Yes?'

'This Peter Chapman fellow did not work alone.'

'You've confirmed Geoffrey Blanchard was assisting him.'

'That's not what I mean. Neither of their fingerprints were a match for the one left on Maggie Keene's shoe. Our real killer is still alive. Peter Chapman was only his assistant.'

He heard the words, but Lean couldn't force his mind to accept their meaning. 'What in blazes are you talking about?'

'The man who killed Maggie Keene and the other women is still out there. And to further muddy the waters, I've spoken with Bishop Healy. The man who died in front of the train in Salem was not the real Peter Chapman.'

'Right,' Lean said, 'he's Jack Whitten.'

'No, the Peter Chapman we met at Father Coyne's was not the same Peter Chapman known to the priests at the cathedral. What it all means, I don't yet know. But for the moment, let's keep our focus on the fact that this Peter Chapman impostor and Geoffrey Blanchard are both dead and we still have a killer at large. In fact, I think he may well have been the man you were suspicious of when we departed Portland. The man in black at Union Station. If the killer is even a man to begin with.'

'What?'

'Nothing,' Grey said. 'In any event, the killer never left Portland. He probably went to Dr Steig's right after we left Portland.'

'We shouldn't discuss this over the telephone. We need to speak in person,' Lean said.

'What about Helen? Do you think she would be up to the task? I know she's been through a terrible loss – but her historical expertise might still be of use.'

428

'We should let her be right now, she has Delia to ...' Lean's voice trailed off as the thought hit him like a shot. He looked down at the paper in his hand, Amelia Porter's page of automatic writing. His eyes scanned across the odd, stilted handwriting: 'The darkness rising beware the Good woman and her child.'

'Holy Mother of God,' he muttered.

'Lean. Are you still there?'

'Meet me at Helen's. And for God's sake, hurry!'

Lean telephoned the police station and ordered a patrolman be sent to his home until he returned. Then he hired a dogcart, eager to make the trip in an open-air carriage that would not obstruct his view. The sporadic gas lighting on the streets gave little aid on this night, just one day prior to the new moon. Even though the streets were thinly populated at this hour, Lean peered at the face of every passerby, desperate for some glimpse of the man in black as he approached Helen's. Once, on Cumberland Street, he was passed by a hackney that came on at a full gallop. The dark figure of the driver, with his black bowler tugged down low upon his brow, had caused Lean to stare suspiciously. But as the carriage went by, he saw that the passenger was a solitary woman in a white poplin dress. Another minute and he arrived on Wilmot Street. He saw Grey's hansom cab pulling up in front of Helen's house. By the time Lean reached the front door, Grey had already knocked several times and was trying the knob.

'Unlocked.'

The two men entered, Lean with his gun drawn, Grey with a steel-handled walking stick at the ready.

'Helen!' Lean shouted. 'Hello! Anyone?' He hurried through the parlor toward the kitchen while Grey went to the second floor. Lean swept through the entire first floor, rushing on ever more quickly as each room turned up vacant. He sprinted to the landing at the top of the stairs. Grey beckoned him to the girl's room at the back of the house. Lean entered and looked around. The bedcovers were lying on the floor, and the window was open. Grey sniffed Delia's pillow, then tossed it over to Lean.

'Ether. Do you think ... ?' Lean couldn't bring himself to finish the question. Not so soon after the murder of Dr Steig. The image of the old man's body sprawled on the floor flitted before his eyes.

'If he meant to kill them immediately, as revenge or whatever passes for a motive in his mind, he'd have done so here rather than risk detection by removing them from the house. He must have some other purpose. Perhaps we interrupted his assistant, Chapman or Whitten, before the full ritual with Geoffrey Blanchard could be completed. He was never burned as we expected. Maybe the killer feels he's required to repeat the final murder, to correct his failure.'

'Or he knows we're onto him. Perhaps they're hostages to ensure safe passage while he flees town.'

Grey shook his head. 'He'd know we can't identify him accurately. He could vanish from town at any time, and no one would try to stop him. No, they're not mere hostages.' Grey picked up the young girl's short dress and stockings from where they'd been left, neatly folded, on a small wooden chair. 'Her school clothes – so she's still in her nightdress.'

'Good. Even easier to spot.'

'Precisely,' said Grey as he led the way back downstairs. 'Which means he does not intend for them to be seen publicly. If he is fleeing, it will be alone, or by private means. Either way, it doesn't bode well for the Prescotts.'

'I'll put men at every depot anyway. Maybe he's fool enough to try it.' Lean stopped downstairs in the parlor to seize photographs that showed Helen and Delia. The two detectives exited into the dark night, then rode toward the police station on Myrtle Street. The silence was broken only by the occasional piece of strategy.

'I'll send a man to Lizzie Madson's rooms,' Lean said. 'If he's on the run, he may take refuge at his old haunt. Dr Steig's as well; he may have missed something he was looking for.'

'While you're at it, get a man over to your own house too. In case your theory on hostages or revenge against us happens to be true.'

'There's an officer there already,' Lean said. 'I'll have him escort Owen and Emma to her sister's.' The carriage pulled up just short of the station, and Lean jumped out, calling back over his shoulder, 'I'll meet you as soon as I can.'

71

The clock on the mantel over Grey's fireplace struck the half hour. Even though Lean was painfully aware of the exact time, he still glanced at the glass face set in the small maple housing. He was beginning to truly hate that clock. One thirty in the afternoon. They'd been at this since before sunrise, and nothing to show for it except piles of papers and books that had been read, then moved from one side of the table to the other.

A sense of futility was beginning to encircle Lean's mind.

Helen and Delia were in the hands of a madman, and even if they were still alive, their chances of remaining so dwindled with each passing hour. And what was he doing? Rummaging through old transcripts looking for some hint that might not even exist, to unlock a riddle that might not mean at all what Grey said it did. How could Grey be so sure of it, when just days earlier he'd been positive it meant something else entirely?

'We've wasted too much time already.'

'How so?' Grey asked, glancing only for a second from the text he was perusing.

'Why, everything. We haven't accomplished anything since leaving Helen's.'

'On the contrary, I think we've made excellent use of our time. You've arranged for your family's temporary relocation and safety. You've gotten a bit of sleep, without which I daresay you'd be of little service. And just look at the progress we've made getting through the material.'

Lean stood up from the table and moved to the windows looking down on High Street outside Grey's building. He hoped the change of scenery would do some good, reveal some hidden meaning or clue in the page that he held: 'The Trial of George Burroughs at a Court of Oyer and Terminer, in Salem, 1692 by Cotton Mather.' He glanced down and read it again.

This G.B. was Indicted for Witchcraft, and Accused by the Confessing Witches as the head Actor at their Hellish Rendezvouses, and one who had the promise of being a King in Satan's Kingdom, now going to be Erected. One of the Bewitched Persons, testified a little black Hair'd Man came to her, saying his

Name was B. and bidding her set her hand to a Book which he shewed unto her; and bragged that he was a Conjurer, above the ordinary Rank of Witches. This G.B. ensnared himself by several Instances of a Preternatural Strength. He was a very Puny Man, yet had often done things beyond the strength of a giant. A Gun of about seven foot Barrel, and so heavy that strong Men could not steadily hold it out with both hands; there were Testimonies that he made nothing of taking up such a Gun with one hand, and holding it out like a Pistol at Armsend. G.B. in his Vindication, was so foolish as to say, that an Indian was there, and held it out at the same time: Whereas none of the Spectators ever saw any such Indian; but they supposed the Black Man, (as the Witches call the Devil; and they say he resembles an Indian) might give him that Assistance.

Useless. The same as the hundreds of other court records, depositions, journal entries, and whatever else they had accumulated in the past two months relating to the witch trials and the Reverend George Burroughs.

'We should be out searching,' Lean said, anger creeping into his voice.

'Where? Even if we knew they were still inside the city, we could never hope to find them before tonight. No,' Grey assured him, 'the answer is in the riddle and in the history of George Burroughs.'

'We don't know that. The riddle could well end at four victims. We don't know that it mentions a fifth.'

'Dr Steig believed it did,' Grey said. 'Whitten may well have revealed it before he killed the doctor.'

'The mark he made on the floor could have been an "S". You thought so yourself.'

'It was a "5". And we were foolish not to see it before in the riddle.' Grey snatched up a page that had been set aside. 'We saw the word "fourth" mentioned in the last paragraph and assumed that four murders was the end. We jumped to the wrong conclusion. A preconceived theory took hold. We didn't read closely enough.'

He pinned the page to the table with his finger, as if accusing it of perjury. 'The fourth month *and* the last. Where the master died *and then* where his blood flowed. There the fourth, *then* the last offering. There the cup emptied *and then* the vessel held ready. It's all in pairs. The final clue is a dual one. Two mysteries wrapped together in the last paragraph, in the final month. First where the master died and then where his blood flowed. Two different locations. Gallows Hill was the first, where Burroughs died. Wherever he shed his blood will be next.'

'He never did, though,' Lean declared. 'That's just it. All through the wars and not a scratch. Another reason they thought he was in league with the Indians and the devil.'

Grey shook his head. 'No. I know there was a mention of it somewhere.'

'"Somewhere"? *That's* what you're pinning Helen and Delia's lives on? *Somewhere* there's a mention of George Burroughs's blood?'

'Yes, Lean. Somewhere. Now, if you don't mind. We've quite a bit left to get through.'

Lean glanced at the clock yet again. He tried to calm his own breathing, and as he did so, the terrible, incessant ticking of the clock came into his ears. He focused on the words in front of him, begging them to have meaning, to reveal something. He fought

434

his way through several more entries, each equally irrelevant to the present crisis.

The clock struck the hour, and Lean just couldn't take it anymore. He slapped the page down, stood up, and made it to the mantel in three long strides. The clock was suddenly in his hand, and, somewhat detached in his own mind, he saw his arm rising up and then rushing down. The clock shattered on the hearthstones. The anger drained out of him, and he was left staring at the small wood-and-glass carcass on the floor.

'Better?' Grey asked.

'Yes. Quite a bit.' Lean contemplated making an effort to clean up the mess but instead settled back into his seat to resume the work. 'Sorry about the clock.'

'You'll get the bill once this is all done,' Grey said with the hint of a smirk.

'Fair enough'

Grey's eyes never left the papers in front of him, and while he continued to read, his hand slipped into his vest pocket. He removed his watch, which he opened and set before him on the table. Its miniature clicking filled the air between the men.

Lean picked up the next entry from his assigned stack. A deposition from the Essex County Archives entitled *Mercy Lewis v. George Burroughs.* He took a deep breath and turned his attention to the item.

The deposition of Mercy Lewis who testifies and says that on the 7th of May 1692, at evening I saw the apparition of Mr George Burroughs whom I very well knew which did grievously torture me and urged me to write in his book and then he brought to me a new fashion book which he did not use to bring and told me I

might write in that book: for that was a book that was in his study
when I lived with them. But I told him I did not believe him for
I had been often in his study, but I never saw that book there. But
he told me that he had several books in his study which I never
saw in his study and he could raise the devil. And now had
bewitched Mr Sheppard's daughter and I asked him how he could
go to bewitch her now he was kept at Salem. And he told me that
the devil was his servant and he sent him in his shape to do it.
Then he again tortured me most dreadfully and threatened to kill
me for he said I should not witness against him. Also he told me
that he had made Abigail Hobbs a witch and several more then
again he did most dreadfully torture me. The next night he told
me I should not see his two wives if he could help it because I
should not witness against him. This 9th May, Mr Burroughs car-
ried me up to an exceeding high mountain and showed me all the
kingdoms of the earth and told me that he would give them all to
me if I would write in his book. And if I would not, he would
throw me down and break my neck. But I told him they were
none of his to give and I would not write if he threw me down on
100 pitchforks.

Mercy Lewis ag'st Burroughs.

'No mention of Burroughs's blood, but it smacks of this investigation.' Lean reread the passage aloud while Grey sat silent with
his eyes closed. When he finished, Lean set the page down.
'Breaking her neck and casting her down on pitchforks. All kinds
of promises to get her name in his book. It all sounds like Maggie
Keene, doesn't it?'

'That bit again about a secret book in his study that he could
use to raise the devil.'

Lean nodded. 'Perhaps a grain of truth in some of these girls' wild testimony. Did she just make that up, or did she really know something about that same book mentioned by the other fellow Meserve told us about, the one Burroughs entrusted to hide the Black Book before he was arrested as a witch? It makes you wonder.'

Grey bolted from his chair and grabbed the telephone receiver. He clicked the lever twice and waited.

'Grey? What is it?'

He held up a finger toward Lean, then spoke into the receiver. 'Telephone exchange 5328, please.' Grey waited, his finger tapping on the side table that held the phone. He glanced up and saw Lean waiting for an explanation. 'Pierce. That other man's name was Pierce. The one who wrote about Burroughs giving him the Black Book and all that.'

Lean waited for something further, but apparently that bit of information was supposed to be enough to explain Grey's sudden frantic behavior.

'Thank you, Operator. No, I won't need to place the call again.' Grey hung up the receiver and then grabbed his coat from a hook by the door.

Lean rushed after Grey, who barreled down the stairs. They nearly knocked over Mrs Philbrick, who had poked her head out of her ground-floor apartment to see about the commotion. Lean tipped his hat in apology as he passed the poor woman, her eyes still wide in terror from the previous incident with a blood-spattered Tom Doran.

Outside on the front steps, Grey waved frantically for a cab.

'Where the blazes are we going?'

Grey didn't look back. A cab was pulling up, and he climbed

aboard before it had even stopped. 'The historical society – to see Meserve!'

They entered the historical society on the third floor of the Portland Public Library building. The room was empty, and the door to the back research room was closed. After finding it locked, Lean pounded several times on the wooden door.

'Meserve's not here,' Grey said. 'How are you with busting doors down?'

'I've done a few in my time.'

'I'll defer to you, then.'

Lean stepped back, girded himself, and then rammed his right foot straight ahead, just next to the doorknob. The frame splintered. A second kick sent the door slamming inward, knocked off its top hinge. Lean stepped into the room with Grey right behind.

'I'm coming ...' F. W. Meserve called as he came bustling down the outside hallway and entered the front room. 'Just a second ...' He had his glasses in hand, cleaning them with a handkerchief. He let it drop and set his glasses on his face as he approached the ruined door, his mouth agape.

'Oh, there you are, Meserve,' Grey said from inside the research room. His head turned this way and that, looking over the various piles of books and bound stacks of paper. 'Sorry about the ...' He waved in the general direction of the entry.

'Door,' Meserve muttered as he stepped into the room. His eyes flitted back and forth between the doorway and his visitors. At a loss to explain events, Meserve fell back into old habits. 'Is there something I can help you with today, gentlemen?'

'Yes, actually,' Grey said. 'That collection of papers you told us about before. Caleb Pierce's writings. There was mention in there of an Indian attack. Pierce, George Burroughs, and some other English settlers took refuge on an island in Casco Bay.'

'Yes, that's true. On Andrews Island.'

'Can we please see the actual document?'

'Of course.' Meserve smiled, so pleased by their interest in the subject that he seemed to momentarily forget about his shattered door. He moved to a bookshelf, ran a finger along several aged spines, and selected one. He set the volume on a table and gently turned through the pages.

'Here we go.' Meserve took half a step to the side, his finger still lingering at the bottom of the page. 'There's the spot where Pierce mentions the island.'

Grey stepped forward and bent in close. He scanned the page, then read aloud: '"On our return to Andrews Isle, I was gladdened to find the Reverend Burroughs having by virtue of his own hands begun construction of a stone wall for defense. You yourself know the surprising strength in the Good Reverend's frame. The business was trying enough that all our hands were sorely cut by the jagged rocks and work of digging out the stones for use. It is to be hoped that no more English blood shall stain that wall before the Lord sees fit to favor us with redemption."'

Grey closed the book. 'Burroughs's blood was shed there. That's our spot.'

Lean puzzled over the name. 'Andrews Island? I'm not familiar with it.'

'It hasn't been called that for a hundred years,' Meserve explained. 'It's Cushing's now.'

'We haven't much time,' Grey said. He stood still, his hand on his chin while he thought. 'We're going to need assistance. Tom Doran.'

'Probably find him at Jimmy Farrell's place,' Lean said.

'A quick stop back at my rooms first.' Grey and Lean started toward the door.

Meserve picked up the book and cradled it like a prized possession. He watched his sudden visitors step around the splintered remains of his door. 'You gentlemen will just show yourselves out, then?'

72

Grey and Lean stood just inside the doorway to James Farrell's basement place. The leader of one of Portland's Irish factions ran a cavernous hall that serviced almost every vice a man could ask for, provided the man in question wasn't too imaginative and mostly liked to drink cheap whiskey and rum. The few narrow windows set high in the walls were too filthy to let in more than an ounce of sunlight. It was still afternoon, but the place was already well on its way to a good night's business. The smell of whiskey, beer, new sweat, and piss almost covered up the stale versions of those same smells that had lingered from the night before.

A doorman with scars visible on his close-shorn scalp approached. He was wide enough across the chest that Lean almost didn't see the man behind him. Jim Farrell hadn't bothered to don his coat but looked dapper all the same in a light blue silk vest over a crisply starched shirt and navy cravat. His face was well lined, and his bristly hair was more than halfway given over to gray. He'd led a hard life and looked older than Lean knew him to be.

'Deputy. You shouldn't be here. I have an arrangement.'

'This isn't official business,' Lean said.

Farrell looked Grey over. The man made little effort to hide the threat of violence lurking close behind his eyes. 'Well, I'm afraid you came down here for nothing, then. Tom Doran ain't taking social calls right now. Sorry, gents.' He gestured toward the door.

'I think you should reconsider,' said Grey.

'Do you, now? And why's that?'

'Because after so many years of loyal service, I suspect you've come to rely on the sturdy support of a man like Tom Doran. You might even, in your own way, consider him a friend. More important to you, it's simply in your best interests.'

Farrell tilted his head slightly; there was a gleam in his eye. Lean could tell that the man was trying to figure whether there was a threat or a proposition coming from Grey.

'Doran's started drinking again,' Grey continued, 'heavily. Dr Steig saved his life years ago. Cured him, in a manner of speaking. At least helped him keep his demons at bay. Steig's dead now. Doran is a man standing at the edge of the abyss. If he goes over, he's no use to you. Eventually he may even become too dangerous to keep around.'

'And what are you proposing to do about it?'

Grey slipped a manila envelope from his inside coat pocket. 'I propose to pull him back. And I have here the one last thing in this world that just might save the man's very soul.'

Lean struggled to contain his own surprise at what Grey was saying. He couldn't tell if it was a ploy. For Doran's sake, and their own, he hoped it was the truth. He knew that Farrell had managed to survive and flourish in his own dangerous profession due, in large part, to his ability to know how much a man was lying to him.

'All right. You got five minutes. Any trouble and it'll be your own souls you'll need to worry about.' Farrell nodded toward the burly doorman, who proceeded to lead Lean and Grey to a semi-private booth in a back corner of the hall. After a minute, the doorman reappeared, holding an unsteady Tom Doran by the elbow.

Doran slumped into the seat across from them. Even in this stench-filled room, Lean could smell the whiskey on the giant Irishman.

'Hello, Tom.'

'What do you fellows want?'

'We need your help,' Grey said.

'Hah, that's rich. I can't help no one.'

'We need to get out to Cushing's Island tonight. Unseen, after dark,' Lean told him.

'So hire a boat.'

'We also need a couple of men who can be relied upon. Sure men.'

'You're the cop,' Doran said. 'Take some of your own.'

'This isn't police business, officially. This is about the guy who killed Dr Steig.'

Doran's eyes flashed at the mention of the name.

'Right now, this is about Helen Prescott. The man who killed Steig has taken her,' Lean said.

'And her little girl,' added Grey. 'If we don't stop him, he'll kill them both. Tonight.'

'You're messing around with me now.'

'No, Tom. We need your help. Farrell's got boats and men

who know their way around every inch of these islands in the dark and can do it without being seen or heard.'

Doran was wavering. Lean could see that it was too much for him to consider in his current state. Grey slid the manila envelope across the table.

'Open it.'

Doran glanced back and forth between Grey and the envelope several times before picking it up and fumbling with the opening, trying not to rip the thing in two. He managed to get a thumb inside and tore away the top. A photograph slid out. Lean caught a glimpse of a woman in the picture. Doran stared at it, and a knot appeared between his eyebrows. 'She's ...'

'She goes by the name of Dunleavy now. Katie Dunleavy. The family lives over near Libby's Hill. She's engaged to a young man by the name of Mullen. A fine Irish lad. He's a bank clerk.'

'Katie?'

'Yes, Tom, your daughter.' Grey let the news sink into Doran's whiskey-clouded brain for a moment longer. 'She's living a very happy life. Dr Steig helped set her on that path twenty years ago. Back when you were in no condition to help her. Your little girl, all grown up and happy. Maybe you could meet her someday, if you were up to it.'

Lean's mind was racing. Steig had kept Doran's jail sentence down after his drunken rampage over his wife's death. The child was to be taken to the Female Orphan Society, but Dr Steig instead made arrangements for a favorable adoption. Had he kept tabs on her ever since, without ever mentioning it to Doran, and then told all this to Grey? Or had Grey ransacked the doctor's papers and found the information? Then the image flashed into Lean's brain. Grey copying down a name and slipping it into his pocket that day in the records room, when they'd been searching for the orphaned son of Old Stitch. He'd been looking for Doran's child. Since then he'd held on to the information that could free Doran from the pain of not knowing that his only child was safe and happy. Grey had kept it up his sleeve until it was needed. But what if it hadn't been needed for another year, or five, or never? Lean wondered how long Grey would have waited to ease Tom Doran's burden.

Doran looked up at them, tears in his eyes. 'She's beautiful. Looks just like her mother.'

Lean felt a vicarious stab of guilt and glanced at Grey. There was no sign of remorse on the man's face, no shame at having just seen the pure joy on Doran's face and knowing he could have delivered the news earlier.

'Tom, Dr Steig's niece is going to die tonight. Her little girl is going to be murdered. She'll never grow up and turn into a beautiful, happy young woman. Don't let that happen to her. You can help this little girl. Right now.' Grey was staring into the massive Irishman's eyes.

'Cushing's?' said Doran.

'Tonight,' Grey said. 'Just after sunset.'

'What time is it now?'

'Four,' said Lean, and then, remembering Doran's condition, he added, 'p.m.'

'Meet me at the bottom of Clark Street in two hours. We'll take the bridge. There's a house on the shore in Cape Elizabeth we can leave from.'

Making their way back through Farrell's place, Lean could feel many eyes on them, men staring like salivating dogs awaiting their master's order. When they reached the street, Lean took several deep breaths, the fresh air like a bit of redemption.

'That wasn't right in there. Holding that all back from Doran until now. You know that, don't you?'

'Right? I fear there's very little right in all that's about to happen. But ask me again come sunrise – if we're both still living.'

The fourteen-foot rowboat scraped onto the rocky gravel of the unlit beach. Tom Doran and his two men dropped their oars so that the handles fell into the bottom of the boat, leaving them leveraged in the oarlocks, the heads lifted high out of the water. Lean did likewise. Doran's rowers were men who didn't look like they spent much time sober or out of doors, but they were adept at handling the boat, and Lean didn't have to ask why. With only four oarlocks, there was plenty of space left for cargo. Tonight, with the four of them manning the oars and the boat not hauling a single barrel of smuggled whiskey or beer, they'd made good time from the mainland. Lean scrambled over the side, splashing down in ankle-deep water. Doran single-handedly drew the boat up onto shore. They left one man there to stand guard, with explicit orders to shoot anyone – particularly a short, dark-haired man – who tried to gain passage on the boat. Two hundred yards north along the shore, they spotted a small dinghy, hidden under a tarp. Doran ordered the second man to stand watch there, with similar orders to the first.

Moving away from the rocky shore, with its cluster of summer cottages, Lean led Doran north. The island was more or less level, with scattered stands of woods in front of them, allowing a decent view of the landscape, though it was dark beneath the new moon.

As they moved closer to the point, still unable to make out any clear details, Lean felt his heart begin to thump louder and louder in his chest. He was trying to move through the tall grass and brush quietly but was struggling to restrict his pace to a brisk walk. His eyes scanned the dark horizon, searching for any spark or sign of flame. There was nothing, and his gaze drifted north-west to the lights visible across the water in Portland. Grey was there, still analyzing the evidence, searching for anything they had missed, guarding against the possibility that they had once again misjudged their man and left him alone in the city to wreak havoc as he'd done with the murder of Dr Steig.

'Damn!' Doran roared past him in the second it took for Lean to detect the source of the giant man's sudden outburst. One hundred yards ahead, a red spark appeared, flickered out, then reappeared. The small dot of fire rushed sideways in both directions and quickly began to climb.

Lean sprinted forward, arms pumping. His gaze was fixed on the spreading flames, though Doran partially blocked his view. He was amazed at how quickly the Irishman's massive strides were outpacing his own. Ahead, in the light of the building flames, Lean saw the form of a small body supported a few feet above the ground. Panic seized his mind, but he clung to one thought, inarticulate but all-encompassing: Delia herself was not yet on fire.

A shot exploded from straight ahead, and Tom Doran went down, tumbling violently head over feet in the tall grass. Lean instinctively threw himself down on the ground, rolled, and got to one knee, pistol in hand. In the fleeting seconds it had taken him to rise, he saw that Doran had regained his own feet and was sprinting forward again.

Lean heard a furious scream pierce the darkness. A woman in a long white dress appeared in the light of the flames. She grabbed a stick of wood from the fire and bolted forward, swinging the flaming brand at Tom Doran. He flung an arm out, knocking the blow aside and sending the woman tumbling. Three more strides and Doran was rushing into the fire, madly kicking both legs, sending flaming branches in every direction. He reached in and swept Delia's limp form from the center of the blaze. The hem of the little girl's dress had caught fire, but Doran extinguished it as he engulfed the small figure within his own massive bulk.

'She alive?' Lean shouted.

'Yes! Yes, she's good!' Doran sank to his knees, still cradling Delia.

Lean exhaled, part of the horrible weight falling from him in an instant. His eyes darted all around the rocky point. Helen was nowhere. He dashed off again, veering to his left in pursuit of the woman in the white dress. She was easy enough to follow; she still clutched the burning torch that she had used to attack Doran. The woman was not a fast runner, and Lean quickly closed the gap between them. As he approached, he saw the flame rise higher. He momentarily thought that she was raising it over her head before he realized that she was scampering up a short rise of smallish, sharply angled rocks.

They were very near the ocean now; the craggy outcropping on which the woman stood stretched a short way out into the water. Lean quickly bounded up the rocks in pursuit. The woman reached the end and turned to face him. In the light of the torch, standing just twelve feet away, she bared her teeth in a twisted, furious snarl. Her red hair was pulled back, and her eyes were sheer hatred. He recognized her as the woman who had chastised Peter Chapman on the rail platform in Salem. He raised the pistol, aiming directly at her chest.

'You're under arrest!'

Her snarl eased and spread into a menacing grin.

'Give it up. I won't think twice of killing you after what you tried here tonight.'

'Tried?' the woman hissed. 'Fool – the Master is rising even now. You can't stop him.'

'The girl's alive.'

'He doesn't need her' – the woman spit out the last word – 'that useless rag doll. Any life will do. And the stronger the spirit offered up, the brighter the flame calling him back to us.' The woman dropped her arm.

'Don't!' Lean made it one step forward before the torch flame touched the bottom of the woman's dress, then blazed upward.

Lean whipped his coat from off his back, thinking to tackle the woman and smother the flames, but her hair was already burning. She screamed, and her arms shot skyward like two fiery pillars. Lean tried to move closer, but the woman was stumbling backward, still shrieking in horrific pain and trailing a strong scent of burning oil. She must have doused the wood when she planned to sacrifice Delia and stained her own dress in the process. Lean swung his coat, striking the woman's side. He was about to attempt a tackle when she turned and ran headlong off the rocks. She dropped down into the ocean, leaving a sickening hiss in her wake. After several seconds, the charred form drifted back to the surface. The dead body, and with it the knowledge of Helen's whereabouts, lay in the dark water, motionless except for the bobbing of the waves.

Lean's knees started shaking as the rush of the immediate danger faded. He sat on the rocks and glanced out over the water at the lights of Portland. Grey was there. There was still hope for Helen.

73

The throbbing ache in her wrists drew Helen back, through a foggy haze, to consciousness. She felt hard boards beneath her, pressing into her hip, as the gauzelike shroud fell away from her mind. She tried to remember where she was. Maybe in her house – or Delia's room. An image came storming back: the woman was standing in her doorway, and then she was lunging forward. Delia! Helen tried to call out but was stifled. She worked her jaw to and fro and pressed her tongue forward. A cloth had been stuffed into her mouth. She gagged and coughed.

Tears dripped out of her eyes and ran across her face. She was on her right side. She opened her eyes, and after a few moments the blurry picture of the dark, confined world came into focus. There were a few points of light. She stared at them until the candle flames became clear. At first she thought there were a dozen, but soon she realized it was only the same two candles, reflected back many times over in the dusky panes of glass that surrounded her.

She could see that she was in a small room, circular, with a short wall of exposed planks about three feet high, above which the room was lined all around with windows. There was only darkness beyond. A droning sound was coming from somewhere behind her head: a voice, almost singing, but the words were difficult to discern, foreign, and all running into one another.

Above her, in the flickering candlelight, she could make out a painted compass on the circular ceiling. A metal hook in the center supported a long brass telescope. As she continued to glance about the room, Helen guessed that the entire space was perhaps eight or ten feet across. There was a narrow door directly opposite her, and to one side was a raised platform, the edge of which held a sort of trapdoor that swung up to allow entry from a stairway below. On the other side of the doorway was a bench, upon which was a coiled length of rope and several half-gallon glass jars. These were filled with liquid, and each appeared to hold some dark mass.

A man entered the room and moved to where a candle sat on the black bench. He loosened the belt of his long, dark robe and wriggled out of the garment. Beneath, he was wearing a dark vest over a long-sleeved white shirt and black trousers. The man had a thick, curved blade tucked into his waistband. The sight of it sent a shock through Helen's mind: the billhook used to carve the cross on Maggie Keene's chest.

'Your friend is an unexpectedly troublesome man ... No bother, though.' The man grinned at Helen. 'No bother at all.'

He took up the dark cloak and one of the candles. Helen watched him as he exited the room and made his way around, on the walk outside, to a spot directly opposite the door. She twisted her body and craned her neck. From the light of the man's candle, Helen was able to make out that he had some wooden stick or pole around which he draped the cloak. Then he set about positioning the pole so that, in the candlelight, it cast a shadowy outline of a man. She could hear the man's light footsteps moving back around until he was just outside the door to the small room. Then there was silence.

Helen's heart was racing, and she fought to keep her own muffled breath in check as she listened for any sound. Soon there came a slight creaking noise. The trapdoor in the floor opened an inch or so. There was a pause, and it opened several more inches. Helen saw a face appear. The head turned quickly, shooting glances all around to take in as much of the scene as possible. Perceval Grey.

She tried to scream at him through her gag. Still supporting the trapdoor with his left hand, Grey raised his right, revealing a gun. He held the barrel vertically to his lips, motioning for silence, then eased his way into the room. Grey was only a few feet from her, and Helen continued to try to shout warnings as he looked around the room. She saw his eyes linger on the windows opposite the door, where the fake shadow of a man flickered through the glass.

Grey slid over to her, keeping low to the floor. He set his gun down beside her and then bent over to reach the knots that bound her wrists behind her back. Helen began to thrash her body, desperately shaking her head in the direction of the door. She realized a second too late that her own struggle to alert Grey had obscured the sounds of the killer entering the room. She saw the dark figure rise up swiftly behind Grey.

Grey's head swiveled around as his hand shot out for his pistol. There was a quick movement, and then Helen heard a sickening thud. Grey released a surprised grunt that was cut short. His body slumped forward onto Helen. The sudden weight of him knocked the wind from her. Grey's head came to rest upon her collarbone, and a few seconds later she felt warm, thick drops of his blood trickling down her neck.

74

Lean urged the horses on, though he was hard-pressed to ignore their protests any longer. The beasts' sides heaved and glistened with sweat after the mad dash of several miles from the shore in Cape Elizabeth. Doran's two men had been left behind there. The lightened load let them make good time, with Lean cracking the whip more often than he should, across the bridge and along the winding path up Commercial Street.

Doran cradled Delia the entire ride. The girl had obviously been drugged, and she fluttered in and out of consciousness during the frenzied boat crossing back to the mainland. When first asked about who had taken her, the girl had mumbled something that included the words 'black coat,' before her quivering lip crumpled into a series of sobs. Lean and Doran had gently but relentlessly pressed her for information on her mother's whereabouts, even though each attempt eventually led to tears, the child whimpering for her mommy.

Finally, when Lean asked, 'Did he say anything? What did the dark man say?' he was rewarded with one more cryptic muttering: 'The lord of the air.' The girl's eyes, already closed, had squinted tighter, her brow furrowing slightly. Lean realized that the phrase had confounded her, a reference queer enough to lodge itself deep in the child's mind, where she could secretly puzzle over the literalness of the statement.

Once ashore, Lean had turned his attention to driving the carriage and Doran had settled into silence with Delia slumped in his arms. Makeshift bandages of knotted handkerchiefs were tied around the big man's left thigh. The leg had bled freely, but

Doran was lucky in that the crazed woman's bullet had only cut a line along the meaty portion of his leg. Although Doran denied any need for medical attention, Lean could see that the man's face had gone a shade paler from his normal ruddy complexion. On the few occasions when Lean glanced at the pair huddled behind him, he could see Doran grimacing as they rumbled over the uneven road.

They went directly to Helen's house in the hope that she might miraculously turn up there at some point. More realistically, the girl was sure to come around sooner or later and be hysterical at the absence of her mother. Lean hoped that familiar surroundings might lessen the fear, even a tiny bit.

After depositing Doran and Delia, Lean came outside and climbed on top of the cab. He was still wrestling with that phrase: 'the lord of the air.' Was it just a passing remark, meaningful only within the impenetrable darkness of the killer's mind? Or was it possibly an actual clue? For lack of anything else that offered any glimmer of hope of finding Helen, Lean immediately attached a great importance to the phrase. He turned the words over, letting the phrase chase its tail round and round in his head. He recognized the title from his readings on the Salem witches; it was a moniker that the Puritans had attached to Satan. But there had to be something more to it. Otherwise he was lost – and so was Helen.

Maybe Grey could pull a linguistic rabbit from his hat and ascribe some concrete meaning to 'the lord of the air.' On his way toward Grey's High Street rooms, Lean passed a police call box. He thought of stopping to telephone ahead to Grey, but the idea of standing still for so long, waiting for the operator to connect the call, was unbearable. Minutes later he was rapping at the door, in nearly as much of a lather as the horses, waiting for the landlady to undo the latch. He heard Mrs Philbrick puttering about just inside the doorway, and then the door inched open and a wary eye appeared.

'Oh, it's you, Deputy Lean. What a relief.'

'Mr Grey in?' Lean said as he barged past into the hallway.

'No.' Then she muttered, 'Thank heavens.'

'How long ago did he leave?'

The landlady shrugged. 'Under an hour, I suppose.'

'Did he say where he was going?'

'No. He was in a right frenzy, but not a word about where he was headed.'

'Did he say anything at all?'

Mrs Philbrick was shrinking back, her eyes edging wider at Lean's barrage of questions. 'Nothing that I can recall.'

'Well, what was he doing in his rooms just before he left?' Lean started up the stairs and heard Mrs Philbrick plodding after him.

'That's the odd part. He wasn't in his rooms.'

Lean stopped short on the stairs, and the landlady bumped into him.

'I went to his door, and I heard him thumping around above,' she said. 'So I went down the hall to the ladder that leads up to the roof door. He comes clambering down, nearly landed on me.'

'What was he doing up there?'

'I'm certain I'd have no idea.'

Lean saw a flicker in her eyes, a look perhaps of embarrassment at having to answer these questions about her peculiar tenant.

'Come now, Mrs Philbrick. This is a matter of the gravest importance. Tell me what he was doing.'

'Seemed to be reading. Had some papers with him.'

'Anything else?'

Her head started to shake, denying any complicity in what she was about to reveal. 'And he was spying on people.'

'Spying on people? What are you saying? Come on now, out with it.'

'It's true. He came rushing down from the roof, hands me some papers and a telescope.' She nodded at the last bit for emphasis. 'Then he dashes into his rooms, comes bolting out again, in a fierce rush for the street.'

'Telescope? Where'd you put it? And the papers.'

'I left them just inside his door. I don't like to go in there when he's out. Course, going in when he's home isn't much to grin at either.'

'How do I get to the roof?'

'Up there, past Mr Grey's. There's a closet door in the hallway.'

Lean bolted up the rest of the stairs. Grey's door was unlocked. Just inside was the telescope and a few pages. Lean seized up the papers, a grand total of three. They were crumpled; Grey had clutched them, perhaps in excitement at having discovered something. Lean pored over them by the light of a gas jet inside Grey's parlor. Each page held a single entry.

The first page was Amelia Porter's warning to Lean: 'The darkness rising beware the Good woman and her child.' Grey had dismissed the woman as a charlatan, but there was no denying that this very writing is what had tipped them to Helen and Delia's abduction. The second page was more from Amelia Porter, one of the quotes they had recorded from her séance: 'A tower standing in a pool of darkness. It's thick like blood and filling with darkness. There's a spark there. I can see a flame. There's still time. Dear God, please hurry.'

The third paragraph was the last entry from the Riddle of the Martyrs. Lean didn't have to read it – he'd long ago memorized every word – but his eyes raced over the page once more, hoping some new idea would make itself known. The words from the pages flowed through his mind. Blood, fire, tower, darkness, rising, empty, filling, time, hurry. No answer came to him, but the same must have been true for Grey until he'd seen something from the roof. Lean shoved the pages into his pocket and snatched up the telescope. In the hallway a narrow door he'd never noticed before blended in with the drab wallpaper. Inside the small closet, wooden rungs nailed into the wall formed a ladder. Lean made his way up and emerged onto a flat rooftop. At first it appeared empty except for chimneys and vent pipes. Then Lean noticed papers lying scattered around. He seized up a few and by match light recognized them as more notes from the investigation. Grey had tossed these aside, so Lean did the same.

He raised the telescope and aimed it toward the harbor, only to be met with disappointment. He'd guessed that Grey might have seen the fire lit by the redheaded woman on Cushing's Island, but that was impossible. The city's hilly topography and several taller buildings blocked the view of Casco Bay. Panic began to flood into his mind, a fear that Helen would die tonight because of his inability to see what Grey had seen. He took several deep breaths, then slowly turned about, staring at the skyline all around him. Buildings, lights, stars clear in the moonless sky. Nothing obvious.

He drew Grey's three pages from his pocket. The first page

must be a reference to Helen and Delia. The third page was the riddle's clue to the location of the final murder on Cushing's Island. But how did the second paper fit? Lean lit another match to see that page again. He read it aloud under the flickering light.

"'A tower standing in a pool of darkness. It's thick like blood and filling with darkness. There's a spark there. I can see a flame. There's still time. Dear God, please hurry.'"

Grey didn't believe in the medium; there had to be another, hidden meaning. Or perhaps the plainest meaning: the words themselves, stripped of any superstitious attachments. The match burned down close to Lean's fingers. He shook out the tiny flame, leaving himself in darkness once more.

"'I can see a flame.'" His voice was quiet, almost pleading with himself. A new thought rattled in his head, like hearing another voice. Words seeped into his mouth, half forming, making his tongue move behind closed lips. They were the words of the mad devil-woman on the island.

'The stronger the spirit offered up, the brighter the flame calling him back to us.'

A flame, not to see by but to be seen. The fire on Cushing's was a marker, a beacon, but for whom? For the devil that they hoped to raise in the form of George Burroughs? Was it all just symbols created to appease the fevered mind of the killer? Or was it an actual sign that the sacrifice was complete? The flame on the tip of the island would certainly be visible, but from where? The killer could be on a boat, intending to land back on Cushing's Island. No – he was the lord of the air. Up high. The fiery beacon on Cushing's Island had to be visible from up high, where he'd be watching. A tower in a pool of darkness.

Lean turned northeast and looked across the city: the

Portland Observatory. It was the highest point in Portland, specifically designed to watch the harbor. Tonight, as usual, the domed top was shrouded in darkness. The maritime flags that were set there, visible throughout the harbor by day, were unlit at night.

Lean brought the telescope to bear on the dark tower. After a moment he saw it. A spark in the observatory. A flicker of light where there should be none.

75

At last there was a movement from Grey. Helen turned her head toward the center of the room to watch him. She was still gagged but noted with a mix of hope and annoyance that the killer hadn't bothered to do the same to Grey. He was lying on his back, hands bound before him. His head tilted one way, then the other, as he got his bearings. Helen looked to confirm that their captor was still outside the small room. She could see glimpses of his shadowy figure as he moved on the other side of the panes of glass. From behind her gag, Helen tried to ask Grey a one-word question: 'Delia?'

Grey turned to face her and responded by raising a finger to his lips. He began to fumble with his hands. Helen's heart leaped at the hope that the killer had been careless with tying Grey's wrists. After a few moments, she discovered that Grey was not wriggling his hands free from his knots. He was digging for his pocketwatch. He flipped it open and raised his head, apparently enough to catch a glimpse of the time by the faint, flickering candlelight inside the room. Helen herself had lost all concept of time; judging by the darkness of the sky, she imagined that it was sometime well after midnight.

After watching Grey replace his watch, Helen waited for him to do something, all the while fighting back her urge to unleash a muffled scream. Her patience was rewarded when Grey simply shifted onto his right side, so that he was now facing away from her. The urge to scream ebbed, replaced by a sudden desire to kick the man and force him to whisper something about Delia – whether her daughter was alive, where she was, and how the two of them might escape.

The wind picked up, and the short gusts rattled the panes of glass that encircled the room. Helen could still hear the killer's voice; it was growing louder as he approached the door.

'Hemen Etan! Hemen-Etan! Hemen-Etan! El Aozia Teu Achadon! El A Hy! Aie Saraye! By Eloym, Archima, Rabur Bathas over Abrac ... flowing down, coming from above Aheor upon Aberer Chavajoth! I command thee ... by the Key of Solomon and the great name Semhamphoras.'

The man entered the room and set his long wooden staff down on the bench. He was again wearing his dark robe, which stretched to the floor. The hood over his head kept his face mostly in shadow. 'By Adonai Eloim, Adonai Jehova, Adonai Sabaoth ... Metraton On Agla Adonai Mathon, the Pythonic word, the Mystery of the Salamander ... the Assembly of Sylphs, the Grotto of Gnomes, the demons of the heaven of Gad ... Almousin, Gibor, Jehosua, Evam, Zariatbatmik: Come, Come, Come!'

'Most tiresome,' Grey declared. 'Are these incantations supposed to be so repetitive, or is that just part of your stammer? Did

459

you have that trouble speaking fluently since birth, or was it a result of the trauma to your neck? Probably all in your head. Product of a fragile mind, I'd suspect.'

'Mr Grey, you've chosen to' – their captor paused, appearing to struggle with the selection of his next word – 'rejoin us. How nice ... that you'll bear witness to the Master's rising. It will be the last thing you ... see on this earth. But what a wondrous sight to behold.' The man pushed back the hood of his robe, revealing a somewhat handsome face topped with black hair. Helen had never seen him before in her life.

'I'm all aflutter with anticipation, Father Coyne. Oh, I suppose you've abandoned that identity now. You've emerged from the ashes of that man's home like the phoenix reborn.'

'Something like that.'

Helen listened in disbelief. She wanted to scream at Grey, tell him to shut up and stop antagonizing the killer.

'What's that, Mrs Prescott?' Grey said. 'Oh, how rude of me – you haven't been properly introduced. Allow me to present Jack Whitten.'

For a second, Helen wondered if she had made some noise earlier to indicate her annoyance. But then she realized that although Grey had said her name, he was really addressing the killer the entire time he spoke.

'I'm sorry I didn't see it sooner,' Grey said. 'That ridiculous headdress of bandages you wore when we came to see you at Father Coyne's hid your black hair. You reclined the whole time to hide your height. And your faked consumptive cough provided excellent cover for your inconsistent, stammering speech.' Grey shot the quickest of glances at Helen. 'Yes, he's the real Jack Whitten. Oh, don't be embarrassed, Mrs Prescott; he's been rather clever in hiding his identity all this time. It's certainly no poor reflection upon you to be a bit confused at the moment.'

Helen shifted her own body, trying to get a better look at the men without having to crane her neck so awkwardly. The effort of moving while tied up caused the release of several quick grunts.

'Hmm? Oh, you thought Jack Whitten died in front of a train in Salem the other night. Well, to tell the truth, so did I. For a while, anyway. The man who was posing as Peter Chapman, Father Coyne's not-so-gracious assistant, was not actually Jack Whitten, as I had originally surmised. But that was your younger brother, wasn't it?' Grey said to the robed man. 'What was his name? I never did see it recorded anywhere.'

'Peter. His . . . given name really was Peter.'

'Clever. You recall, Mrs Prescott, that Old Stitch, or Black Lucy Whitten, had two sons. But, as an Indian fortune-teller who knew her explained, they had separate fathers – and the two boys couldn't have looked more different. The eldest was supposedly hanged by Colonel Blanchard's mob when they burned the family out. That was after the colonel's wife died from Old Stitch's poisons. Was it the abrus seeds that killed Mrs Blanchard?'

'My mother didn't kill Mrs Blanchard. She took her own life once she learned the truth about her husband, and me.'

'Is that it?' Grey asked. 'Your mother worked as a servant for the Blanchards. She was let go when she became pregnant with you. But Mrs Blanchard didn't know the truth, did she?'

'He paid her to keep quiet about it all . . . to say the father was some foreign sailor. It wasn't till the end that she figured it out . . . Came to see my mother one last time, to hear the truth for herself.'

461

'Then she took her own life, and the colonel had to hide the reason. He came to kill you and your mother, so there would be no one left who knew the truth of his sins.' Grey considered this new information for a moment. 'I see, and so the elder boy was hanged and the younger was turned over to the orphanage, to be held until the age of sixteen. But the younger boy, Peter, didn't miss a trick, did he? Claimed to be the elder son, Jack, to shave a few years off his time in captivity. And the elder boy ... well, they never did find a body. Because there was none. There was a hanging, though. So what happened? They left you for dead and you managed to wriggle out?'

'It's easy enough to kill someone ... when you know what you're about.' Jack Whitten reached down beneath the bench and picked up the coiled rope that Helen had noticed earlier. 'But that lot was useless. Couldn't tie a shoe, let alone a ... noose. Besides, I did have some magical protections. By the time they set the fire and got me strung up, Mother and ... Peter had both gone off. Nothing for that mob but to stand and stare at me dying. Lost their stomach for it. The rope was ... cutting into me, but I just played dead and waited.' Whitten measured out about half the length of rope, maybe twenty-five feet. 'When they were gone, it was ... no trouble to get my boot knife and cut myself down.'

'And then the real Jack Whitten slipped away,' Grey said. 'Never noticed. Never missed. To scratch out a life and cause what trouble he may. You might even have rejoined your mother during her time spent in the traveling Indian shows. Is that where you picked up the Abenaki language? And your contempt for them?'

'Your people are a pitiless and savage race, Mr Grey.' Jack Whitten smiled down at him. 'I learned many useful things there.'

Grey continued, 'Meanwhile, Peter, using Jack's name, began to find a bit of religion under the tutelage of Father Coyne. Until one day when he got into a bit of trouble with another boy. Geoffrey Blanchard, wasn't it?'

Whitten nodded. Helen thought the man was enjoying Grey's recitation of the facts, which went on in a dry, professorial tone.

'They broke in to the cathedral library and found the Black Book. Passed it off as a bit of mischief, no doubt, but it was more than that. The men from Harvard had come to the cathedral back then to make a copy. It would have been quite a business, all hushed up and secret. Seems Peter hadn't gotten so much religion that he could just ignore it when he knew there was something in there worth taking a look at. But the boys got caught, and Peter was blamed. He was banished from the cathedral to the boys' home in Cape Elizabeth to serve out the remainder of his time until, in the guise of Jack, he reached sixteen and was released into the world.'

'Blanchard recognized the Whitten name. Made him nervous, and he demanded Peter be sent away,' said Jack.

Grey paused, his mouth starting to go dry. He kept his eyes focused, refusing to divert his attention from Whitten to Helen. 'Years go by, and our little saga lies dormant. Jack and Peter are reunited and get on with their lives, such as they are. Father Coyne goes on preaching. Old Stitch goes on with her hocus-pocus performances. Colonel Blanchard continues his war on alcohol and sin. All of those involved in the death of Agnes Blanchard, and the attempted lynching of young Jack Whitten, go on with their lives. Until these many years later, something happens. Something that sets the wheel in motion again.'

Whitten looped the middle section of rope around the hook in the ceiling that held the observatory's telescope. He tied a knot there so that two long sections of rope dangled from the hook and landed in piles on the floor.

Grey cleared his throat. 'What's that, Mrs Prescott? You're quite right; I've neglected your excellent bit of detective work with Rachel Blanchard at her mother's grave. Not everyone in our story did get on with life. The son, Geoffrey Blanchard, was never able to overcome the loss of his beloved mother. It consumed him, drove him mad. It's when he turns to the occult to reach his departed mother that the colonel's had enough. He keeps Geoffrey locked away in asylums, well out of view. But from what I saw, he didn't put his son away soon enough. At some point Geoffrey Blanchard learned a fair amount about witchcraft.

'And that, I think, brings us to the point where our current little mystery begins to play itself out. Witchcraft and the Black Book. That's where all our strands connect. Of course, you knew all about witchcraft, Jack. You grew up with it. And you learned that Geoffrey had became a student.'

Whitten smiled. 'I'd been keeping my eyes on the Blanchards . . . father and son. They were there that day. They were the ones who . . . did this to me.' He tugged his collar down to reveal a line of scar tissue around his neck. 'The colonel's always surrounded by his . . . old army men. And too visible. But the son could be gotten to . . . made to pay for what they did.'

'So you followed Geoffrey Blanchard when he made his way to Jotham Marsh's magical society. And the subject of the Black Book came to light again.'

'With all I knew, it was easy enough to fit in with Marsh's

foolish order. I was a star pupil. And Blanchard ... well, he was still obsessed with his dead mother. Talked of nothing else. He wanted to know everything about contacting spirits. Marsh knew all about it. He mentioned the Black Book. Blanchard got to talking, mentioned the book at the cathedral, and soon enough we all put two and two together.'

'You needed access to the cathedral to get at the book. It was you who went there as Peter Chapman,' Grey said, 'since Father Coyne would have recognized your brother.'

'But I couldn't pick the lock. So I needed to find the copy ... Eventually I won Father Coyne's confidence. He revealed that the copy was kept at Harvard.'

'You got to it first, figured out which section was the Riddle of the Martyrs, and destroyed the rest, so no one could follow what you were doing and stop you.'

'Or try to repeat my efforts.'

Helen's mind had been floating back and forth between the conversation and images of Delia. She was desperately hoping there was a reason Grey wasn't talking about her daughter: because he already knew whether she was still alive. Or perhaps that's why he hadn't bothered even looking her in the eye for more than a second. He knew that Delia was already gone. Helen pushed the idea out of her thoughts. He was distracting Whitten from the rescue that must be coming.

'Marsh demanded ... I turn the riddle over to him, but he was a fraud.' Whitten was answering some question from Grey that Helen had missed. 'He wouldn't have ever dared to perform the ritual. I think he was glad I refused. But he talked about mutiny ... turned the others against me.'

'Including Lizzie Madson?'

'Even Lizzie,' Whitten said.

'And that's why she deserved to die?'

'It seems she was always one of Marsh's.' Jack Whitten shrugged. 'Student ... or lover. Just another soul for him to ... toy with.'

'What about Maggie Keene and Hannah Easler?'

'Who's that?' Whitten asked

'The pregnant woman in Scituate.'

'They ... served the purpose. Sinners. Fallen souls ... needed for the ritual.'

'The red ink on Maggie Keene's hand. You had her sign in a book of some sort.'

'I needed her soul, a witch's soul.' Whitten picked up one of the glass jars that Helen had seen on the bench inside the room. He lifted it to eye level and considered the contents. The candle-light was too dim for her to make out anything with certainty, but Helen thought she saw shapes like protruding fingers.

'And prying up the floorboards at the Portland Company?' Grey asked.

'The riddle required it. That was the one sacrifice that was required to be on the very ground where the Master first took a life.'

'And you believe Burroughs's old meetinghouse was that site.'

'Precisely.'

'And the billhook, the cross cut into her, the pitchfork – those guarded against her witch's powers being used against you. The same as the bottle you buried beneath your mother when you killed her. But that's one piece I don't quite understand. Your mother died months before the ritual began. Why kill her at all – just to gain the abrus seeds?'

'The abrus seeds were only a ... a pleasant aside to killing her. You fail to understand the basic principles of magic, Mr Grey. The Riddle of the Martyrs is a most ... demanding ritual. Success requires the ultimate focus of the Mage's powers. His energies must be ... entirely pure, unfettered. Mother had placed many ... spells on me over the years. Her interference – those spells – they had to be removed.'

'No qualms about murdering your own mother?' Grey asked.

'Every man must be thrust into this world in a spasm of blood and pain. I suppose she spilled her blood for me then ... the same as any mother. But there was scarce little given after that moment. She hadn't enough of a proper soul in her ... to spare any for my birth. And what little soul there was in me, she did her best to drive out soon enough.'

'She didn't come back for you. Didn't try to save you when you were being hanged.'

'Why would she?' Whitten answered.

'But now, all these years later, you found people who would stay with you. All through this ritual.'

'Peter was never a true believer, but he'd do whatever I told him ... always did. Blanchard was true, even though he was a fool. He thought all this, all the work I was doing, was to bring his mother back. That I would waste my time ... to bring back such a plain and useless spirit as that.'

'You've chosen George Burroughs's spirit instead. Why?'

'Why?' Whitten set the jar holding one of his gruesome trophies back down on the bench. His attention was now squarely on Grey. 'He is the Master. The greatest conjurer that's ever lived in this country ... that has ever set foot within a thousand miles of here. He was appointed, he would rule as king when the new

order was raised. The Master brought the Black Book, his book . . .
into my hands exactly two hundred years after his betrayal and
hanging. The Riddle of the Martyrs . . . declares that the ritual is
to be performed on the cycle of the Master's death. And here it is.'

There was silence for a few moments. Helen thought she
heard a voice call out in greeting, alongside the rumble of passing wheels, but the sounds held a distant, airy timbre.

'You realize, of course,' Grey said, 'that you're a lunatic. To
believe in witchcraft and all this, your master, Reverend
Burroughs. It's madness.'

Whitten's eyes darted back and forth between Grey and
Helen. She felt a palpable knot of fear the moment she met his
stare. *At least Delia's not here.* No matter where she was, it had to
be better than being trapped in this tiny room with Jack Whitten
and his insane, murderous eyes.

'Madness? Consider this, Grey. If you speak . . . a few lines to
her today' – Whitten nodded toward Helen – 'tomorrow she tells
them to a friend, who relays them to me. Next week . . . I repeat
them back to you. Probably half the words are changed. Would
you wager five dollars, let alone your . . . eternal soul, on how well
those words were kept in just one week?

'Yet you worship a god nailed to a post nearly two thousand
years ago. You follow the words of a man that were written down
after his death . . . by men who did not know him, in a language
you cannot speak. Words passed from mouth to ear how many
times? Passed through how many languages? Subject to the
whims of how many men's tongues and pens? You cast yourself
out onto the sea . . . and cling to that wreckage: the misheard and
mangled words of your crucified god, corrupted over centuries to
the point where they are no more credible than barroom

hearsay ... backyard gossip. And you believe that those words will save your soul. I call that madness.'

Whitten's voice was getting louder, stronger as he went on, a spark growing in him. 'Tell me, have you ever heard your god's voice? Has he ever even spoken to you? And not in some ... some ridiculous sign you create for yourself: a drop of water on a statue's face ... a rainbow or a sudden piece of good fortune. I mean an actual voice ... speaking directly to you? No? Well, my god speaks to me. His words are given to me every day, to heed and follow. So I ask you, which one of us is truly mad to do our god's bidding?'

'So after you got a hold of the Riddle of the Martyrs,' Grey said with no more outward excitement than if he'd been asking for a recipe or the steps to some chemistry experiment, 'why bother killing Father Coyne?'

'I thought he might be growing suspicious.'

'And you poisoned him with the abrus seeds.'

'He retreated to his family's home, and I accompanied him. It was a perfect cover from which to conduct our affairs.'

'How long until you murdered him?'

'Not long – months ago. I let Peter kill him. He'd earned it.'

'You kept his body, and that was what they pulled from the ashes of his house. And what about Geoffrey Blanchard on Gallows Hill? You let Peter carry out that murder as well, even though it was you the Blanchards hanged all those years ago.'

'Not murder, Mr Grey, sacrifice. And that pained me. I'd have liked to slit the little toad's throat myself. But' – he motioned toward his leg – 'I was unable to go so soon after I was shot. It was disappointing, but now I see the Master's hand in it all. I am still alive to complete the ritual and accept his return.'

'You seem to have little remorse over your brother's death.'

'Sacrifices are required of us all,' Whitten said.

'So Geoffrey Blanchard had arrangements at the hospital to come and go – bribed a guard, I suppose. His excursion out a week ago was to communicate with you, make final plans for the last phase of the ritual. You made assurances, lured him to Gallows Hill with the promise of a ritual he believed would bring his mother back to him.'

'He never understood the true purpose of the riddle. He actually thought, when all was done, he'd see her risen in the flesh once more.' A twisted grin spread across Whitten's face.

'So you admit that the Riddle of the Martyrs doesn't produce the dead?'

'In the flesh? Of course not,' Whitten said. 'The called spirit of the Master exists again within the flesh of the Servant.'

'Within you? Ah, so that's the purpose of the disappearing moon. And the riddle's references to the vessels being poured out. Emptied and prepared. Some sort of symbolic wearing away of your soul, making room for the spirit of the Master.'

'Not symbolic, Grey. My soul will give way before the Master. He shall live in me.'

'And what becomes of your soul?'

'Sacrifices are required of us all.'

'I do have one final question,' Grey said. 'What exactly do you plan to do when your invocation fails? When you realize you're still the same weak, ineffectual, stuttering child you've always been. The memories of beatings, the constant hunger, strange men grunting and rutting in the room beside yours, separated by that tattered curtain. The feel of that rope burning into your neck. No one coming to save you. There's no one coming to save you now, either.'

470

The hint of a smile that had flickered across Whitten's face for much of their conversation now vanished. 'Soon you will see, Grey ... Then you will believe ... in those last few moments before you die. You will know the truth of all things. Your god's empty promise. There will be no judgment ... no redemption. And my god will rule over you. My spirit will pass into ... nothingness, and I will be joined with the Master. He will complete his work. The world wasn't ... ready two hundred years ago; it is now.' Whitten stepped back and spread out his arms.

'And there shall be the trumpet sounded, and it will be heard many miles off ... and then they all come one after another to be made witches. And the Master will pull down the Kingdom of Christ and raise up the Kingdom of the Devil ... who was always the true teacher and rightful God of Man. And the Master will abolish all these false churches in the land, and so go through the country. And the Master has ... has promised that all his people should live bravely, that all persons should be equal, that there should be no day of resurrection ... or of judgment, and neither punishment nor shame for sin.' Whitten fell silent, still staring at Grey.

'You know,' Grey said, 'you just reminded me: since Geoffrey Blanchard is dead, there'll be a vacant room at the Danvers Lunatic Hospital It's rather luxurious inside. And the grounds are lovely. Depending on your behavior, you'd have upwards of an hour a day of outside time. Supervised, of course.'

Whitten took a small step forward and launched a boot into Grey's midsection. 'I thought perhaps to spare you ... for a while, anyway. You seemed to fit. With your Indian blood, ... so like the Master's shadow helper. But I can see now that you deserve to die as much as the others ...' Jack Whitten struggled to produce the

471

next word, and as he did, there was a noticeable thud from below. His eyes went wide. Whitten tilted his head and listened for several seconds before leaning in toward Grey again.

'Oh, you're a clever one. Distracting me so. You will suffer for this.' He stepped over to Helen, bent down to grab her by the arm, and thrust his billhook close to her face. 'Up!' he hissed. 'Any trouble and I'll slice your throat.'

Her legs were not bound, but she was still a bit unsteady from the aftereffects of the chloroform. Whitten held her in front of him and stepped toward the trapdoor, so he could look down the short, curved staircase. He waited there half a minute, blade poised at Helen's neck.

'I know you're there,' he finally called out. 'My god reveals your secrets to me. Step forward or I'll kill her.'

76

From where he stood, beside the final set of steps, Lean could see the shadow of a human form within the rectangle of faint light coming down from the trapdoor. He took a deep breath and whirled around into view, his pistol aimed up to where a dark-haired man wielding a billhook held Helen before him.

'Toss that up here!' Whitten shouted down to Lean.

Lean didn't flinch. Helen shook her head at him, pleading with her eyes for him not to listen to the madman. The blade pressed into her neck, and she let out a stifled yelp. Lean lowered the gun slowly, then tossed it up the staircase. It landed beside the killer's feet.

'Delia's alive!' Lean called out.

Helen's eyes went wide with unmistakable joy. She didn't seem to notice the killer's recoil that caused him to poke her neck again, hard enough to draw a bead of blood.

'You lie!' Whitten shouted.

'We pulled her from the pyre on Cushing's.'

'I saw the blaze,' Whitten said.

'You saw that red-haired witch of yours. She went up fast, whoever she was.'

The killer pushed Helen aside and bent to grab Lean's pistol. Lean ducked back into the shadows, grabbing a loose piece of wood from one of the shelves that held the observatory's signal flags. He expected to see the killer descend, but instead the room went dark as the trapdoor slammed shut.

Inside the observation platform, Grey watched as Jack Whitten set Lean's pistol aside and grabbed his long wooden staff. The man struggled to get the wooden bar into place above the trapdoor. He wedged the top beneath a windowsill and started forcing the base under the lip of the door leading outside. With one fluid motion, Grey rolled himself up to a sitting position, got his weight over his crossed ankles, and forced himself upright. His hands were bound before him, but he had enough mobility to grab the rope Whitten had tied to the hook in the ceiling. Grey took hold of it and looped the rope twice. As Whitten finished jamming the trapdoor closed, Grey dropped the rope circle over the man's head and yanked the ends, drawing the cord tight about Whitten's neck.

Whitten spun around and was met with a backhanded blow from Grey's bound fists. He fell back against the doorframe, then drew the billhook from his belt. Grey was on him in an instant, seizing Whitten's wrist and slamming it through a windowpane. The billhook clattered to the floor. The trapdoor banged, and Grey realized that Lean was throwing his weight against it, not realizing it was blocked.

Whitten tried to reach Lean's pistol on the floor. Grey slipped his foot forward and kicked the gun, which slid over the door-jamb out onto the deck. The attempt to grab the weapon had put Whitten off balance, and Grey threw his weight forward. Whitten clutched at Grey, but the momentum carried both men through the open door.

The two men spilled out onto the narrow walkway sur-rounding the observation platform. Grey was on his side as he grappled with the killer. He saw his pistol nearby, where it had slipped out the door during the struggle. He let go of Whitten and stretched for the gun. He just reached the butt with his fin-gertips when Whitten clasped his wrist. There was a stinging on the back side of his hand as Whitten dug his nails into Grey's flesh.

Grey jerked his body, flailing forward toward the gun. Whitten released his wrist and also grasped for the gun. The two of them struggled for control of it for a second before it slipped away, toward the edge of the deck. It passed under the bottom edge of the railing that circled the deck. The gun wobbled there for a split second, then disappeared over the side.

Whitten pushed away and scrambled to his feet. Grey bolted up as well but, hampered by his bound wrists, he was a half second too late. The man was on him again, pushing him back to the waist-high railing. Grey's foot slipped out from under him. The deck was not level; it sloped away slightly from the building. The unexpected slant caught him off guard and gave

Whitten the advantage needed to overpower him. Grey's lower back pressed into the rail. The killer's hands were at his throat, pushing, forcing his head back so that Grey arched out over the railing. He grabbed at Whitten's hands, trying to break the man's grip.

Jack Whitten was small but surprisingly strong. Grey didn't have enough leverage; he was losing the battle, unable to pry the killer's hands from around his neck. Grey stuck his right foot between two of the railing's balusters, twisting his lower leg around for support. Then he let go of Whitten's grip and went for the throat instead, his fingers clutching, searching for the man's windpipe, desperate to crush it. Grey strained to work his thumbs between the double strands of the rope that he had tightened around the killer's neck.

He tried to force the killer back, to gain equal footing. The two stood that way for several seconds, each pushing at the other, both with every bit of strength they possessed. Grey was struggling to draw enough breath through his clenched teeth. At some point he bit his tongue, and blood-specked spittle flew from his mouth with each fierce exhalation.

Grey stared into the man's eyes. There was a crazed glee there, a dark, bottomless rapture. Each man continued to choke the other, but the length of rope around the killer's neck was interfering, keeping Grey from getting a solid grip.

Where the hell was Lean? Grey glanced through the glass, into the observation room. He saw Helen there on the floor, kicking with both legs, trying to snap or dislodge the solid wooden staff that was jamming the trapdoor shut. He saw her look out toward them. By the flickering candlelight, Grey caught Helen's stare: equal parts fierce determination and terror.

He turned away, looking back into the face of Jack Whitten. Lack of oxygen was making dark spots appear before his eyes. He would be done soon. Beaten. Dead. Fear began to well up inside Grey, quickly boiling over into a fury, a burning, consuming anger toward the inhuman murderer who, with every second, was strangling the life out of him. Grey tried to focus. His eyes locked onto the length of rope that was angled toward them, dangling from the hook inside the observatory.

In an instant, Grey shifted his hands, from trying to clasp the man's throat to instead clutching Whitten's robe. He twisted his ankle free from around the baluster and jerked up and backward, yanking the killer toward him. The sudden, unexpected reversal in weight completely surprised Jack Whitten; he had no time to react. With their combined effort pushing back against the rail, the momentum was too strong.

Grey's feet left the deck, and he teetered on the rail, then toppled backward, yanking on Whitten as he went. The killer's body came with him over the side. As they fell, Grey released the robe and grabbed the man's body in a bear hug, tighter than he had ever clasped anything in his life. They fell clean through the air for another second before the rope around Whitten's neck snapped them back. There was the clear sound – a sickening crack – and then the momentum slammed them into the outward-sloping side of the building.

Grey struck against the observatory sideways, his left shoulder taking the force of the blow. That arm went dead, and he slipped down, with only the grip of his right hand on the killer's belt to support him. He took several deep gasps of air, then pulled himself up enough so that he could wrap his own legs around those of the dead man to whom he clung. Finally he glanced down – there was nothing but hard ground five stories below. Looking up, he saw Lean at the railing, fiddling with the rope.

'Hurry!' called Grey.

Grey's strength was fading, and he couldn't hold on much longer. Within seconds another length of rope came cascading down the side of the building.

'Take hold of this one,' Lean called out to him.

Grey flexed his leg muscles, tightening the grip on Whitten's body. Then his right hand shot out to grab the new length of rope, and he wrapped it around his forearm several times. He reached out with one leg, then the other, snaking each around the dangling rope. Grey began to rise, and at the same time Whitten's body sank toward the ground. He realized that they were both suspended by separate ends of the same rope. The deadweight of Whitten's body, along with Lean's pulling, was hoisting Grey back up toward the observation deck. He gave another look down and watched Whitten's dark form dropping in jerky motions toward the earth.

A few more pulls and Lean was able to tie off the rope, then reach over the rail to grab hold of Grey. Once he was safely onto the deck, Lean slipped back into the observation platform to loosen Helen's gag.

'Where's Delia?' she pleaded as Lean cut away the ropes from her wrists.

'Home. Tom Doran's there with her.'

'Oh, thank heaven!' Helen clasped Lean in a hug, then started shaking her arms, trying to regain circulation. She breathed deeply several times as she fought to control the wild pendulum of emotions she had endured that night. Then she caught sight of

Grey standing in the doorway. She struggled to her feet, with Lean's assistance.

'Are you out of your mind! How could you – What were you thinking? Were you trying to kill yourself? And before ... that whole time ... just ignored me ... Why were you ... blathering on and provoking him ... ? Lucky he didn't kill us both.'

Grey was in visible pain from his left shoulder, but a smirk appeared as he listened to Helen's rant.

'This is not funny. I watched you throw yourself over the edge. I thought you were dead! Do you understand – How could you? You are so ...' Helen stepped forward with her hand raised, about to slap Grey cross the face. 'So absolutely maddening.' Instead of striking, Helen reached out, grabbed Grey's lapels, yanked him down to her, and kissed him full on the lips.

After a few seconds, Lean forced an awkward cough. Helen released her hold on Grey.

'Forgive me,' she said. 'I don't know what came over me. It's just—'

'No need to apologize.' Grey gave her an appreciative smile. 'It's been a most trying night. But if we stay here much longer, we're going to have to answer a lot of difficult questions.'

'What do we do with his body? We could call it a suicide,' Lean said.

Grey shook his head. 'We'll need a carriage or wagon.'

'I spotted one around the side,' Lean said. 'I think it's the one he used to bring Helen here.'

'Excellent. Help me get him loaded, then get Miss Prescott home. I'll see to the body.'

77

Lean eyed the pair of gravediggers. They were a matched set: stout workmen with caps slanted to keep the sun off their faces and cigarettes dangling from the corners of slack jaws. Their frock coats would be set aside as soon as the last of the crowd dispersed, revealing soil-encrusted work clothes. Lean could see they were restless, eager to begin filling the hole before the late-August heat worsened. It was only eleven o'clock, but the sky was already developing a haze. It was the kind of day that begged for something other than a black suit, regardless of the occasion. While many of the mourners had shed genuine tears, Lean had noticed more than one who dabbed their eyes as an excuse to continuously wipe beads of sweat from their brows.

The last few tearful hugs were bestowed on Helen by some more distant relatives of Dr Steig. The preacher had finished several minutes earlier, and most of the large crowd had already dissipated, moving up the slope toward the main gate of the Western Cemetery. A row of carriages, many lined with black crepe, waited there like so many hovering crows.

Emma turned to Lean. 'Are you ready?'

'I'll be right along.'

She gave his hand an encouraging squeeze. Emma led Owen to where Helen and Delia stood, not far from the double plot where Dr Steig, after more than a dozen years, would join his late wife. Emma exchanged hugs and quiet words with Helen. Her departure left a small company of five: those whose lives had been threatened by Jack Whitten and his unknown female devotee the night before last. Lean supposed that it was the shared horror, as well as the confused manner in which that night had ended, that now left them clustered beside Dr Steig's grave.

After Whitten's death they had located that man's cab and deposited the former owner's body inside. Grey had taken the reins and disappeared into the night. Lean had managed to hail another cab and get Helen back to her house. Not much had been said on that ride, other than repeated assurances that Delia was fine and the ordeal was truly over. Upon arrival, they found Doran inside, standing guard over the girl. There hadn't been much opportunity or need for further discussion after the reunion of mother and daughter.

Now Lean, Tom Doran, and Grey, with his left arm in a sling, stood a few steps removed and waited for Helen to ready herself. With her daughter by her side, Helen gave the men a wide smile, tears welling up in her eyes once more. 'Gentlemen. Thank you for coming. Thank you for everything.' She reached out her hand. 'I'm so grateful to you, Mr Grey. And, Archie, thank you ever so much.'

'I only wish . . .' Lean glanced at the grave, where the diggers were getting ready.

'I know. But still, for my daughter. And for letting me keep a promise to her.'

Lean clasped her hand and gave her a smile, not needing to know exactly what she'd meant. Helen then took Doran's massive hand in her own and looked up into the man's eyes. He was clearly uncomfortable with the entire scene.

'Tom, I can't thank you enough. If anything had ever happened to Delia . . .' Helen's voice began to crack, and she stepped back.

Doran's ruddy complexion darkened a shade or two as he stammered out some muddled acceptance of thanks while also trying to ask if she was all right and then throwing in his own expression of gratitude, just in case one was warranted. Doran was then mercifully rescued from his own verbal efforts by Delia Prescott, who bolted forward to bear-hug the man.

'Thank you, Mr Dor – Can I call you Uncle Tom?'

'Hmm? Err, well, sure, I s'pose. I mean . . .'

Delia had already moved on to Lean. 'Thank you, too. Can I call you Uncle Archie?'

'Course you can, dear.'

She gave Lean a wide grin, then turned to face Perceval Grey, who regarded the girl with an expression that landed somewhere between embarrassment and the surprise of seeing a knife pulled from a hidden pocket.

'And thank you as well . . . Mr Grey.' She did a little curtsy.

Grey tipped his hat in appreciation of the girl's choice to restrain her youthful enthusiasm.

Before heading up the slope to where Rasmus Hansen had already climbed back atop the doctor's old carriage, Helen invited them all over to Dr Steig's house for refreshments with the family. Lean accepted, while Grey merely gave a vague nod and Doran begged off, muttering something about staying behind to make sure the grave men did their piece right.

After Helen took her leave, Lean and Grey strolled casually toward the gate. Grey seemed particularly hesitant to leave the cemetery, his eyes constantly searching along Vaughan Street, both sides of the entrance.

'You expecting someone?' Lean asked.

'Yes, actually.' Grey walked on, offering no further details.

'Speaking of missing people, we haven't really talked. You never told me of the final resting place of Jack Whitten.'

'Here we are!' Grey's eyes were fixed on a hackney that had just parked by the cemetery's front gate.

Two men emerged and entered the cemetery. As they approached, Lean recognized them as Dr Jotham Marsh and his lackey Jerome, the one who had visited this cemetery to deposit the body of Whitten's third victim in the Marsh family tomb.

'Why, if it isn't my favorite pair of bloodhounds: Lean and Grey. What a surprise to find you here,' said Marsh.

'I take it you haven't come to pay final respects to Dr Steig.'

'What? Oh, no. Unfortunate bit of news, that. No, I didn't personally know the man. I understand he did some good work with troubled veterans and whatnot. But our professional interests didn't overlap.'

'Oh, I'm sure you could have found some topic of shared interest,' Grey said. 'After all, you study the arts of controlling those evil spirits that rage around us in the air unseen. Dr Steig practiced in how to subdue those evil forces that rage inside us. In a sense, you were both fighting the same battle, only on different fields.'

'Well stated, Mr Grey.' Marsh regarded Grey with a thin smile and a slight arch of one eyebrow. 'Perhaps I've underestimated the depth of your understanding as to my work.'

Grey nodded, gave a smile rife with mock civility, and answered, 'It's certainly my pleasure to disabuse you of any misconceptions about the depths of my understanding.'

There was a moment of certain recognition between the two men, which Lean interrupted by asking, 'If you didn't come for Dr Steig's funeral, then what brings you down here?'

'Unfortunately, I received word from the groundskeeper that there's been some attempted mischief at my family's tomb.

Someone tampering at the lock – vandals, robbers, kids on a dare. It happens every so often.'

Marsh started to turn and go on his way, but Grey called his attention back. 'Dr Marsh, do you know a man by the name of Whitten? An acquaintance of Lizzie Madson, I believe.'

'Whitten? Yes, I do recall the man, vaguely. Not a particularly memorable fellow.'

'He studied with you?' Grey said.

'Briefly. Why, is he in some sort of trouble?'

Grey gave a shrug. 'According to some theories.'

Marsh's face curled up in a crooked smile. He tipped his hat to both of them and said, 'Gentlemen. Always a pleasure, but I do have business to attend to. Good luck with that Whitten character.'

'I'm sure he'll turn up,' called Grey as Marsh walked away.

'Some type of vandalism at his tomb.' Lean looked at Grey with an eyebrow arched. 'You kept the tomb key.'

'Yes, but I had to make it obvious. Simply unlocking the door would not have gotten Dr Marsh's attention. He might never have received the message I left for him.'

'Which is what?' Lean imagined the body of Jack Whitten lying in the tomb. He wondered if the rope was still tangled about the man's neck. 'Besides the obvious, I mean.'

'That I've taken an interest in his activities.'

They passed out under the stone archway of the cemetery. 'How much of a role do you think Jotham Marsh actually had in all this?'

'Based on what Whitten said at the observatory, I think Marsh played a part. He dirtied his hands in setting this dark ritual into motion. He doesn't deserve to walk away entirely clean of all the tragic consequences.' Grey raised his arm to signal an approaching hackney cab.

'I'm not sure,' Lean said. 'Granted, he's a bit odd with all that occult gibberish, but to hear him tell it, he seems to mean well. Love and spiritual understanding and such.'

'What was it the old Puritan, Cotton Mather, said? Something about the devil's never being more dangerous than when he transforms himself into an angel of light. Marsh's ongoing activities bear watching.'

'But it's almost September. You said you'd be heading back to Boston.'

'Did I?'

'You did,' Lean said. 'Quite emphatically.'

'Funny, I don't recall.' Grey cast a glance back over his shoulder, in the direction of the line of tombs. 'In any event, I think Portland might hold my interest after all.'

They climbed into the carriage and settled themselves in the seats. As the driver started the horse forward, Lean let out a chuckle. 'Well, your landlady, Mrs Philbrick, will be quite thrilled to know you're staying on indefinitely.'

'You know, I think there was actually a tear in her eye this morning when I informed her of my intentions.'

Acknowledgements

I'd like to thank my early readers, Cathy Shields, Jacqueline Morabito, and Benson McGrath. They each provided opinions and support at a time when it was still a possibility that they would be the only three people to ever actually read this book.

My agents, Suzanne Gluck and Erin Malone, deserve a world of thanks not only for their guidance and insight along the way, but first for sharing my vision of what this book could be. Also at William Morris Endeavor, I'd like to thank Sarah Ceglarski and Tracy Fisher. My editor, Sean Desmond, helped shape the work with his perceptive ideas and keen eye. Thanks to Maureen Sugden as well as Rachelle Mandik at Crown Publishers, and Lynne Amft.

I wish to thank a number of authors who made my research so easy and enjoyable. First of all, Dr Hans Gross's seminal work *System Der Kriminalistik* inspired some of the procedures and ideas used by Perceval Grey (even though the English translation, *Criminal Investigation*, was not yet available in 1892). Lawrence Sutin's *A Life of Aleister Crowley* inspired certain elements of Jotham Marsh's character. Deborah Blum's *Ghost Hunters* did the same for Amelia Porter.

I've quoted or paraphrased Charles Upham's treatise on the Salem witch trials, as well as early documents from the likes of Cotton Mather and Robert Calef. I reviewed transcripts of the Salem trial records online at the University of Virginia's Salem Witch Trial documentary archive. Although I was familiar with the historical links between Portland, George Burroughs, the Abenaki Indians, and the witch trials, Mary Beth Norton's *In the Devil's Snare* was a wonderful resource for examining those collective topics. My efforts at incorporating and translating phrases and prayers from the Abenaki language are the result of numerous online resources. I apologize for any inaccuracies or discrepancies that resulted.

Edward Elwell's *Portland and Vicinity*, as well as various other publications by the Greater Portland Landmarks, Inc., proved invaluable in researching the city in the late nineteenth century. Similarly, volumes by David H. Fletcher on the Portland Company and John K. Moulton on the Portland Observatory were highly informative. Although I tried to accurately depict Portland, Maine, as it was in 1892, I did take liberties in other areas as warranted by the needs of the story. Any factual errors, intentional or otherwise, are mine alone.